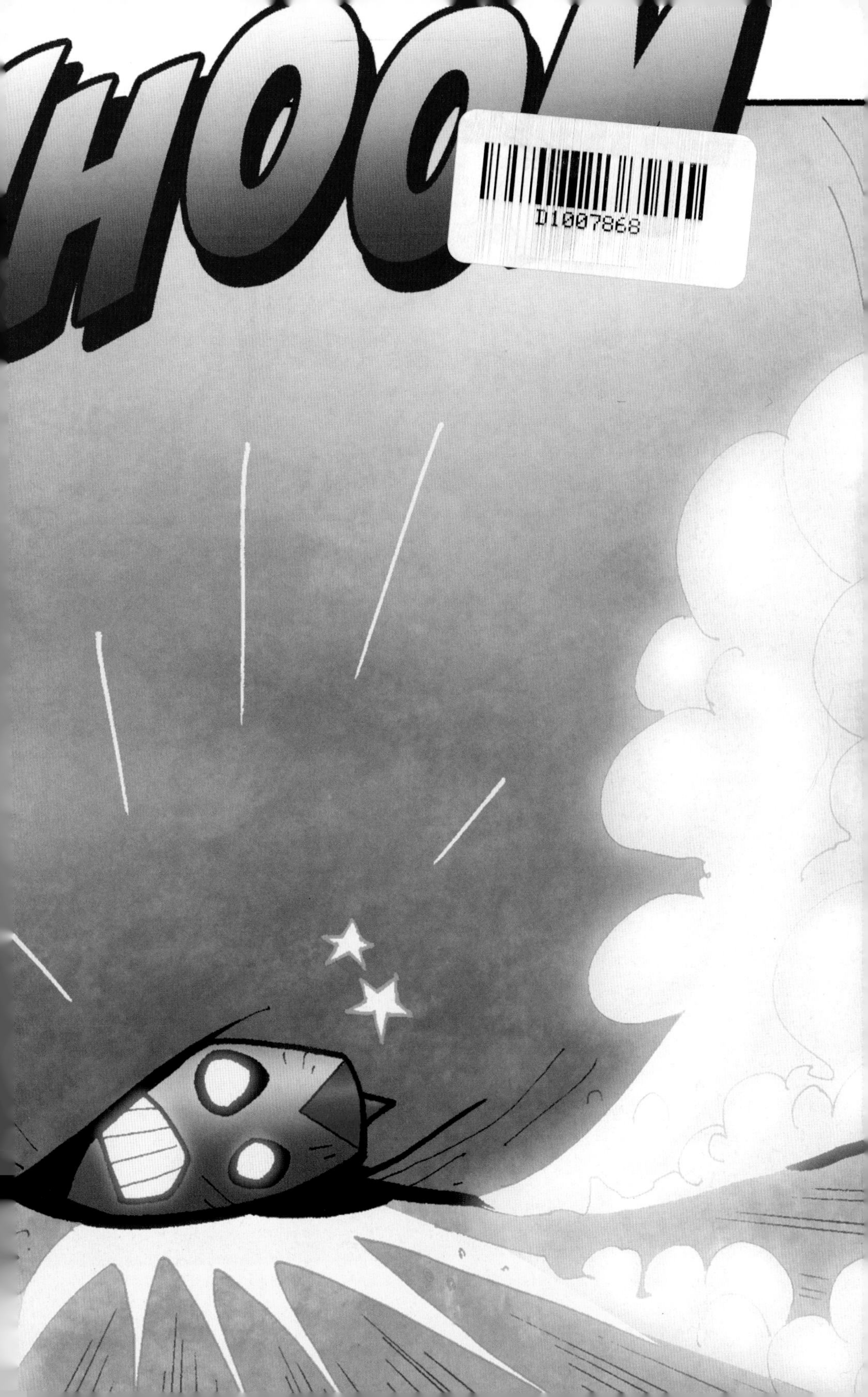
HOO

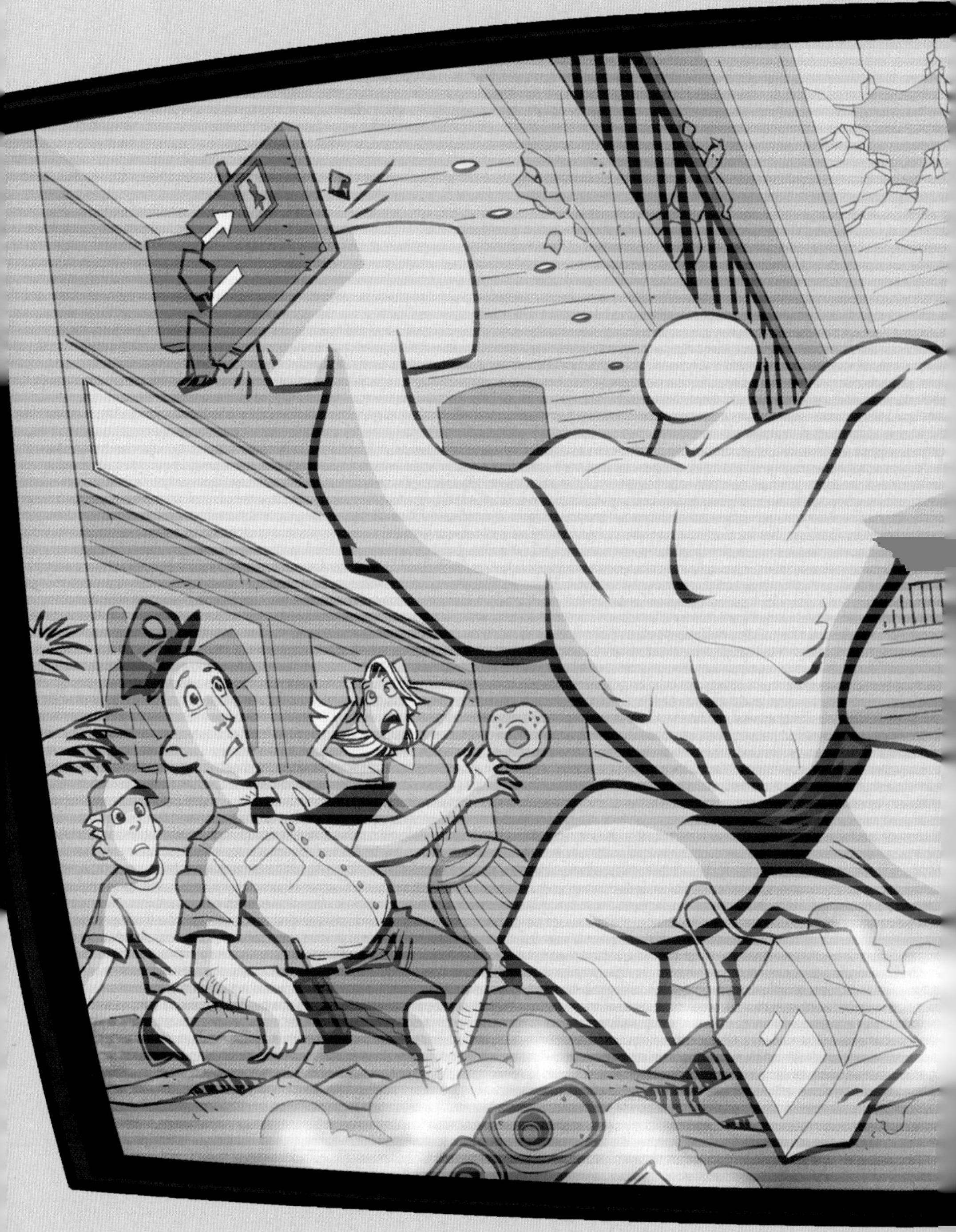

Disney · PIXAR

THE INCREDIBLES

FAMILY MATTERS

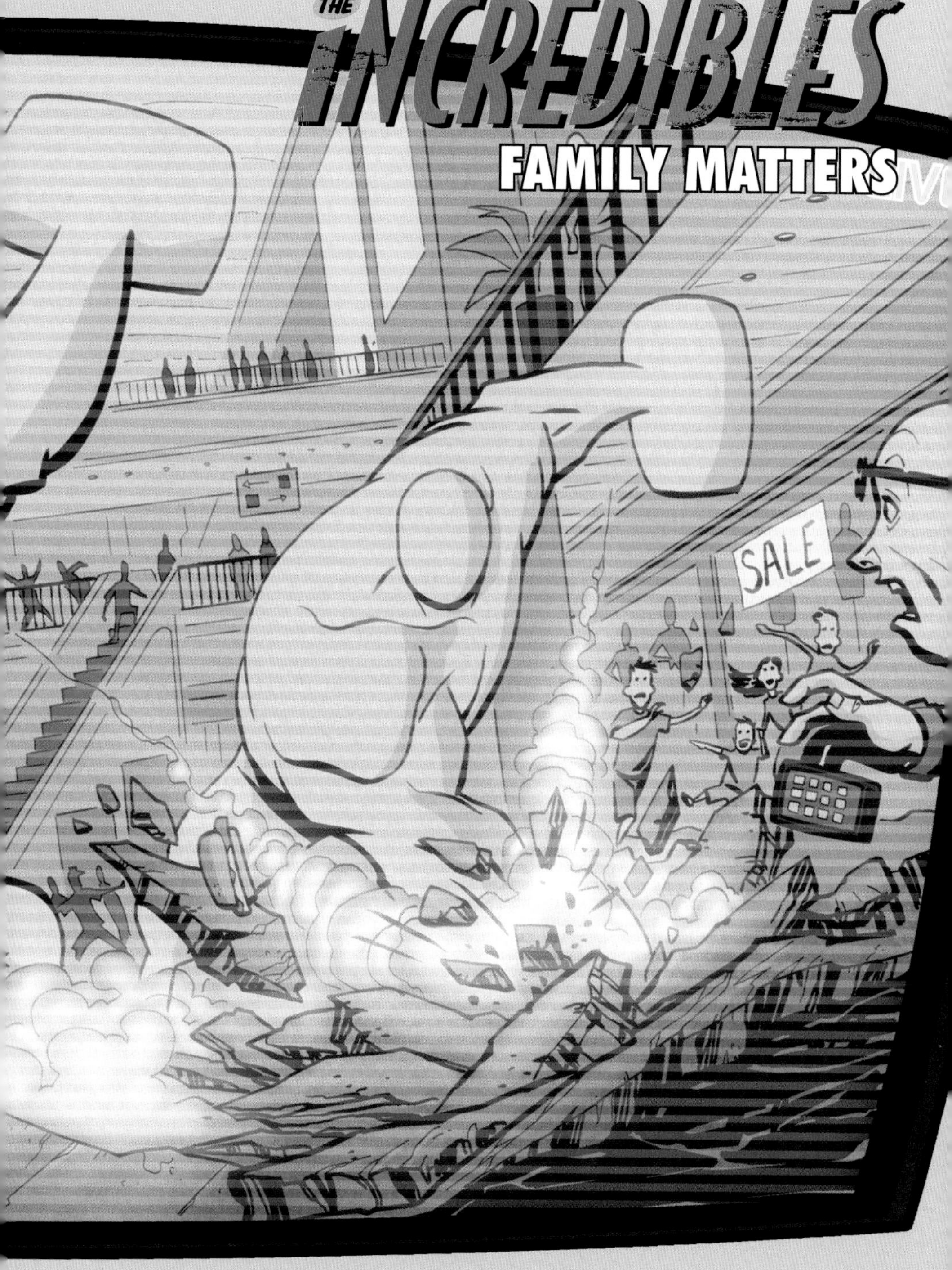
SALE

DISNEY ·

THE INCR

PIXAR

EDIBLES

Disney · PIXAR

THE INCREDIBLES

FAMILY MATTERS

BOOM KIDS!

ROSS RICHIE
chief executive officer

ANDREW COSBY
chief creative officer

MARK WAID
editor-in-chief

ADAM FORTIER
vice president,
publishing

CHIP MOSHER
marketing director

MATT GAGNON
managing editor

FIRST EDITION: JULY 2009

10 9 8 7 6 5 4 3 2 1
PRINTED IN CANADA

Office of publication: 6310 San Vicente Blvd Ste 404, Los Angeles, CA 90048.

WRITTEN BY: MARK WAID

ART BY: MARCIO TAKARA

COLORS: ANDREW DALHOUSE

LETTERS: JOSE MACASOCOL, JR.

EDITOR: PAUL MORRISSEY
TRADE EDITOR: AARON SPARROW

COVER ARTIST: MARCIO TAKARA
COLORS BY: ANDREW DALHOUSE

CHAPTER ONE

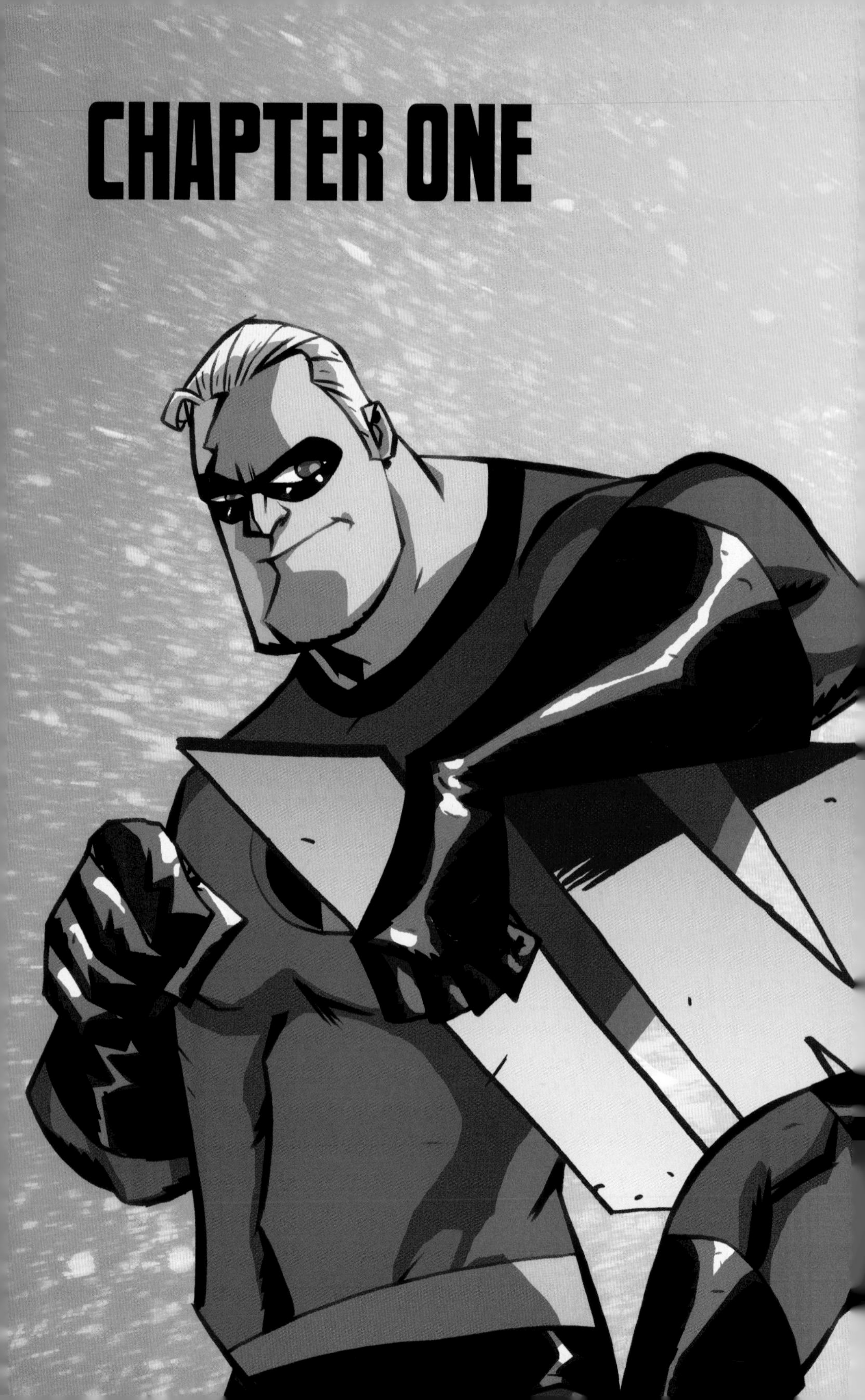

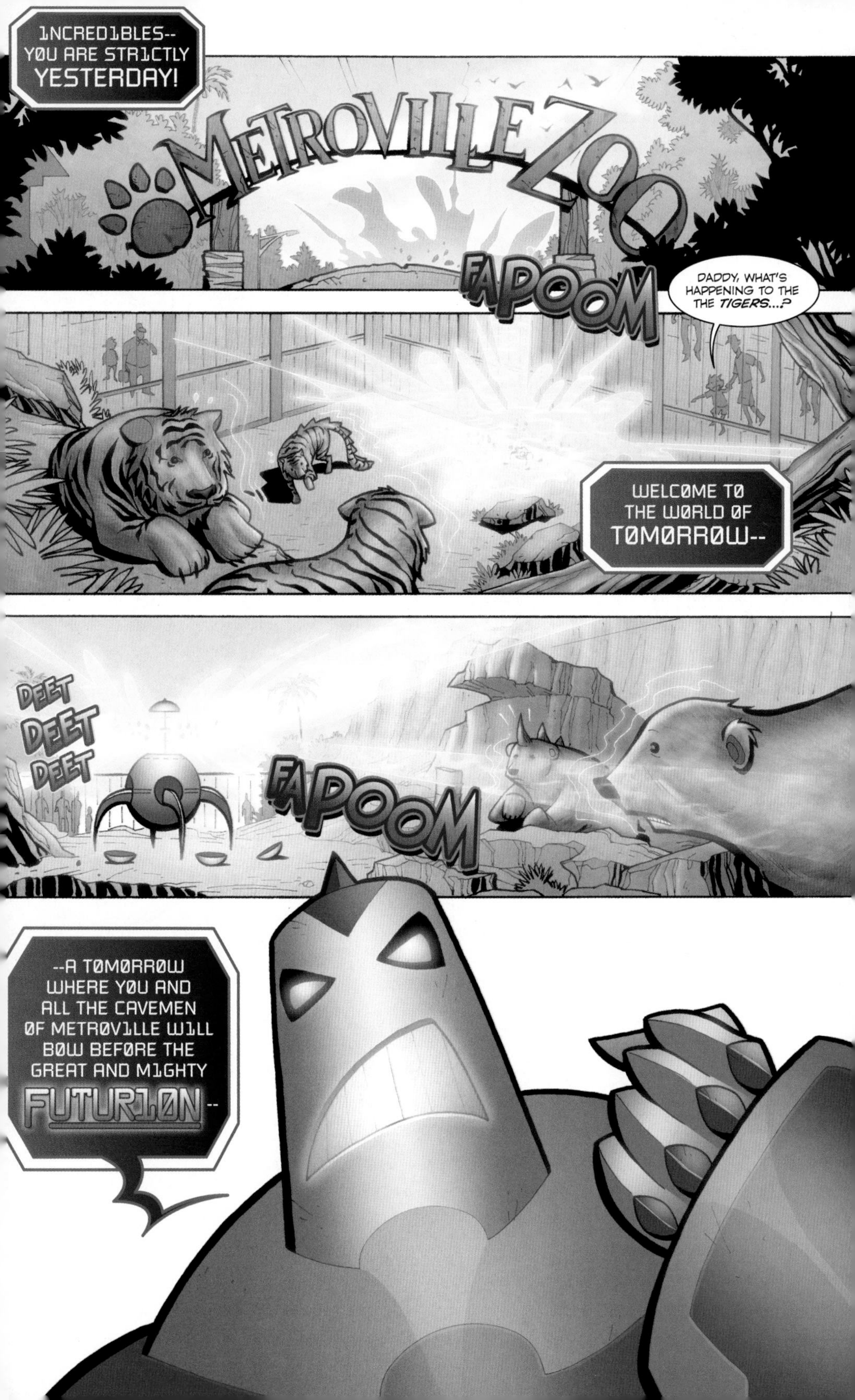
1NCRED1BLES--
Y0U ARE STR1CTLY
YESTERDAY!
METROVILLE ZOO
FAPOOM
DADDY, WHAT'S HAPPENING TO THE THE *TIGERS...?*
WELC0ME T0 THE W0RLD 0F T0M0RR0W--
DEET DEET DEET
FAPOOM
--A T0M0RR0W WHERE Y0U AND ALL THE CAVEMEN 0F METR0V1LLE W1LL B0W BEF0RE THE GREAT AND M1GHTY
FUTUR10N--

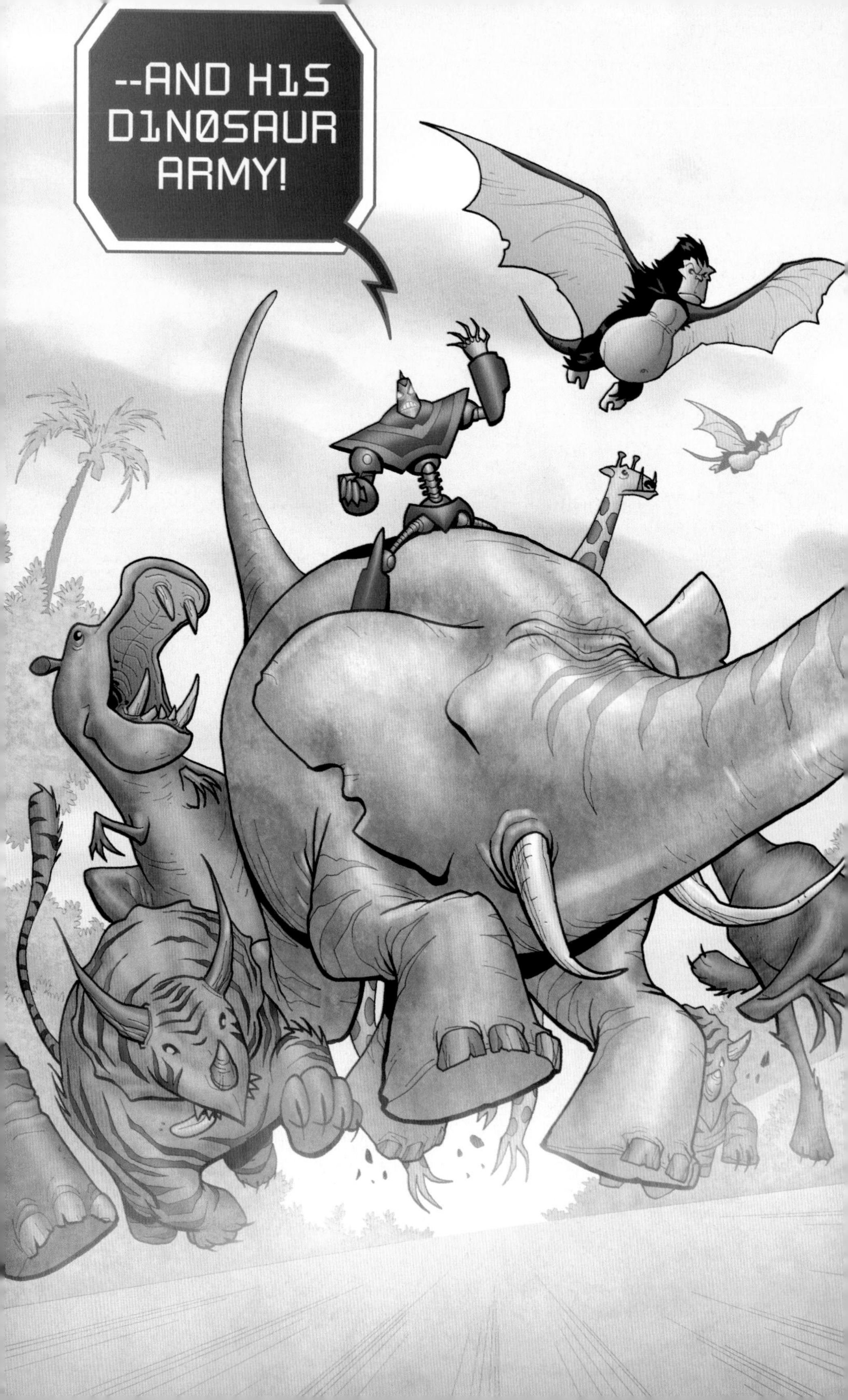
--AND H1S D1N0SAUR ARMY!

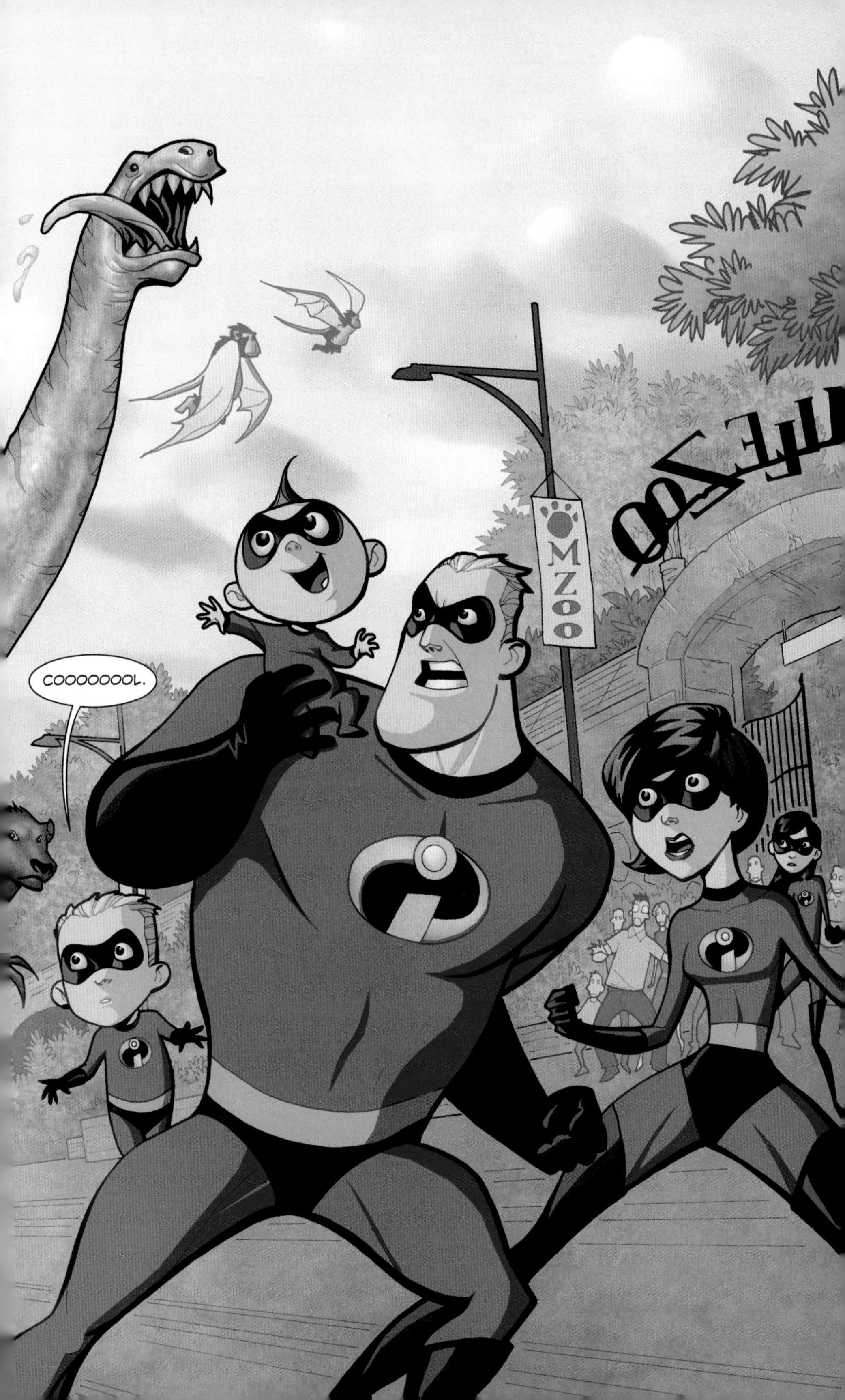
MZOO
COOOOOOOL.

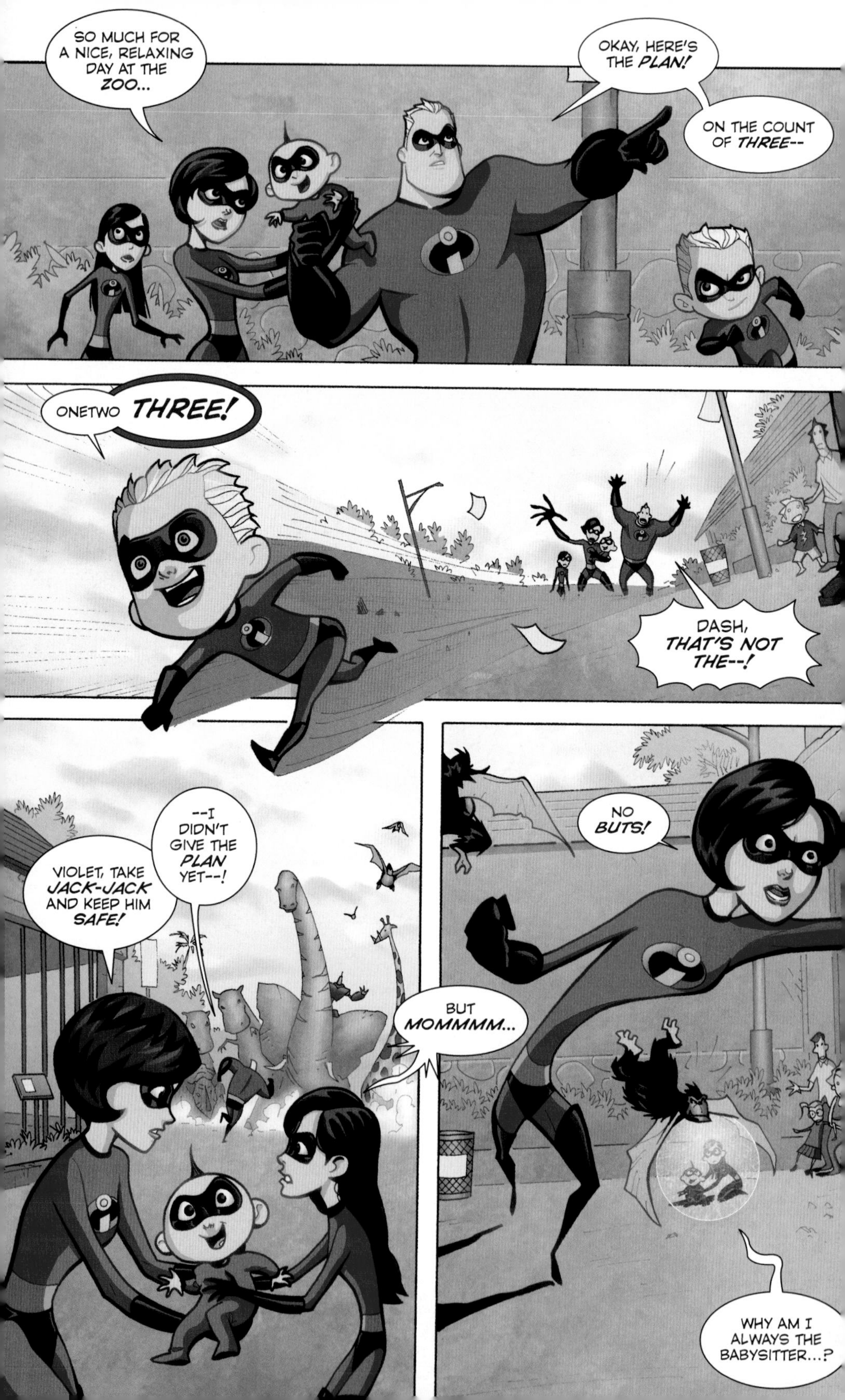
SO MUCH FOR A NICE, RELAXING DAY AT THE ZOO...
OKAY, HERE'S THE PLAN!
ON THE COUNT OF THREE--
ONETWO THREE!
DASH, THAT'S NOT THE--!
--I DIDN'T GIVE THE PLAN YET--!
VIOLET, TAKE JACK-JACK AND KEEP HIM SAFE!
BUT MOMMMM...
NO BUTS!
WHY AM I ALWAYS THE BABYSITTER...?

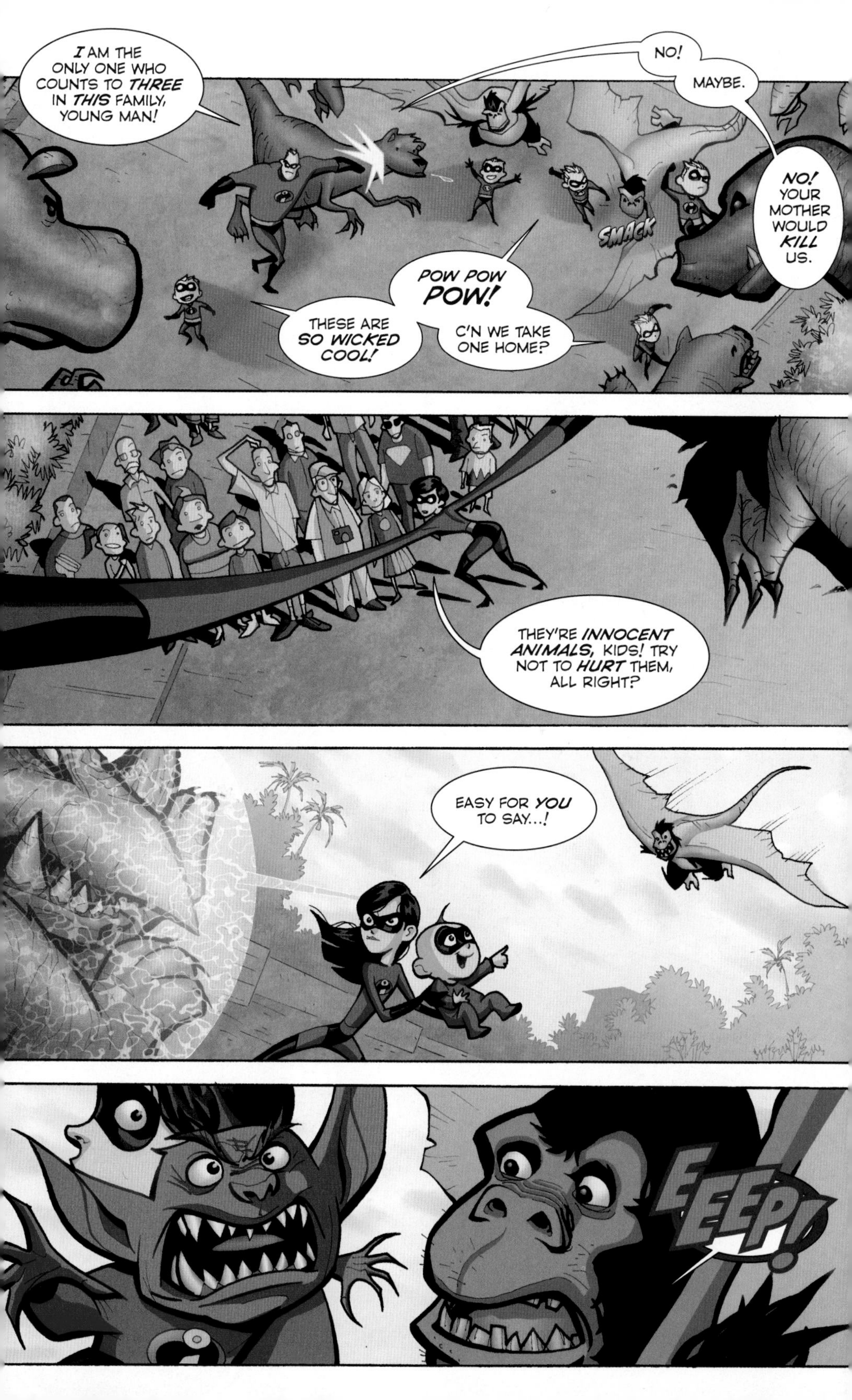

I AM THE ONLY ONE WHO COUNTS TO THREE IN THIS FAMILY, YOUNG MAN!
NO!
MAYBE.
NO! YOUR MOTHER WOULD KILL US.
SMACK
POW POW POW!
THESE ARE SO WICKED COOL!
C'N WE TAKE ONE HOME?
THEY'RE INNOCENT ANIMALS, KIDS! TRY NOT TO HURT THEM, ALL RIGHT?
EASY FOR YOU TO SAY...!
EEEP!

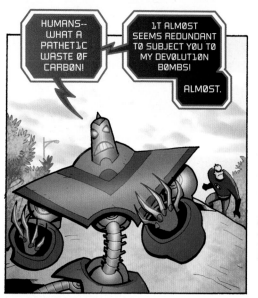

HUMANS-- WHAT A PATHETIC WASTE ØF CARBØN!

1T ALMØST SEEMS REDUNDANT TØ SUBJECT YØU TØ MY DEVØLUT1ØN BØMBS!

ALMØST.

FUTURION. AGAIN.

THANKS FOR RUINING MY DAY OFF.

HOW MANY TIMES DO I HAVE T KEEP KNOCKING YO BACK TO THE 24T CENTURY?

BLANNGGG!

...

OW?

ØDD. LAST T1ME WE MET, THAT WØULD HAVE TAKEN MY HEAD R1GHT ØFF. YØU'RE LØS1NG YØUR TØUCH, CAVEMAN!

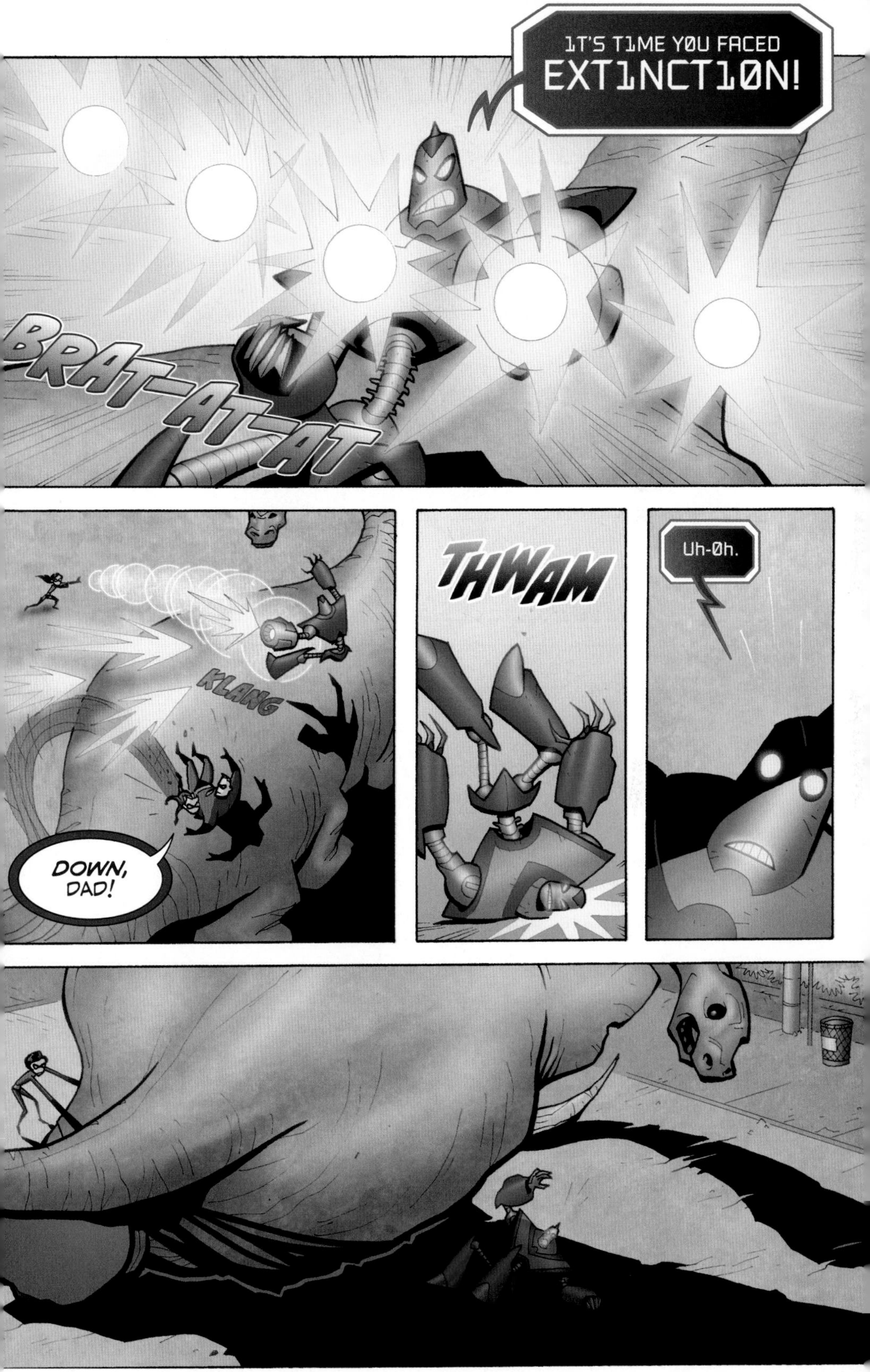
1T'S T1ME Y0U FACED
EXT1NCT10N!
BRAT-AT-AT
DOWN, DAD!
KLANG
THWAM
Uh-0h.

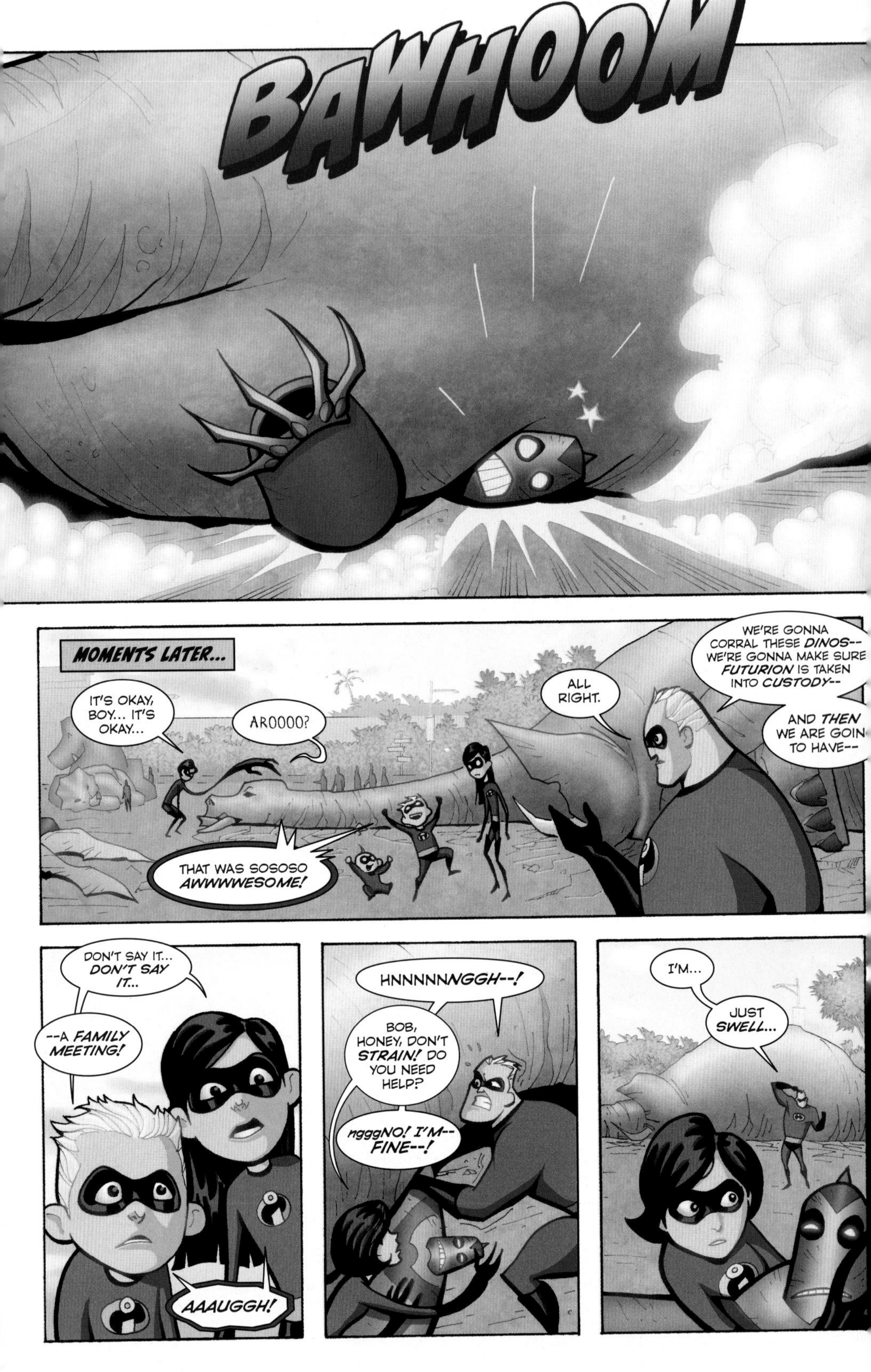
BAWHOOM
MOMENTS LATER...
IT'S OKAY, BOY... IT'S OKAY...
AROOOO?
THAT WAS SOSOSO AWWWWESOME!
ALL RIGHT.
WE'RE GONNA CORRAL THESE DINOS-- WE'RE GONNA MAKE SURE FUTURION IS TAKEN INTO CUSTODY--
AND THEN WE ARE GOIN TO HAVE--
DON'T SAY IT... DON'T SAY IT...
--A FAMILY MEETING!
AAAUGGH!
HNNNNNNGGH--!
BOB, HONEY, DON'T STRAIN! DO YOU NEED HELP?
nggNO! I'M-- FINE--!
I'M...
JUST SWELL...

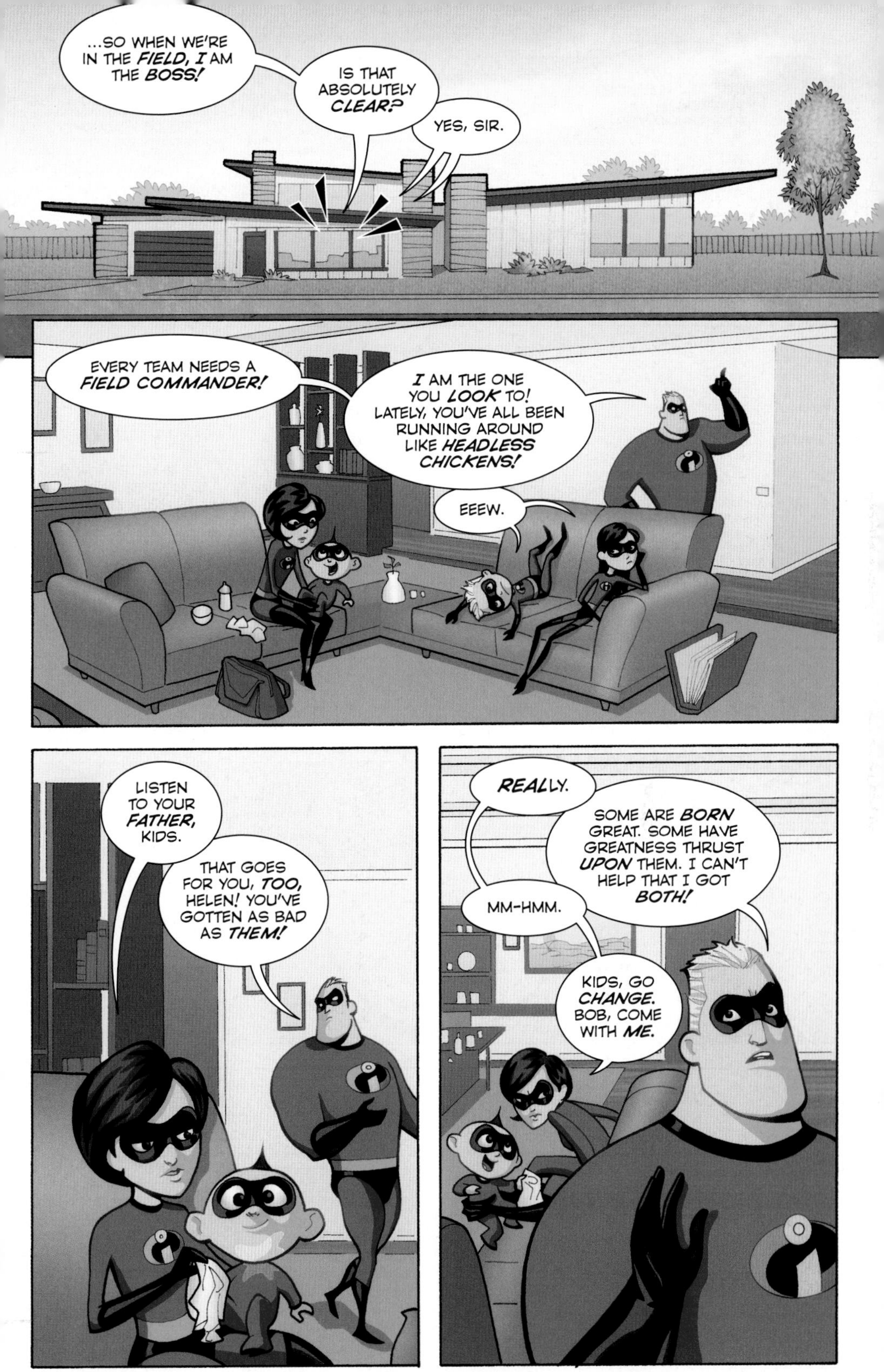
...SO WHEN WE'RE IN THE *FIELD, I* AM THE *BOSS!*
IS THAT ABSOLUTELY *CLEAR?*
YES, SIR.
EVERY TEAM NEEDS A *FIELD COMMANDER!*
I AM THE ONE YOU *LOOK* TO! LATELY, YOU'VE ALL BEEN RUNNING AROUND LIKE *HEADLESS CHICKENS!*
EEEW.
LISTEN TO YOUR *FATHER,* KIDS.
THAT GOES FOR YOU, *TOO,* HELEN! YOU'VE GOTTEN AS BAD AS *THEM!*
*REAL*LY.
SOME ARE *BORN* GREAT. SOME HAVE GREATNESS THRUST *UPON* THEM. I CAN'T HELP THAT I GOT *BOTH!*
MM-HMM.
KIDS, GO *CHANGE.* BOB, COME WITH *ME.*

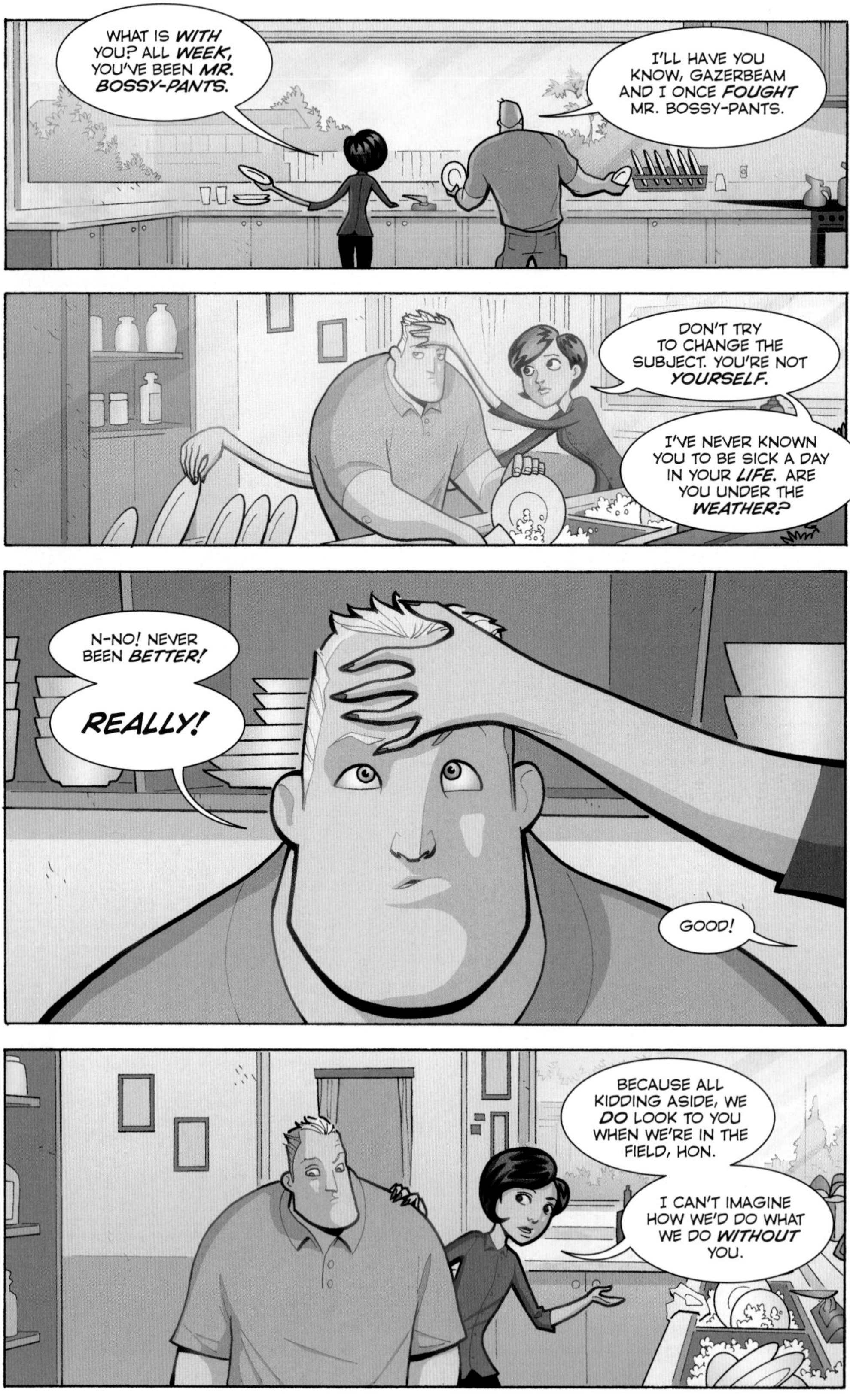
WHAT IS WITH YOU? ALL WEEK, YOU'VE BEEN MR. BOSSY-PANTS.
I'LL HAVE YOU KNOW, GAZERBEAM AND I ONCE FOUGHT MR. BOSSY-PANTS.
DON'T TRY TO CHANGE THE SUBJECT. YOU'RE NOT YOURSELF.
I'VE NEVER KNOWN YOU TO BE SICK A DAY IN YOUR LIFE. ARE YOU UNDER THE WEATHER?
N-NO! NEVER BEEN BETTER!
REALLY!
GOOD!
BECAUSE ALL KIDDING ASIDE, WE DO LOOK TO YOU WHEN WE'RE IN THE FIELD, HON.
I CAN'T IMAGINE HOW WE'D DO WHAT WE DO WITHOUT YOU.

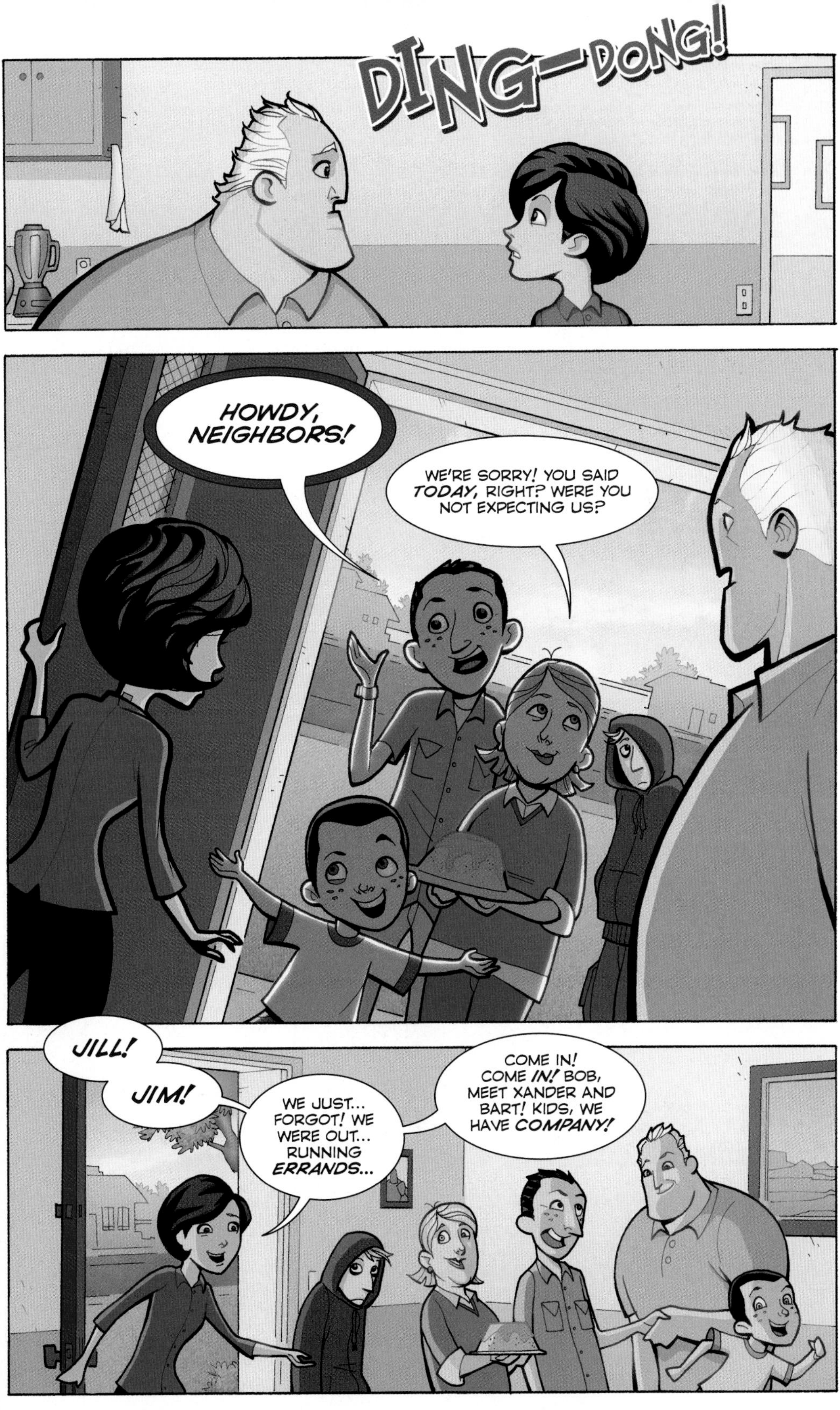
DING-DONG!
HOWDY, NEIGHBORS!
WE'RE SORRY! YOU SAID *TODAY*, RIGHT? WERE YOU NOT EXPECTING US?
JILL!
JIM!
WE JUST... FORGOT! WE WERE OUT... RUNNING *ERRANDS...*
COME IN! COME *IN!* BOB, MEET XANDER AND BART! KIDS, WE HAVE *COMPANY!*

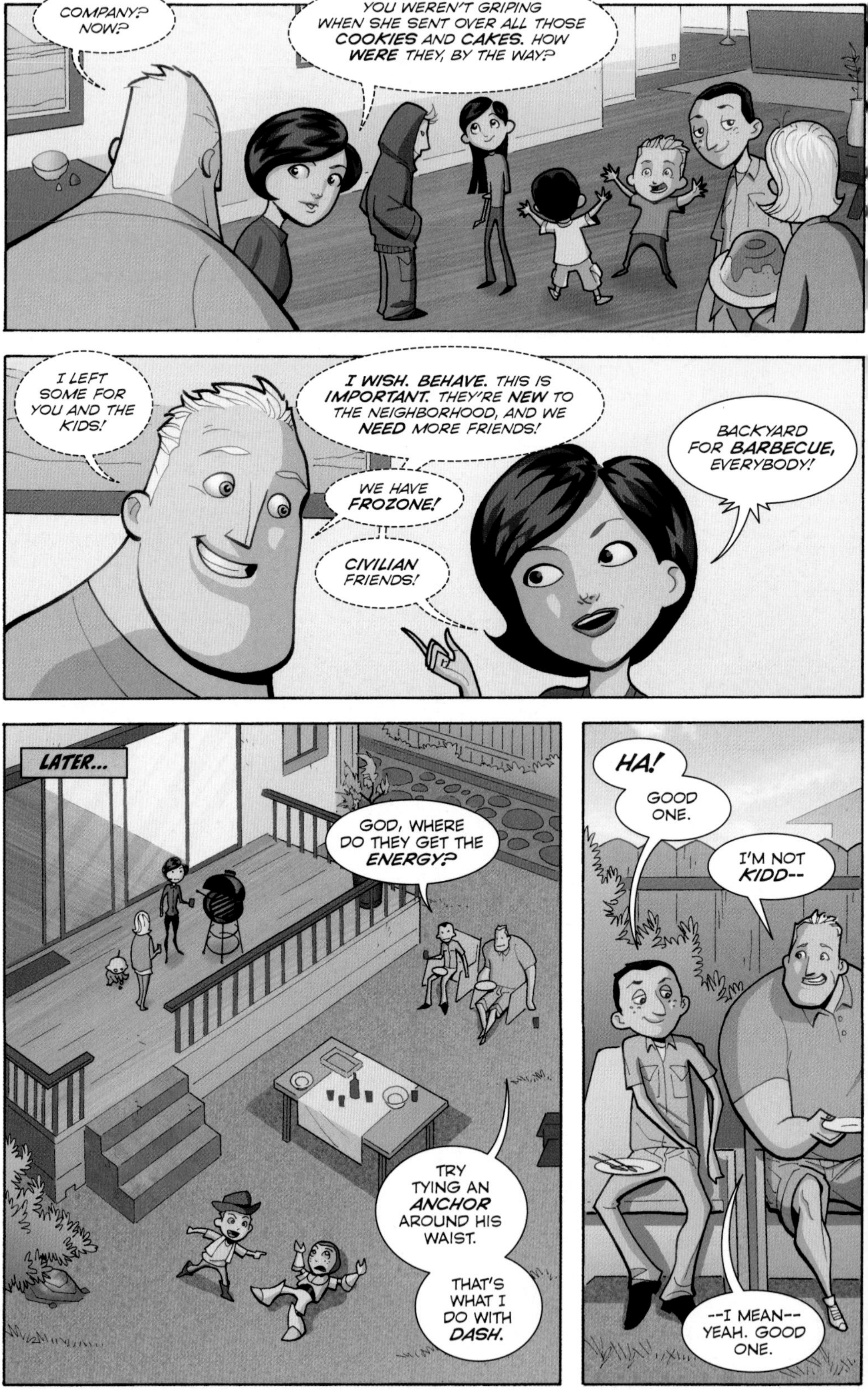
COMPANY? NOW?
YOU WEREN'T GRIPING WHEN SHE SENT OVER ALL THOSE COOKIES AND CAKES. HOW WERE THEY, BY THE WAY?
I LEFT SOME FOR YOU AND THE KIDS!
I WISH. BEHAVE. THIS IS IMPORTANT. THEY'RE NEW TO THE NEIGHBORHOOD, AND WE NEED MORE FRIENDS!
WE HAVE FROZONE!
CIVILIAN FRIENDS!
BACKYARD FOR BARBECUE, EVERYBODY!
LATER...
GOD, WHERE DO THEY GET THE ENERGY?
TRY TYING AN ANCHOR AROUND HIS WAIST.
THAT'S WHAT I DO WITH DASH.
HA!
GOOD ONE.
I'M NOT KIDD--
--I MEAN-- YEAH. GOOD ONE.

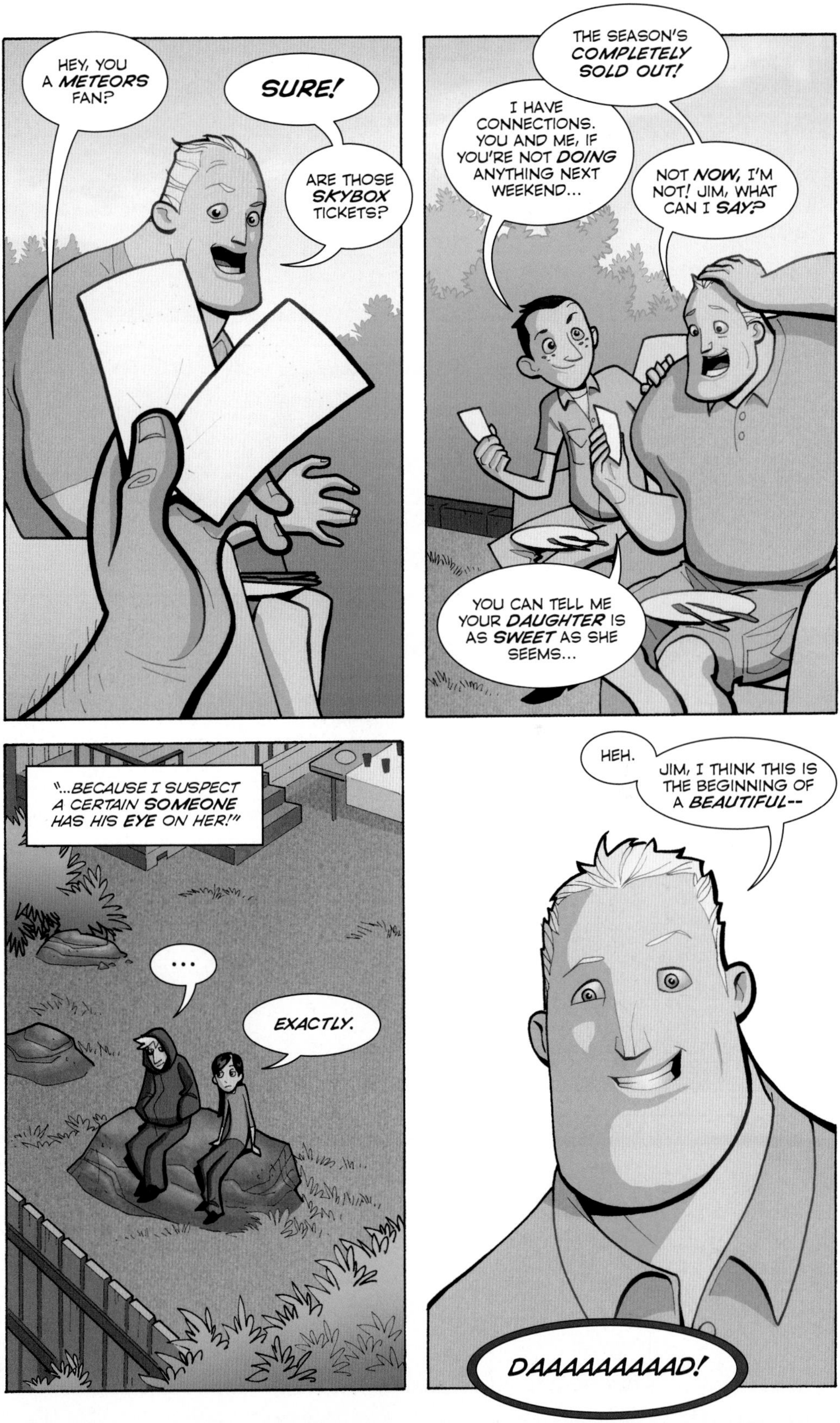
HEY, YOU A METEORS FAN?
SURE!
ARE THOSE SKYBOX TICKETS?
THE SEASON'S COMPLETELY SOLD OUT!
I HAVE CONNECTIONS. YOU AND ME, IF YOU'RE NOT DOING ANYTHING NEXT WEEKEND...
NOT NOW, I'M NOT! JIM, WHAT CAN I SAY?
YOU CAN TELL ME YOUR DAUGHTER IS AS SWEET AS SHE SEEMS...
"...BECAUSE I SUSPECT A CERTAIN SOMEONE HAS HIS EYE ON HER!"
...
EXACTLY.
HEH.
JIM, I THINK THIS IS THE BEGINNING OF A BEAUTIFUL--
DAAAAAAAAAD!

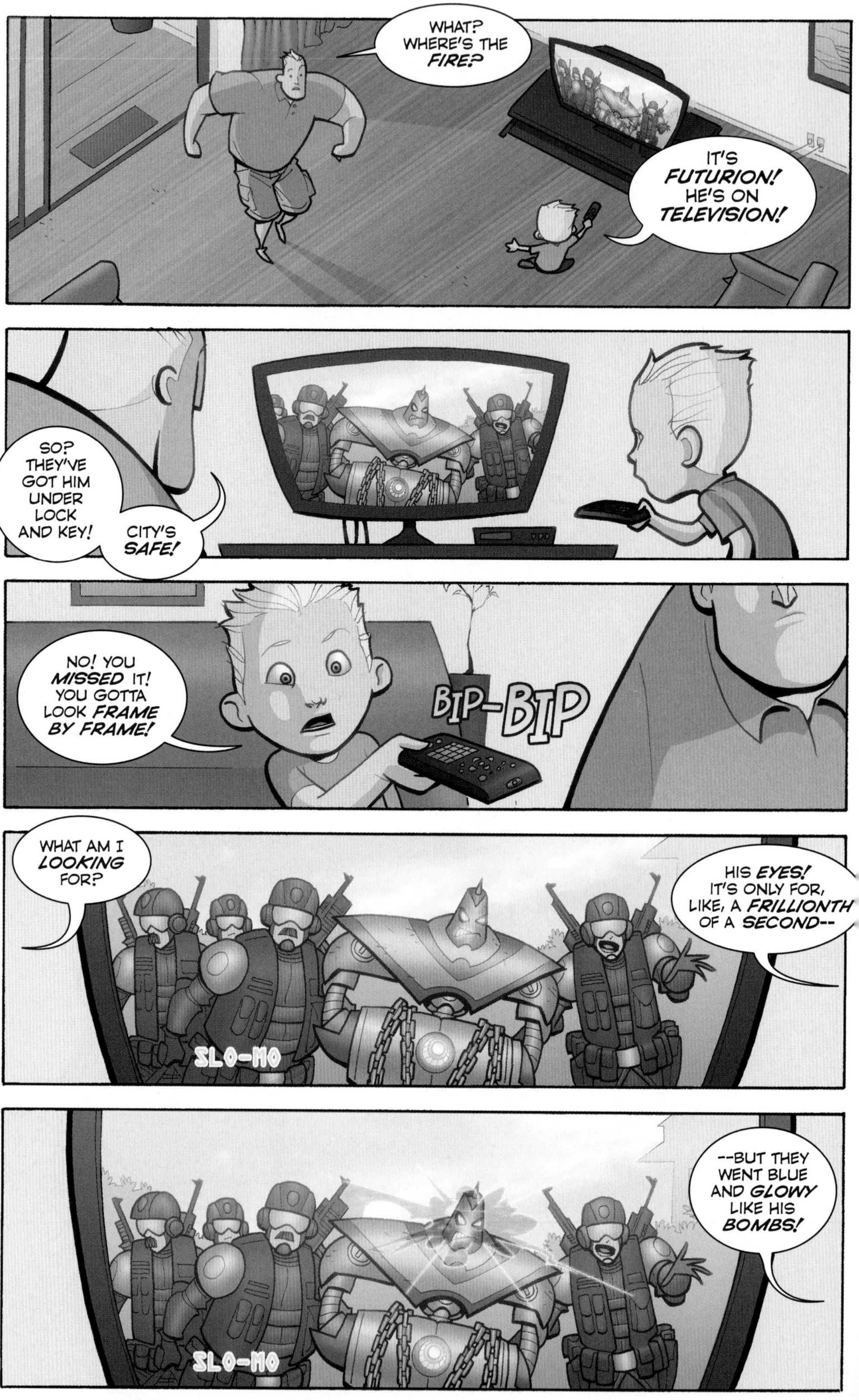
WHAT? WHERE'S THE *FIRE?*
IT'S *FUTURION!* HE'S ON *TELEVISION!*
SO? THEY'VE GOT HIM UNDER LOCK AND KEY!
CITY'S *SAFE!*
NO! YOU *MISSED* IT! YOU GOTTA LOOK *FRAME BY FRAME!*
BIP-BIP
WHAT AM I *LOOKING* FOR?
HIS *EYES!* IT'S ONLY FOR, LIKE, A *FRILLIONTH* OF A *SECOND--*
SLO-MO
--BUT THEY WENT BLUE AND *GLOWY* LIKE HIS *BOMBS!*
SLO-MO

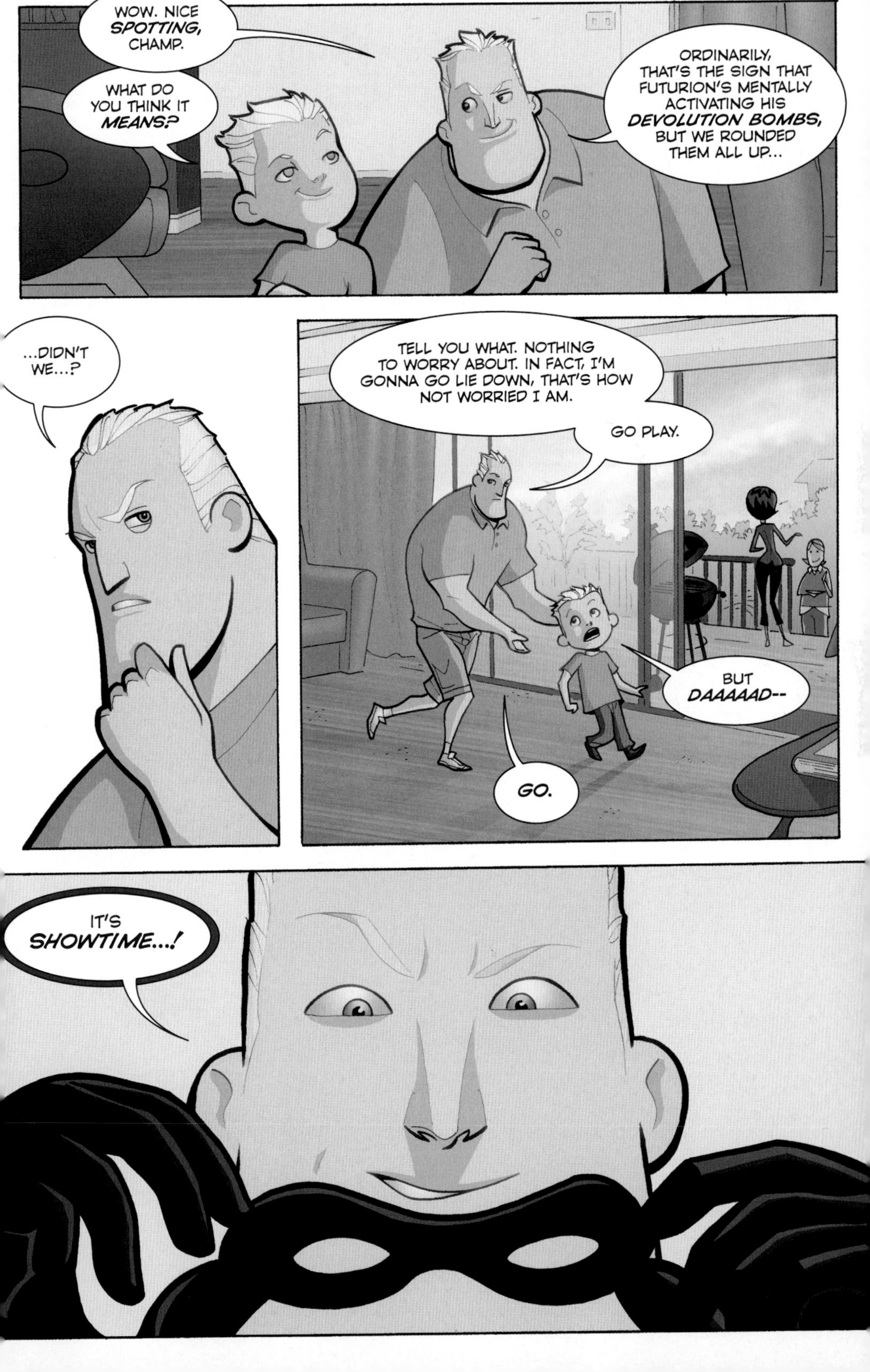
WOW. NICE SPOTTING, CHAMP.
WHAT DO YOU THINK IT MEANS?
ORDINARILY, THAT'S THE SIGN THAT FUTURION'S MENTALLY ACTIVATING HIS DEVOLUTION BOMBS, BUT WE ROUNDED THEM ALL UP...
...DIDN'T WE...?
TELL YOU WHAT. NOTHING TO WORRY ABOUT. IN FACT, I'M GONNA GO LIE DOWN, THAT'S HOW NOT WORRIED I AM.
GO PLAY.
BUT DAAAAAD--
GO.
IT'S SHOWTIME...!

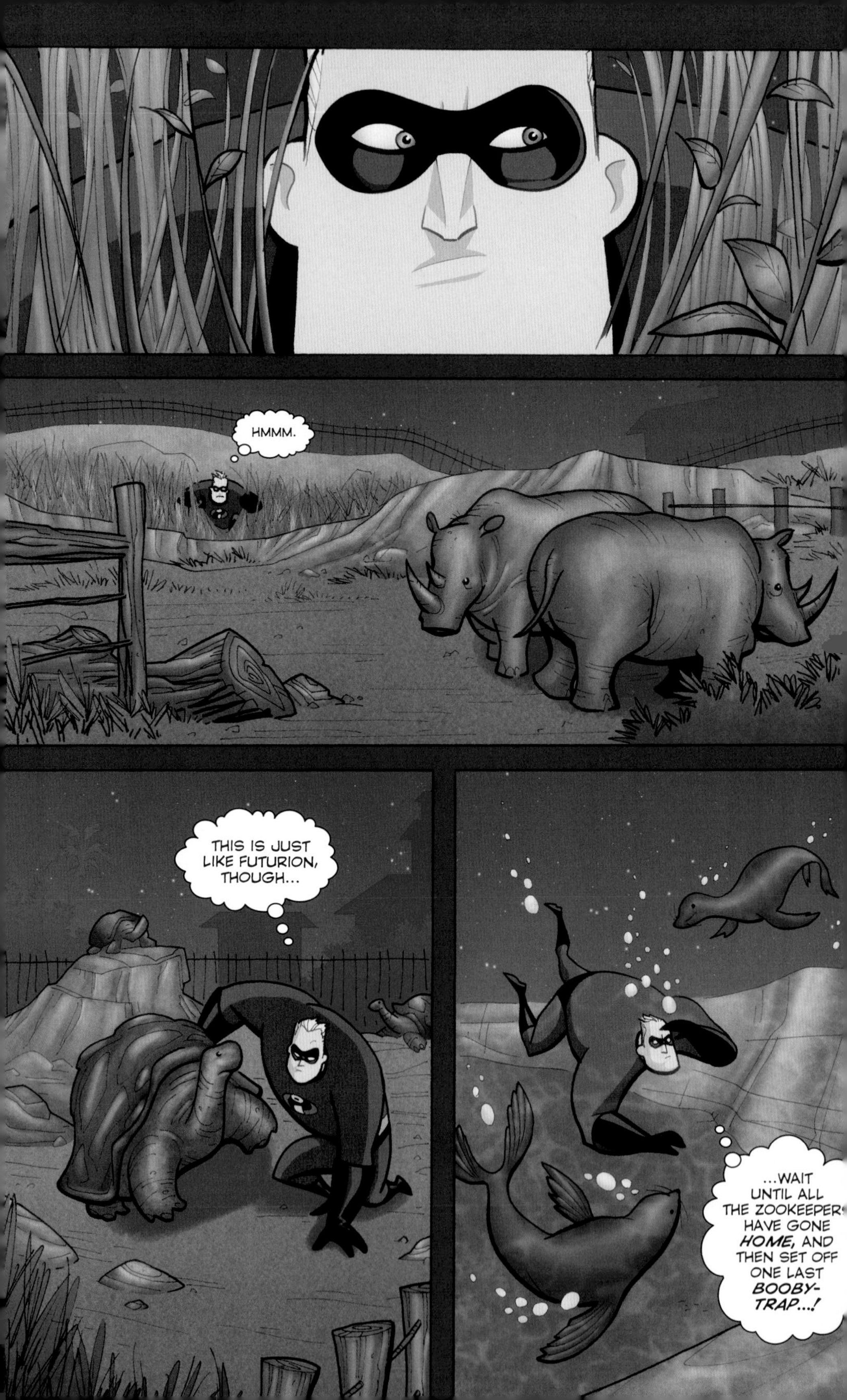
HMMM.
THIS IS JUST LIKE FUTURION, THOUGH...
...WAIT UNTIL ALL THE ZOOKEEPERS HAVE GONE *HOME,* AND THEN SET OFF ONE LAST *BOOBY-TRAP...!*

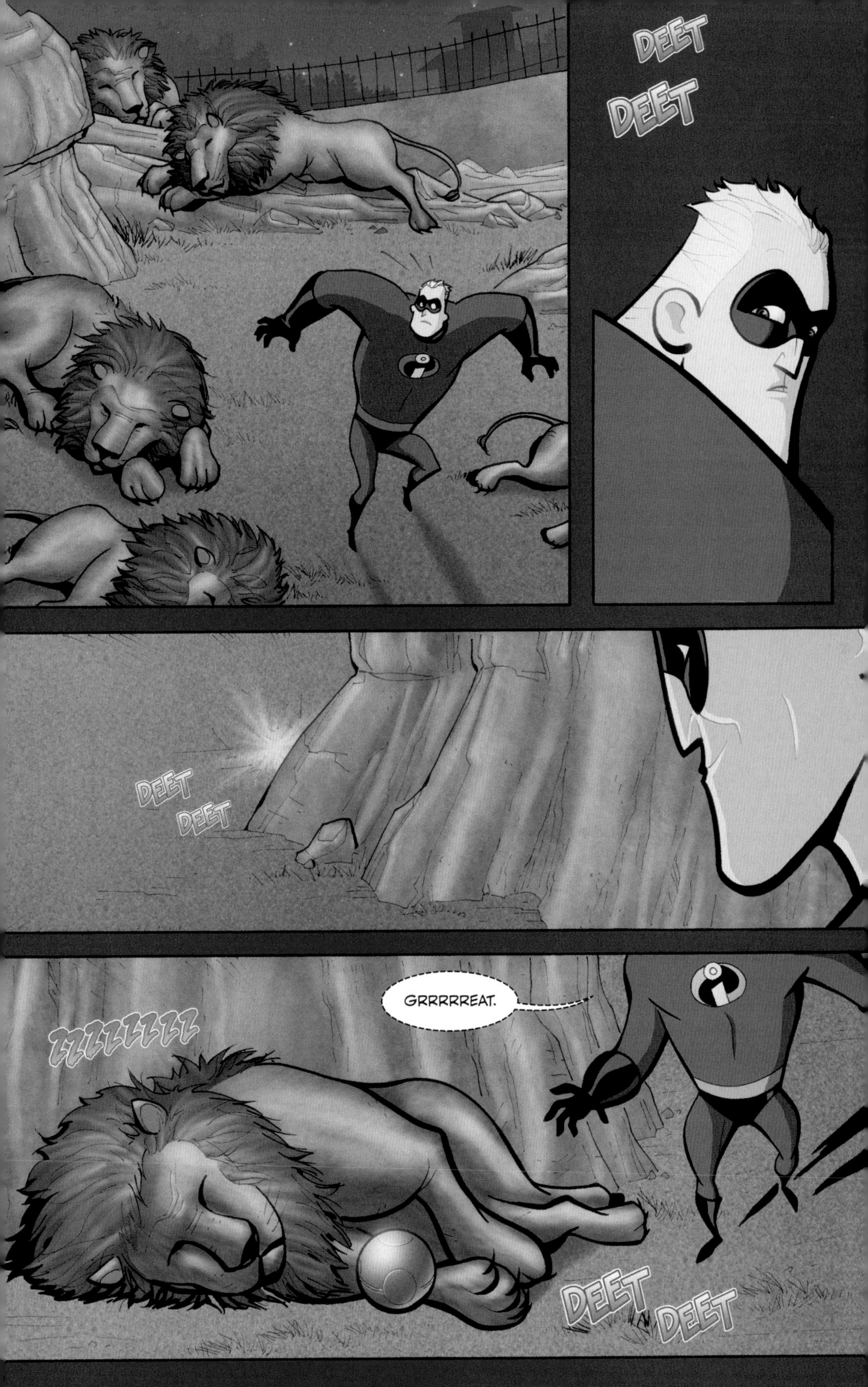
DEET
DEET
DEET
DEET
ZZZZZZZZ
GRRRRREAT.
DEET
DEET

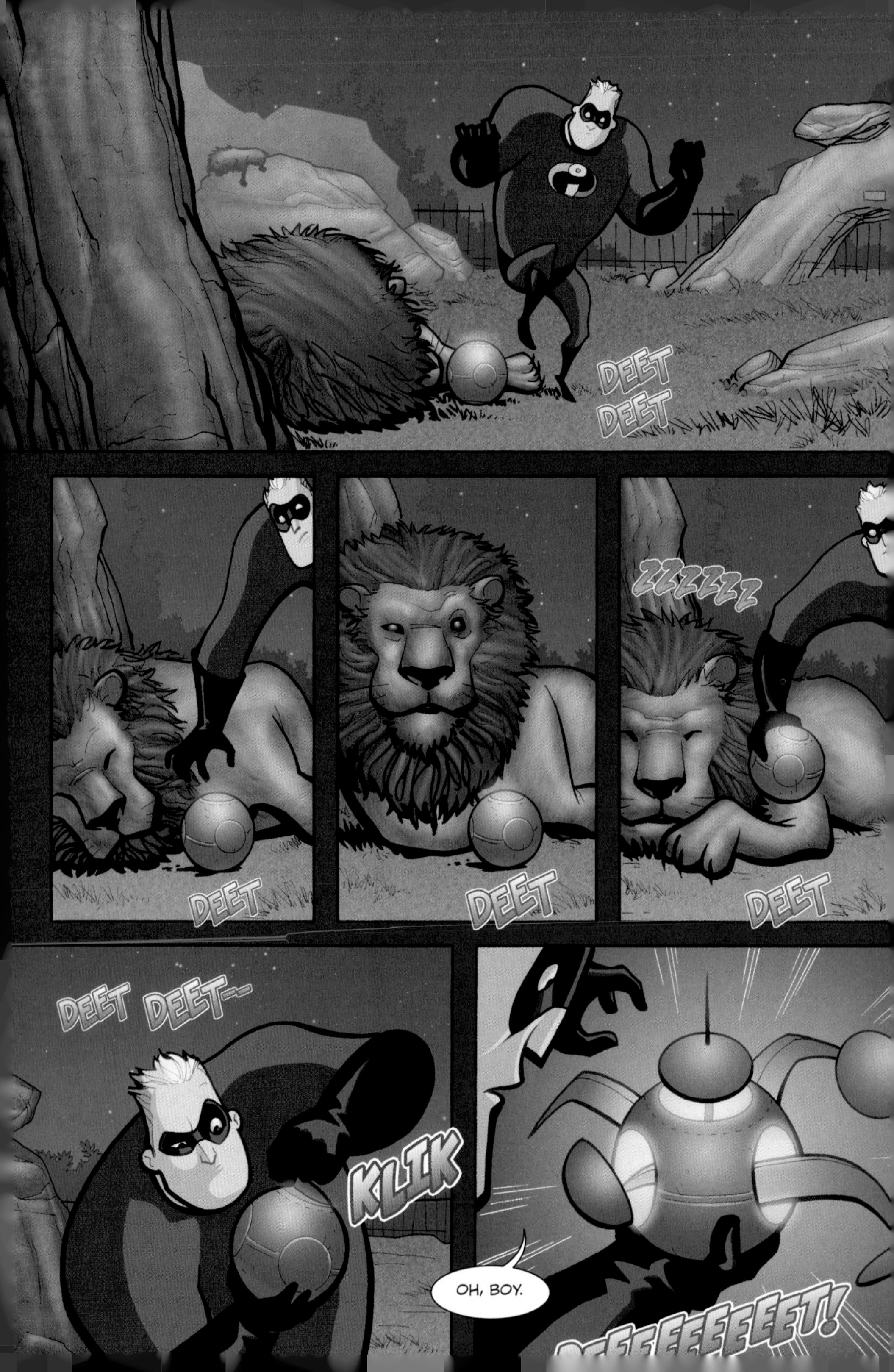
DEET
DEET
DEET
DEET
ZZZZZZ
DEET
DEET DEET--
KLIK
OH, BOY.

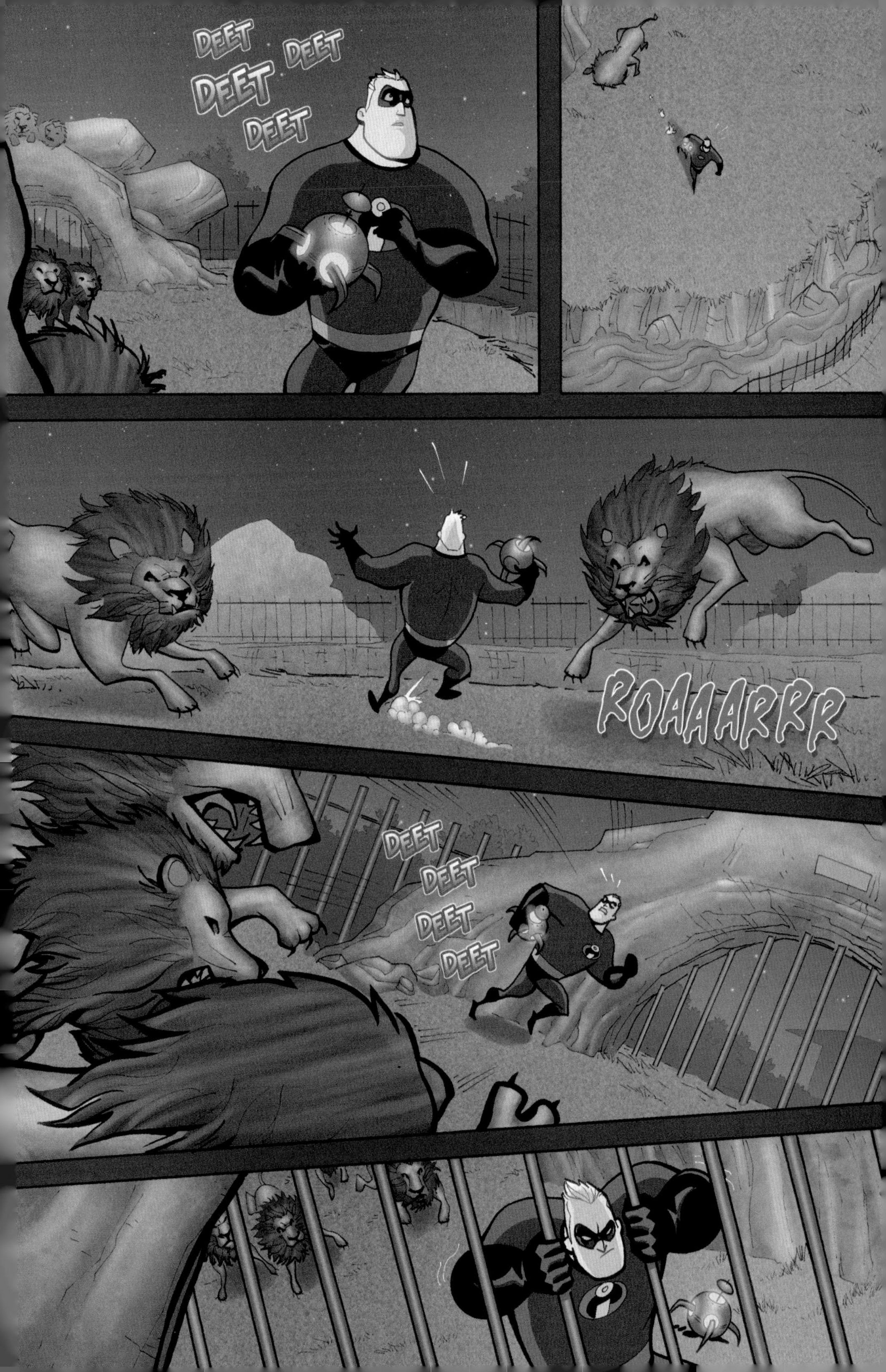
DEET
DEET
DEET
DEET
ROAAARRR
DEET
DEET
DEET
DEET

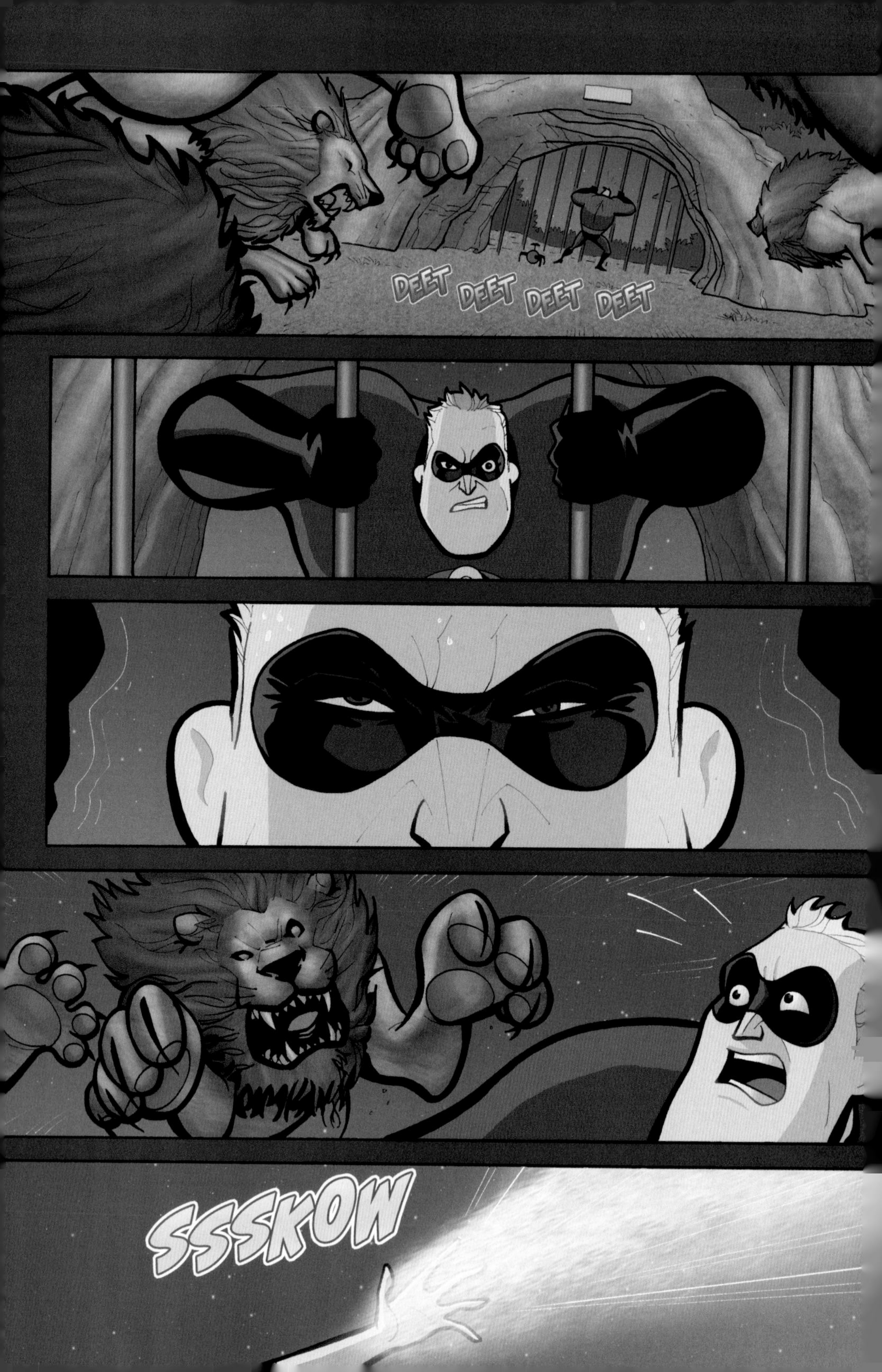

DEET DEET DEET DEET
SSSKOW

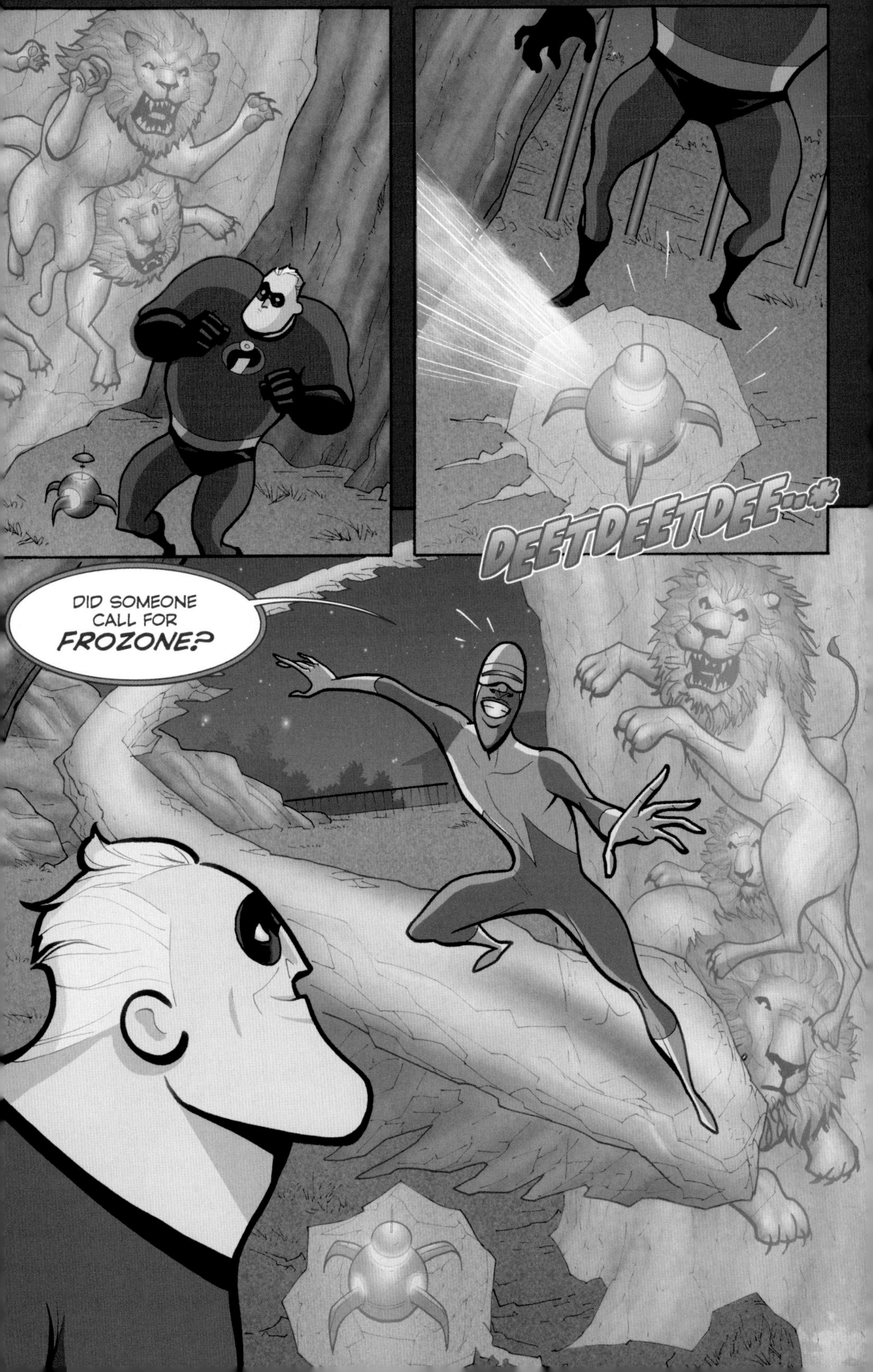
DEETDEETDEE..*
DID SOMEONE CALL FOR FROZONE?

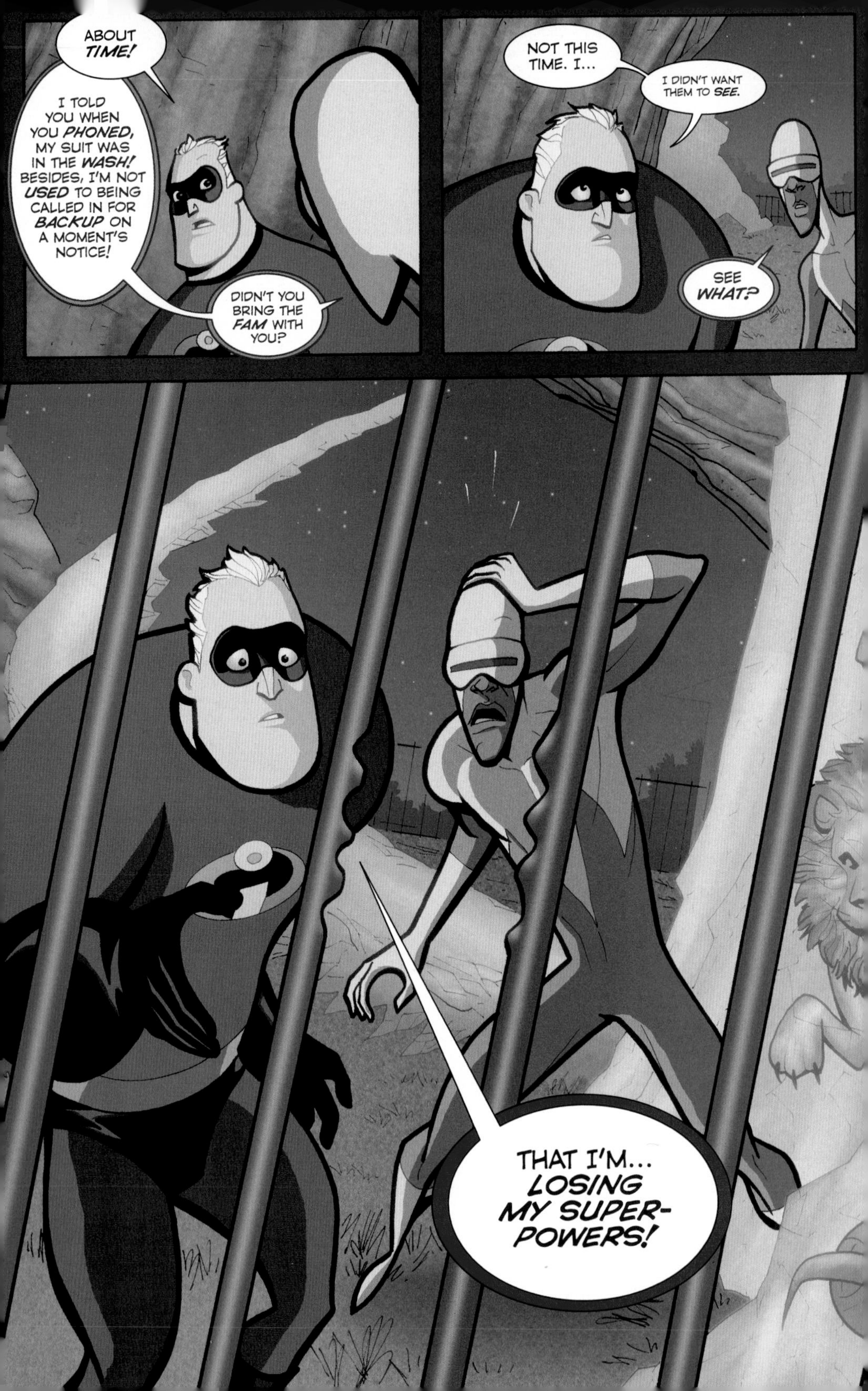
ABOUT TIME!
I TOLD YOU WHEN YOU PHONED, MY SUIT WAS IN THE WASH! BESIDES, I'M NOT USED TO BEING CALLED IN FOR BACKUP ON A MOMENT'S NOTICE!
DIDN'T YOU BRING THE FAM WITH YOU?
NOT THIS TIME. I...
I DIDN'T WANT THEM TO SEE.
SEE WHAT?
THAT I'M... LOSING MY SUPER-POWERS!

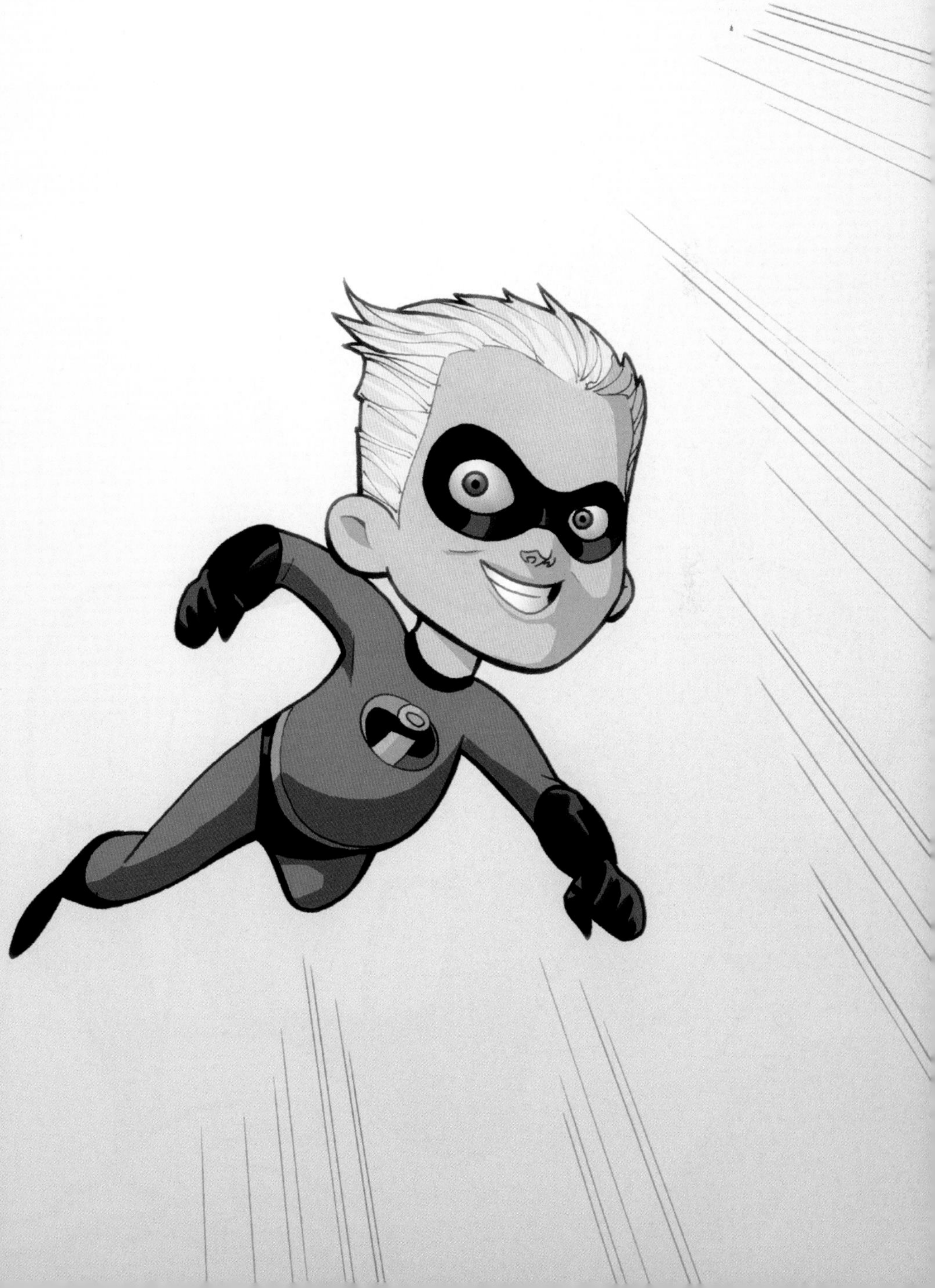

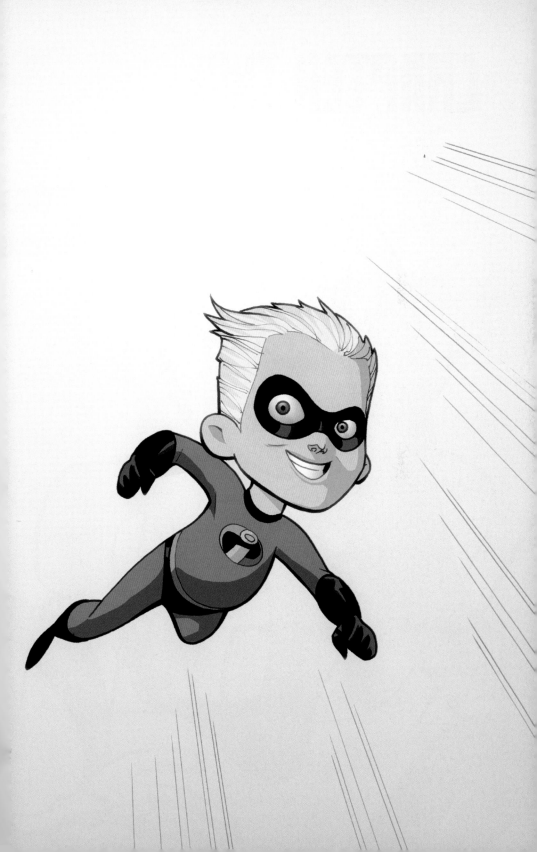

CHAPTER TWO

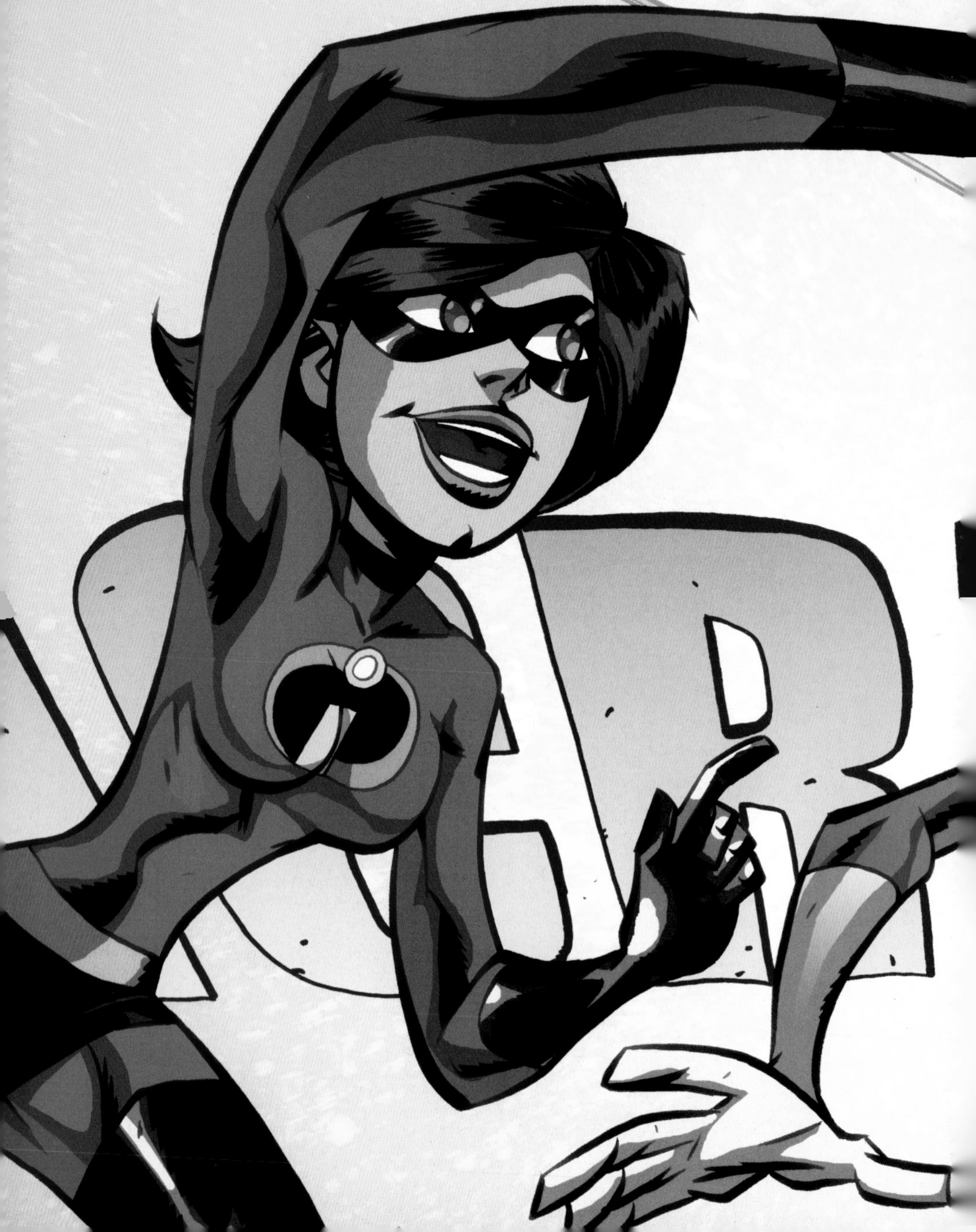

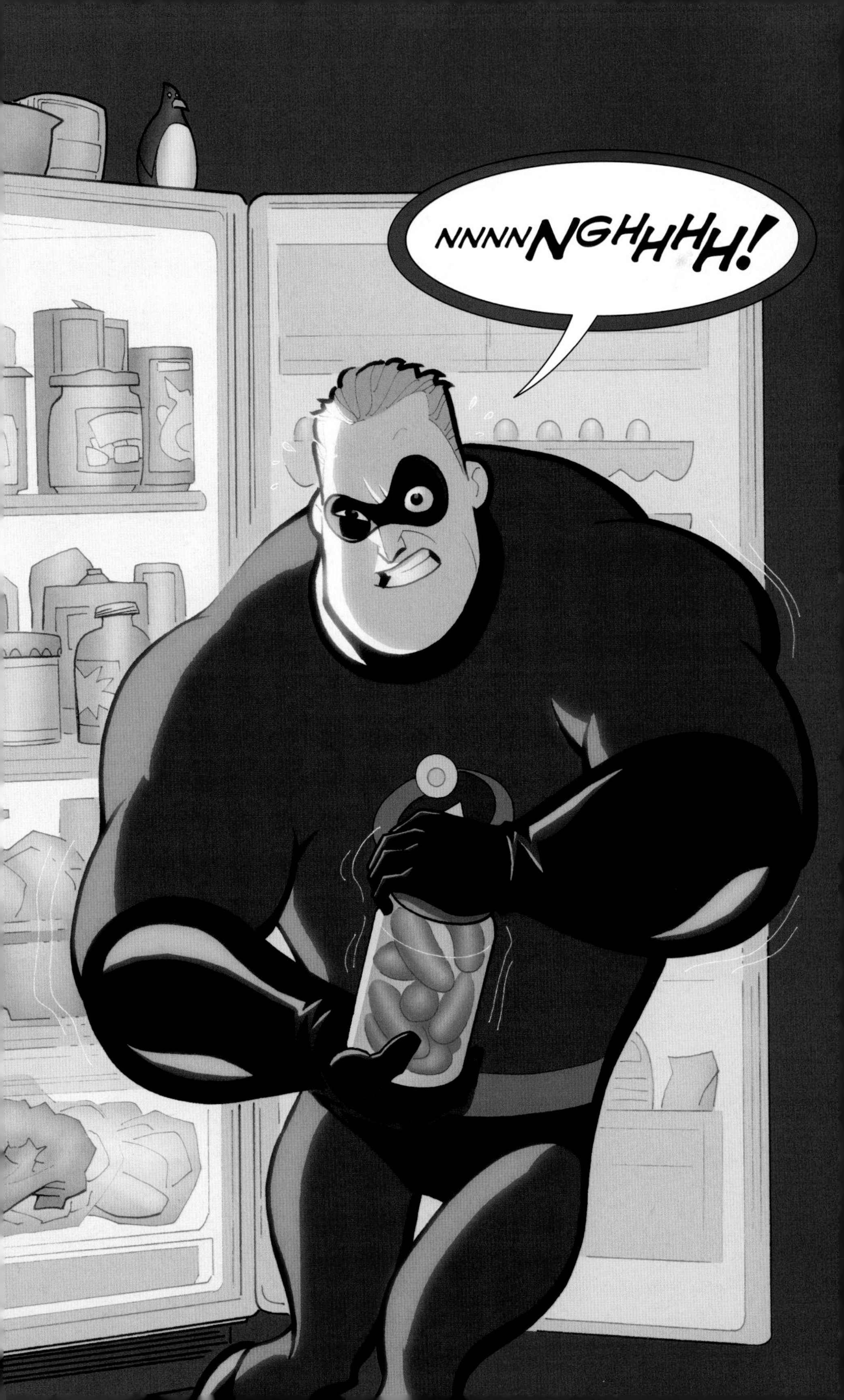
NNNNNGHHHH!

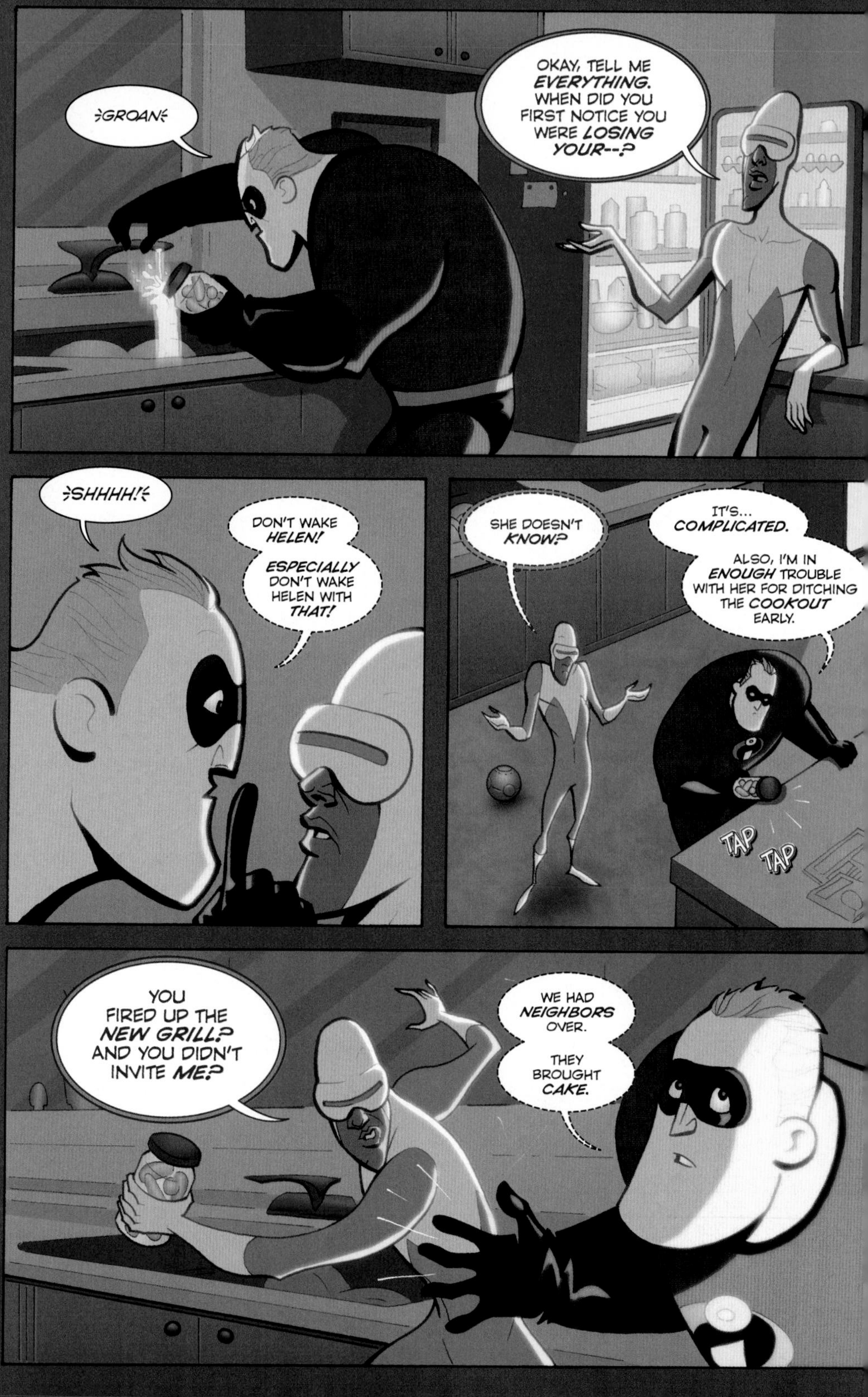
GROAN
OKAY, TELL ME EVERYTHING. WHEN DID YOU FIRST NOTICE YOU WERE LOSING YOUR--?
SHHHH!
DON'T WAKE HELEN!
ESPECIALLY DON'T WAKE HELEN WITH THAT!
SHE DOESN'T KNOW?
IT'S... COMPLICATED.
ALSO, I'M IN ENOUGH TROUBLE WITH HER FOR DITCHING THE COOKOUT EARLY.
TAP TAP
YOU FIRED UP THE NEW GRILL? AND YOU DIDN'T INVITE ME?
WE HAD NEIGHBORS OVER.
THEY BROUGHT CAKE.

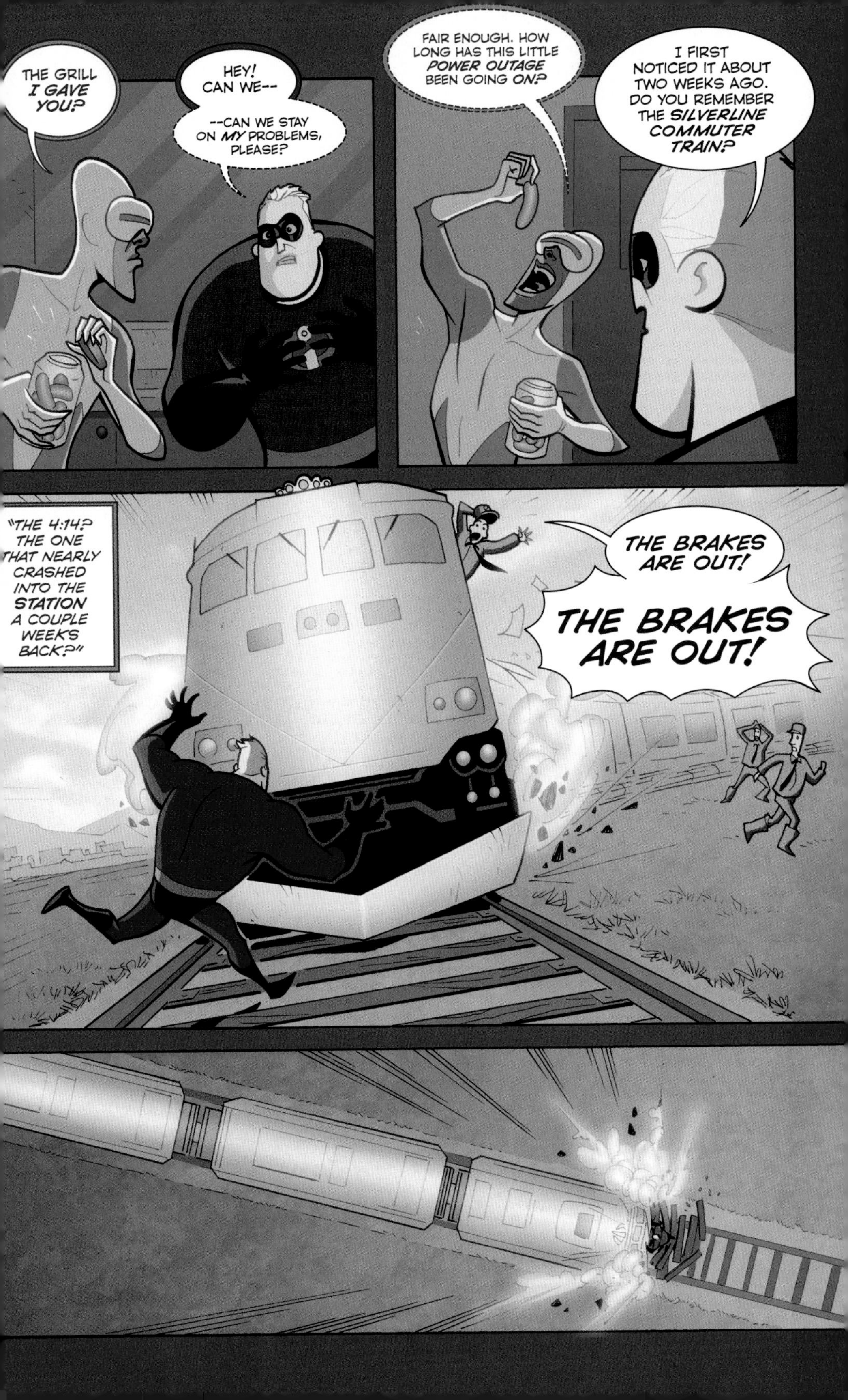
THE GRILL I GAVE YOU?
HEY! CAN WE--
--CAN WE STAY ON MY PROBLEMS, PLEASE?
FAIR ENOUGH. HOW LONG HAS THIS LITTLE POWER OUTAGE BEEN GOING ON?
I FIRST NOTICED IT ABOUT TWO WEEKS AGO. DO YOU REMEMBER THE SILVERLINE COMMUTER TRAIN?
"THE 4:14? THE ONE THAT NEARLY CRASHED INTO THE STATION A COUPLE WEEKS BACK?"
THE BRAKES ARE OUT!
THE BRAKES ARE OUT!

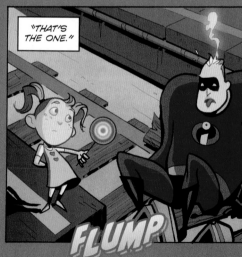

"THAT'S THE ONE."

FLUMP

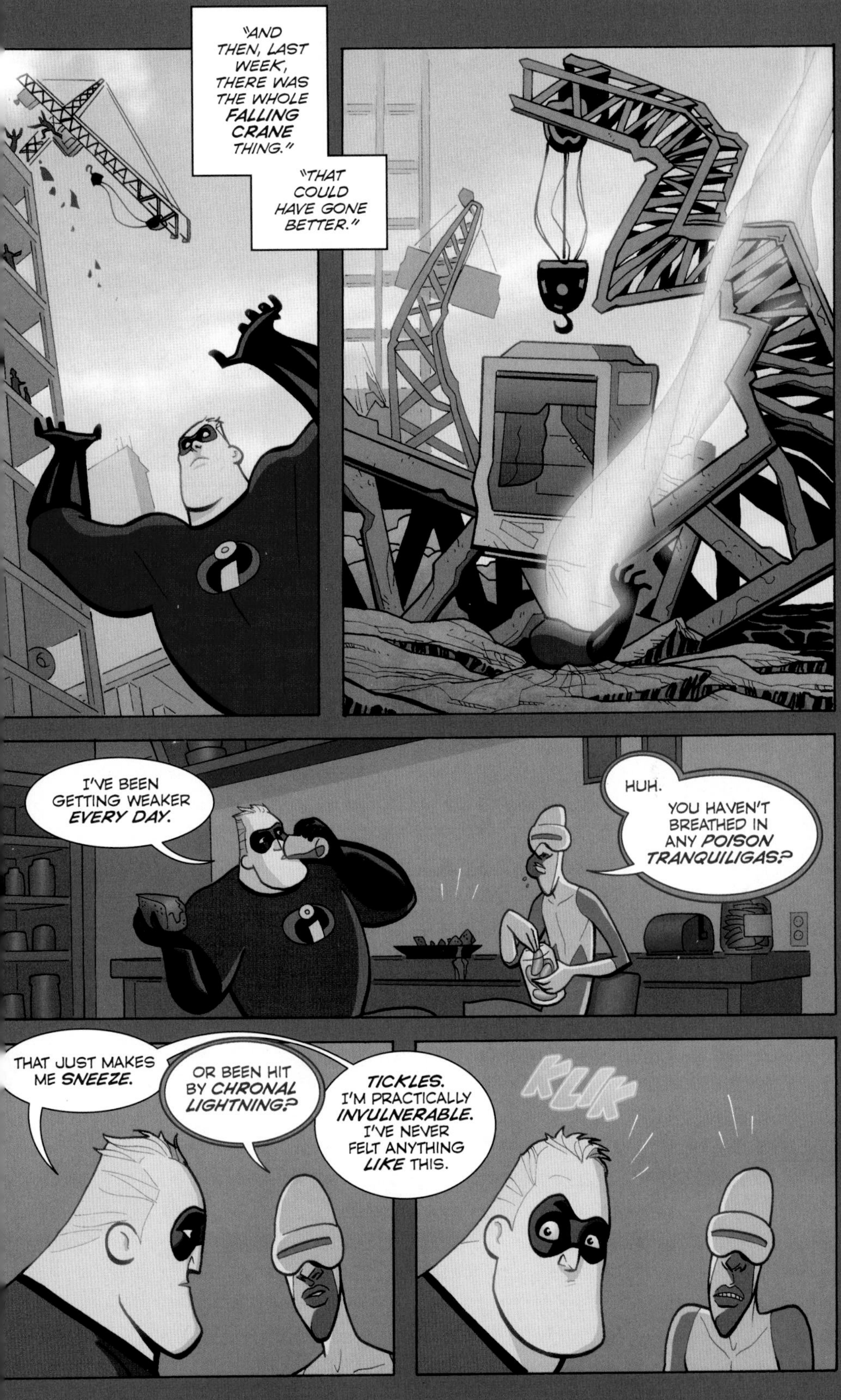
"AND THEN, LAST WEEK, THERE WAS THE WHOLE FALLING CRANE THING."
"THAT COULD HAVE GONE BETTER."
I'VE BEEN GETTING WEAKER EVERY DAY.
HUH.
YOU HAVEN'T BREATHED IN ANY POISON TRANQUILIGAS?
THAT JUST MAKES ME SNEEZE.
OR BEEN HIT BY CHRONAL LIGHTNING?
TICKLES. I'M PRACTICALLY INVULNERABLE. I'VE NEVER FELT ANYTHING LIKE THIS.
KLIK

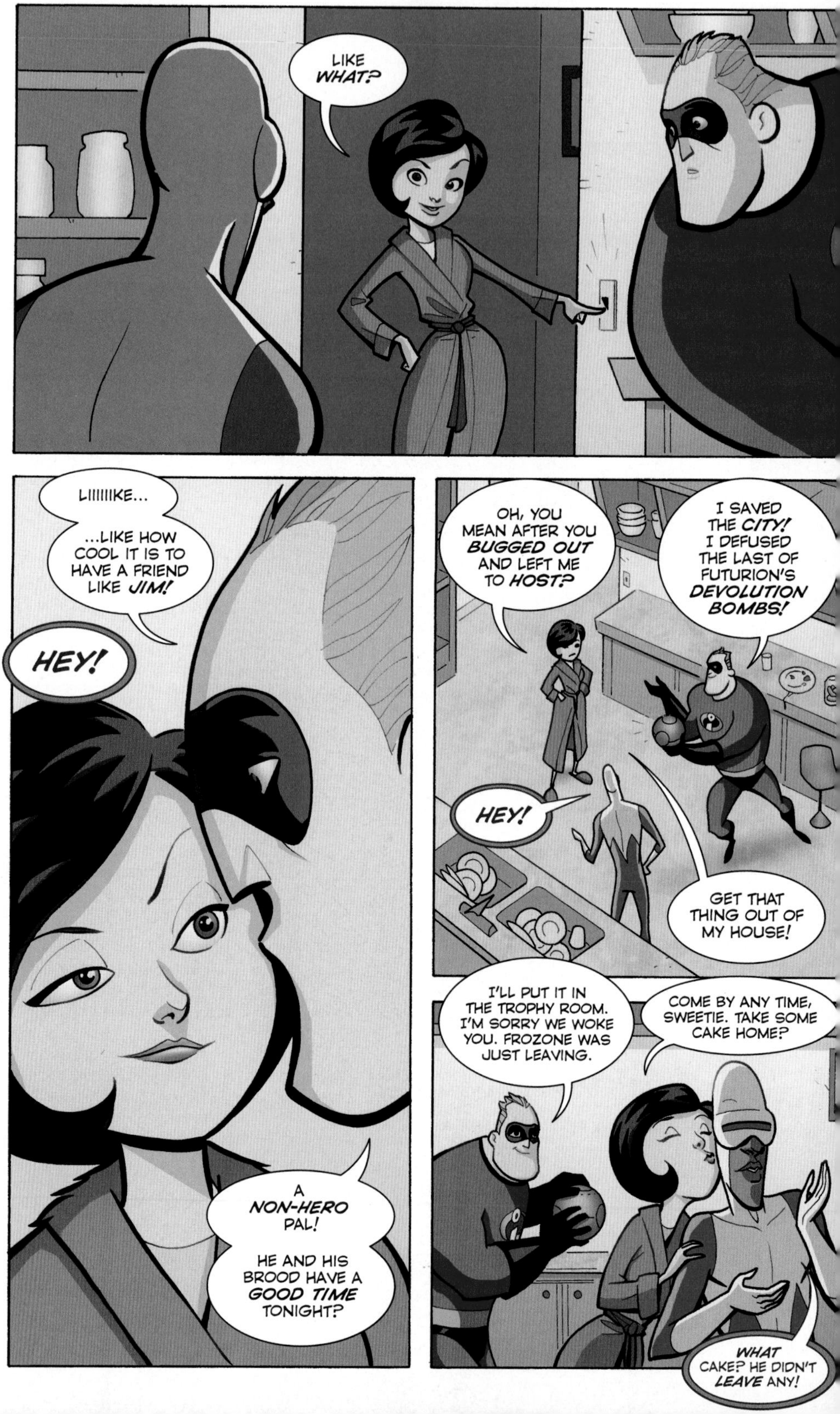
LIKE WHAT?
LIIIIIIKE...
...LIKE HOW COOL IT IS TO HAVE A FRIEND LIKE JIM!
HEY!
A NON-HERO PAL!
HE AND HIS BROOD HAVE A GOOD TIME TONIGHT?
OH, YOU MEAN AFTER YOU BUGGED OUT AND LEFT ME TO HOST?
I SAVED THE CITY! I DEFUSED THE LAST OF FUTURION'S DEVOLUTION BOMBS!
HEY!
GET THAT THING OUT OF MY HOUSE!
I'LL PUT IT IN THE TROPHY ROOM. I'M SORRY WE WOKE YOU. FROZONE WAS JUST LEAVING.
COME BY ANY TIME, SWEETIE. TAKE SOME CAKE HOME?
WHAT CAKE? HE DIDN'T LEAVE ANY!

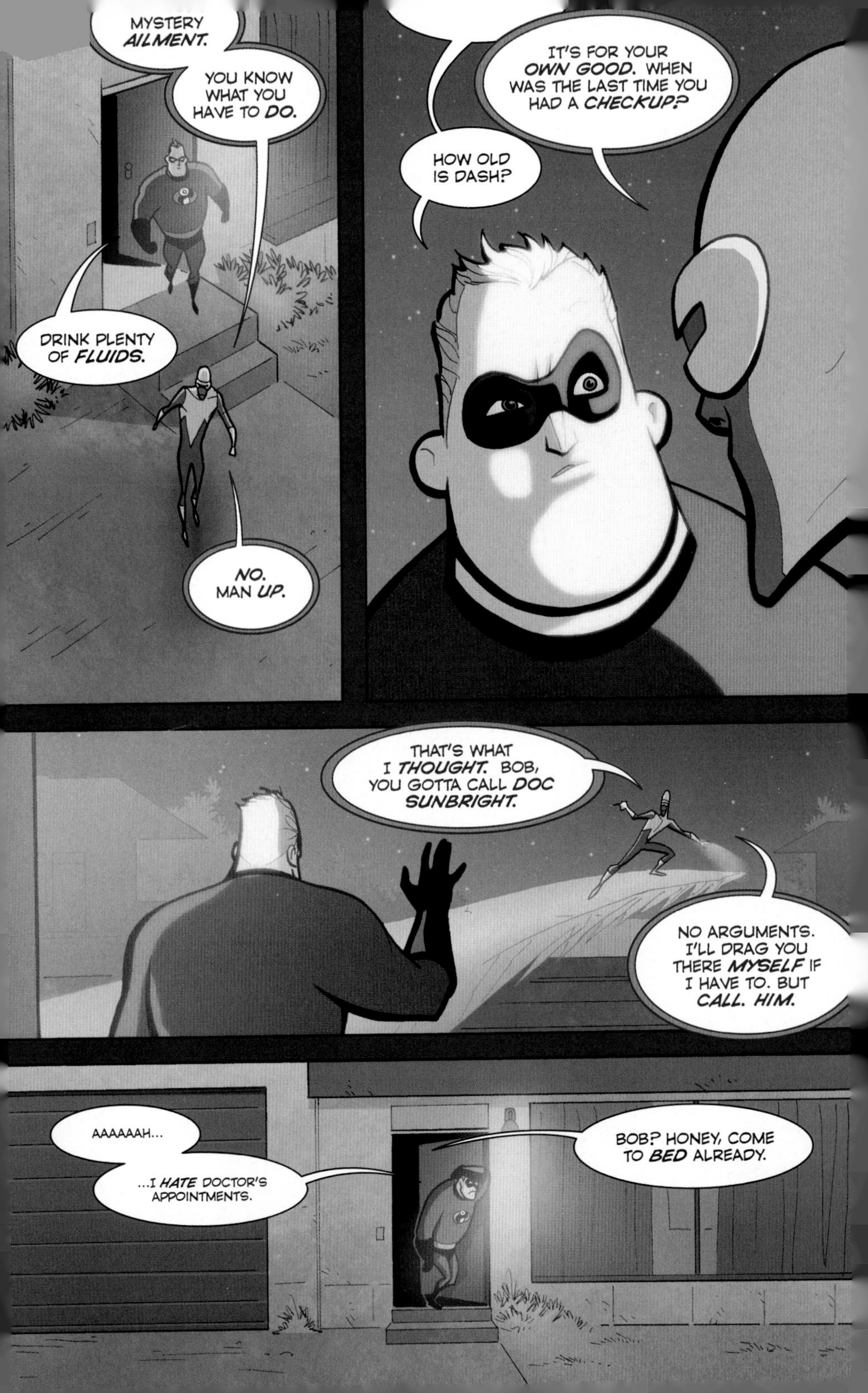
MYSTERY AILMENT.
YOU KNOW WHAT YOU HAVE TO DO.
DRINK PLENTY OF FLUIDS.
NO. MAN UP.
IT'S FOR YOUR OWN GOOD. WHEN WAS THE LAST TIME YOU HAD A CHECKUP?
HOW OLD IS DASH?
THAT'S WHAT I THOUGHT. BOB, YOU GOTTA CALL DOC SUNBRIGHT.
NO ARGUMENTS. I'LL DRAG YOU THERE MYSELF IF I HAVE TO. BUT CALL. HIM.
AAAAAAH...
...I HATE DOCTOR'S APPOINTMENTS.
BOB? HONEY, COME TO BED ALREADY.

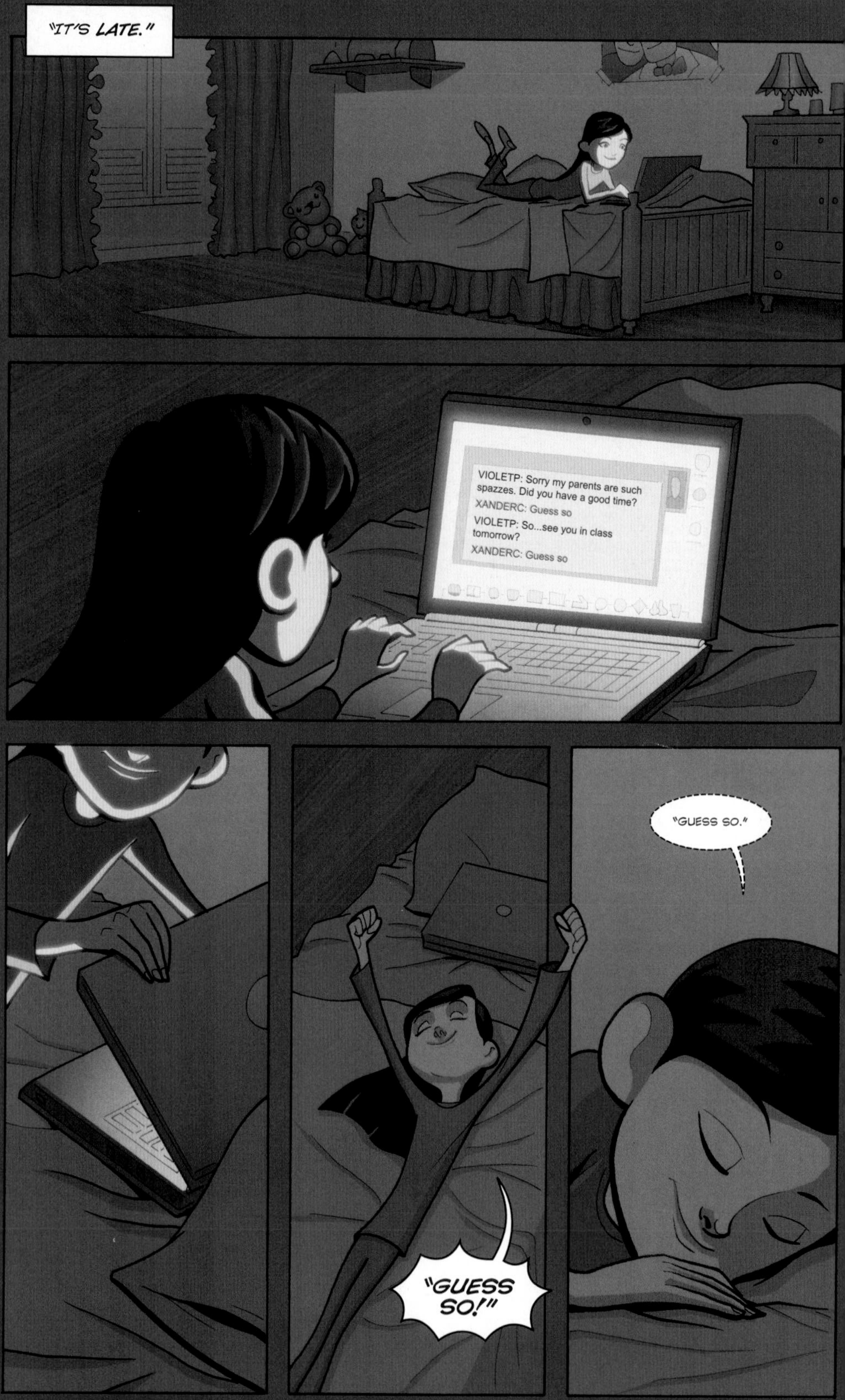
"IT'S LATE."
VIOLETP: Sorry my parents are such spazzes. Did you have a good time?
XANDERC: Guess so
VIOLETP: So...see you in class tomorrow?
XANDERC: Guess so
"GUESS SO!"
"GUESS SO."

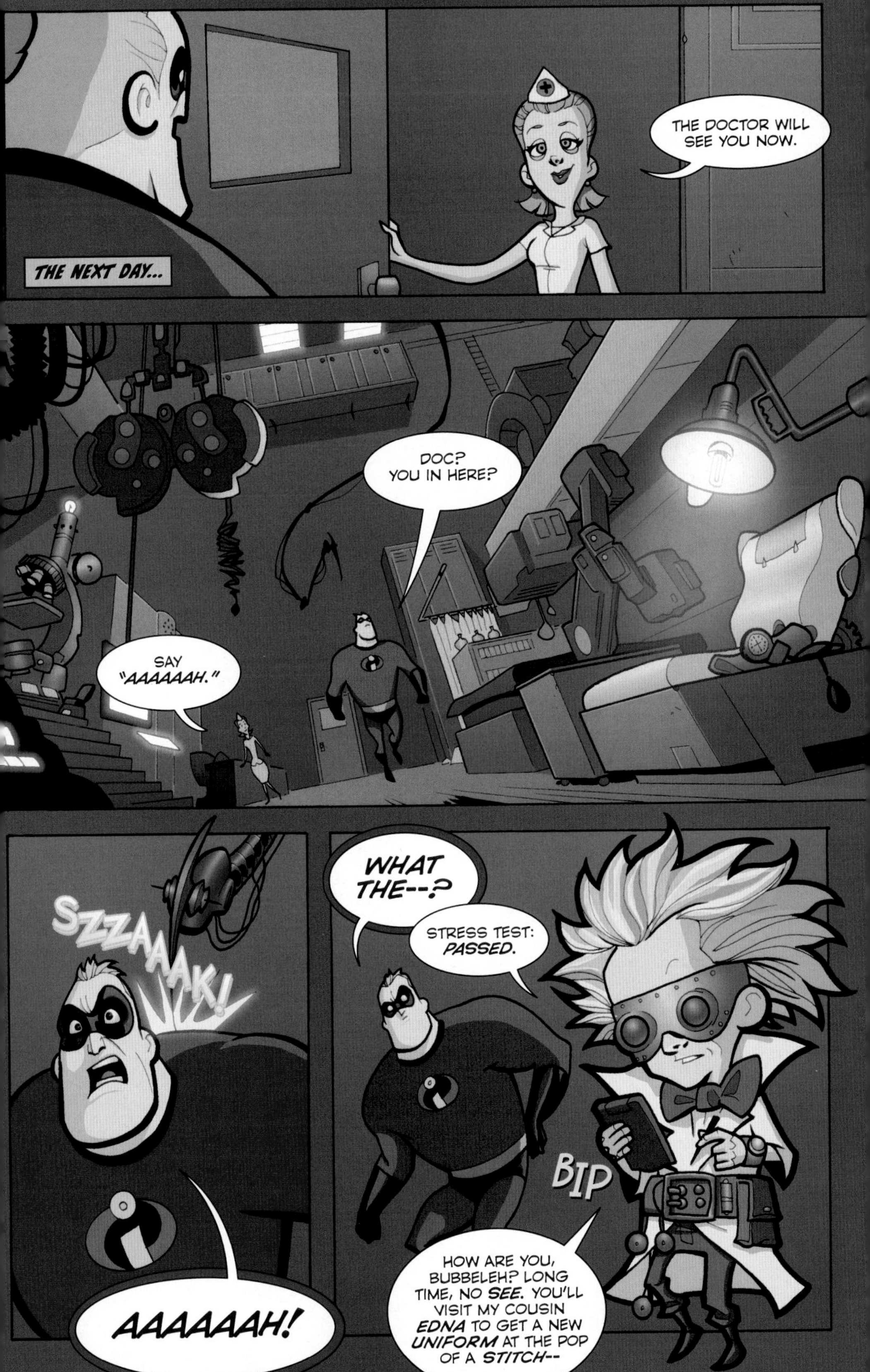
THE NEXT DAY...
THE DOCTOR WILL SEE YOU NOW.
DOC? YOU IN HERE?
SAY "AAAAAAH."
SZZAAAAK!
AAAAAAH!
WHAT THE--?
STRESS TEST: PASSED.
BIP
HOW ARE YOU, BUBBELEH? LONG TIME, NO SEE. YOU'LL VISIT MY COUSIN EDNA TO GET A NEW UNIFORM AT THE POP OF A STITCH--

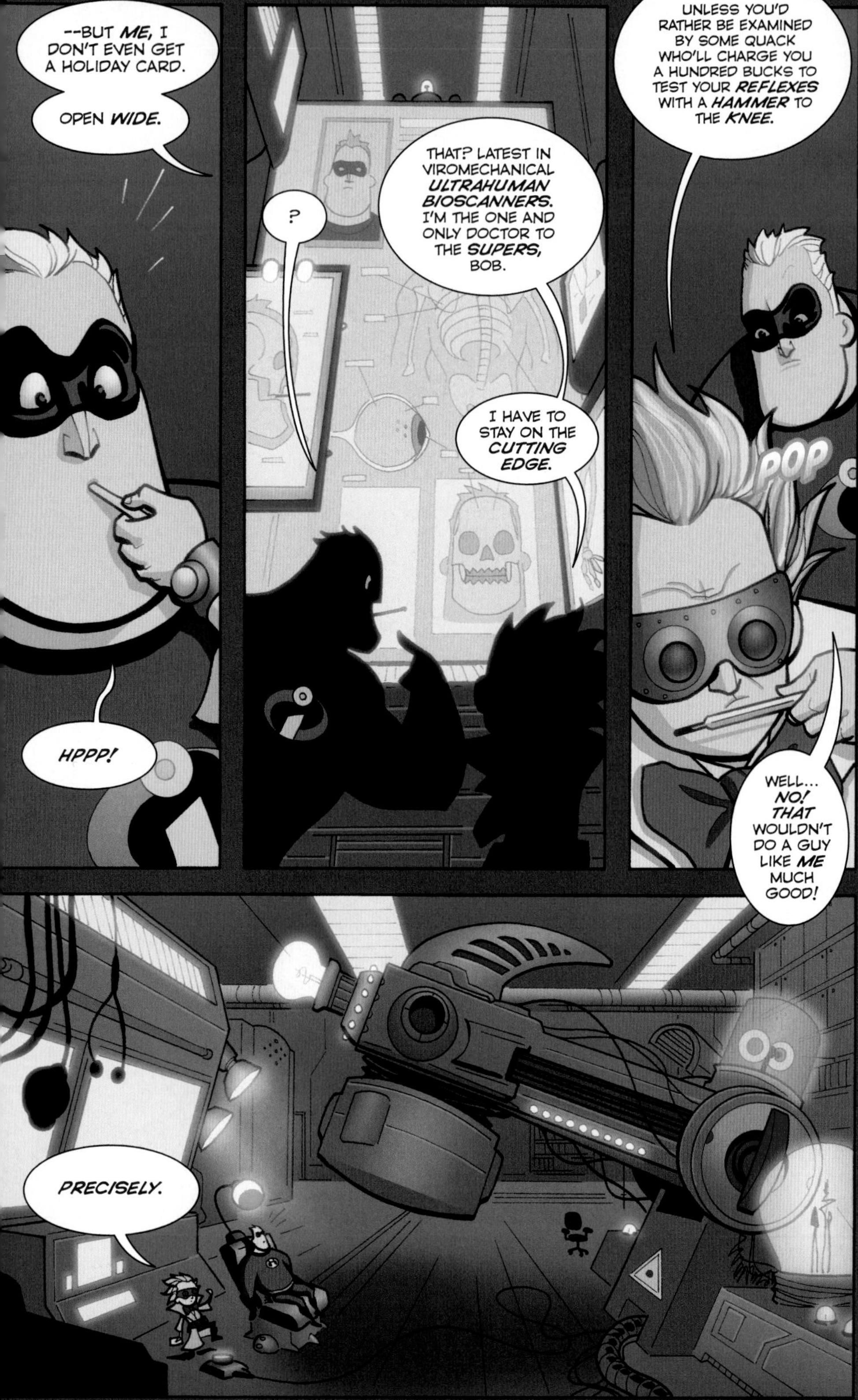
--BUT ME, I DON'T EVEN GET A HOLIDAY CARD.
OPEN WIDE.
HPPP!
?
THAT? LATEST IN VIROMECHANICAL ULTRAHUMAN BIOSCANNERS. I'M THE ONE AND ONLY DOCTOR TO THE SUPERS, BOB.
I HAVE TO STAY ON THE CUTTING EDGE.
UNLESS YOU'D RATHER BE EXAMINED BY SOME QUACK WHO'LL CHARGE YOU A HUNDRED BUCKS TO TEST YOUR REFLEXES WITH A HAMMER TO THE KNEE.
POP
WELL... NO! THAT WOULDN'T DO A GUY LIKE ME MUCH GOOD!
PRECISELY.

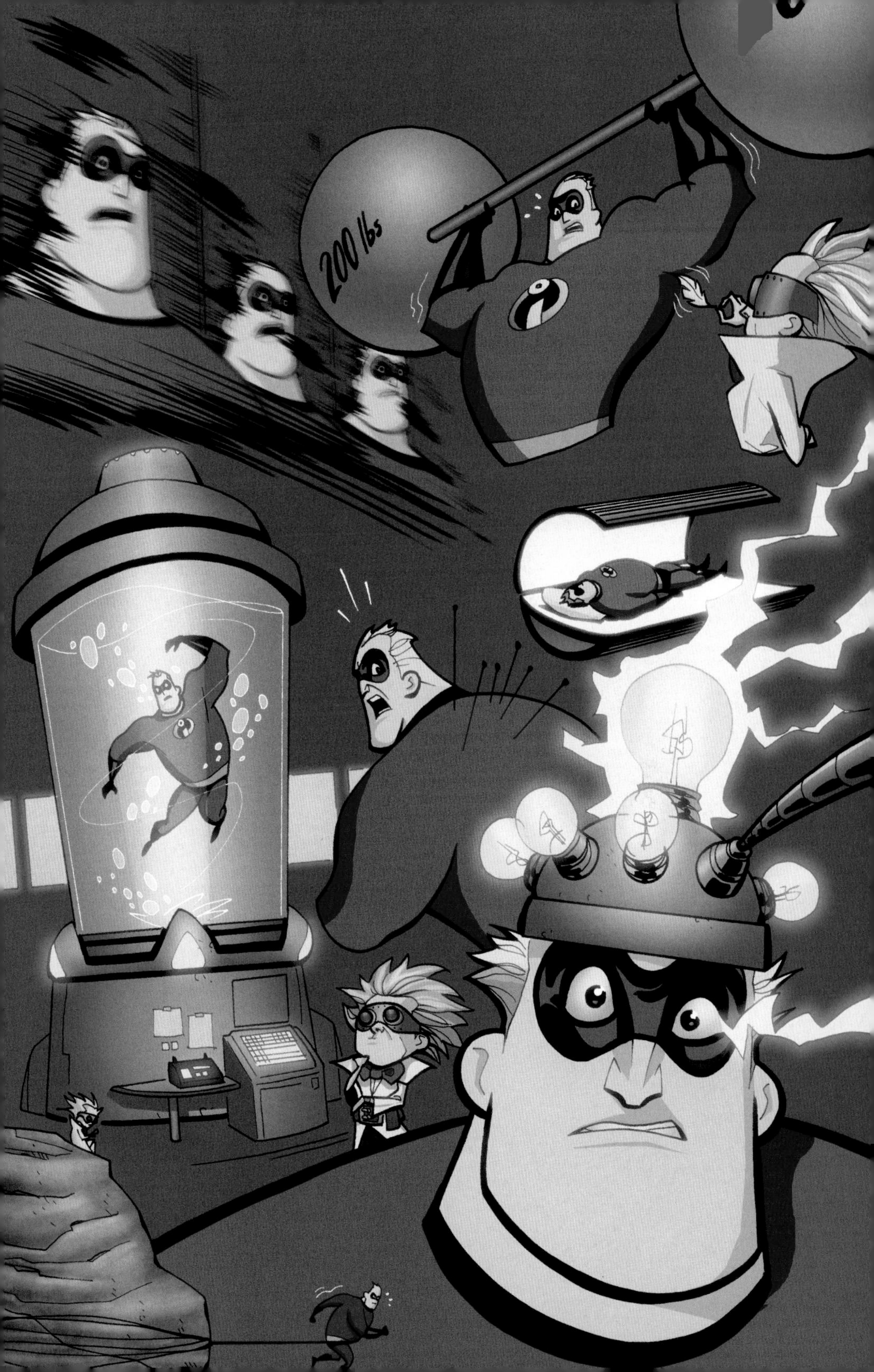
200 lbs

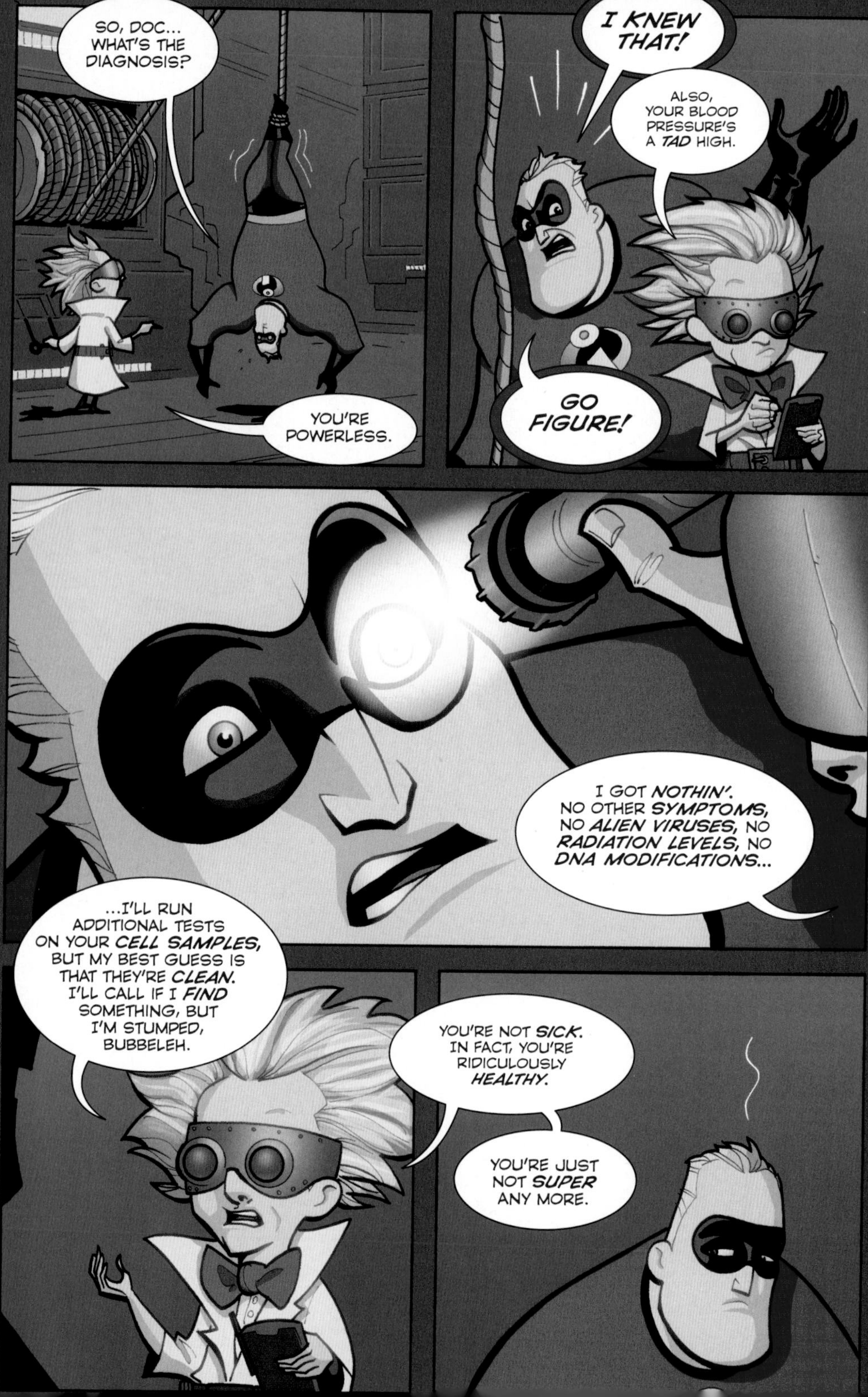
SO, DOC... WHAT'S THE DIAGNOSIS?
YOU'RE POWERLESS.
I KNEW THAT!
ALSO, YOUR BLOOD PRESSURE'S A TAD HIGH.
GO FIGURE!
I GOT NOTHIN'. NO OTHER SYMPTOMS, NO ALIEN VIRUSES, NO RADIATION LEVELS, NO DNA MODIFICATIONS...
...I'LL RUN ADDITIONAL TESTS ON YOUR CELL SAMPLES, BUT MY BEST GUESS IS THAT THEY'RE CLEAN. I'LL CALL IF I FIND SOMETHING, BUT I'M STUMPED, BUBBELEH.
YOU'RE NOT SICK. IN FACT, YOU'RE RIDICULOUSLY HEALTHY.
YOU'RE JUST NOT SUPER ANY MORE.

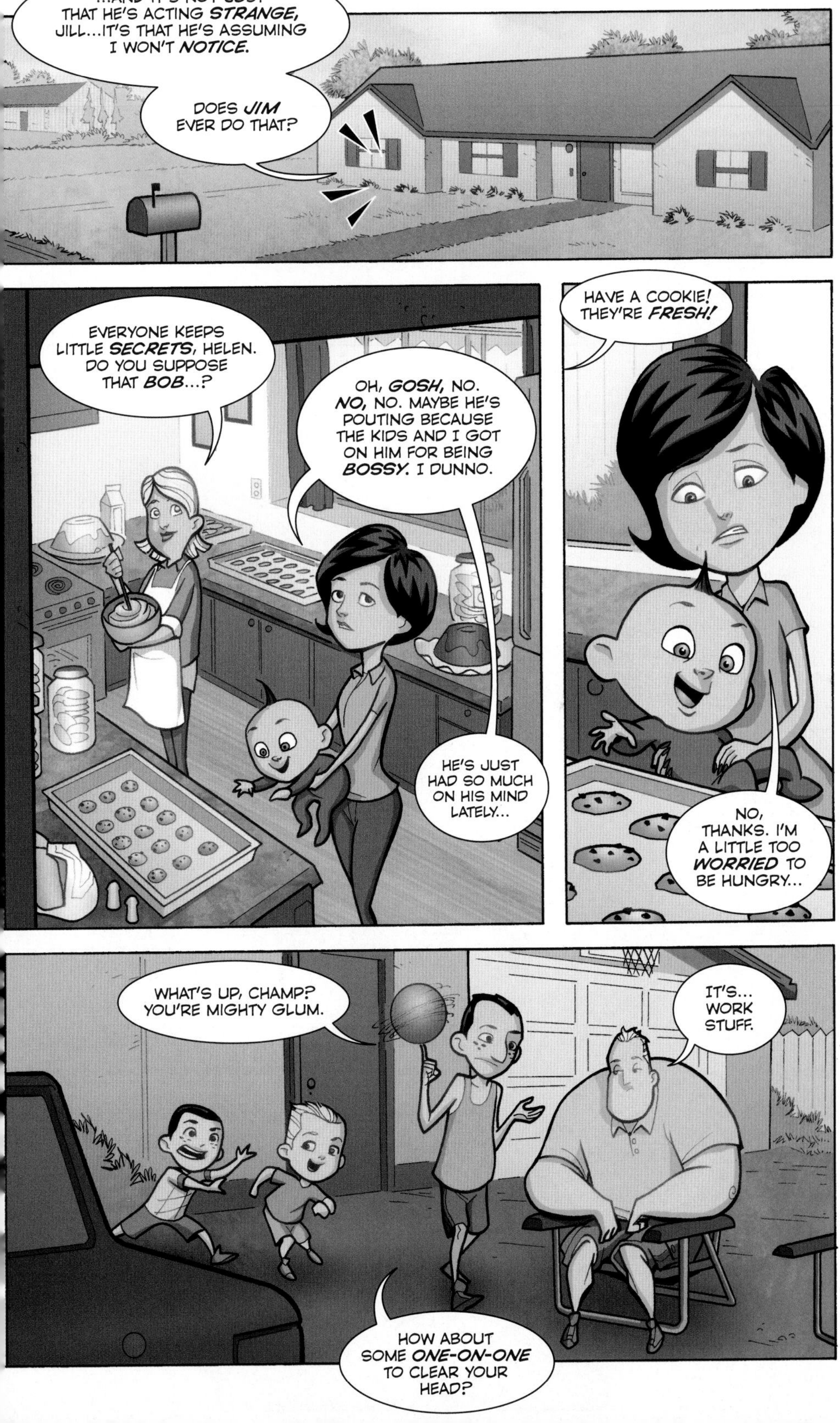

...AND IT'S NOT JUST THAT HE'S ACTING STRANGE, JILL...IT'S THAT HE'S ASSUMING I WON'T NOTICE.
DOES JIM EVER DO THAT?
EVERYONE KEEPS LITTLE SECRETS, HELEN. DO YOU SUPPOSE THAT BOB...?
OH, GOSH, NO. NO, NO. MAYBE HE'S POUTING BECAUSE THE KIDS AND I GOT ON HIM FOR BEING BOSSY. I DUNNO.
HE'S JUST HAD SO MUCH ON HIS MIND LATELY...
HAVE A COOKIE! THEY'RE FRESH!
NO, THANKS. I'M A LITTLE TOO WORRIED TO BE HUNGRY...
WHAT'S UP, CHAMP? YOU'RE MIGHTY GLUM.
IT'S... WORK STUFF.
HOW ABOUT SOME ONE-ON-ONE TO CLEAR YOUR HEAD?

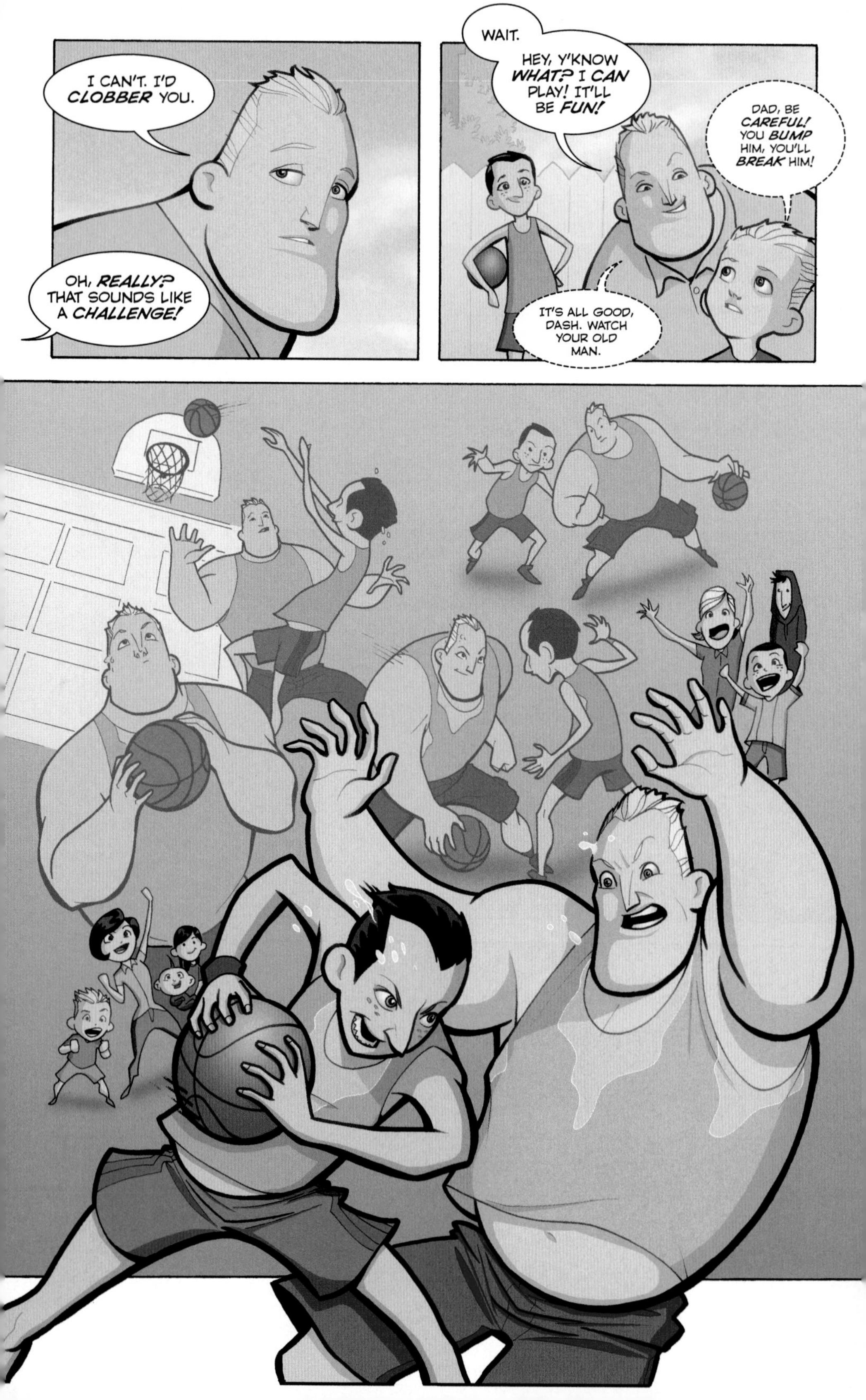
I CAN'T. I'D CLOBBER YOU.
OH, REALLY? THAT SOUNDS LIKE A CHALLENGE!
WAIT.
HEY, Y'KNOW WHAT? I CAN PLAY! IT'LL BE FUN!
DAD, BE CAREFUL! YOU BUMP HIM, YOU'LL BREAK HIM!
IT'S ALL GOOD, DASH. WATCH YOUR OLD MAN.

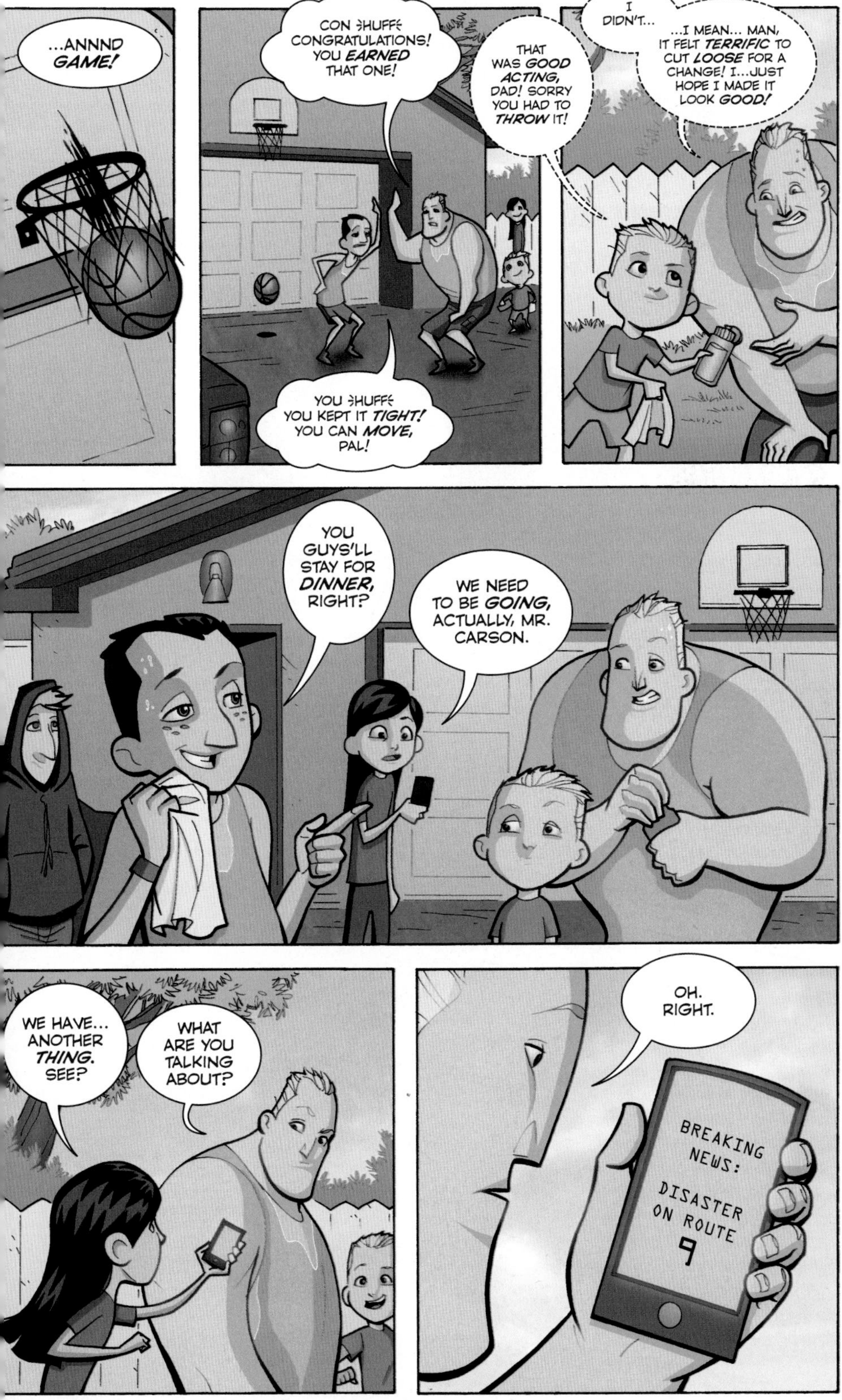
...ANNND GAME!
CON ≶HUFF≶ CONGRATULATIONS! YOU EARNED THAT ONE!
YOU ≶HUFF≶ YOU KEPT IT TIGHT! YOU CAN MOVE, PAL!
THAT WAS GOOD ACTING, DAD! SORRY YOU HAD TO THROW IT!
I DIDN'T...
...I MEAN... MAN, IT FELT TERRIFIC TO CUT LOOSE FOR A CHANGE! I...JUST HOPE I MADE IT LOOK GOOD!
YOU GUYS'LL STAY FOR DINNER, RIGHT?
WE NEED TO BE GOING, ACTUALLY, MR. CARSON.
WE HAVE... ANOTHER THING. SEE?
WHAT ARE YOU TALKING ABOUT?
OH. RIGHT.
BREAKING NEWS:
DISASTER ON ROUTE 9

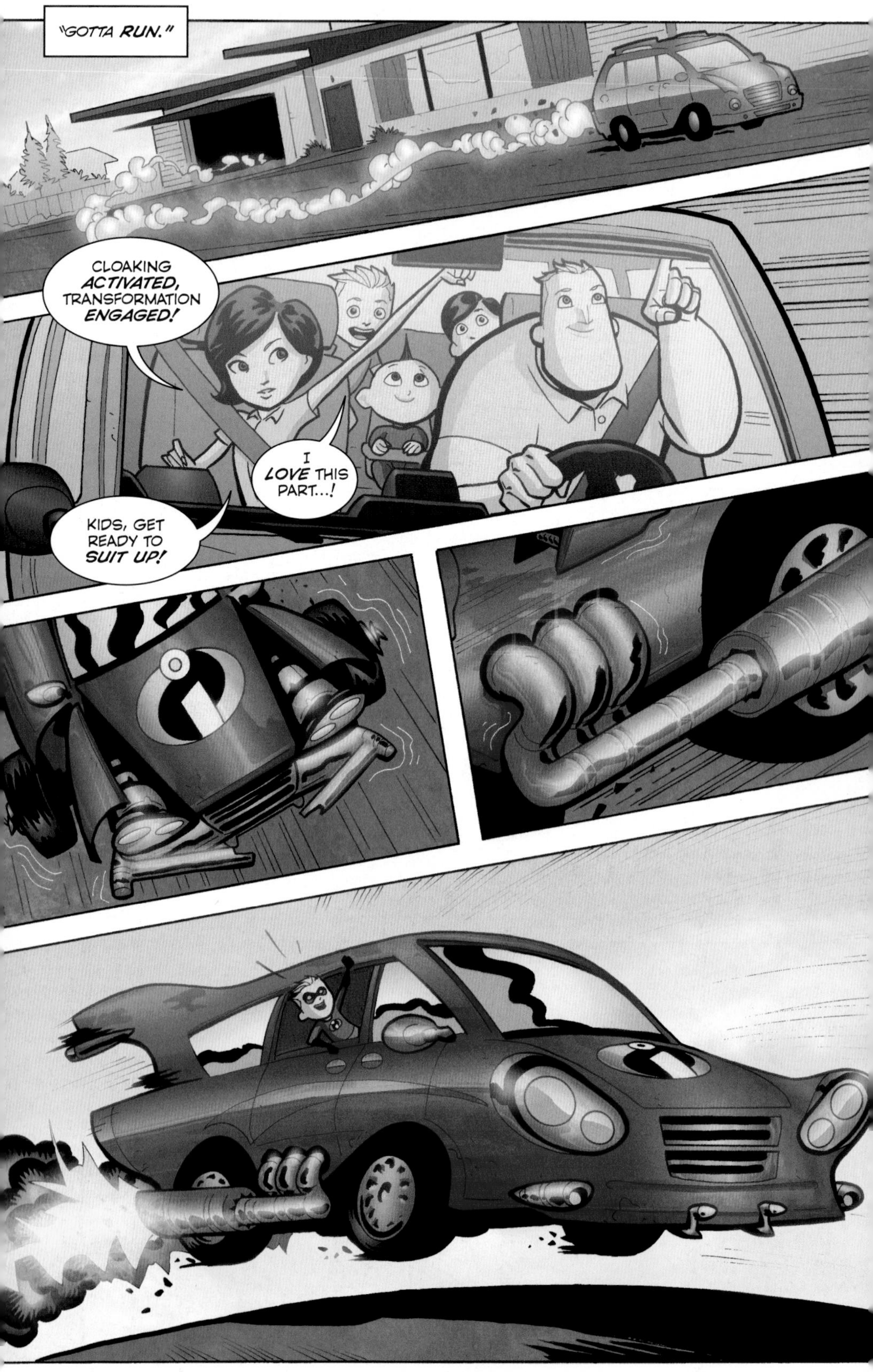
"GOTTA RUN."
CLOAKING ACTIVATED, TRANSFORMATION ENGAGED!
I LOVE THIS PART...!
KIDS, GET READY TO SUIT UP!

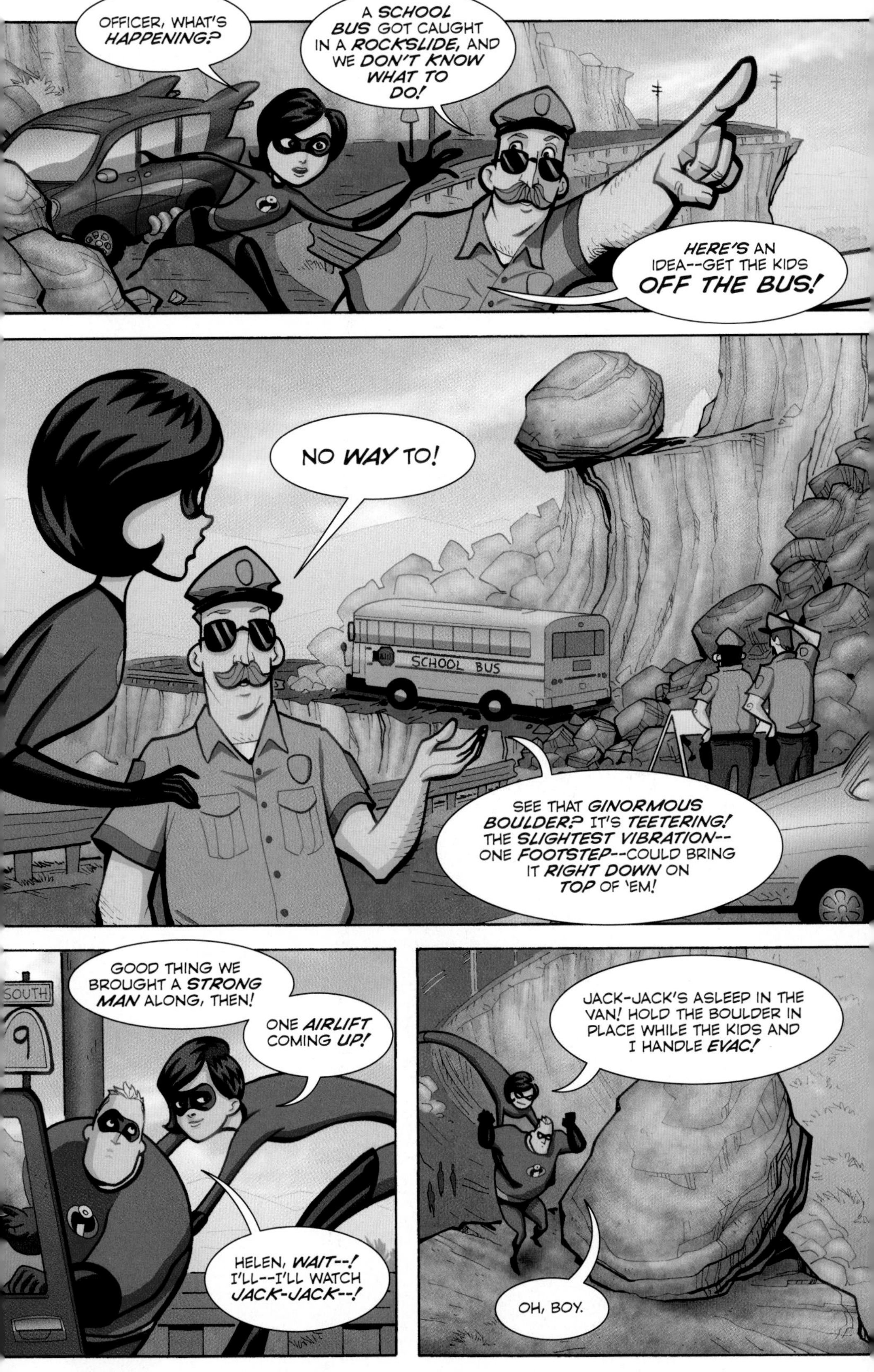

OFFICER, WHAT'S HAPPENING?
A SCHOOL BUS GOT CAUGHT IN A ROCKSLIDE, AND WE DON'T KNOW WHAT TO DO!
HERE'S AN IDEA--GET THE KIDS OFF THE BUS!
NO WAY TO!
SCHOOL BUS
SEE THAT GINORMOUS BOULDER? IT'S TEETERING! THE SLIGHTEST VIBRATION--ONE FOOTSTEP--COULD BRING IT RIGHT DOWN ON TOP OF 'EM!
SOUTH
9
GOOD THING WE BROUGHT A STRONG MAN ALONG, THEN!
ONE AIRLIFT COMING UP!
HELEN, WAIT--! I'LL--I'LL WATCH JACK-JACK--!
JACK-JACK'S ASLEEP IN THE VAN! HOLD THE BOULDER IN PLACE WHILE THE KIDS AND I HANDLE EVAC!
OH, BOY.

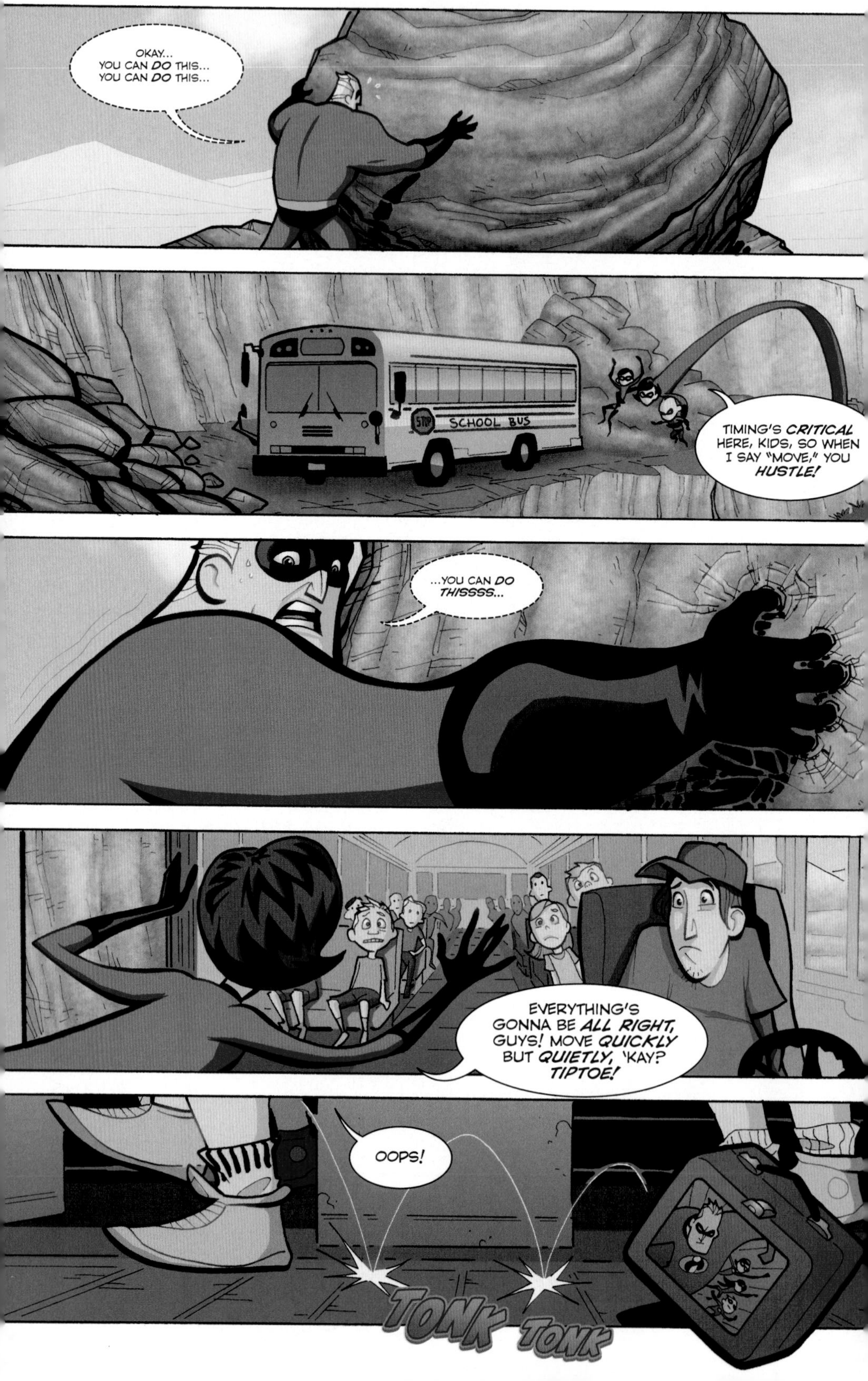
OKAY... YOU CAN DO THIS... YOU CAN DO THIS...
SCHOOL BUS
STOP
TIMING'S CRITICAL HERE, KIDS, SO WHEN I SAY "MOVE," YOU HUSTLE!
...YOU CAN DO THISSSS...
EVERYTHING'S GONNA BE ALL RIGHT, GUYS! MOVE QUICKLY BUT QUIETLY, 'KAY? TIPTOE!
OOPS!
TONK TONK

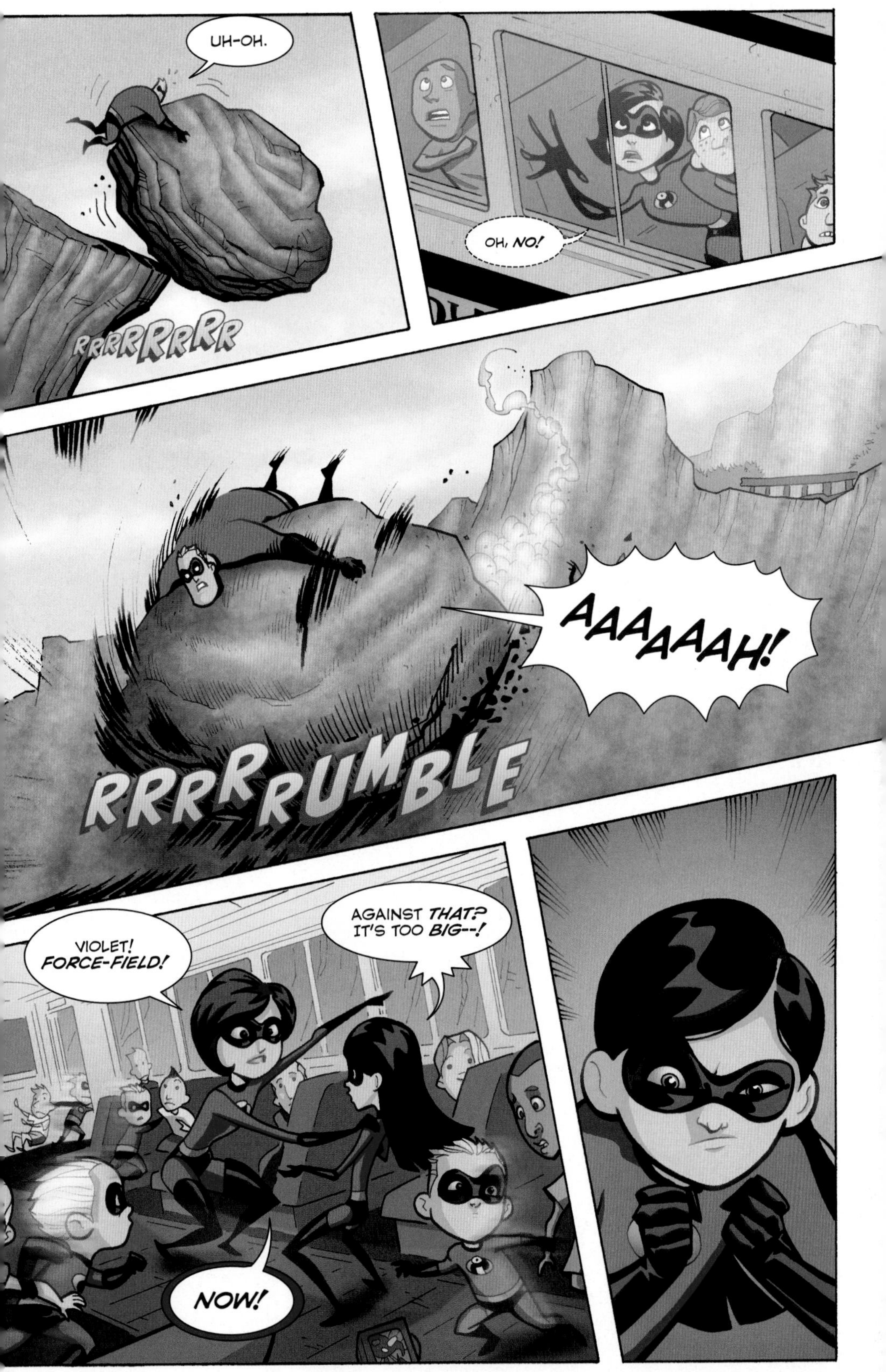
UH-OH.
OH, NO!
RRRRRRRR
AAAAAAH!
RRRRRUMBLE
VIOLET! FORCE-FIELD!
AGAINST THAT? IT'S TOO BIG--!
NOW!

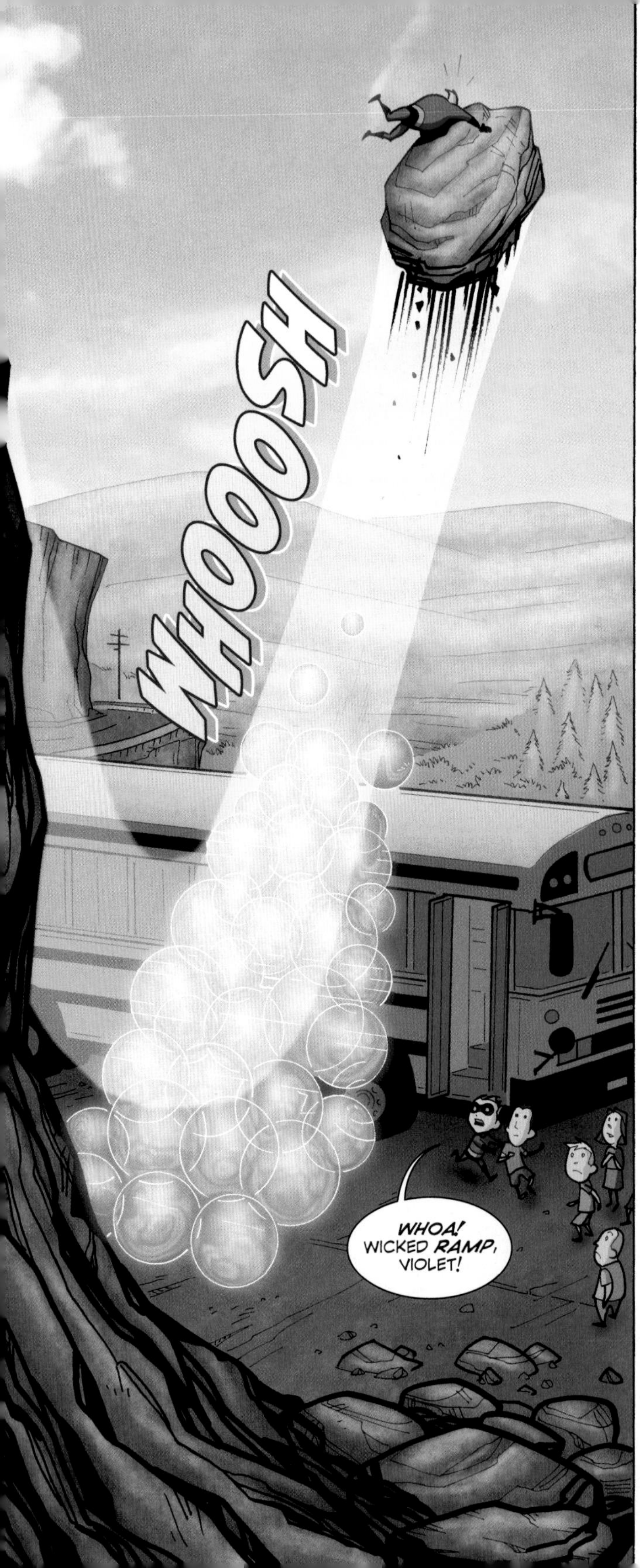
WHOOOSH
WHOA! WICKED RAMP, VIOLET!
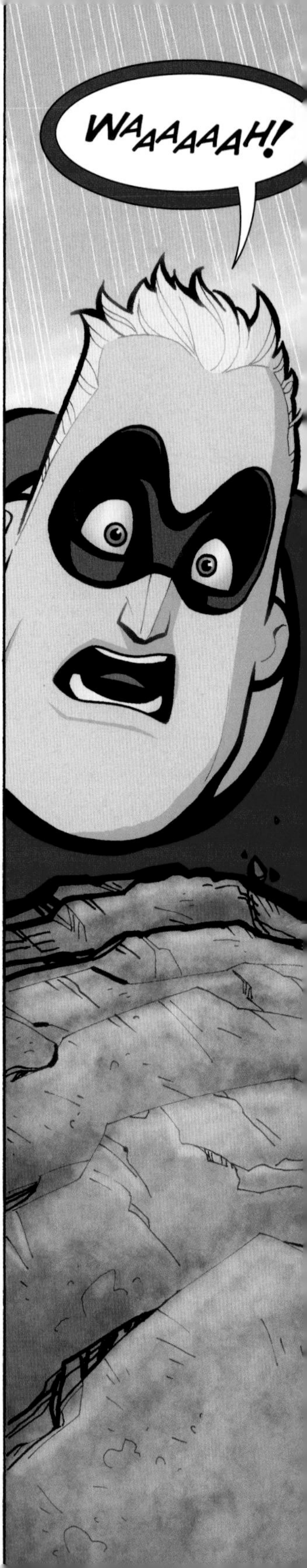
WAAAAAAH!

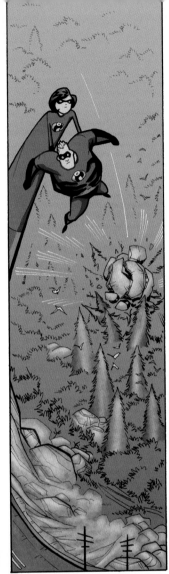

LOSE YOUR *FOOTING?*

I--

I... I WASN'T STRONG ENOUGH.

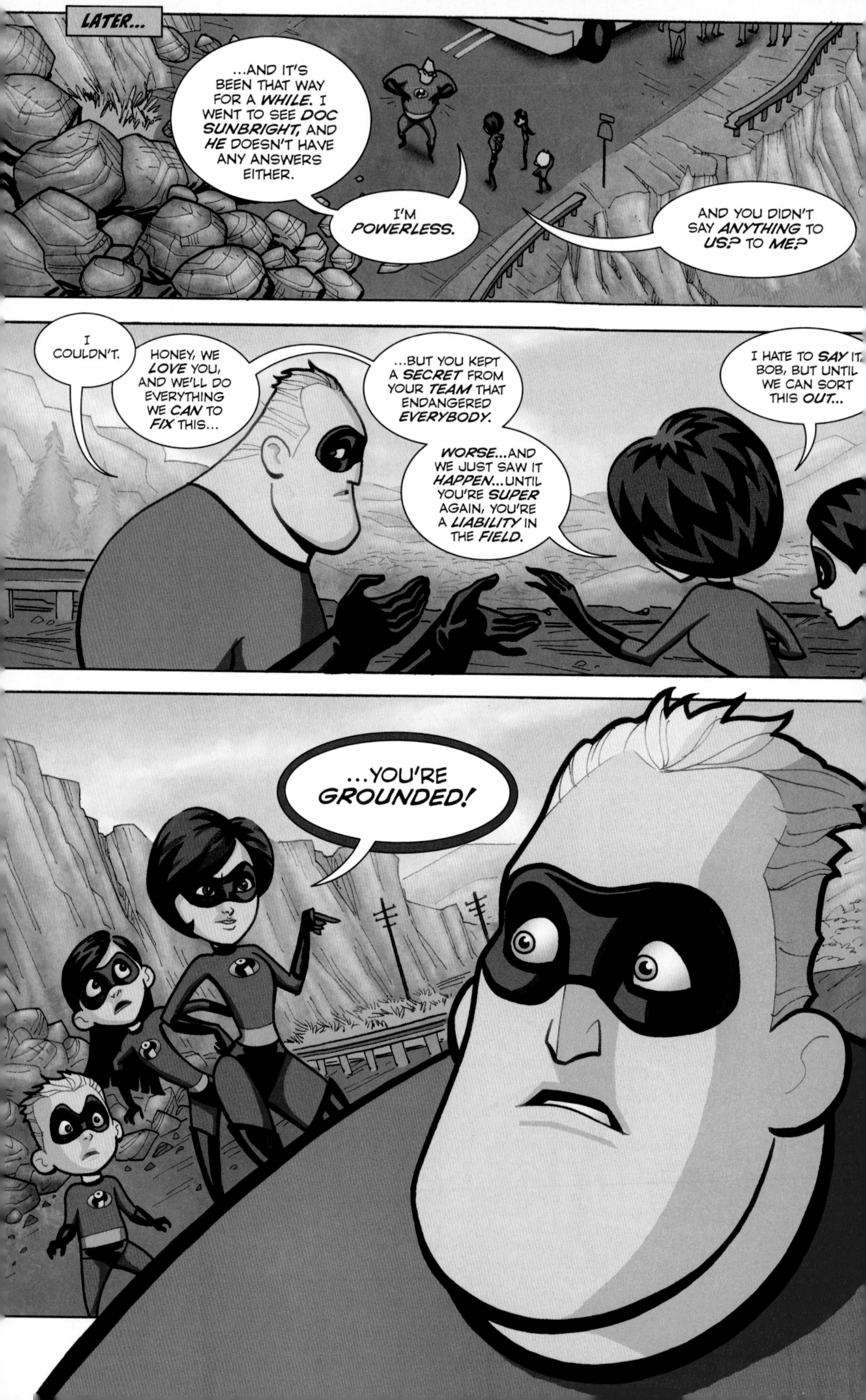
LATER...
...AND IT'S BEEN THAT WAY FOR A WHILE. I WENT TO SEE DOC SUNBRIGHT, AND HE DOESN'T HAVE ANY ANSWERS EITHER.
I'M POWERLESS.
AND YOU DIDN'T SAY ANYTHING TO US? TO ME?
I COULDN'T.
HONEY, WE LOVE YOU, AND WE'LL DO EVERYTHING WE CAN TO FIX THIS...
...BUT YOU KEPT A SECRET FROM YOUR TEAM THAT ENDANGERED EVERYBODY.
WORSE...AND WE JUST SAW IT HAPPEN...UNTIL YOU'RE SUPER AGAIN, YOU'RE A LIABILITY IN THE FIELD.
I HATE TO SAY IT, BOB, BUT UNTIL WE CAN SORT THIS OUT...
...YOU'RE GROUNDED!

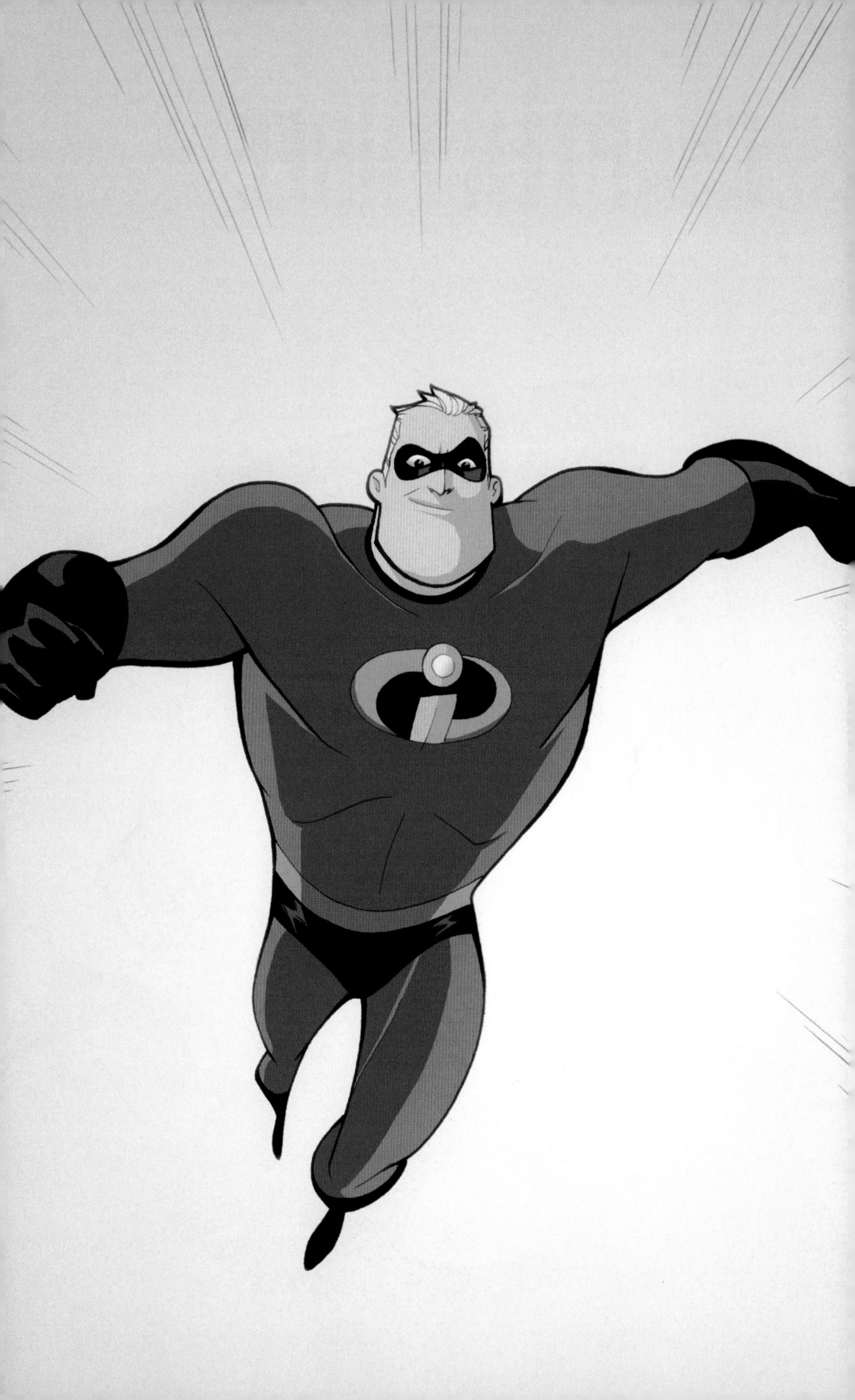

CHAPTER THREE

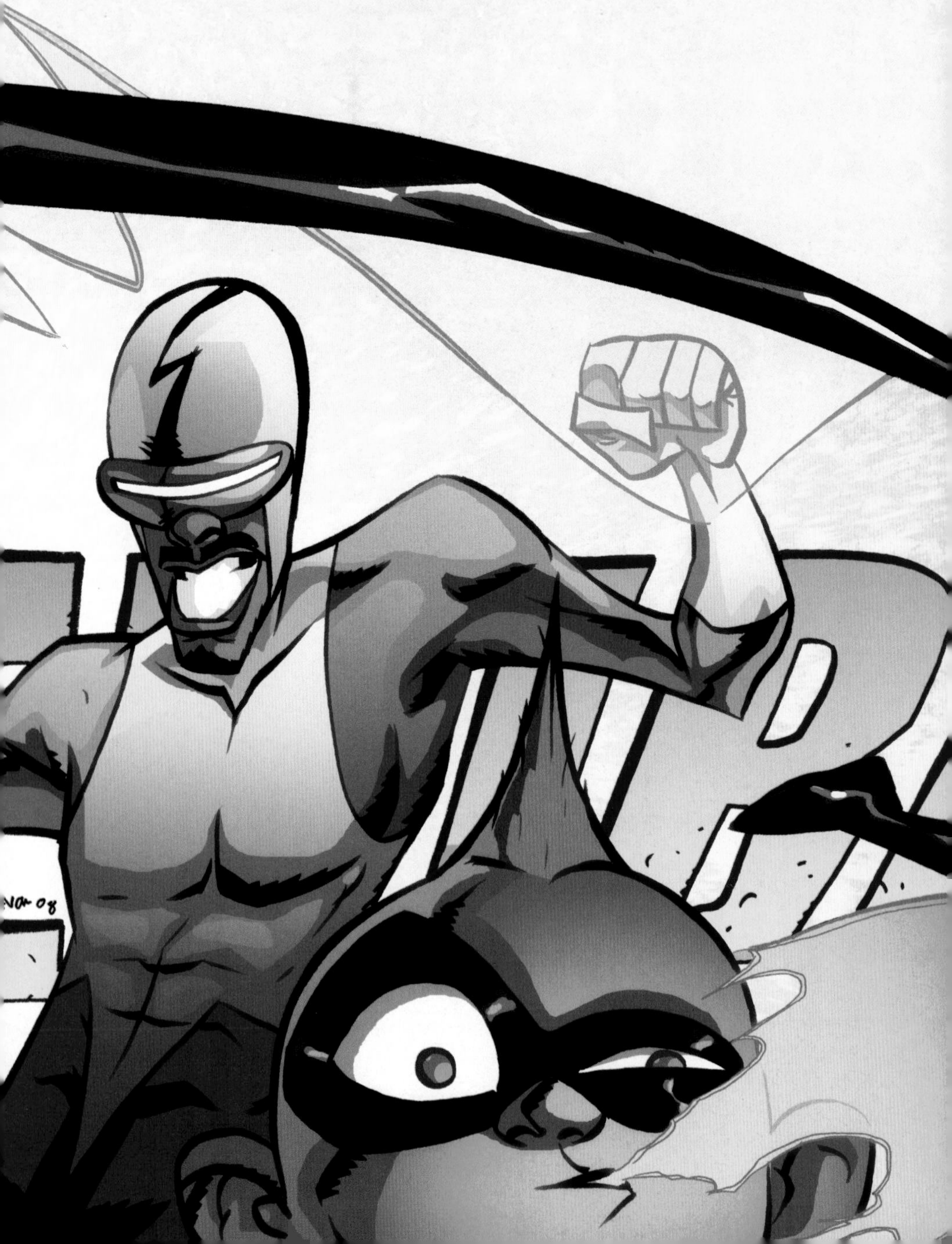

EEEYYEEEEWWWW!

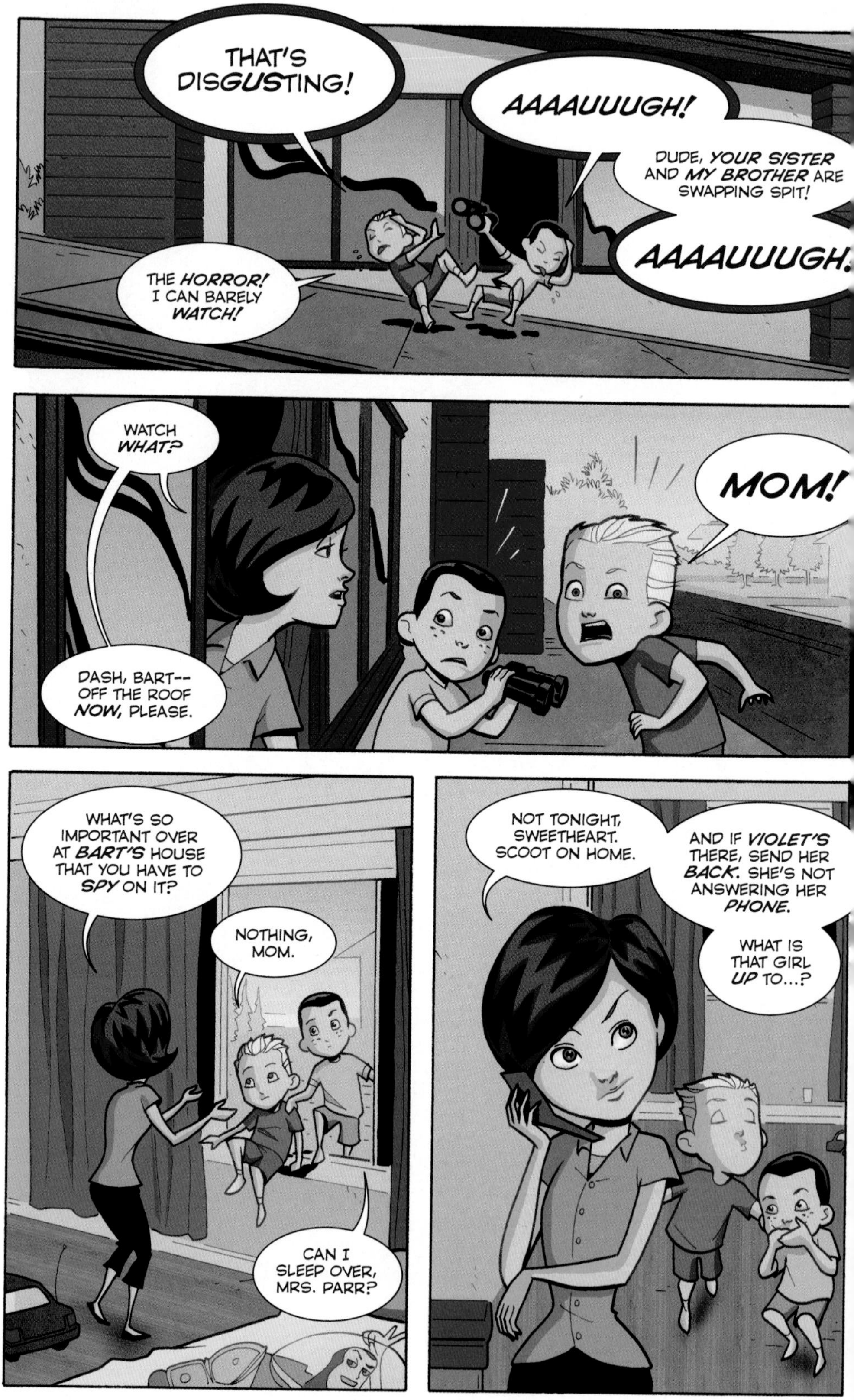
THAT'S DISGUSTING!
AAAAUUUGH!
DUDE, YOUR SISTER AND MY BROTHER ARE SWAPPING SPIT!
AAAAUUUGH!
THE HORROR! I CAN BARELY WATCH!
WATCH WHAT?
DASH, BART-- OFF THE ROOF NOW, PLEASE.
MOM!
WHAT'S SO IMPORTANT OVER AT BART'S HOUSE THAT YOU HAVE TO SPY ON IT?
NOTHING, MOM.
CAN I SLEEP OVER, MRS. PARR?
NOT TONIGHT, SWEETHEART. SCOOT ON HOME.
AND IF VIOLET'S THERE, SEND HER BACK. SHE'S NOT ANSWERING HER PHONE.
WHAT IS THAT GIRL UP TO...?

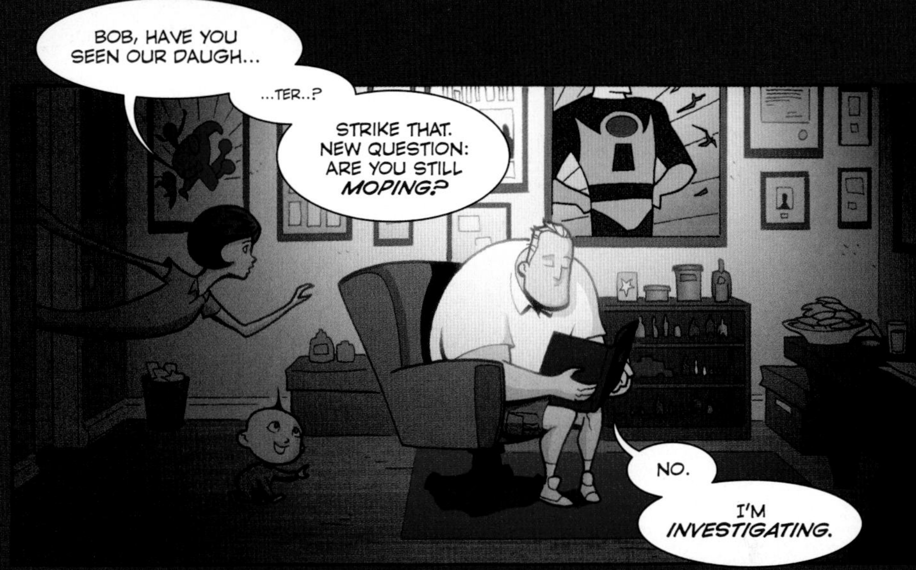
BOB, HAVE YOU SEEN OUR DAUGH...
...TER..?
STRIKE THAT. NEW QUESTION: ARE YOU STILL *MOPING?*
NO.
I'M *INVESTIGATING.*

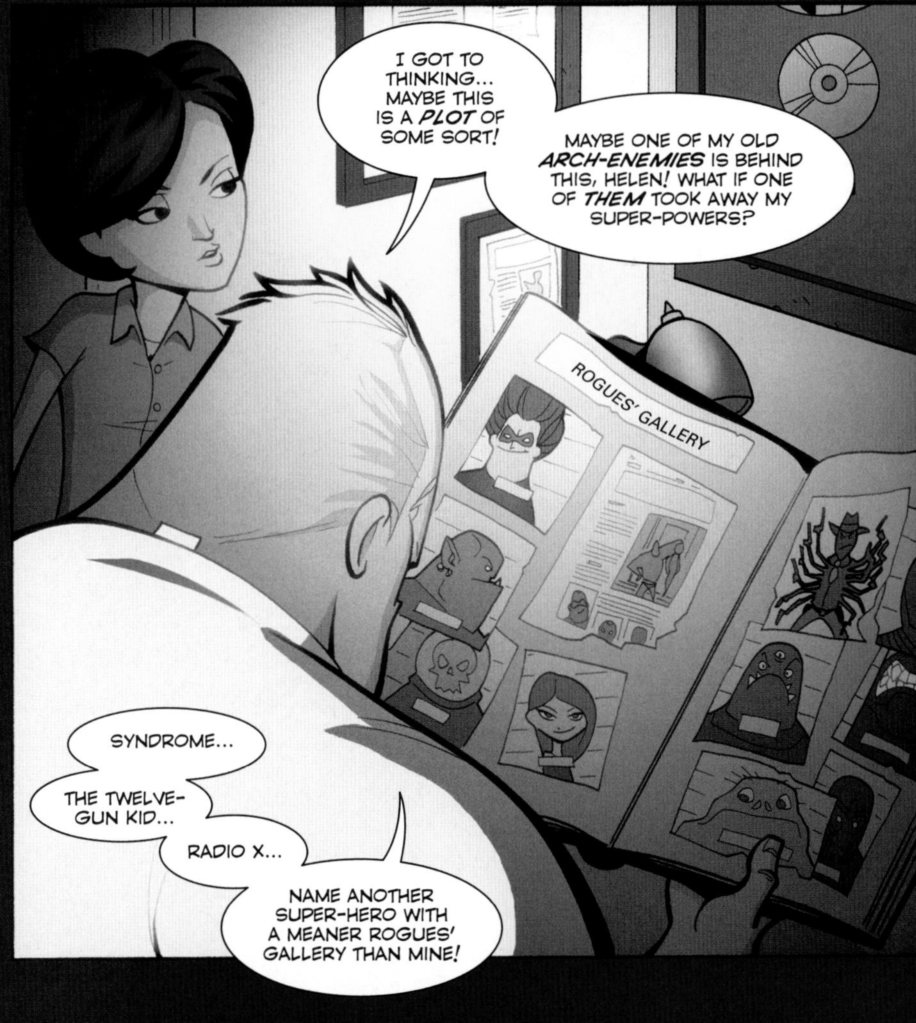
I GOT TO THINKING... MAYBE THIS IS A *PLOT* OF SOME SORT!
MAYBE ONE OF MY OLD *ARCH-ENEMIES* IS BEHIND THIS, HELEN! WHAT IF ONE OF *THEM* TOOK AWAY MY SUPER-POWERS?
ROGUES' GALLERY
SYNDROME...
THE TWELVE-GUN KID...
RADIO X...
NAME ANOTHER SUPER-HERO WITH A MEANER ROGUES' GALLERY THAN MINE!

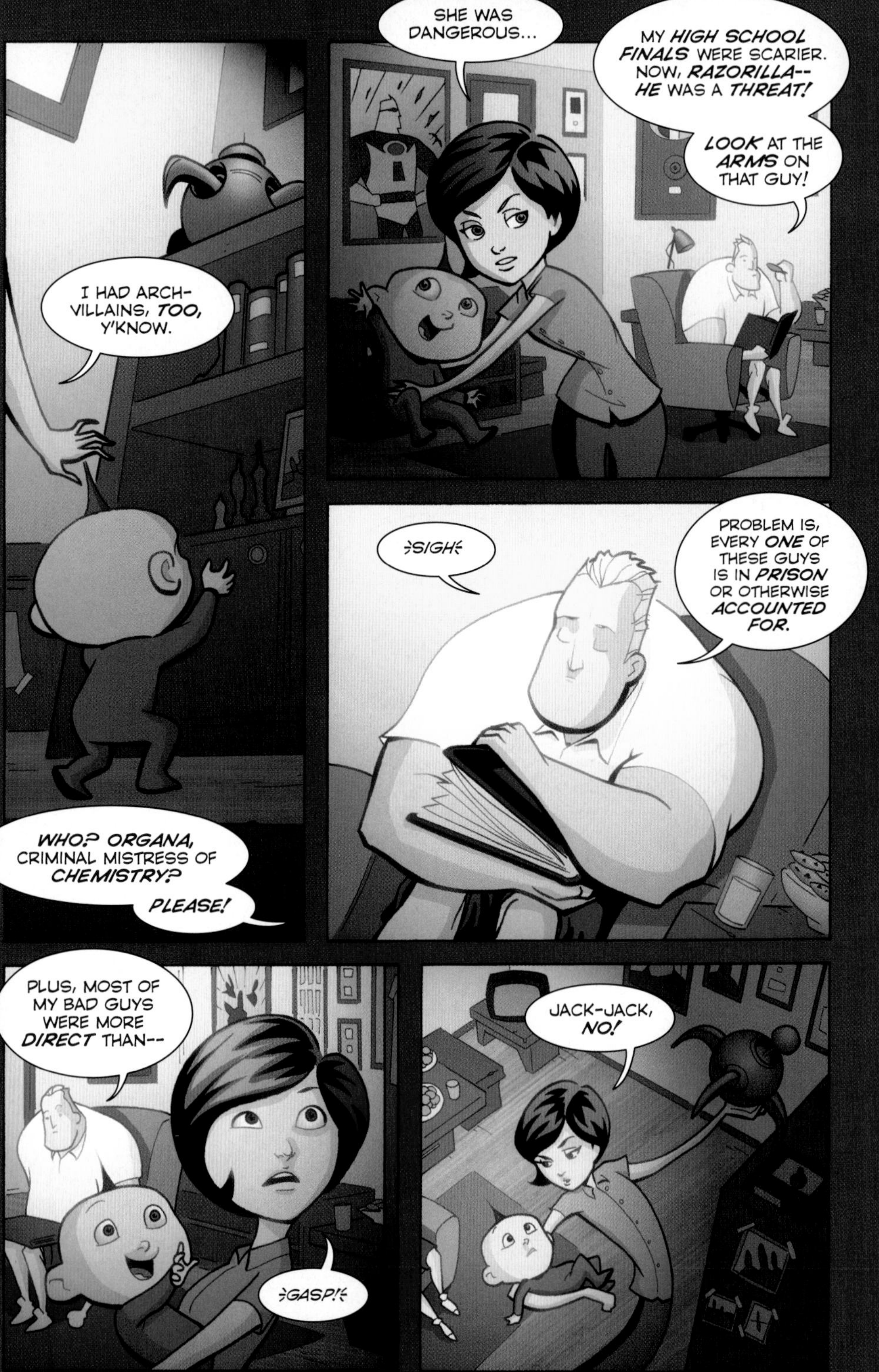
I HAD ARCH-VILLAINS, TOO, Y'KNOW.
SHE WAS DANGEROUS...
MY HIGH SCHOOL FINALS WERE SCARIER. NOW, RAZORILLA-- HE WAS A THREAT!
LOOK AT THE ARMS ON THAT GUY!
WHO? ORGANA, CRIMINAL MISTRESS OF CHEMISTRY?
PLEASE!
SIGH
PROBLEM IS, EVERY ONE OF THESE GUYS IS IN PRISON OR OTHERWISE ACCOUNTED FOR.
PLUS, MOST OF MY BAD GUYS WERE MORE DIRECT THAN--
GASP!
JACK-JACK, NO!

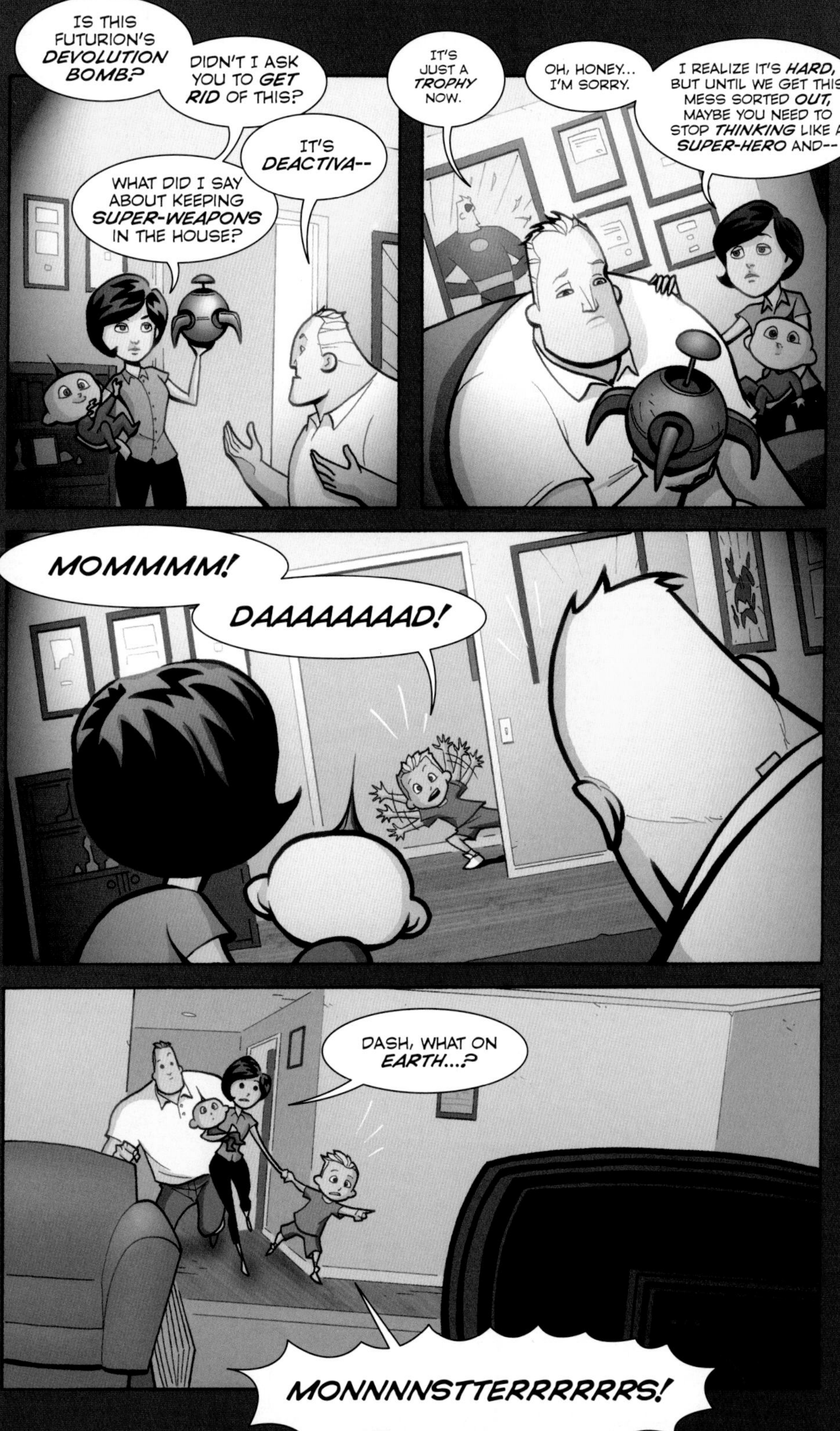
IS THIS FUTURION'S DEVOLUTION BOMB?
DIDN'T I ASK YOU TO GET RID OF THIS?
WHAT DID I SAY ABOUT KEEPING SUPER-WEAPONS IN THE HOUSE?
IT'S DEACTIVA--
IT'S JUST A TROPHY NOW.
OH, HONEY... I'M SORRY.
I REALIZE IT'S HARD, BUT UNTIL WE GET THIS MESS SORTED OUT, MAYBE YOU NEED TO STOP THINKING LIKE A SUPER-HERO AND--
MOMMMM!
DAAAAAAAAD!
DASH, WHAT ON EARTH...?
MONNNNSTTERRRRRRS!

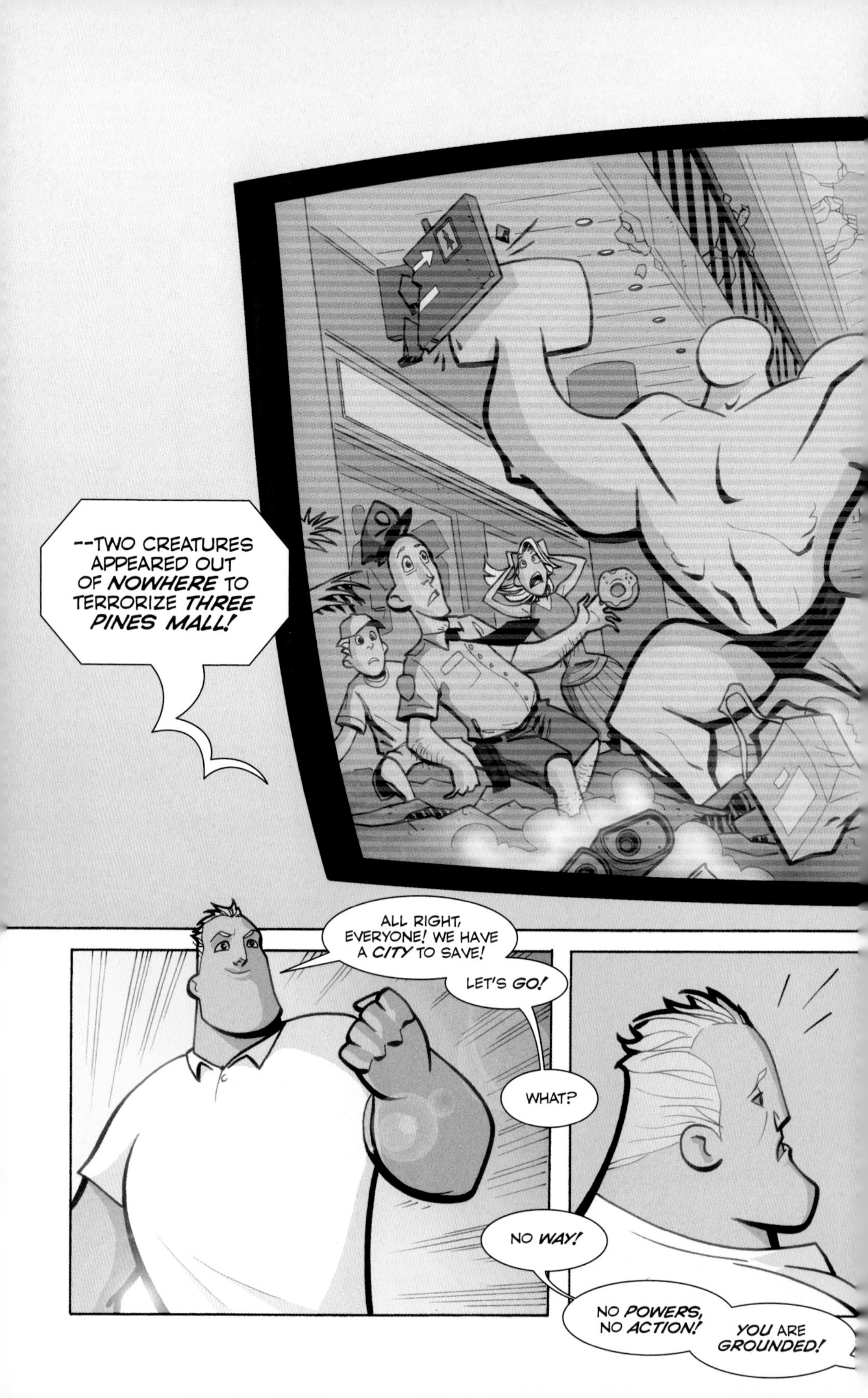
--TWO CREATURES APPEARED OUT OF *NOWHERE* TO TERRORIZE *THREE PINES MALL!*
ALL RIGHT, EVERYONE! WE HAVE A *CITY* TO SAVE!
LET'S *GO!*
WHAT?
NO *WAY!*
NO *POWERS,* NO *ACTION!*
YOU ARE *GROUNDED!*

3 LIVE

WE'RE *LIVE* ON THE *SCENE*--

I CAN BE *USEFUL!*

YES, YOU *CAN!* TAKE *JACK-JACK!* AND REMEMBER THERE'S *LAUNDRY!*

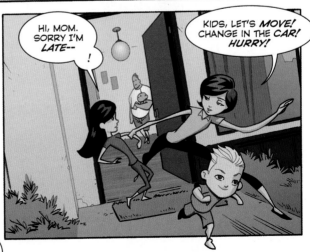

HI, MOM. SORRY I'M *LATE*--

!

KIDS, LET'S *MOVE!* CHANGE IN THE *CAR!* *HURRY!*

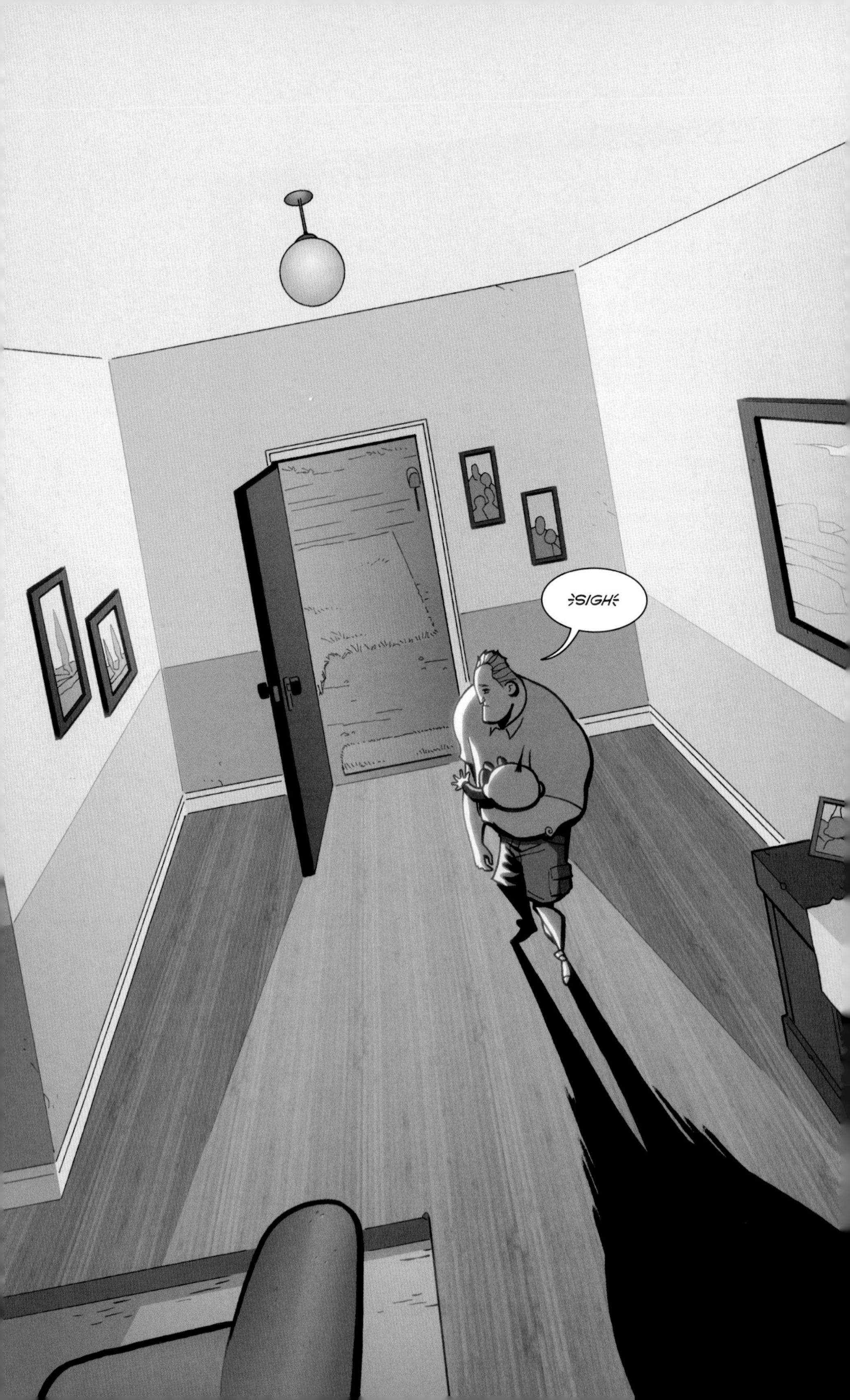
SIGH

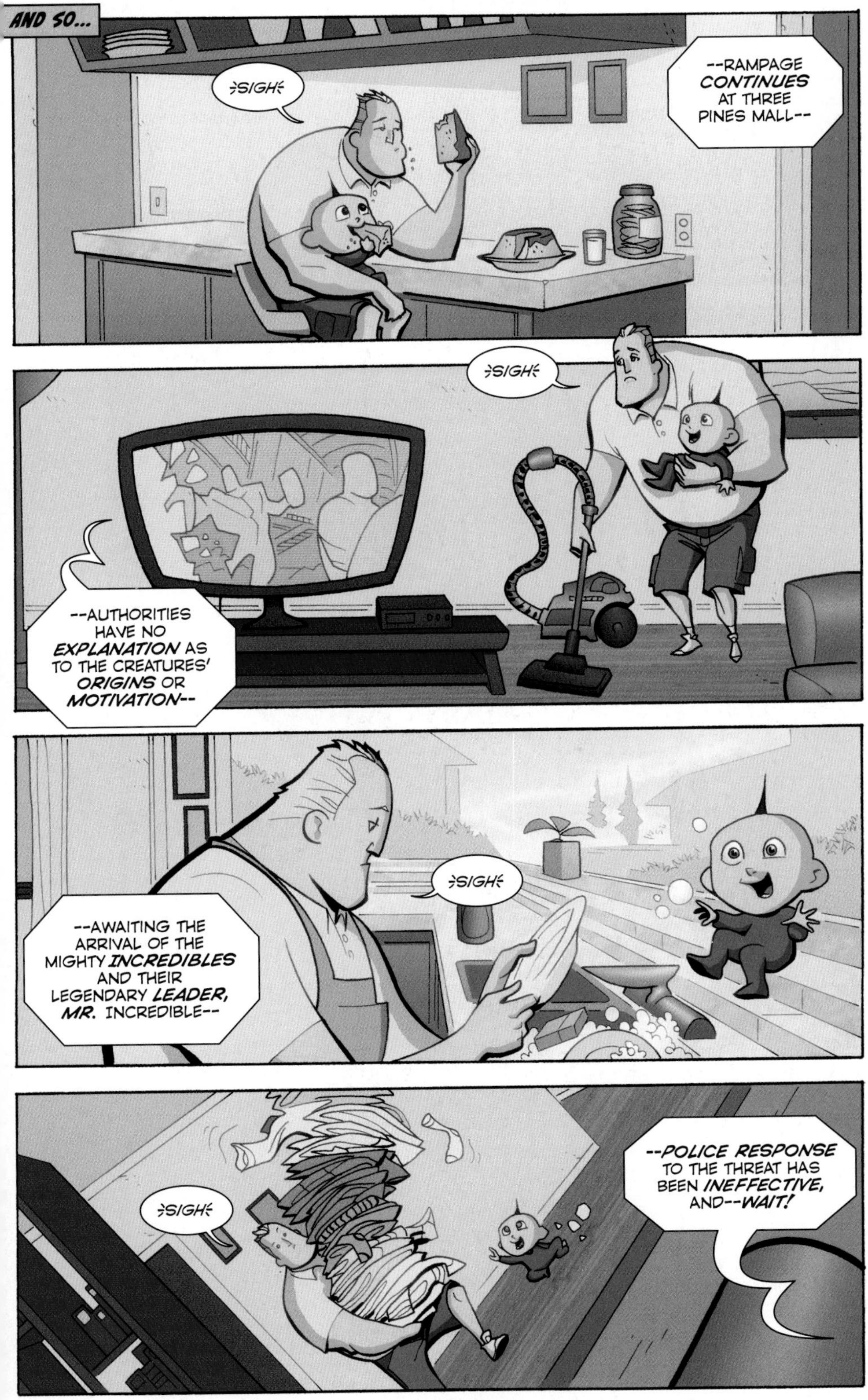
AND SO...
>SIGH<
--RAMPAGE CONTINUES AT THREE PINES MALL--
>SIGH<
--AUTHORITIES HAVE NO EXPLANATION AS TO THE CREATURES' ORIGINS OR MOTIVATION--
--AWAITING THE ARRIVAL OF THE MIGHTY INCREDIBLES AND THEIR LEGENDARY LEADER, MR. INCREDIBLE--
>SIGH<
>SIGH<
--POLICE RESPONSE TO THE THREAT HAS BEEN INEFFECTIVE, AND--WAIT!

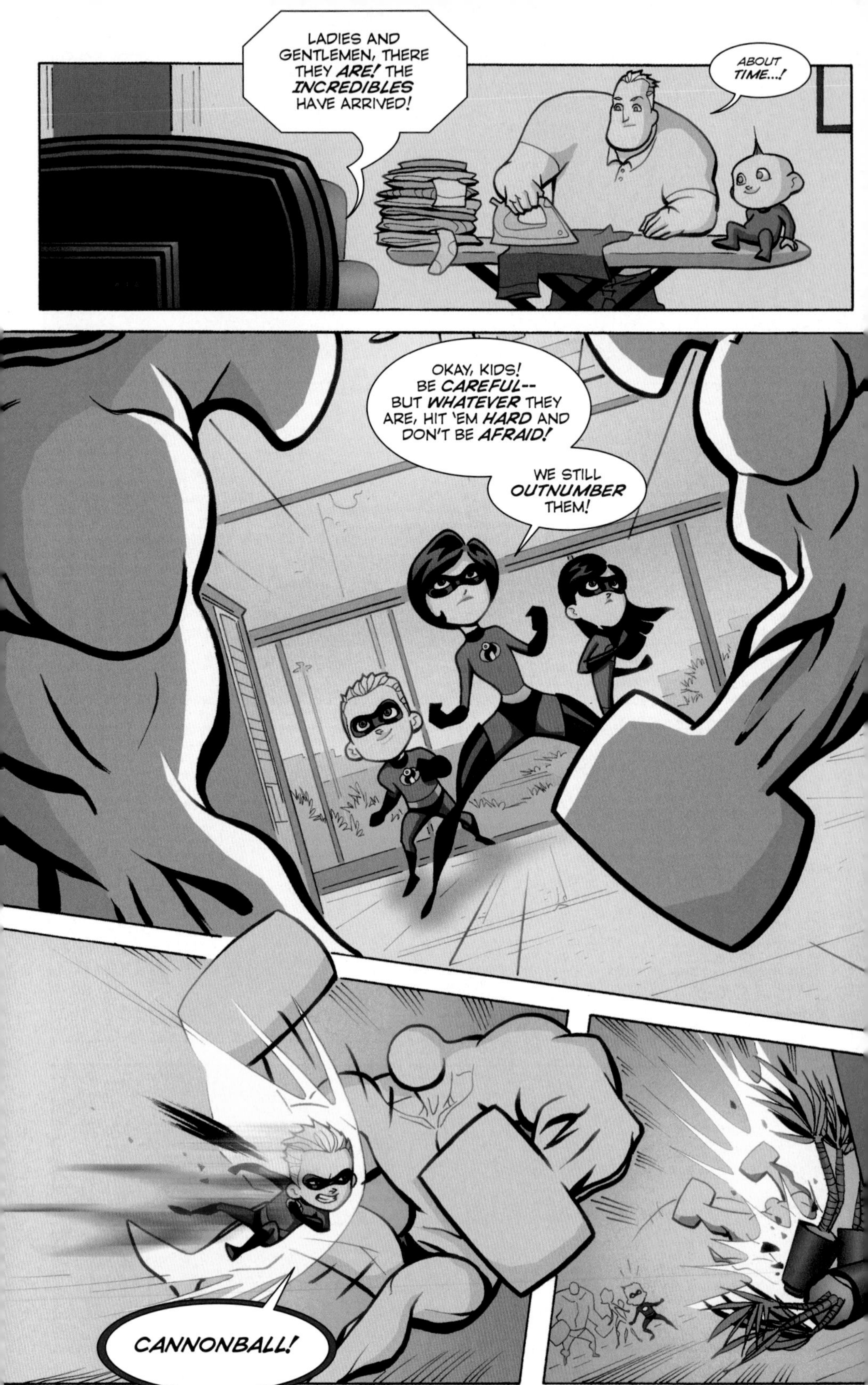
LADIES AND GENTLEMEN, THERE THEY ARE! THE INCREDIBLES HAVE ARRIVED!
ABOUT TIME...!
OKAY, KIDS! BE CAREFUL-- BUT WHATEVER THEY ARE, HIT 'EM HARD AND DON'T BE AFRAID!
WE STILL OUTNUMBER THEM!
CANNONBALL!

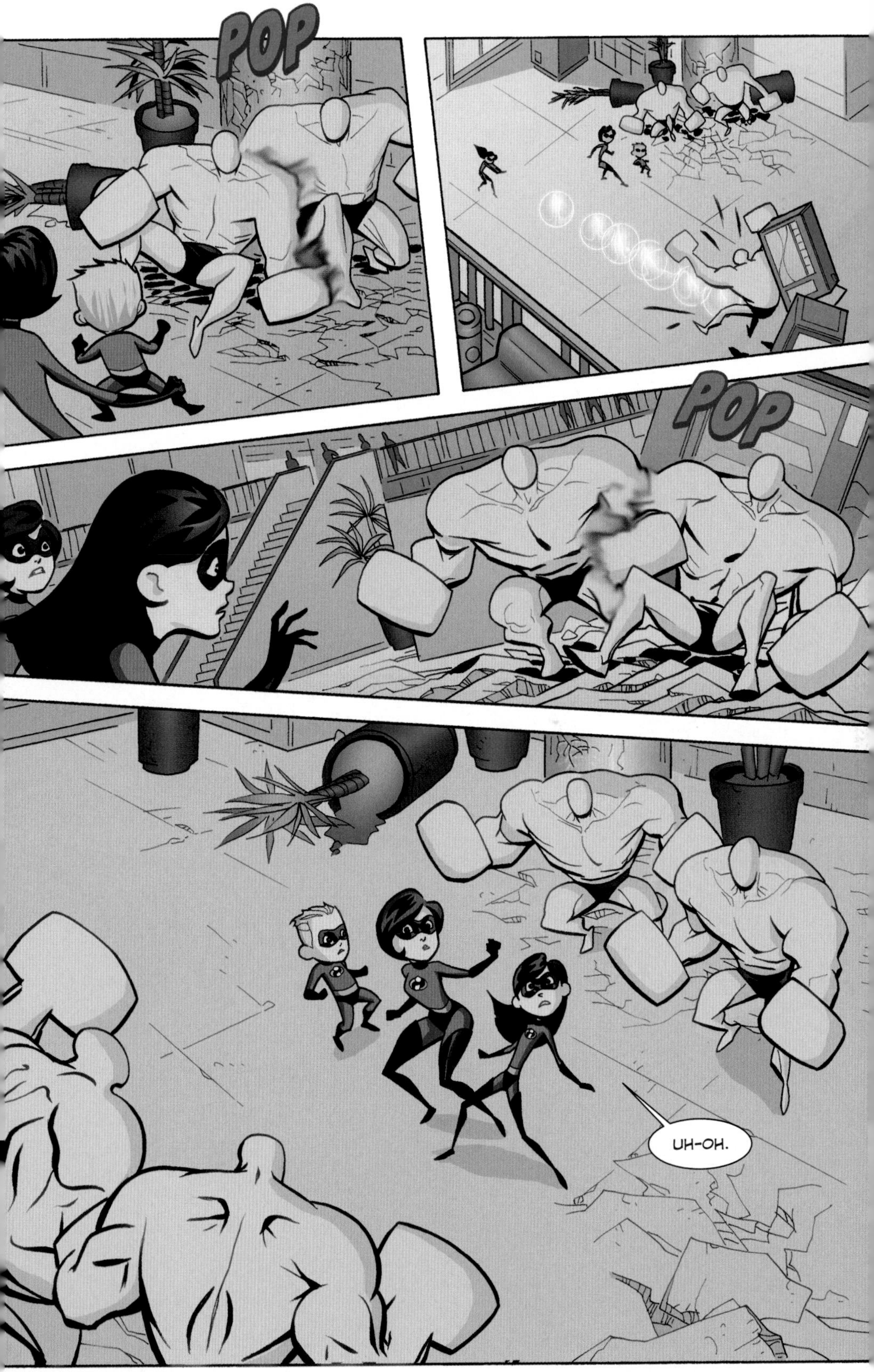
POP
POP
UH-OH.

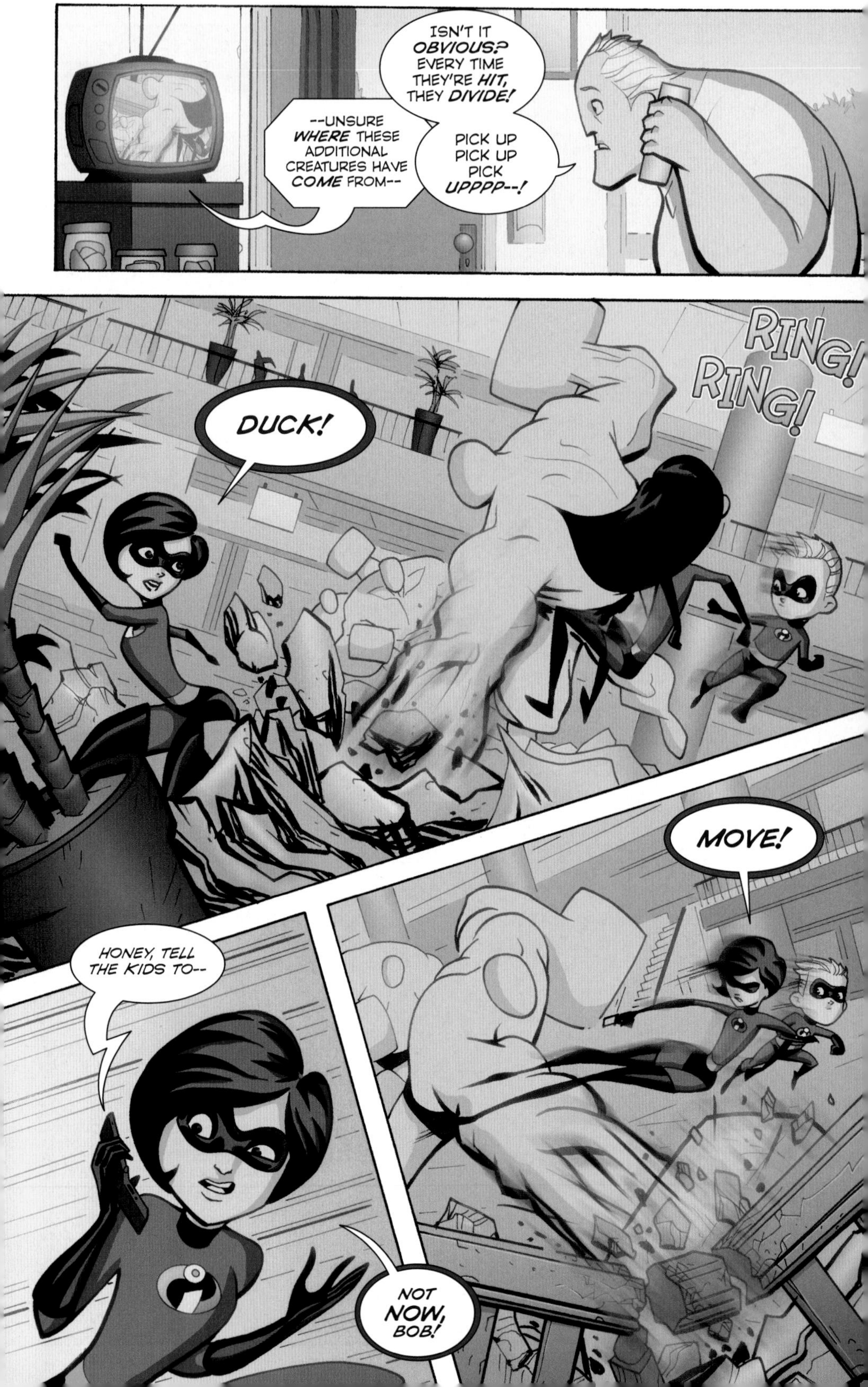
--UNSURE WHERE THESE ADDITIONAL CREATURES HAVE COME FROM--
ISN'T IT OBVIOUS? EVERY TIME THEY'RE HIT, THEY DIVIDE!
PICK UP PICK UP PICK UPPPP--!
RING! RING!
DUCK!
MOVE!
HONEY, TELL THE KIDS TO--
NOT NOW, BOB!

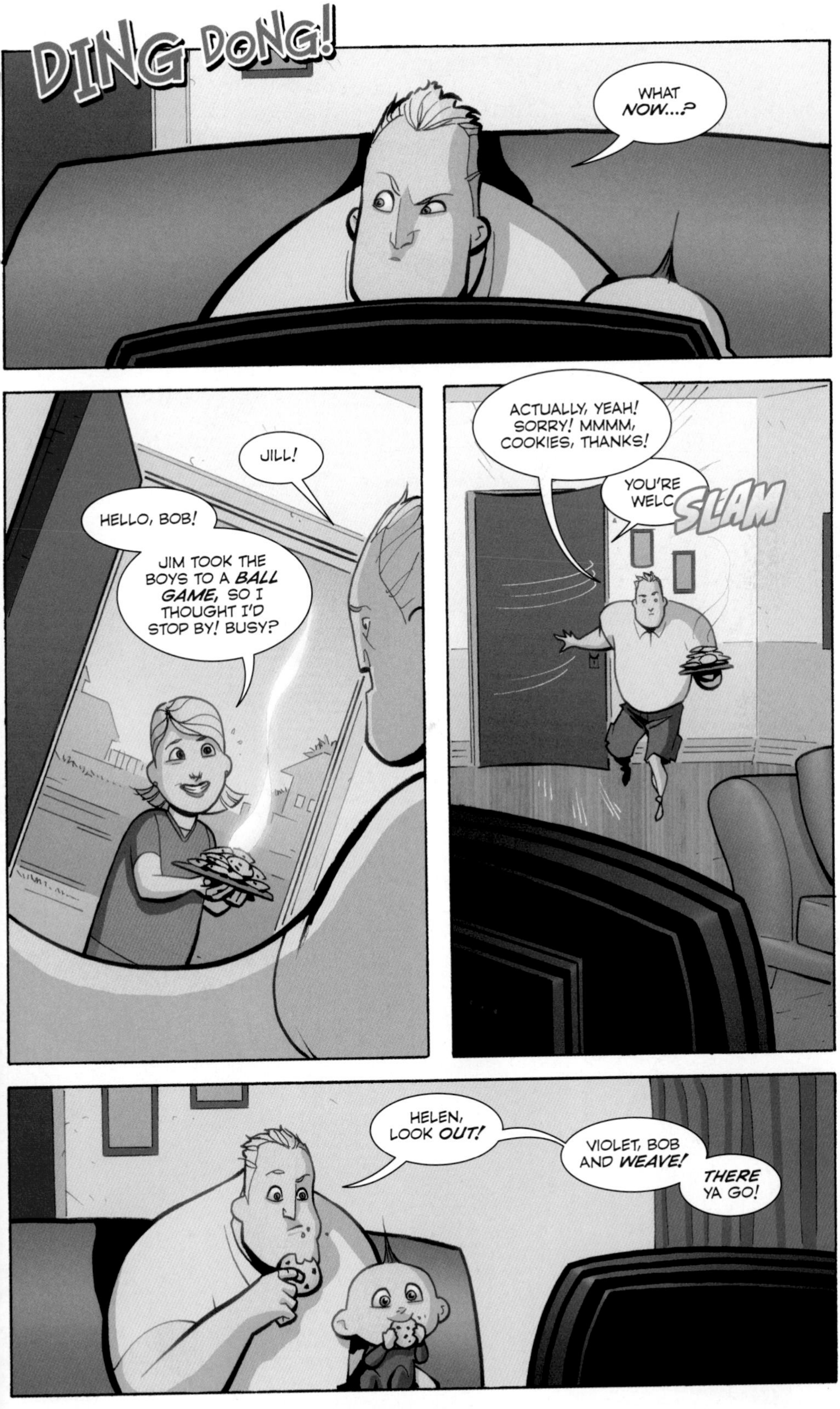
DING DONG!
WHAT NOW...?
JILL!
HELLO, BOB!
JIM TOOK THE BOYS TO A BALL GAME, SO I THOUGHT I'D STOP BY! BUSY?
ACTUALLY, YEAH! SORRY! MMMM, COOKIES, THANKS!
YOU'RE WELC
SLAM
HELEN, LOOK OUT!
VIOLET, BOB AND WEAVE!
THERE YA GO!

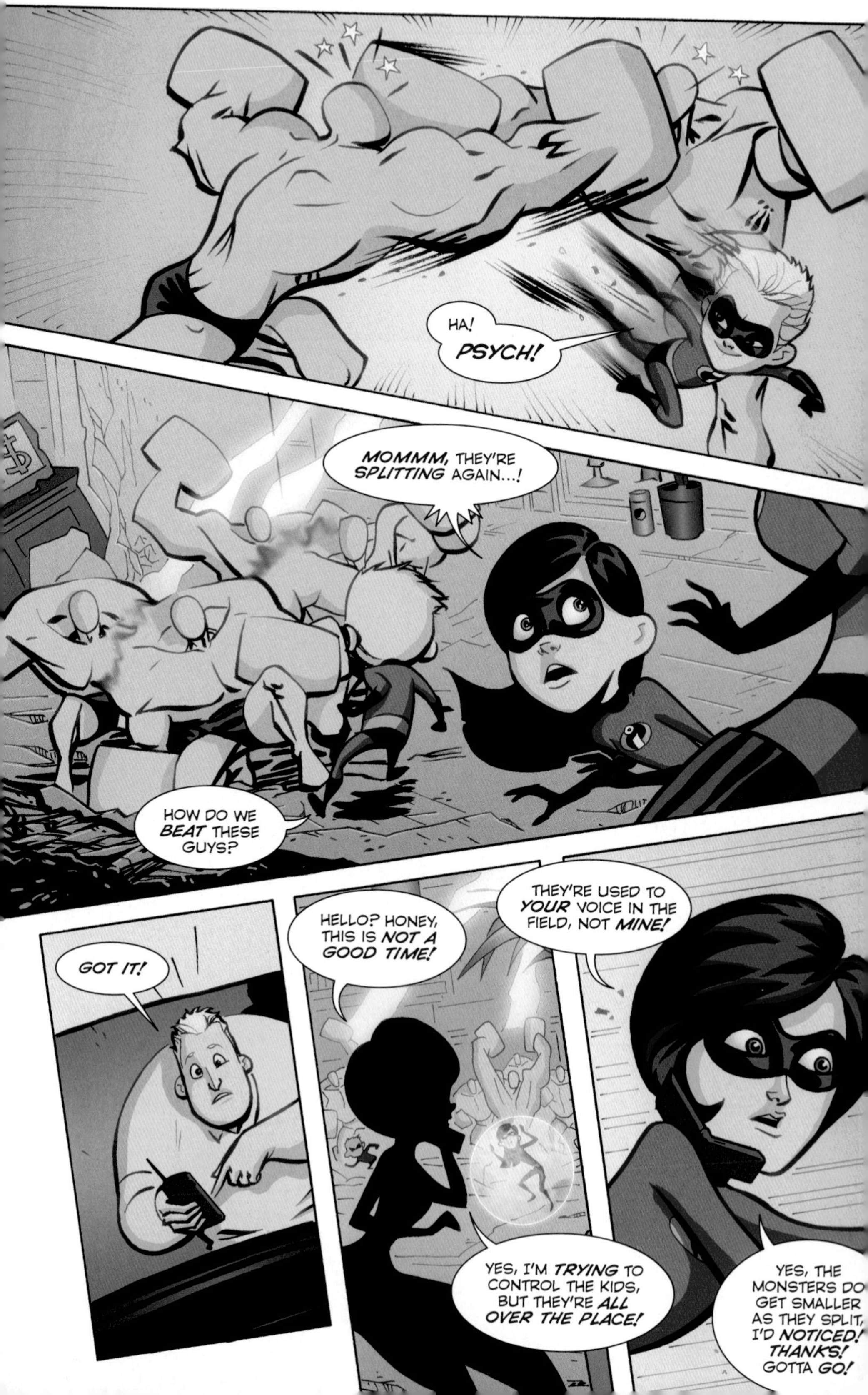

HA! PSYCH!
MOMMM, THEY'RE SPLITTING AGAIN...!
HOW DO WE BEAT THESE GUYS?
GOT IT!
HELLO? HONEY, THIS IS NOT A GOOD TIME!
THEY'RE USED TO YOUR VOICE IN THE FIELD, NOT MINE!
YES, I'M TRYING TO CONTROL THE KIDS, BUT THEY'RE ALL OVER THE PLACE!
YES, THE MONSTERS DO GET SMALLER AS THEY SPLIT, I'D NOTICED! THANKS! GOTTA GO!

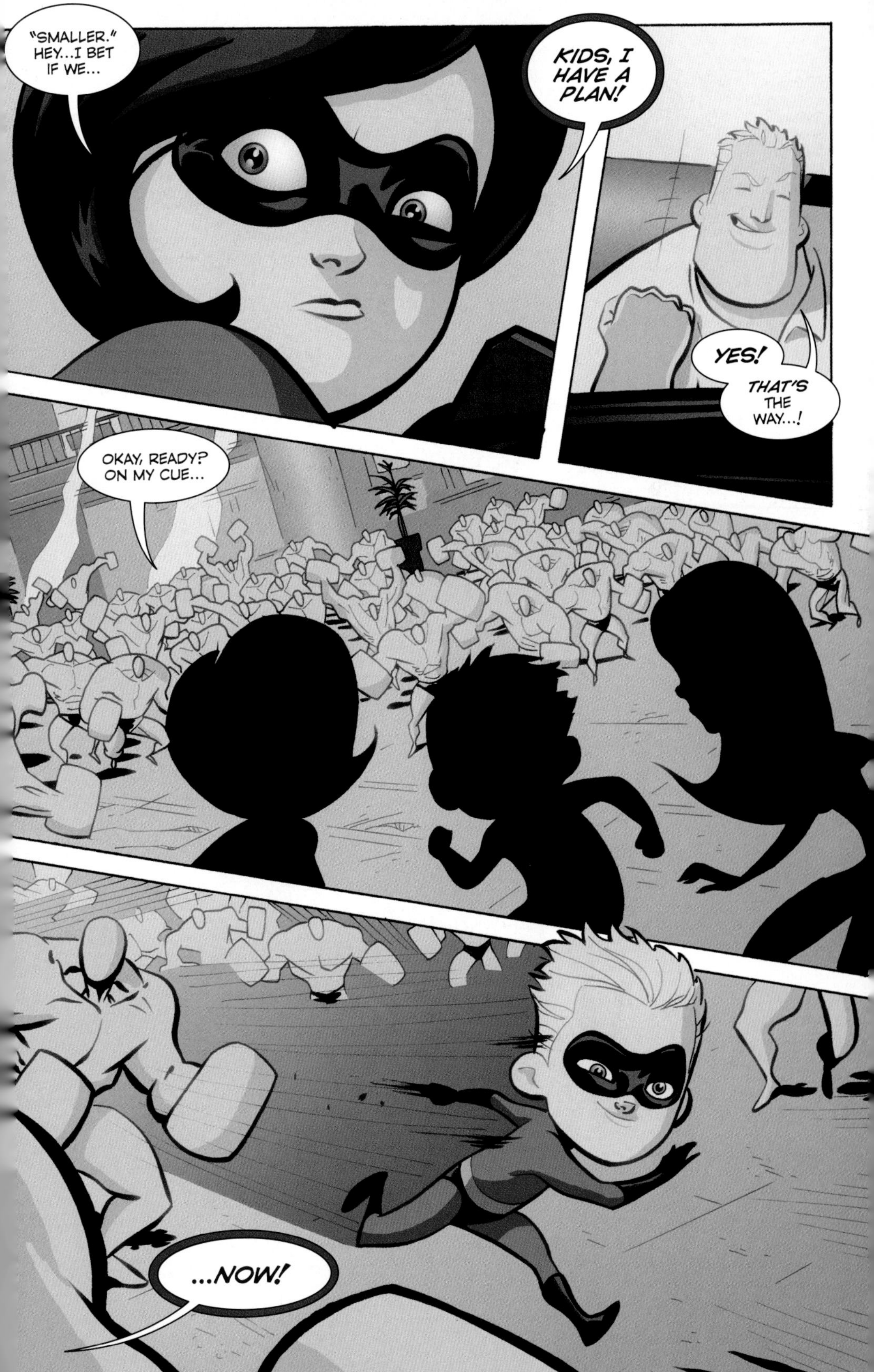
"SMALLER." HEY...I BET IF WE...
KIDS, I HAVE A PLAN!
YES!
THAT'S THE WAY...!
OKAY, READY? ON MY CUE...
...NOW!

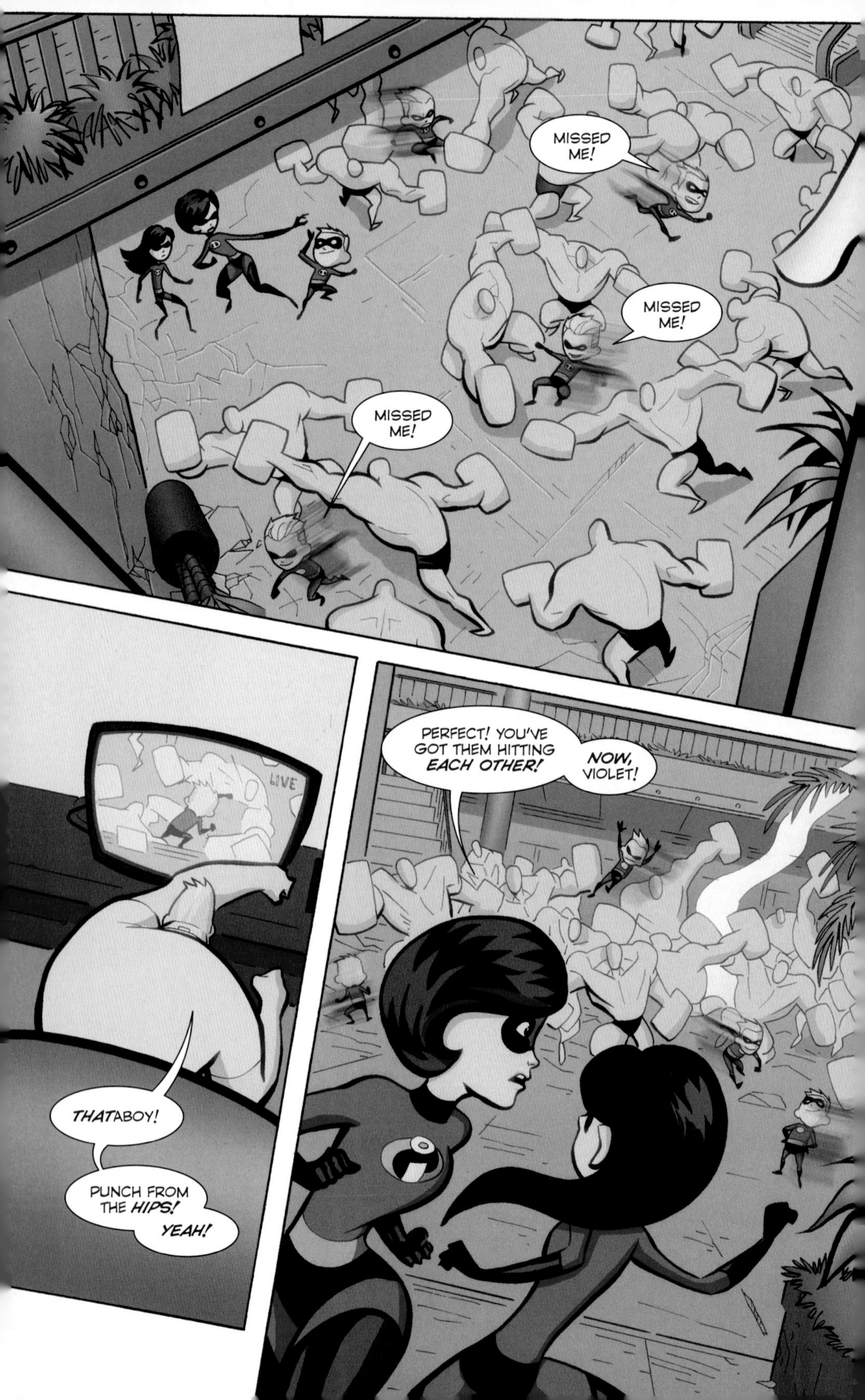
MISSED ME!
MISSED ME!
MISSED ME!
LIVE
THATABOY!
PUNCH FROM THE HIPS!
YEAH!
PERFECT! YOU'VE GOT THEM HITTING EACH OTHER!
NOW, VIOLET!

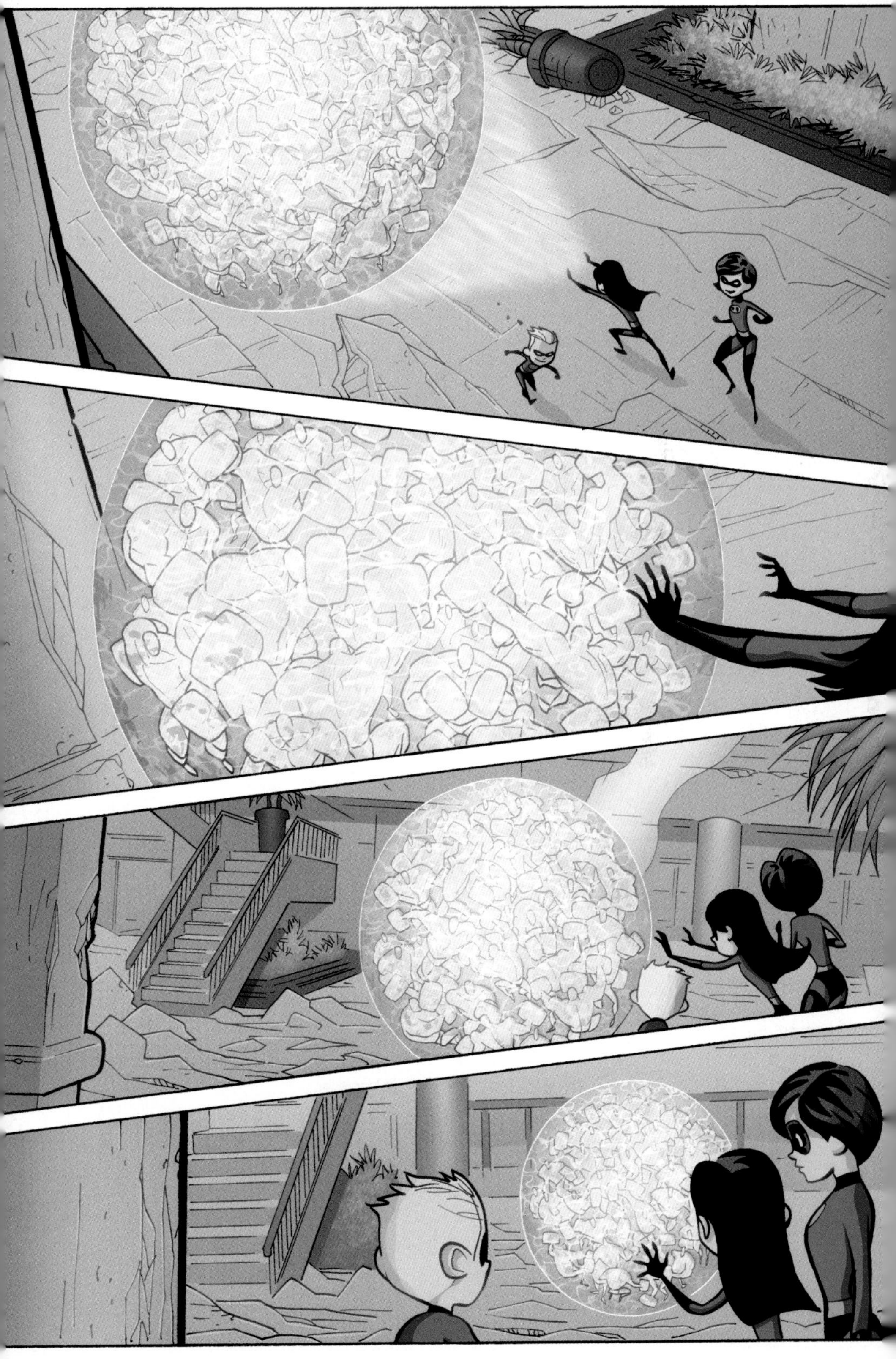

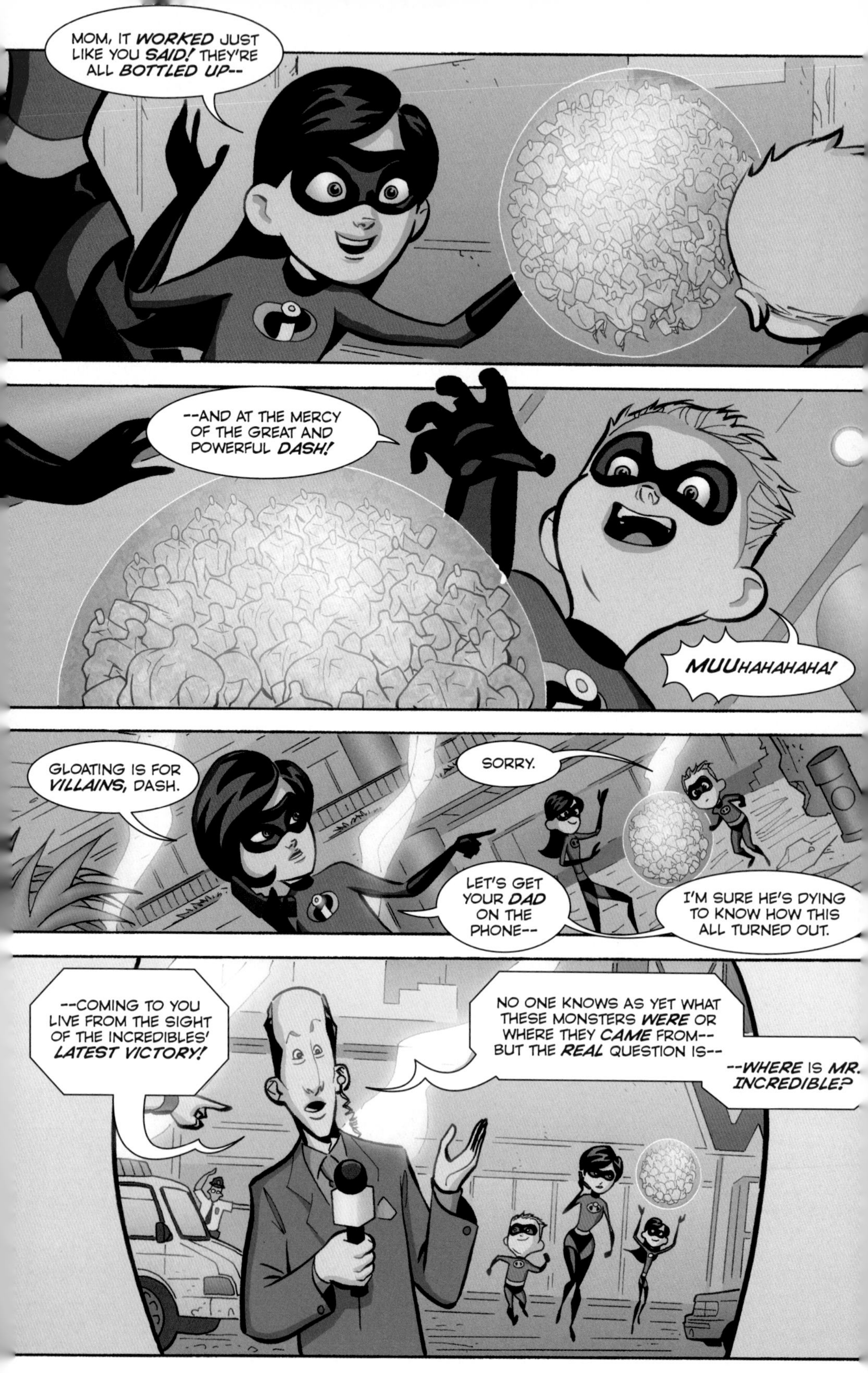
MOM, IT WORKED JUST LIKE YOU SAID! THEY'RE ALL BOTTLED UP--
--AND AT THE MERCY OF THE GREAT AND POWERFUL DASH!
MUUHAHAHAHA!
GLOATING IS FOR VILLAINS, DASH.
SORRY.
LET'S GET YOUR DAD ON THE PHONE--
I'M SURE HE'S DYING TO KNOW HOW THIS ALL TURNED OUT.
--COMING TO YOU LIVE FROM THE SIGHT OF THE INCREDIBLES' LATEST VICTORY!
NO ONE KNOWS AS YET WHAT THESE MONSTERS WERE OR WHERE THEY CAME FROM-- BUT THE REAL QUESTION IS--
--WHERE IS MR. INCREDIBLE?

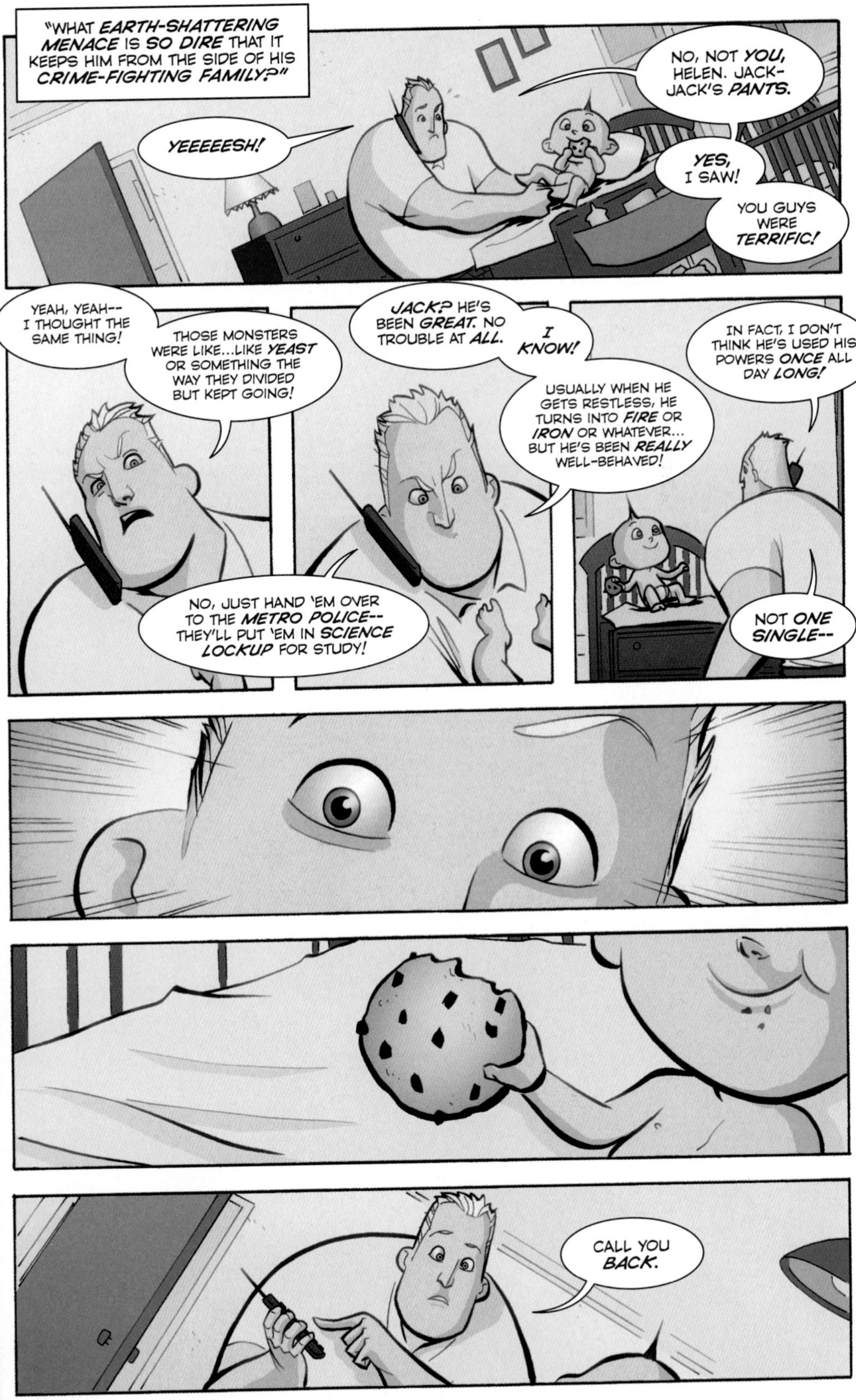
"WHAT EARTH-SHATTERING MENACE IS SO DIRE THAT IT KEEPS HIM FROM THE SIDE OF HIS CRIME-FIGHTING FAMILY?"
YEEEEESH!
NO, NOT YOU, HELEN. JACK-JACK'S PANTS.
YES, I SAW!
YOU GUYS WERE TERRIFIC!
YEAH, YEAH-- I THOUGHT THE SAME THING!
THOSE MONSTERS WERE LIKE...LIKE YEAST OR SOMETHING THE WAY THEY DIVIDED BUT KEPT GOING!
NO, JUST HAND 'EM OVER TO THE METRO POLICE-- THEY'LL PUT 'EM IN SCIENCE LOCKUP FOR STUDY!
JACK? HE'S BEEN GREAT. NO TROUBLE AT ALL.
I KNOW!
USUALLY WHEN HE GETS RESTLESS, HE TURNS INTO FIRE OR IRON OR WHATEVER... BUT HE'S BEEN REALLY WELL-BEHAVED!
IN FACT, I DON'T THINK HE'S USED HIS POWERS ONCE ALL DAY LONG!
NOT ONE SINGLE--
CALL YOU BACK.

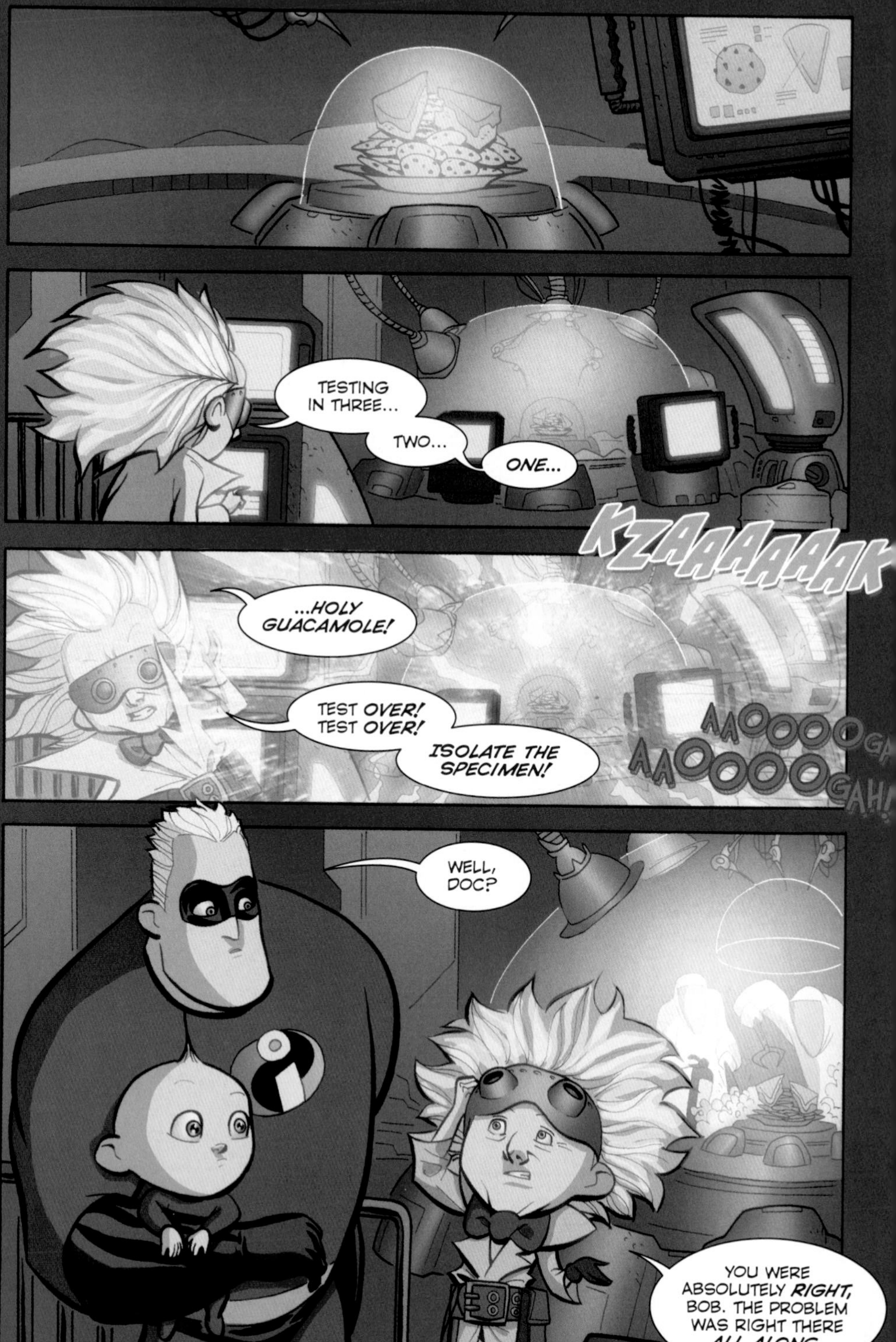
TESTING IN THREE...
TWO...
ONE...
KZAAAAAAAK
...HOLY GUACAMOLE!
TEST OVER! TEST OVER!
ISOLATE THE SPECIMEN!
AAOOOOOGAH!
WELL, DOC?
YOU WERE ABSOLUTELY RIGHT, BOB. THE PROBLEM WAS RIGHT THERE ALL ALONG.

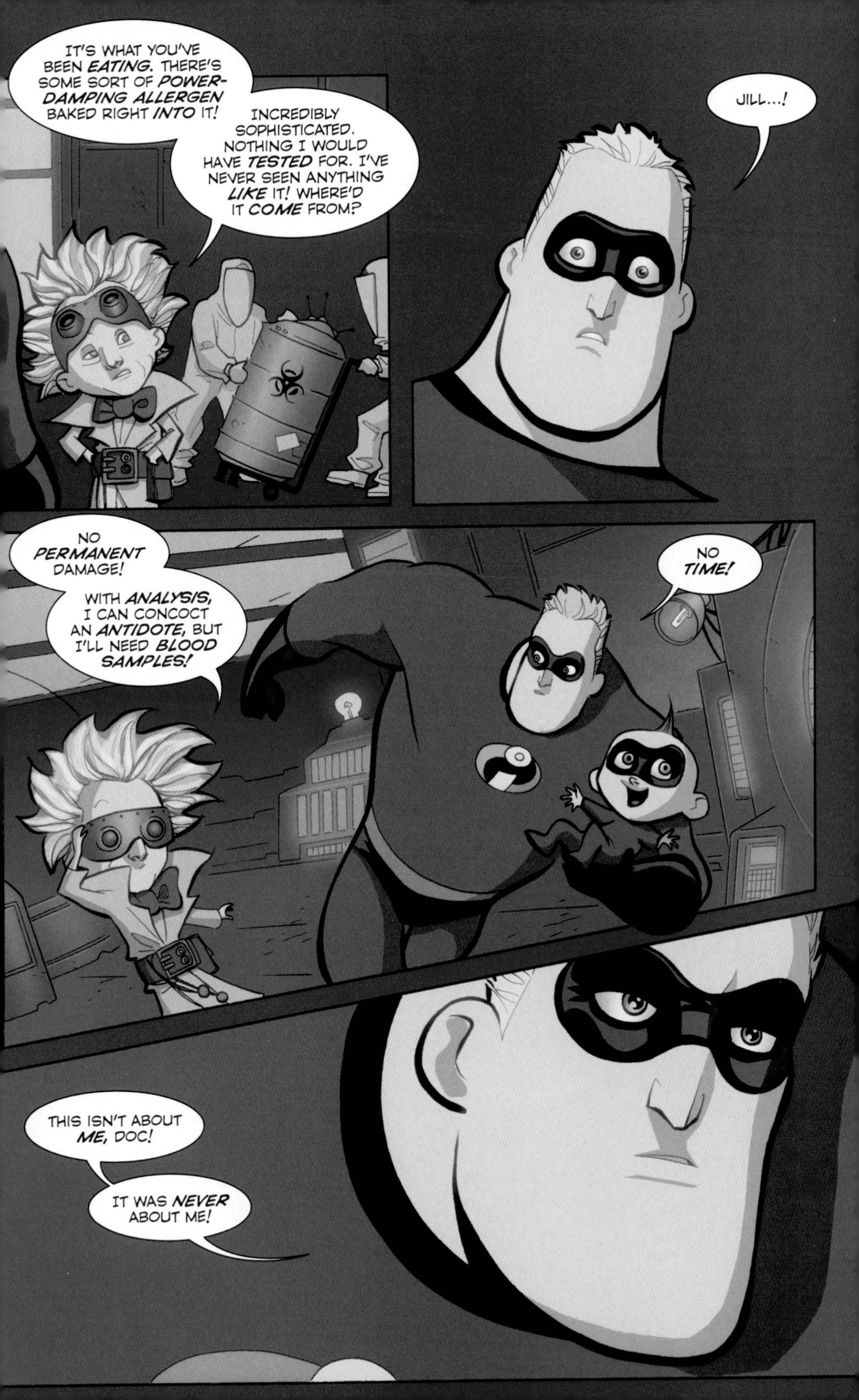
IT'S WHAT YOU'VE BEEN EATING. THERE'S SOME SORT OF POWER-DAMPING ALLERGEN BAKED RIGHT INTO IT!
INCREDIBLY SOPHISTICATED. NOTHING I WOULD HAVE TESTED FOR. I'VE NEVER SEEN ANYTHING LIKE IT! WHERE'D IT COME FROM?
JILL...!
NO PERMANENT DAMAGE!
WITH ANALYSIS, I CAN CONCOCT AN ANTIDOTE, BUT I'LL NEED BLOOD SAMPLES!
NO TIME!
THIS ISN'T ABOUT ME, DOC!
IT WAS NEVER ABOUT ME!

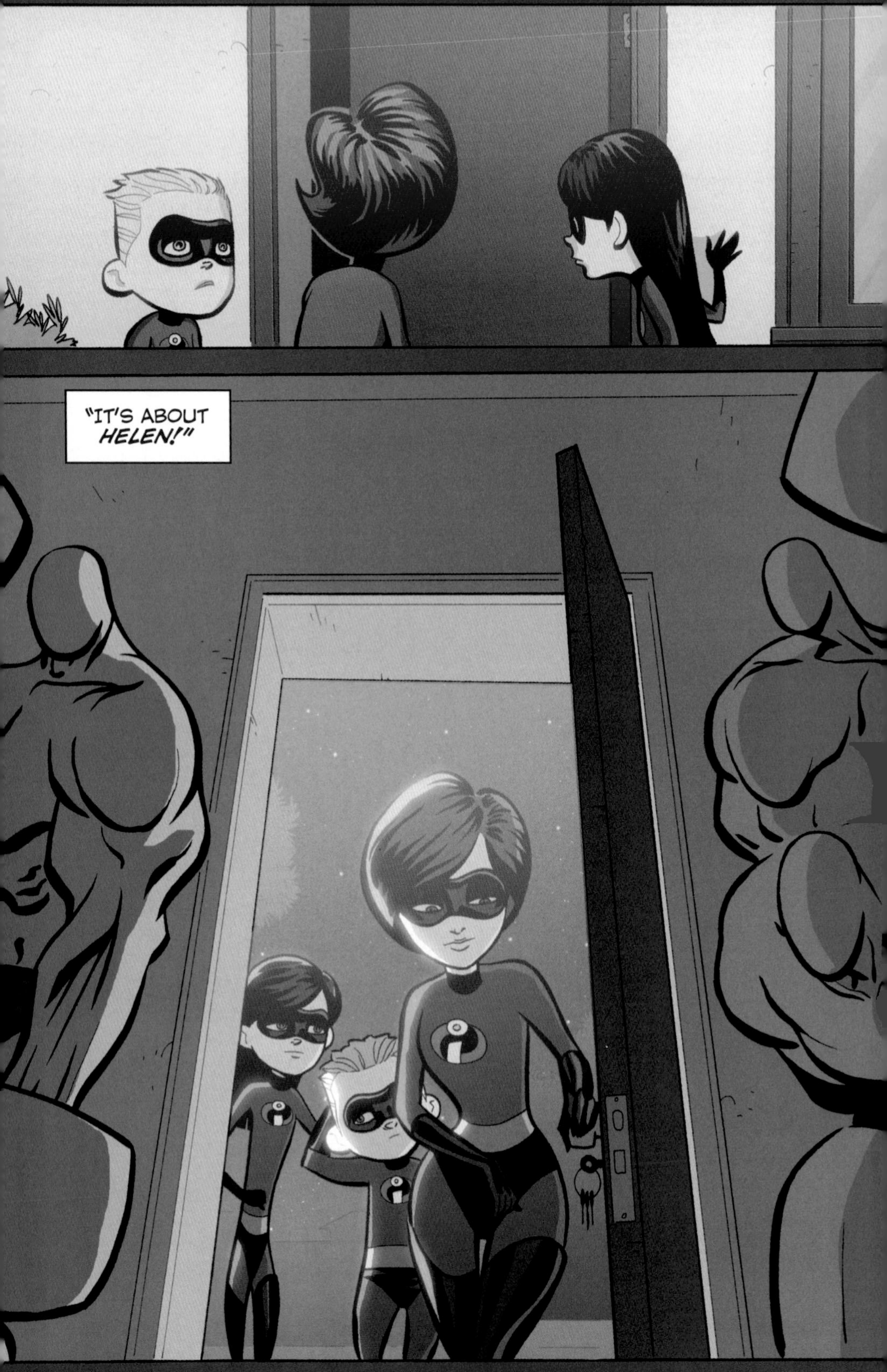
"IT'S ABOUT HELEN!"

CHAPTER FOUR

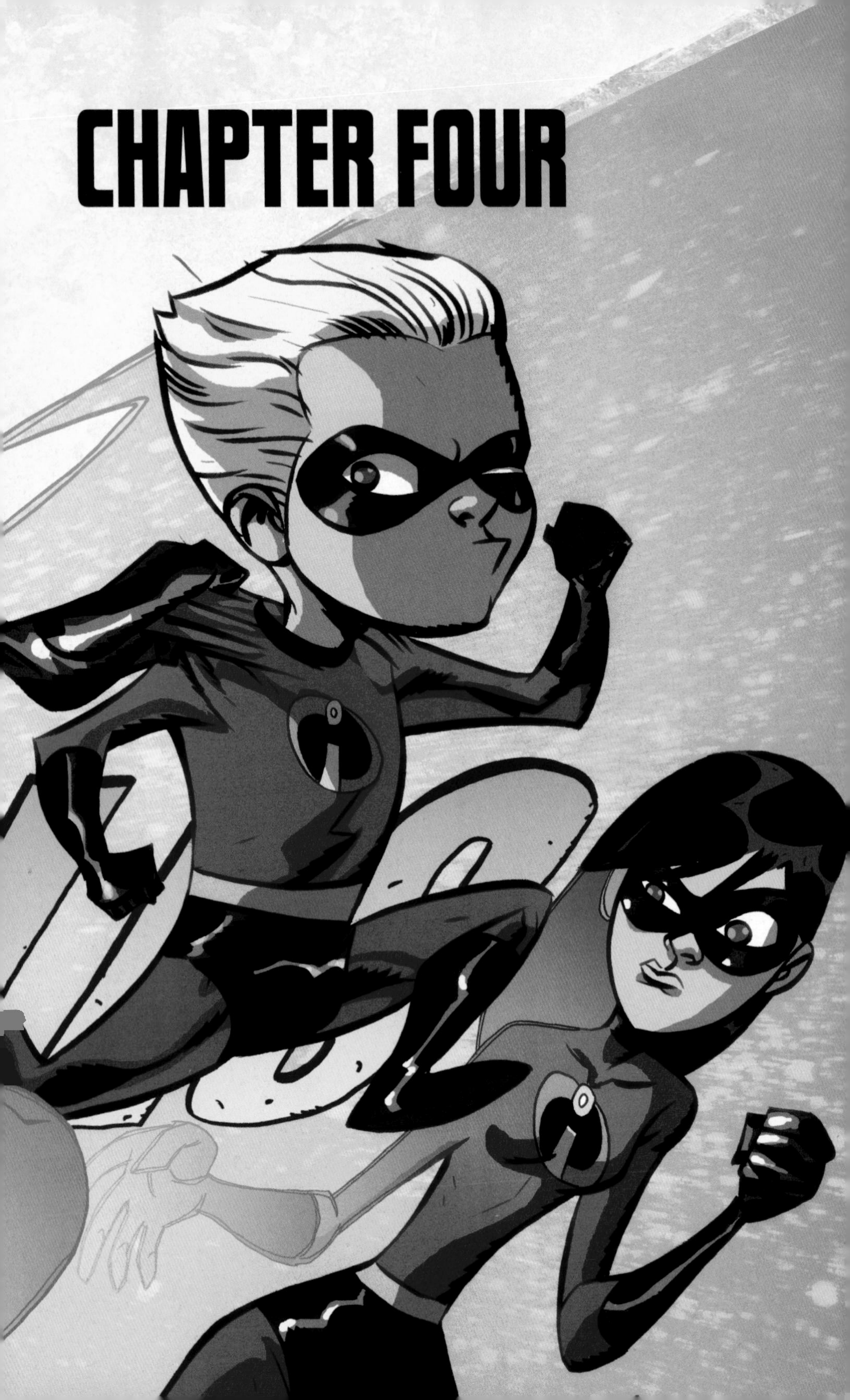

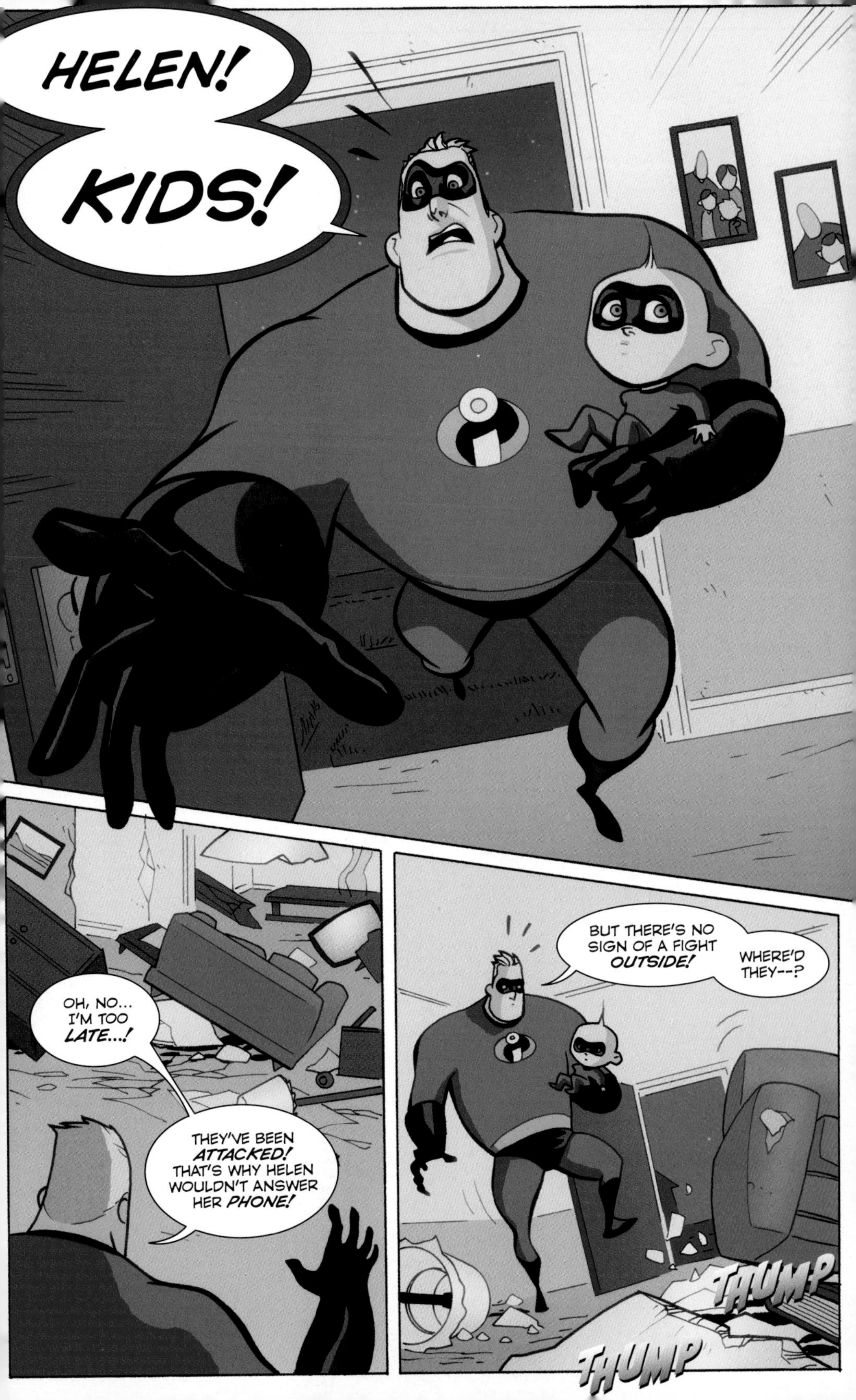
HELEN!
KIDS!
OH, NO... I'M TOO LATE...!
THEY'VE BEEN ATTACKED! THAT'S WHY HELEN WOULDN'T ANSWER HER PHONE!
BUT THERE'S NO SIGN OF A FIGHT OUTSIDE!
WHERE'D THEY--?
THUMP
THUMP

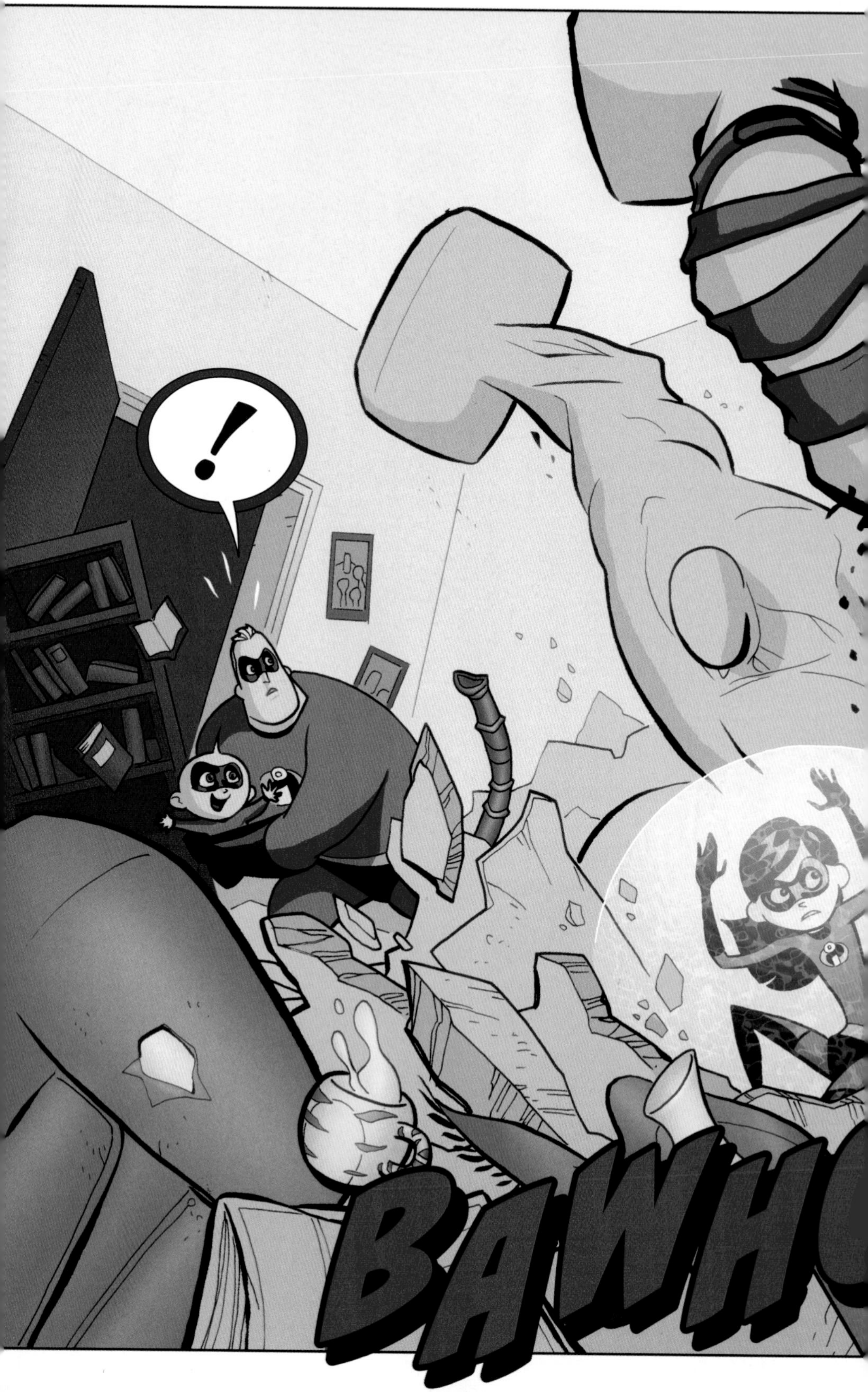
!
BAWH

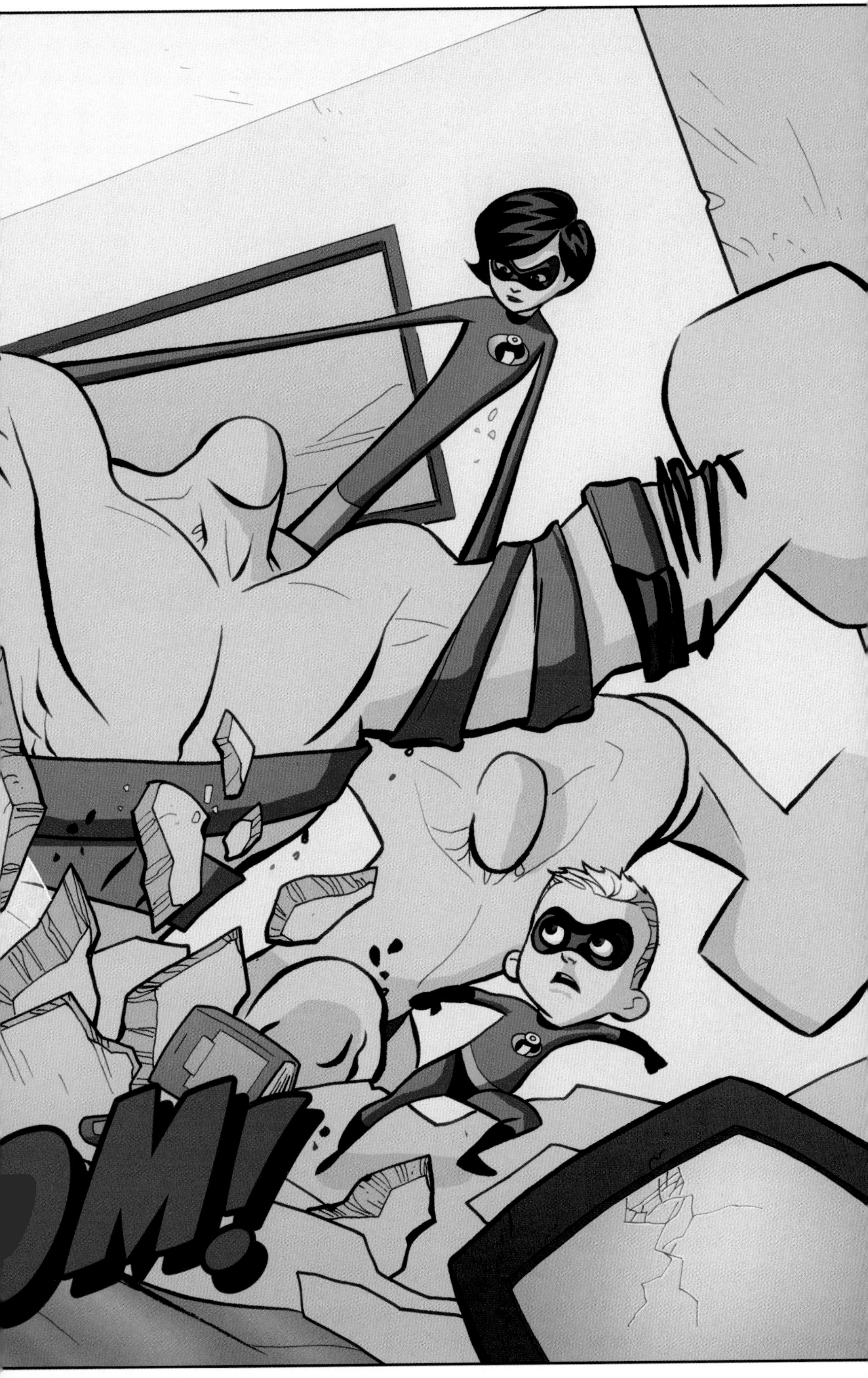
OM!

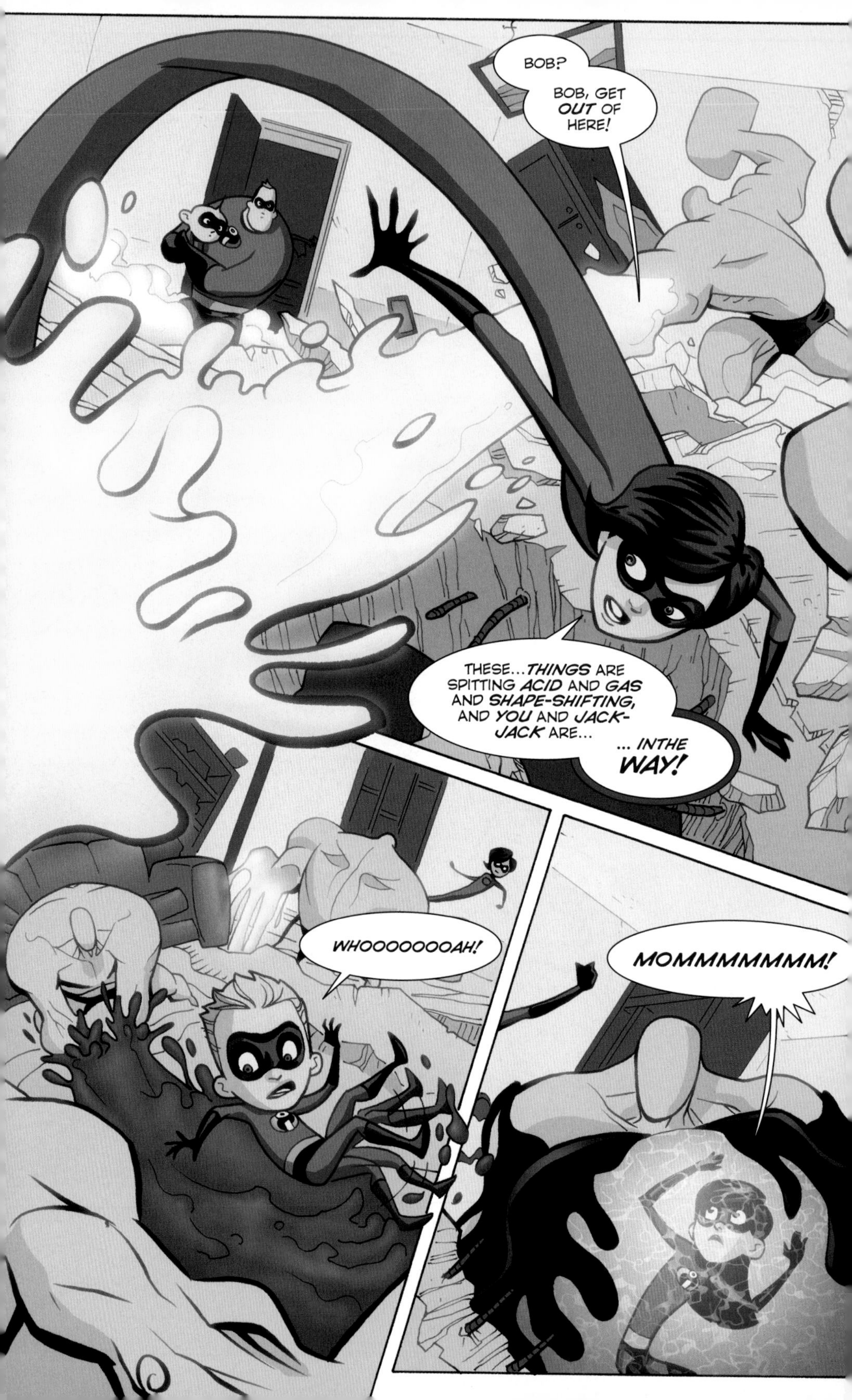
BOB?
BOB, GET OUT OF HERE!
THESE...THINGS ARE SPITTING ACID AND GAS AND SHAPE-SHIFTING, AND YOU AND JACK-JACK ARE...
... IN THE WAY!
WHOOOOOOOAH!
MOMMMMMMMM!

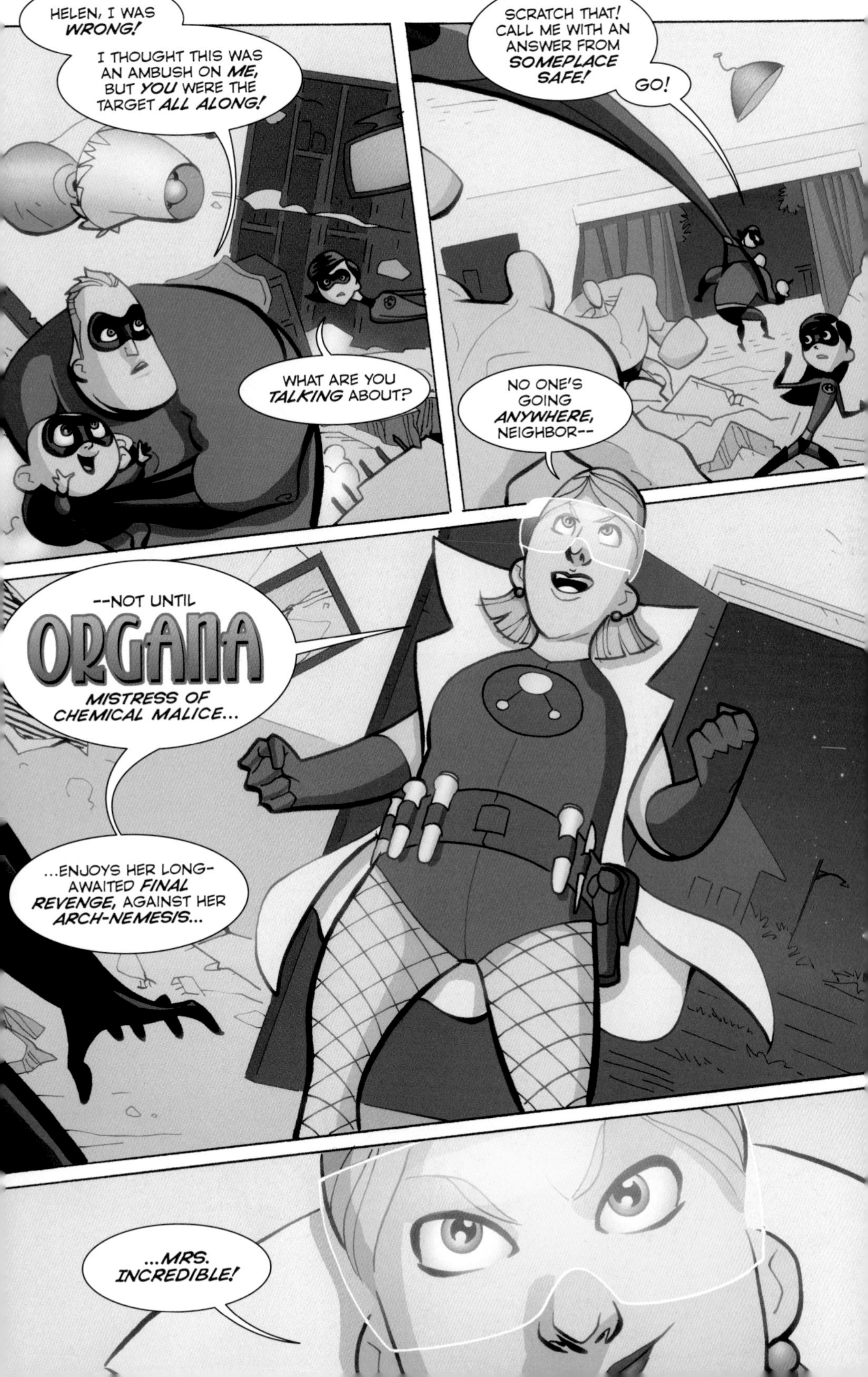
HELEN, I WAS WRONG!
I THOUGHT THIS WAS AN AMBUSH ON ME, BUT YOU WERE THE TARGET ALL ALONG!
WHAT ARE YOU TALKING ABOUT?
SCRATCH THAT! CALL ME WITH AN ANSWER FROM SOMEPLACE SAFE!
GO!
NO ONE'S GOING ANYWHERE, NEIGHBOR--
--NOT UNTIL ORGANA MISTRESS OF CHEMICAL MALICE...
...ENJOYS HER LONG-AWAITED FINAL REVENGE, AGAINST HER ARCH-NEMESIS...
...MRS. INCREDIBLE!

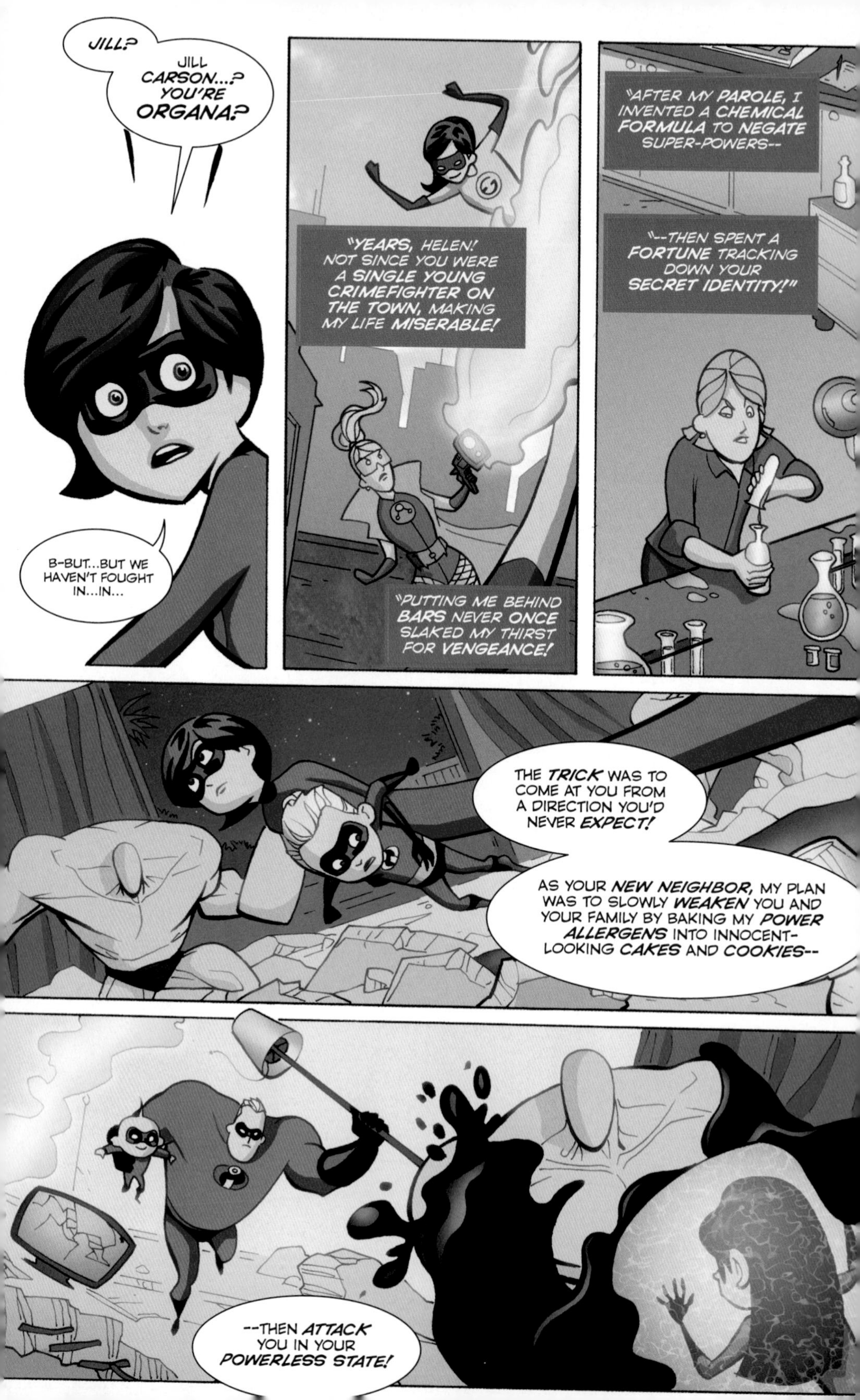
JILL?
JILL CARSON...? YOU'RE ORGANA?
B-BUT...BUT WE HAVEN'T FOUGHT IN...IN...
"YEARS, HELEN! NOT SINCE YOU WERE A SINGLE YOUNG CRIMEFIGHTER ON THE TOWN, MAKING MY LIFE MISERABLE!
"PUTTING ME BEHIND BARS NEVER ONCE SLAKED MY THIRST FOR VENGEANCE!
"AFTER MY PAROLE, I INVENTED A CHEMICAL FORMULA TO NEGATE SUPER-POWERS--
"--THEN SPENT A FORTUNE TRACKING DOWN YOUR SECRET IDENTITY!"
THE TRICK WAS TO COME AT YOU FROM A DIRECTION YOU'D NEVER EXPECT!
AS YOUR NEW NEIGHBOR, MY PLAN WAS TO SLOWLY WEAKEN YOU AND YOUR FAMILY BY BAKING MY POWER ALLERGENS INTO INNOCENT-LOOKING CAKES AND COOKIES--
--THEN ATTACK YOU IN YOUR POWERLESS STATE!

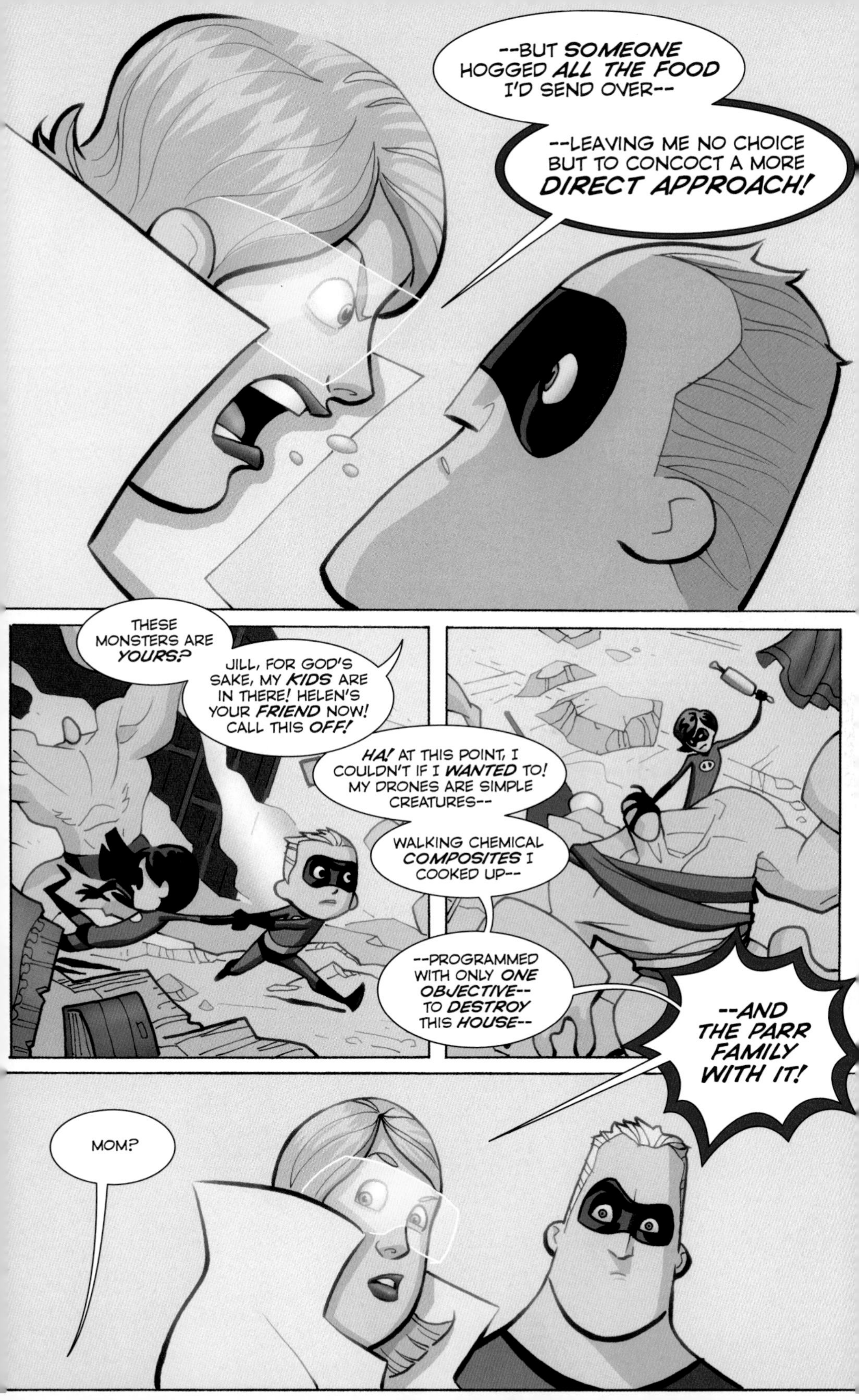
--BUT SOMEONE HOGGED ALL THE FOOD I'D SEND OVER--
--LEAVING ME NO CHOICE BUT TO CONCOCT A MORE DIRECT APPROACH!
THESE MONSTERS ARE YOURS?
JILL, FOR GOD'S SAKE, MY KIDS ARE IN THERE! HELEN'S YOUR FRIEND NOW! CALL THIS OFF!
HA! AT THIS POINT, I COULDN'T IF I WANTED TO! MY DRONES ARE SIMPLE CREATURES--
WALKING CHEMICAL COMPOSITES I COOKED UP--
--PROGRAMMED WITH ONLY ONE OBJECTIVE-- TO DESTROY THIS HOUSE--
--AND THE PARR FAMILY WITH IT!
MOM?

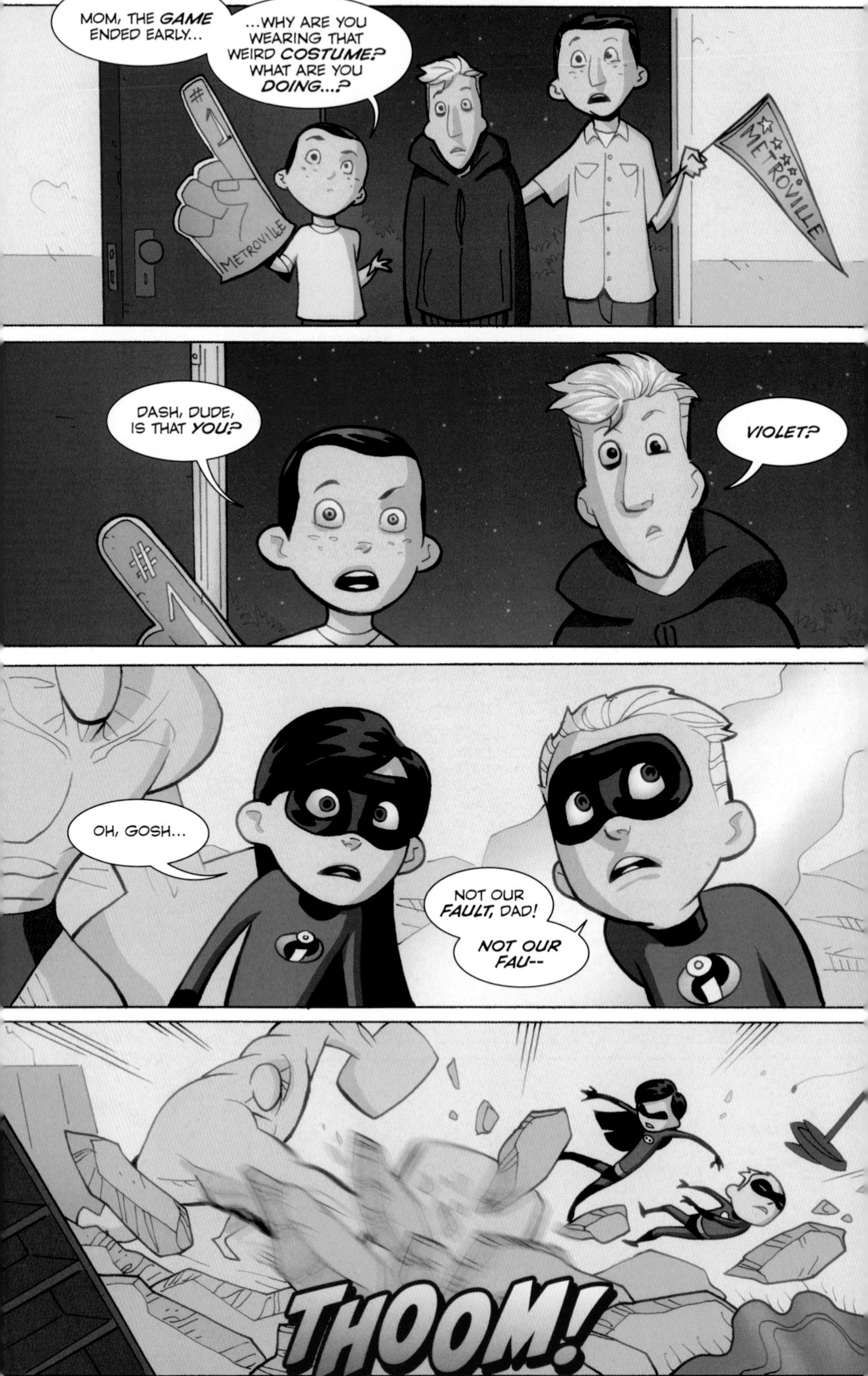
MOM, THE GAME ENDED EARLY...
...WHY ARE YOU WEARING THAT WEIRD COSTUME? WHAT ARE YOU DOING...?
#1
METROVILLE
METROVILLE
DASH, DUDE, IS THAT YOU?
VIOLET?
OH, GOSH...
NOT OUR FAULT, DAD!
NOT OUR FAU--
THOOM!

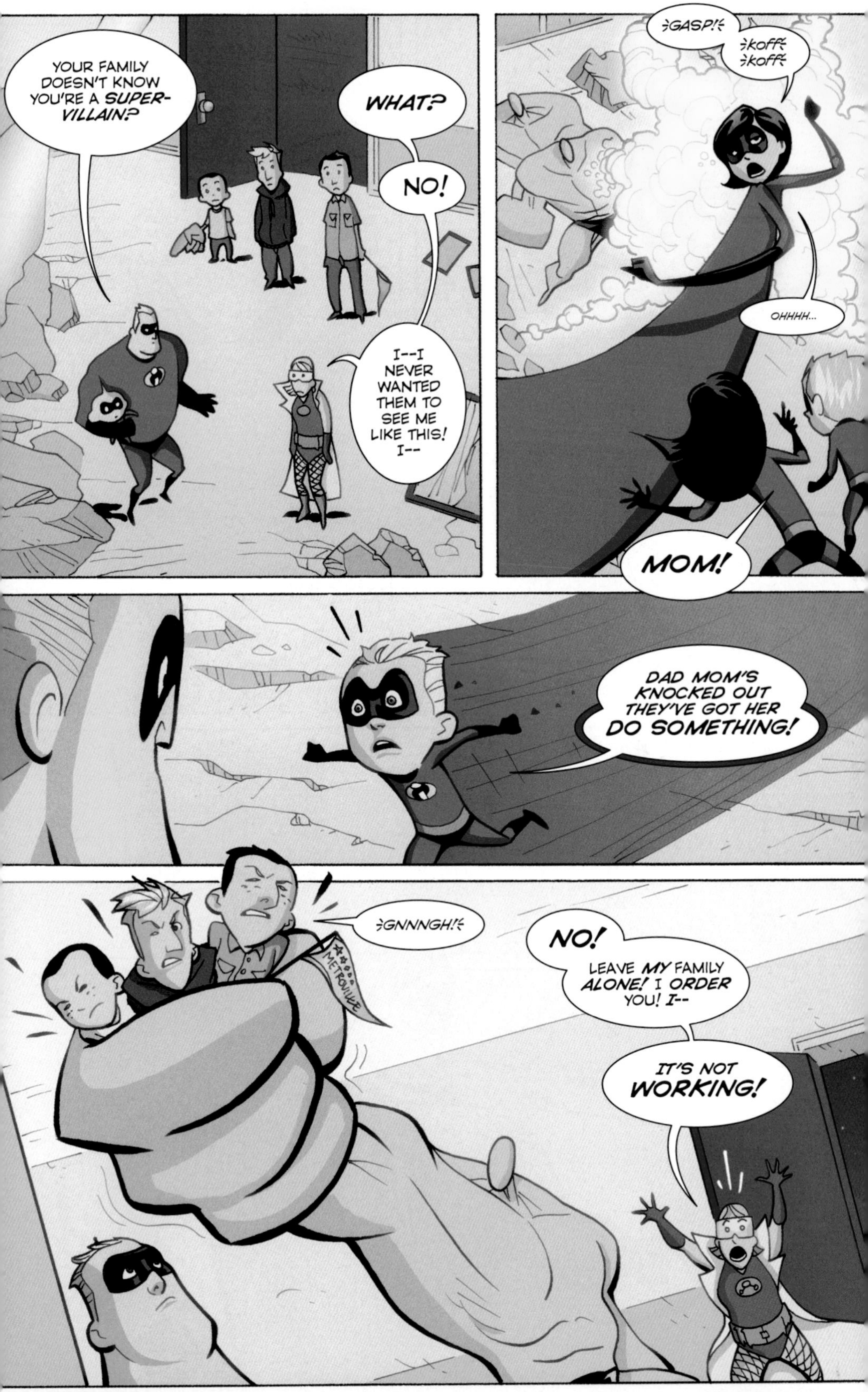
YOUR FAMILY DOESN'T KNOW YOU'RE A SUPER-VILLAIN?
WHAT?
NO!
I--I NEVER WANTED THEM TO SEE ME LIKE THIS! I--
GASP!
koff koff
OHHHH...
MOM!
DAD MOM'S KNOCKED OUT THEY'VE GOT HER DO SOMETHING!
GNNNGH!
METROVILLE
NO!
LEAVE MY FAMILY ALONE! I ORDER YOU! I--
IT'S NOT WORKING!

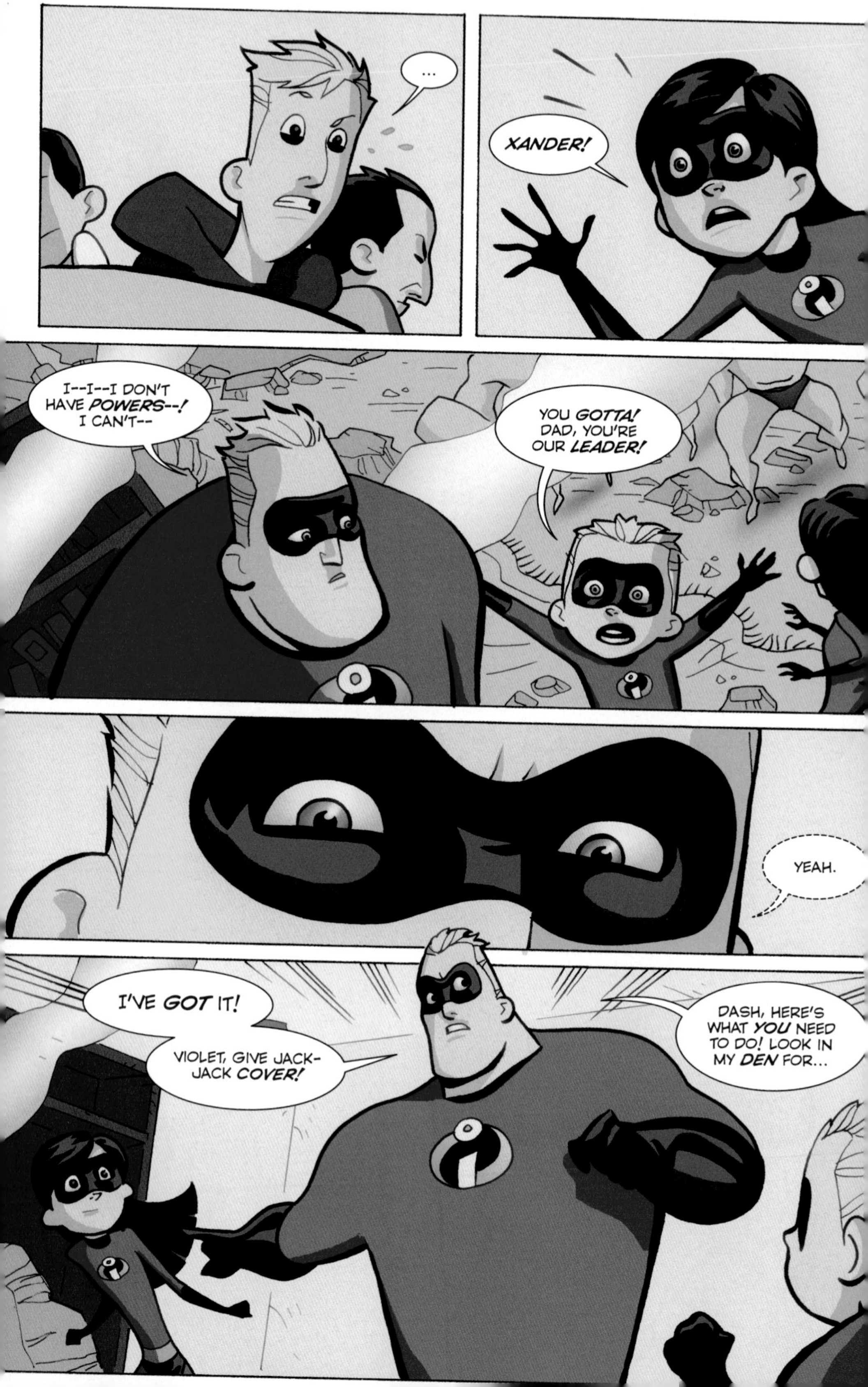
...
XANDER!
I--I--I DON'T HAVE POWERS--! I CAN'T--
YOU GOTTA! DAD, YOU'RE OUR LEADER!
YEAH.
I'VE GOT IT!
VIOLET, GIVE JACK-JACK COVER!
DASH, HERE'S WHAT YOU NEED TO DO! LOOK IN MY DEN FOR...

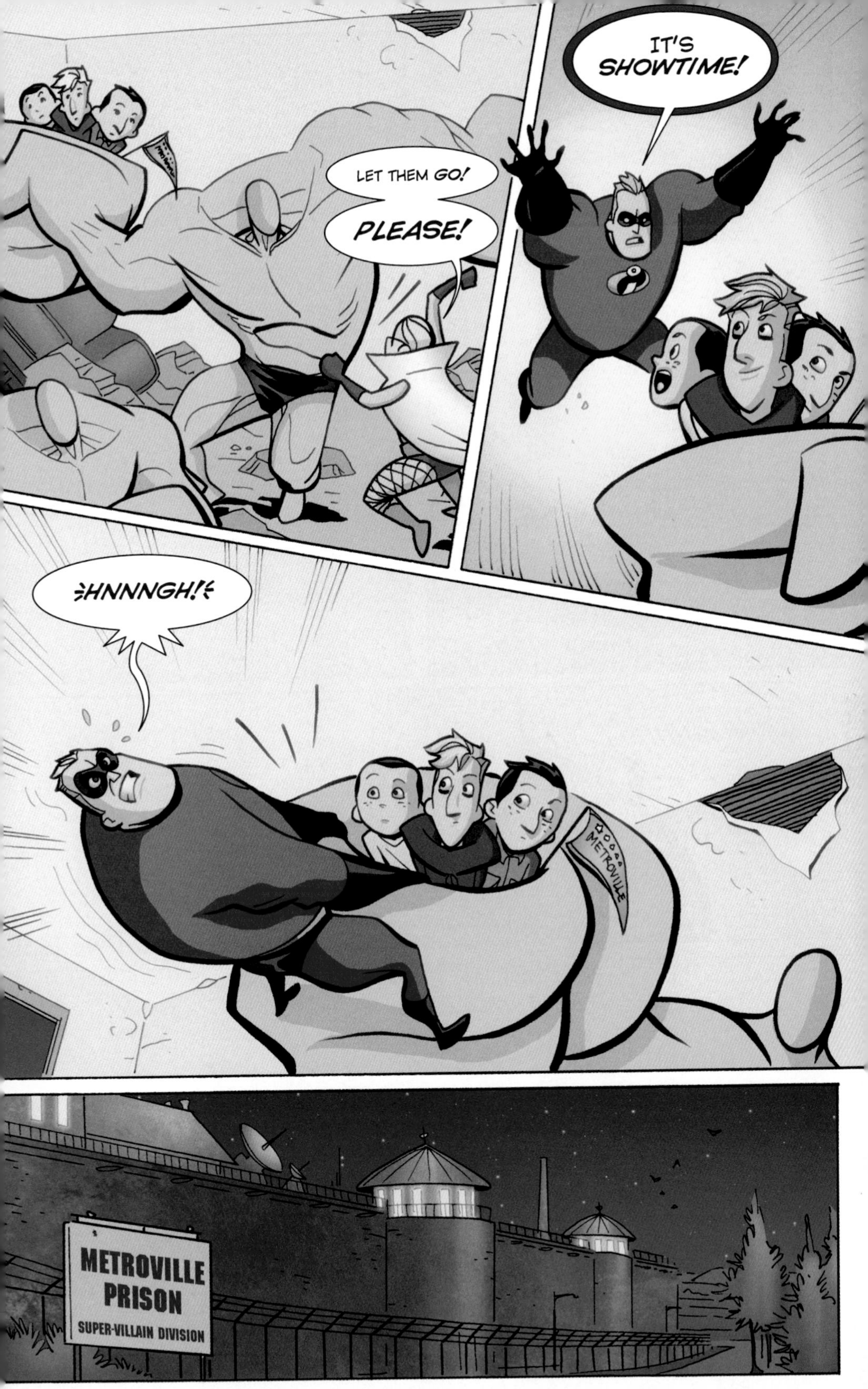
LET THEM GO!
PLEASE!
IT'S SHOWTIME!
METROVILLE
HNNNGH!
METROVILLE PRISON
SUPER-VILLAIN DIVISION

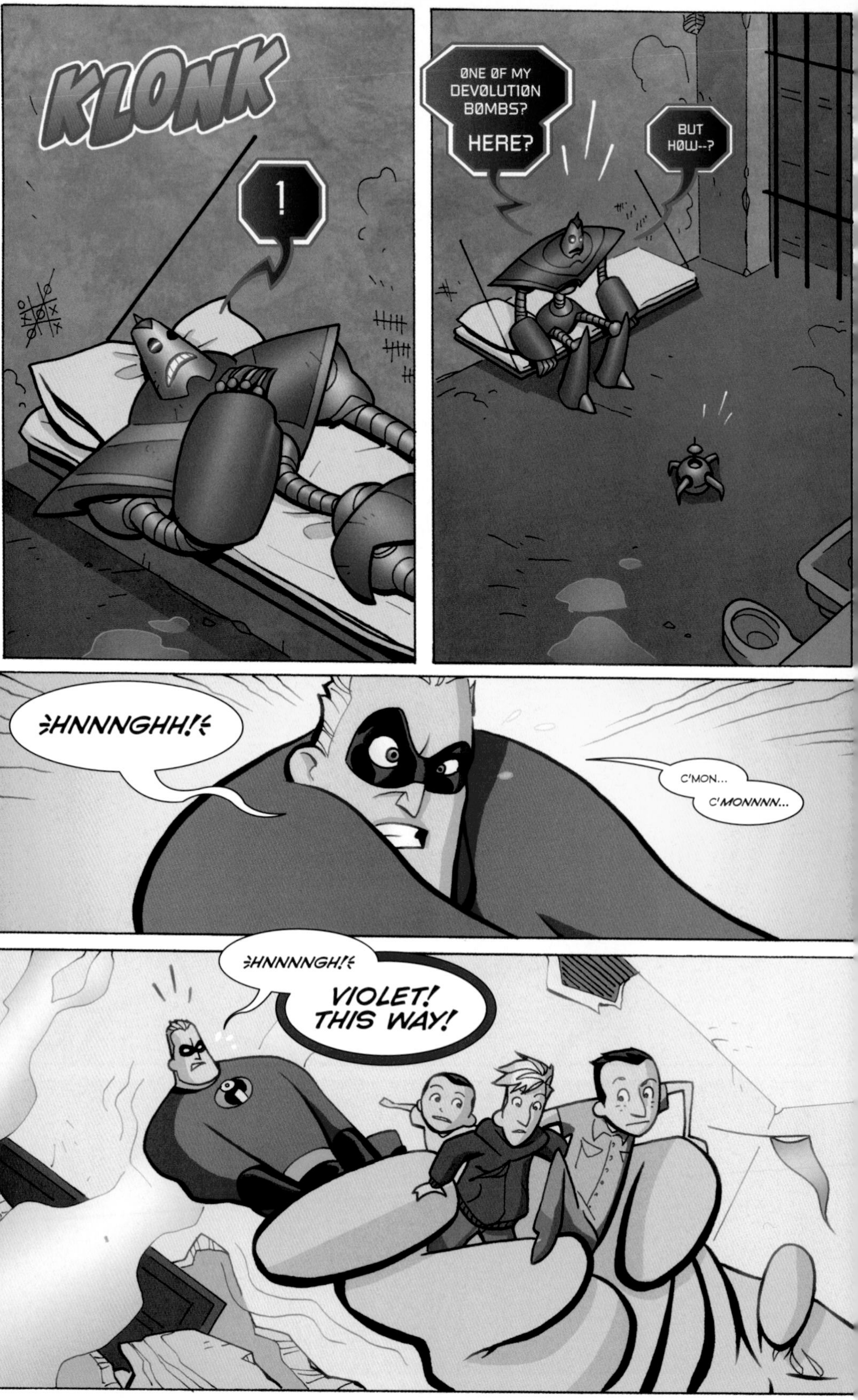
KLONK
!
ØNE ØF MY DEVØLUTIØN BØMBS? HERE?
BUT HØW--?
HNNNGHH!
C'MON... C'MONNNN...
HNNNNGH!
VIOLET! THIS WAY!

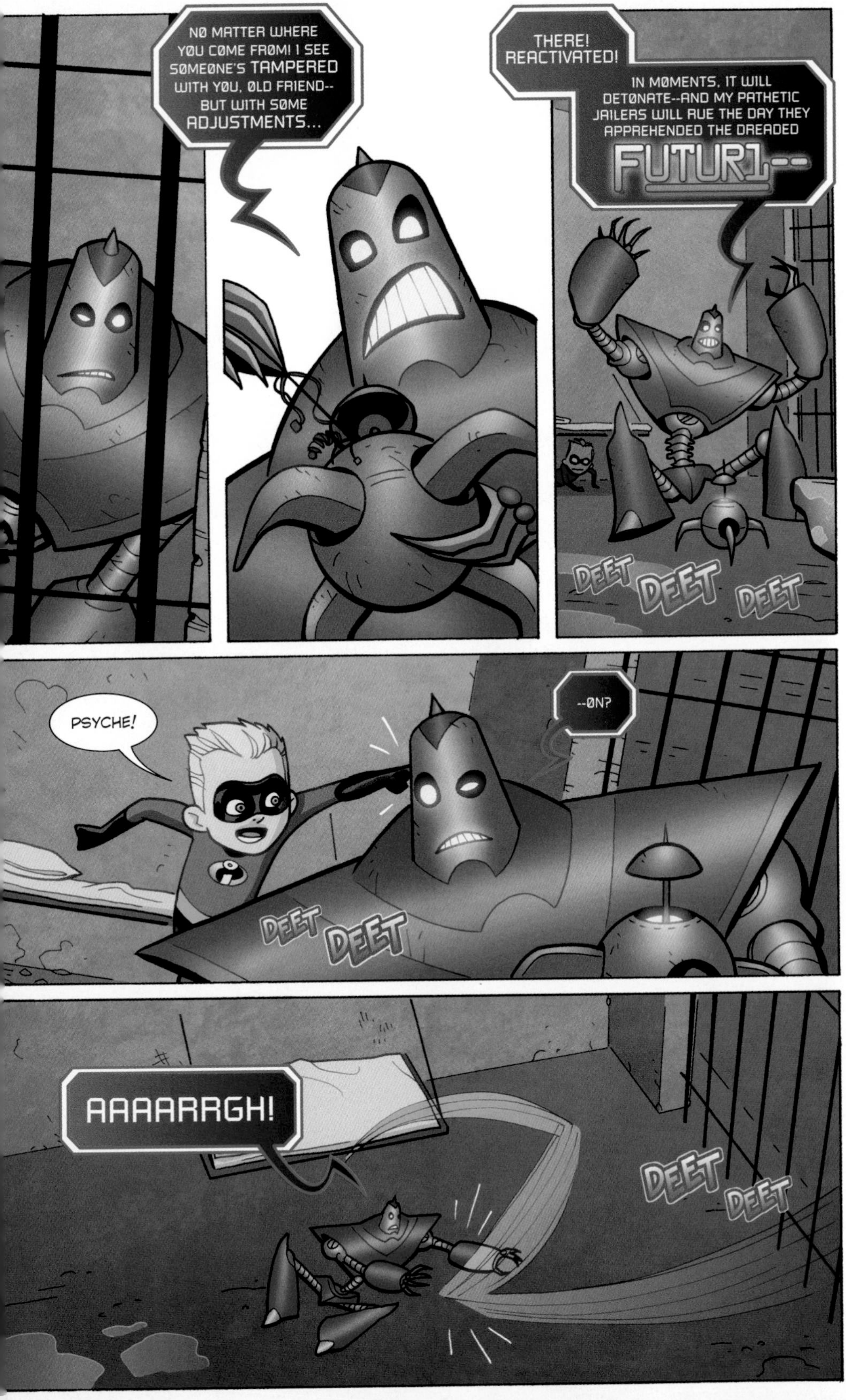

NØ MATTER WHERE YØU CØME FRØM! I SEE SØMEØNE'S TAMPERED WITH YØU, ØLD FRIEND-- BUT WITH SØME ADJUSTMENTS...
THERE! REACTIVATED!
IN MØMENTS, IT WILL DETØNATE--AND MY PATHETIC JAILERS WILL RUE THE DAY THEY APPREHENDED THE DREADED
FUTUR1--
DEET DEET DEET
PSYCHE!
--ØN?
DEET DEET
AAAARRGH!
DEET DEET

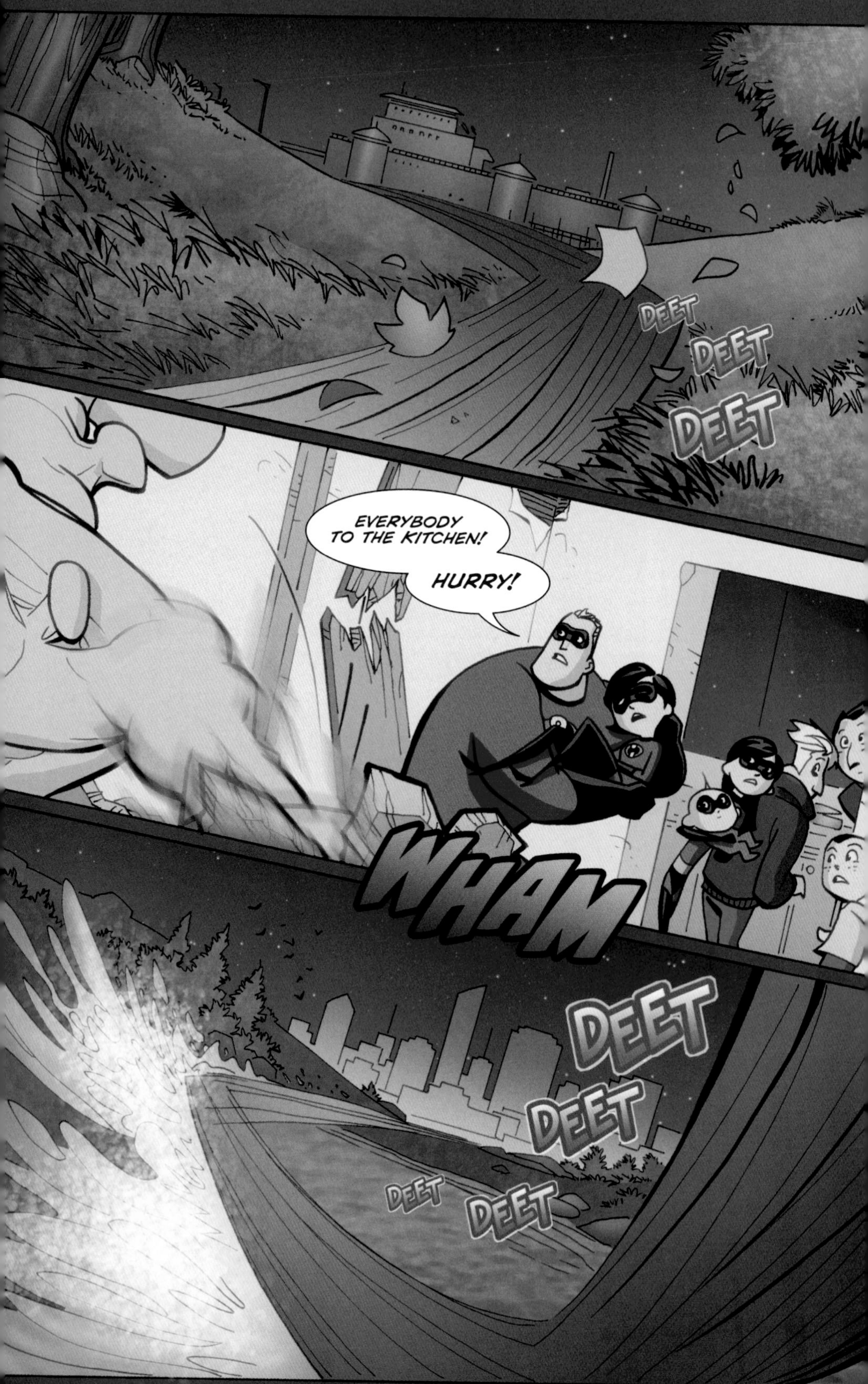

DEET
DEET
DEET
EVERYBODY TO THE KITCHEN!
HURRY!
WHAM
DEET
DEET
DEET
DEET

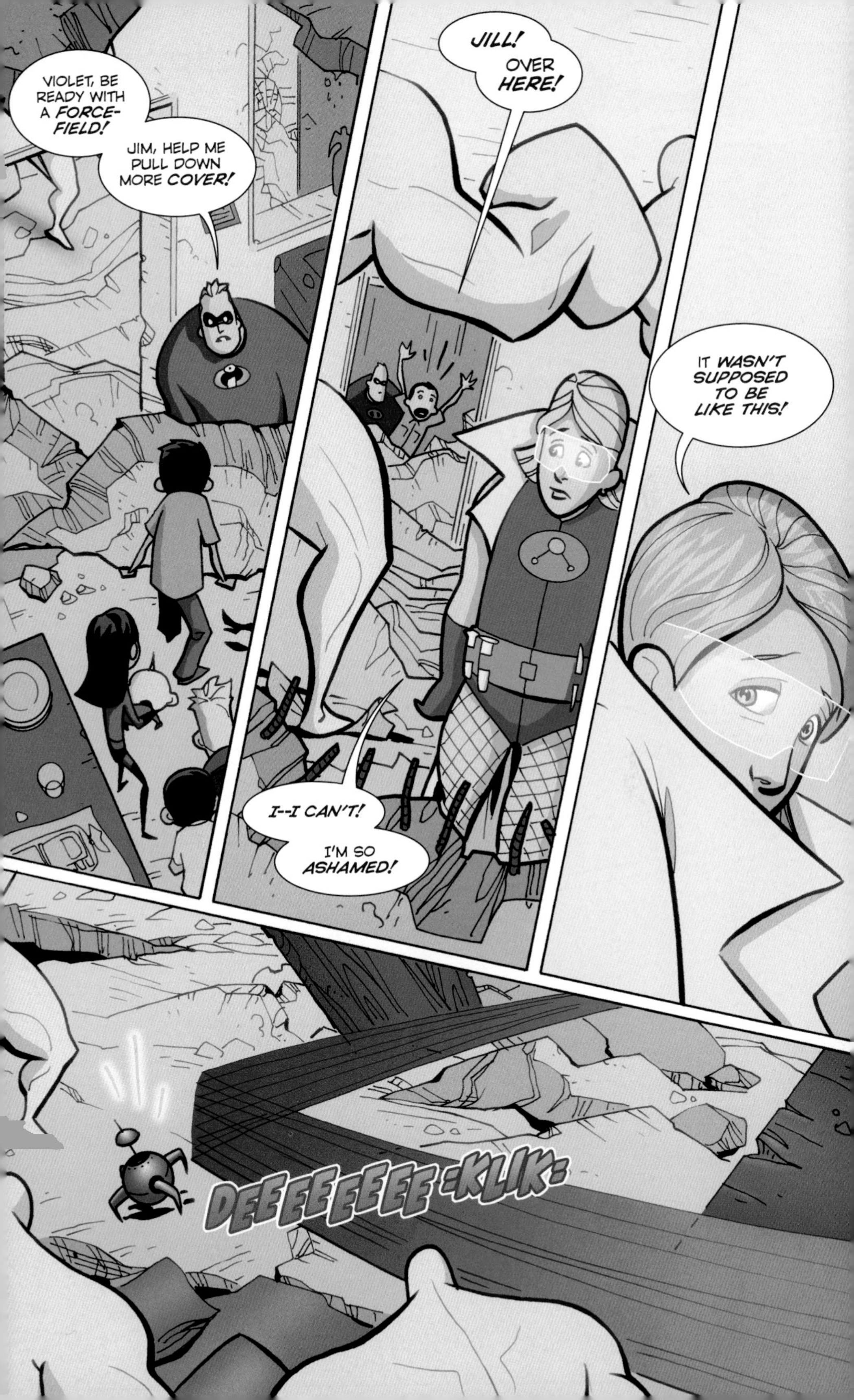
VIOLET, BE READY WITH A FORCE-FIELD!
JIM, HELP ME PULL DOWN MORE COVER!
JILL!
OVER HERE!
I--I CAN'T!
I'M SO ASHAMED!
IT WASN'T SUPPOSED TO BE LIKE THIS!
DEEEEEEEE -KLIK-

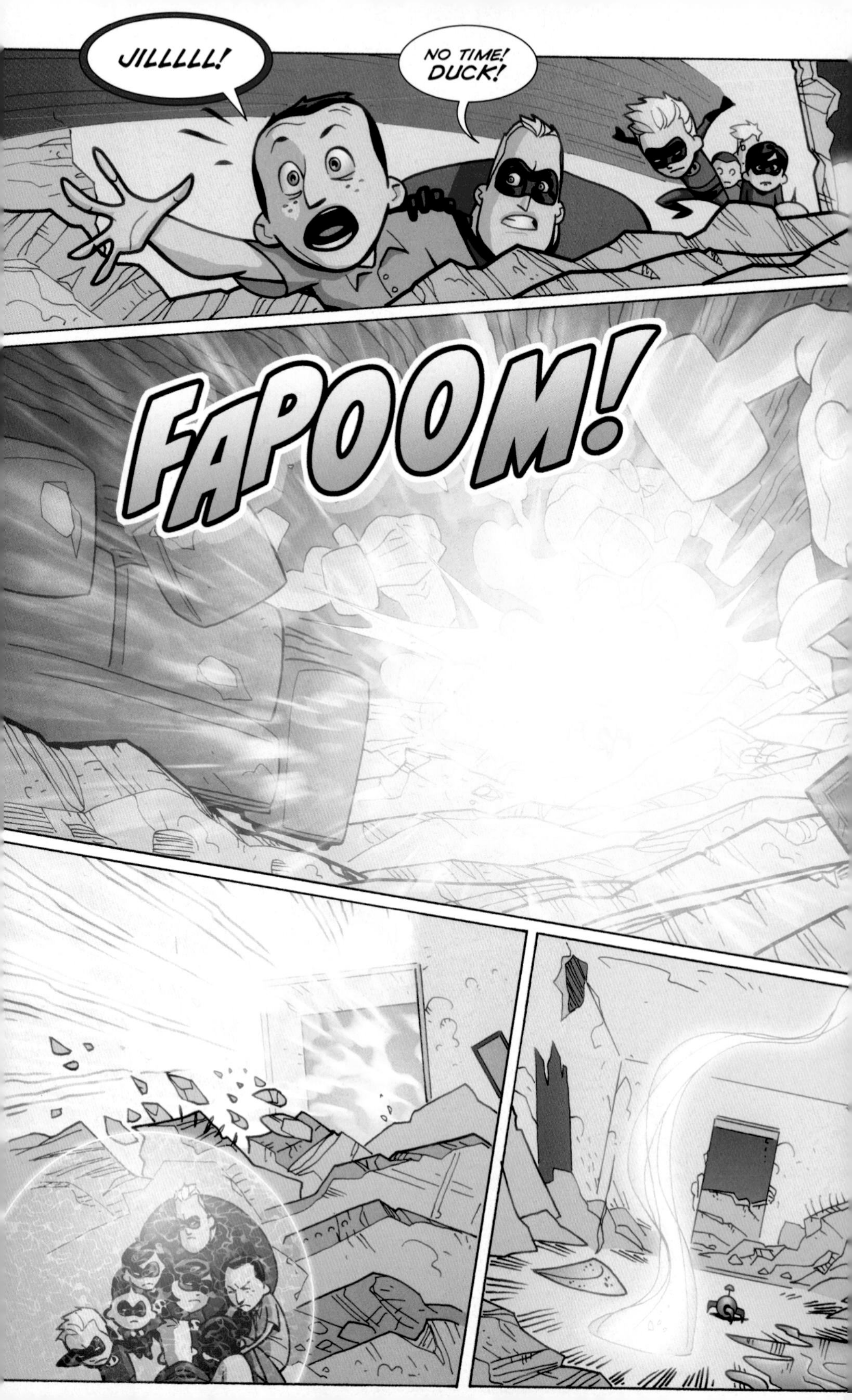
JILLLLL!
NO TIME! DUCK!
FAPOOM!

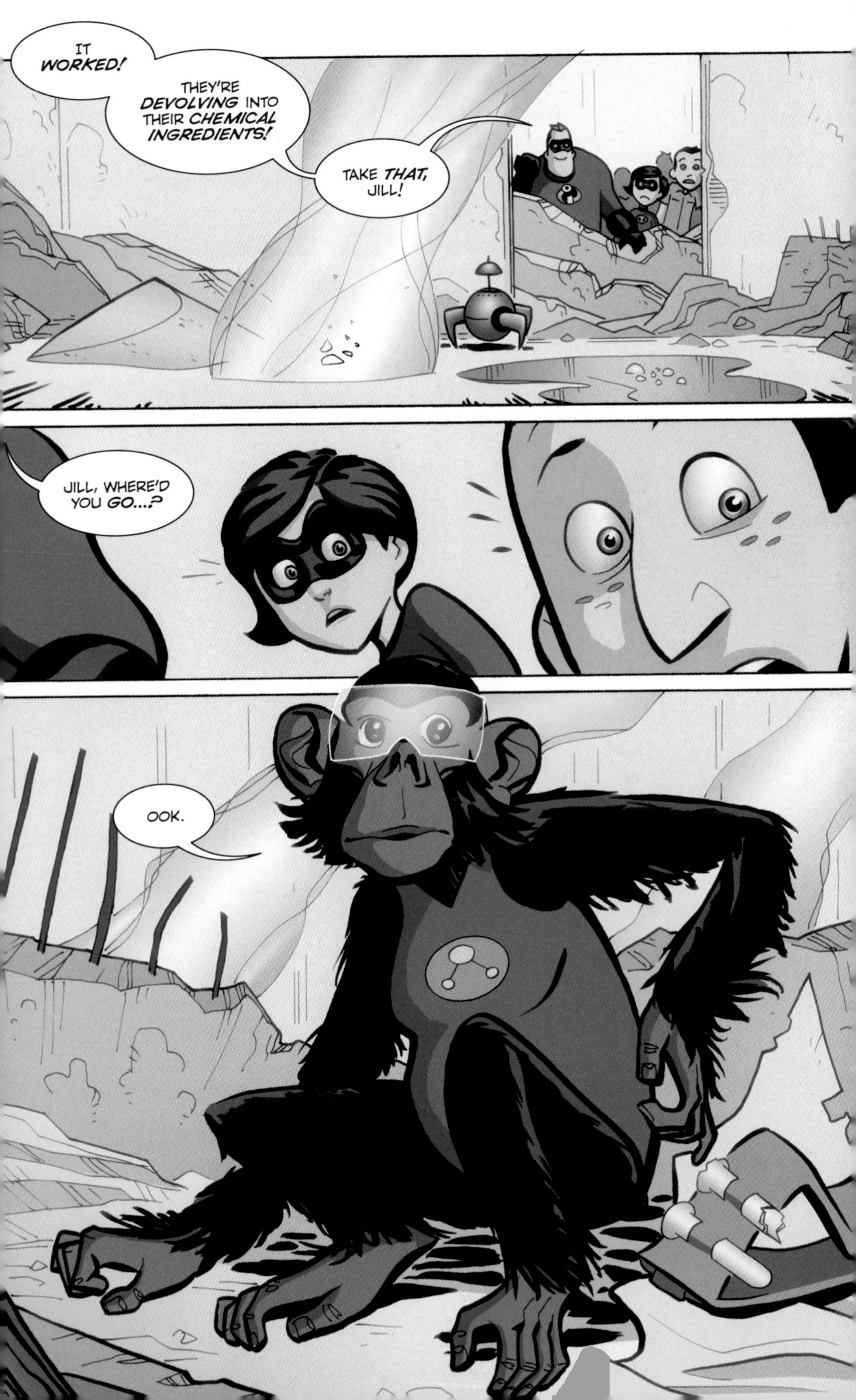
IT WORKED!
THEY'RE DEVOLVING INTO THEIR CHEMICAL INGREDIENTS!
TAKE THAT, JILL!
JILL, WHERE'D YOU GO...?
OOK.

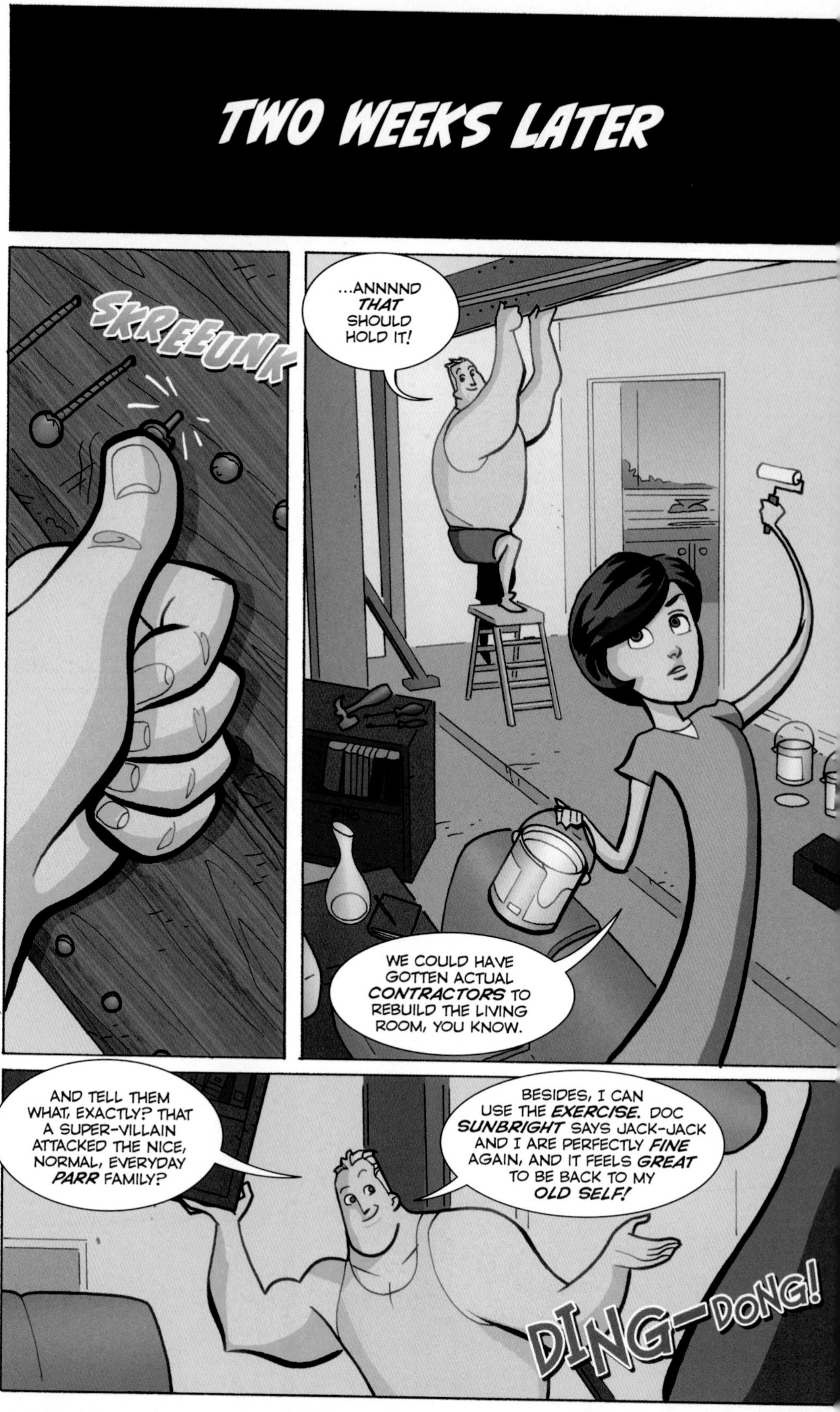
TWO WEEKS LATER
SKREEUNK
...ANNNND THAT SHOULD HOLD IT!
WE COULD HAVE GOTTEN ACTUAL CONTRACTORS TO REBUILD THE LIVING ROOM, YOU KNOW.
AND TELL THEM WHAT, EXACTLY? THAT A SUPER-VILLAIN ATTACKED THE NICE, NORMAL, EVERYDAY PARR FAMILY?
BESIDES, I CAN USE THE EXERCISE. DOC SUNBRIGHT SAYS JACK-JACK AND I ARE PERFECTLY FINE AGAIN, AND IT FEELS GREAT TO BE BACK TO MY OLD SELF!
DING-DONG!

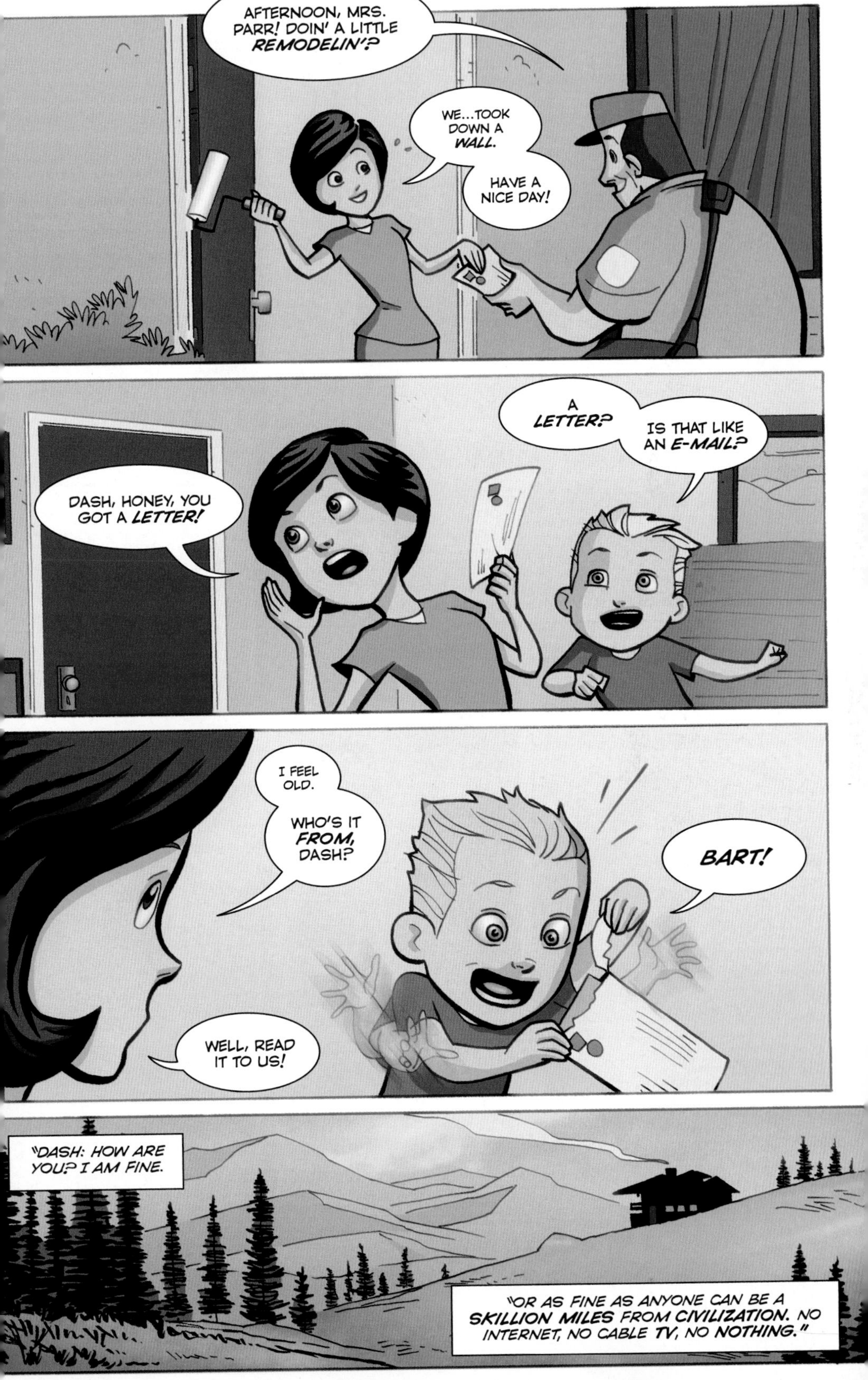

AFTERNOON, MRS. PARR! DOIN' A LITTLE REMODELIN'?
WE...TOOK DOWN A WALL.
HAVE A NICE DAY!
DASH, HONEY, YOU GOT A LETTER!
A LETTER?
IS THAT LIKE AN E-MAIL?
I FEEL OLD.
WHO'S IT FROM, DASH?
BART!
WELL, READ IT TO US!
"DASH: HOW ARE YOU? I AM FINE.
"OR AS FINE AS ANYONE CAN BE A SKILLION MILES FROM CIVILIZATION. NO INTERNET, NO CABLE TV, NO NOTHING."

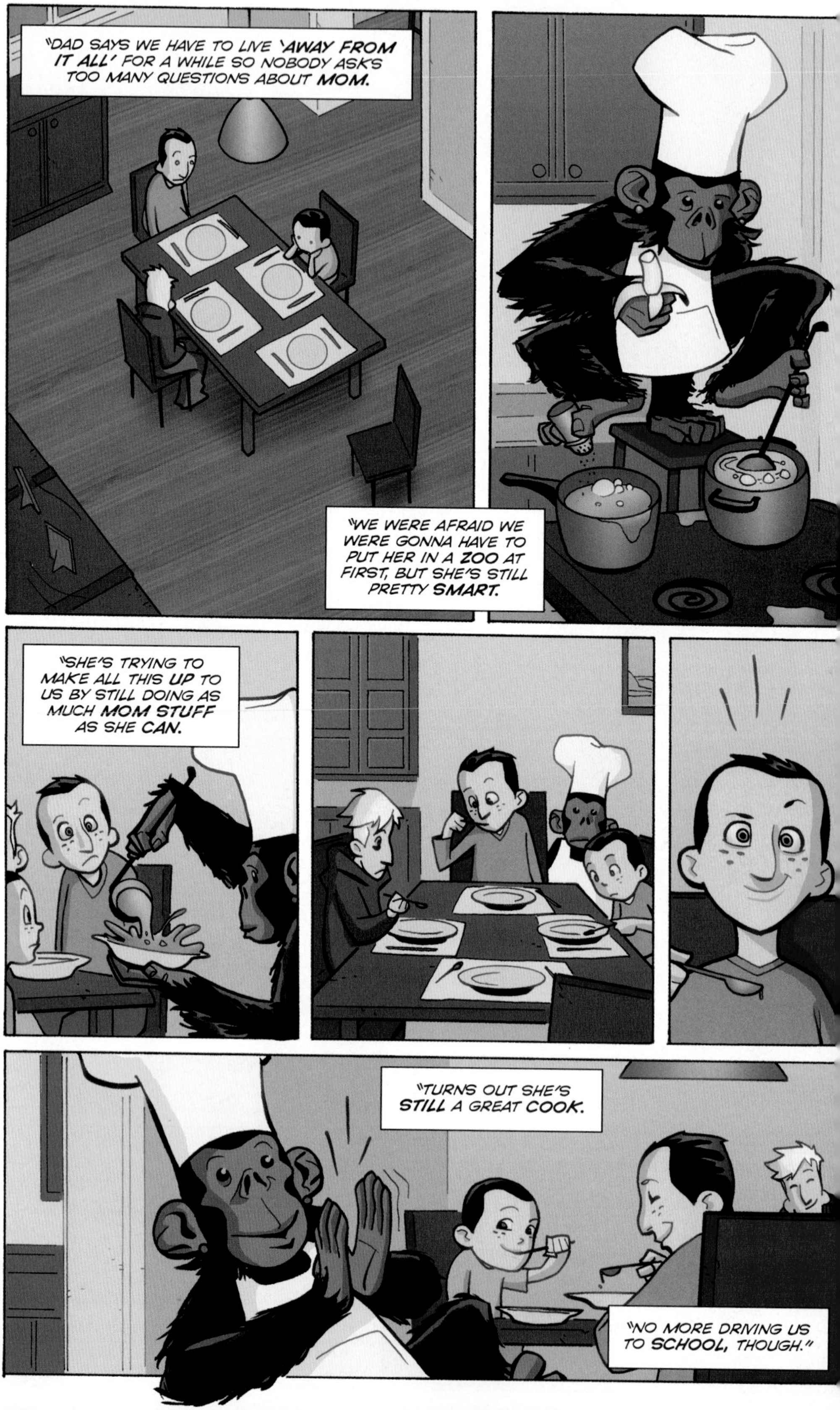
"DAD SAYS WE HAVE TO LIVE 'AWAY FROM IT ALL' FOR A WHILE SO NOBODY ASKS TOO MANY QUESTIONS ABOUT MOM.
"WE WERE AFRAID WE WERE GONNA HAVE TO PUT HER IN A ZOO AT FIRST, BUT SHE'S STILL PRETTY SMART.
"SHE'S TRYING TO MAKE ALL THIS UP TO US BY STILL DOING AS MUCH MOM STUFF AS SHE CAN.
"TURNS OUT SHE'S STILL A GREAT COOK.
"NO MORE DRIVING US TO SCHOOL, THOUGH."

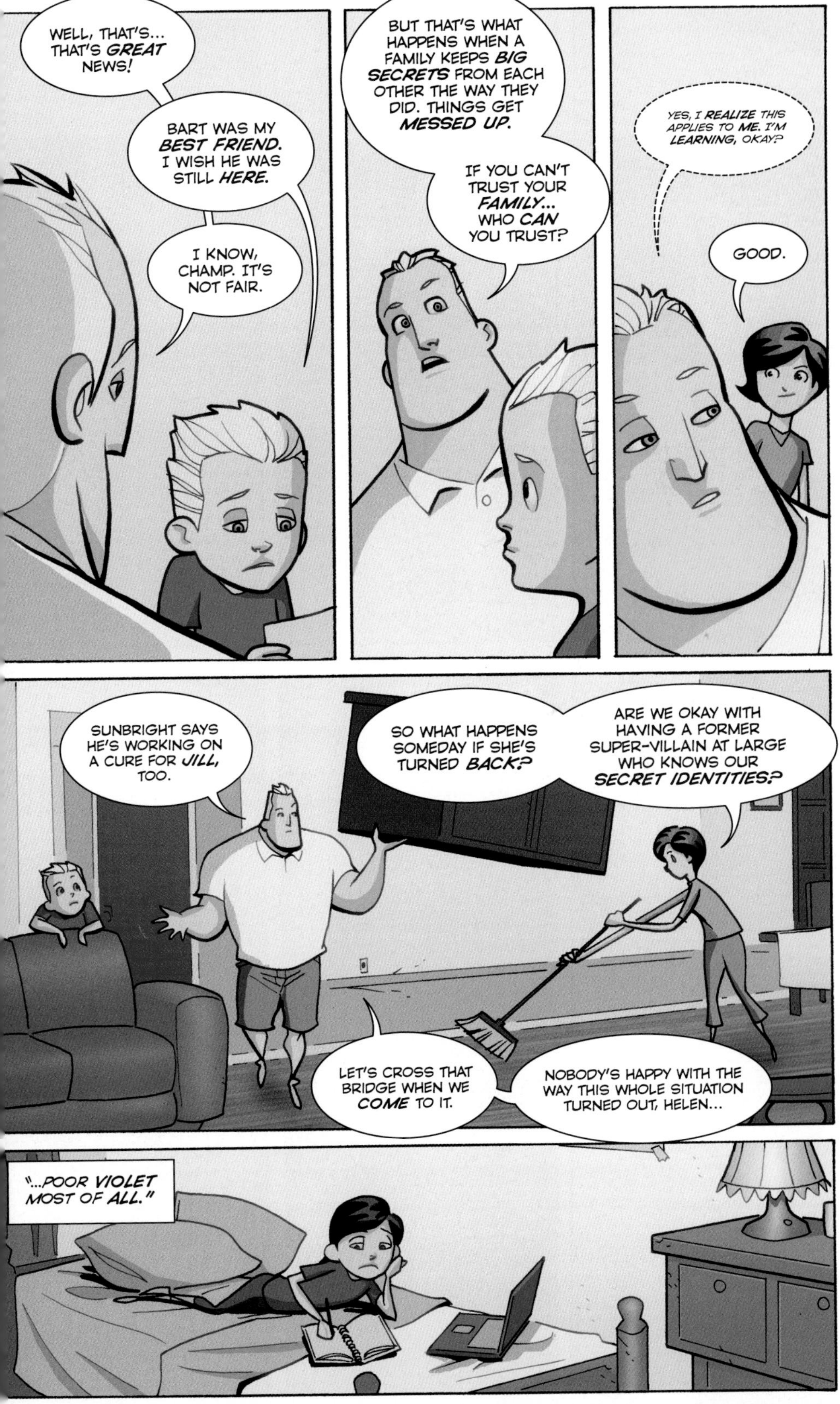

WELL, THAT'S... THAT'S *GREAT* NEWS!
BART WAS MY *BEST FRIEND.* I WISH HE WAS STILL *HERE.*
I KNOW, CHAMP. IT'S NOT FAIR.
BUT THAT'S WHAT HAPPENS WHEN A FAMILY KEEPS *BIG SECRETS* FROM EACH OTHER THE WAY THEY DID. THINGS GET *MESSED UP.*
IF YOU CAN'T TRUST YOUR *FAMILY...* WHO *CAN* YOU TRUST?
YES, I *REALIZE* THIS APPLIES TO *ME.* I'M *LEARNING,* OKAY?
GOOD.
SUNBRIGHT SAYS HE'S WORKING ON A CURE FOR *JILL,* TOO.
SO WHAT HAPPENS SOMEDAY IF SHE'S TURNED *BACK?*
ARE WE OKAY WITH HAVING A FORMER SUPER-VILLAIN AT LARGE WHO KNOWS OUR *SECRET IDENTITIES?*
LET'S CROSS THAT BRIDGE WHEN WE *COME* TO IT.
NOBODY'S HAPPY WITH THE WAY THIS WHOLE SITUATION TURNED OUT, HELEN...
"...POOR *VIOLET* MOST OF *ALL.*"

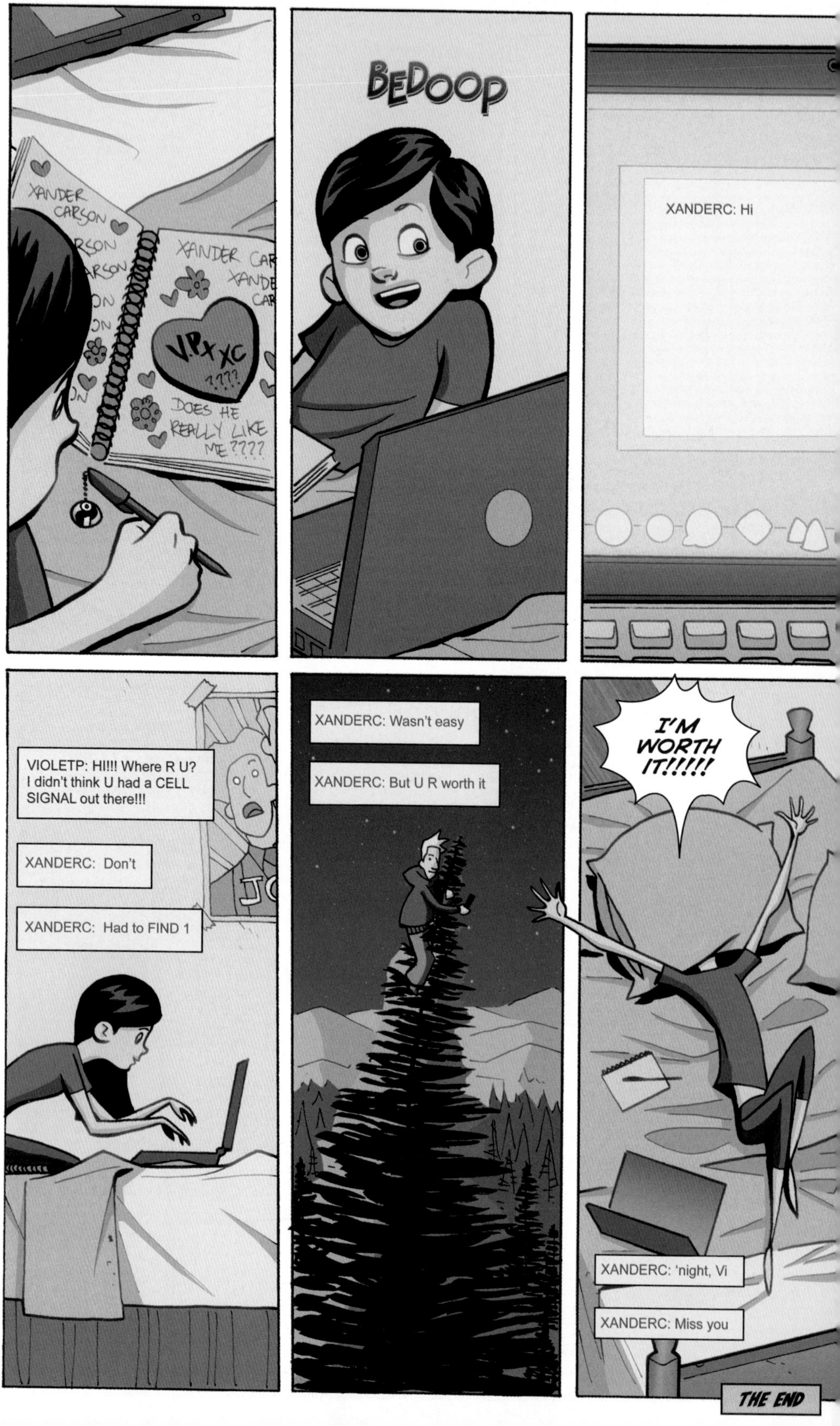
XANDER CARSON
V.P. + XC
????
DOES HE REALLY LIKE ME????
BEDOOP
XANDERC: Hi
VIOLETP: HI!!! Where R U? I didn't think U had a CELL SIGNAL out there!!!
XANDERC: Don't
XANDERC: Had to FIND 1
XANDERC: Wasn't easy
XANDERC: But U R worth it
I'M WORTH IT!!!!!
XANDERC: 'night, Vi
XANDERC: Miss you
THE END

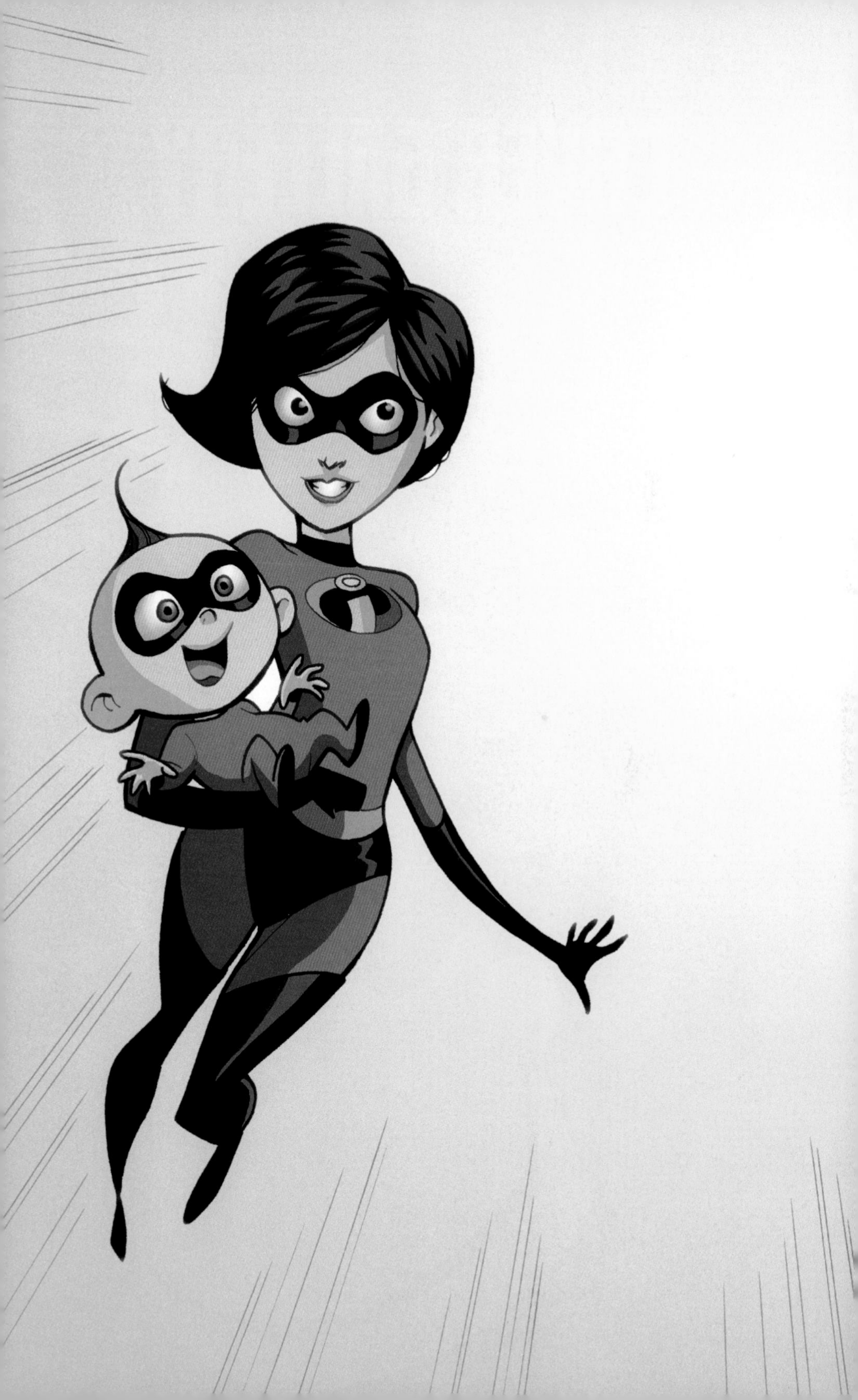

COVER GALLERY

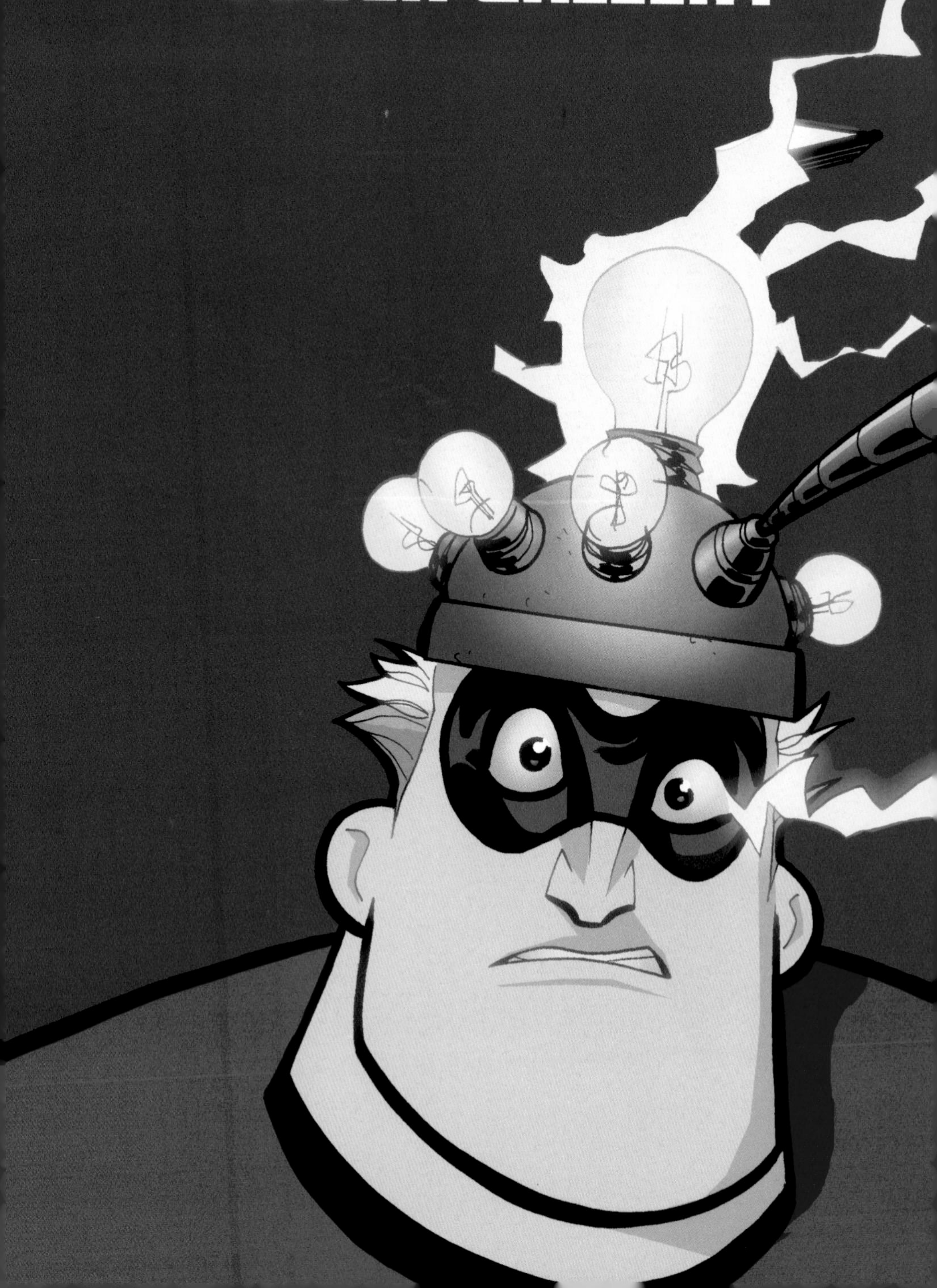

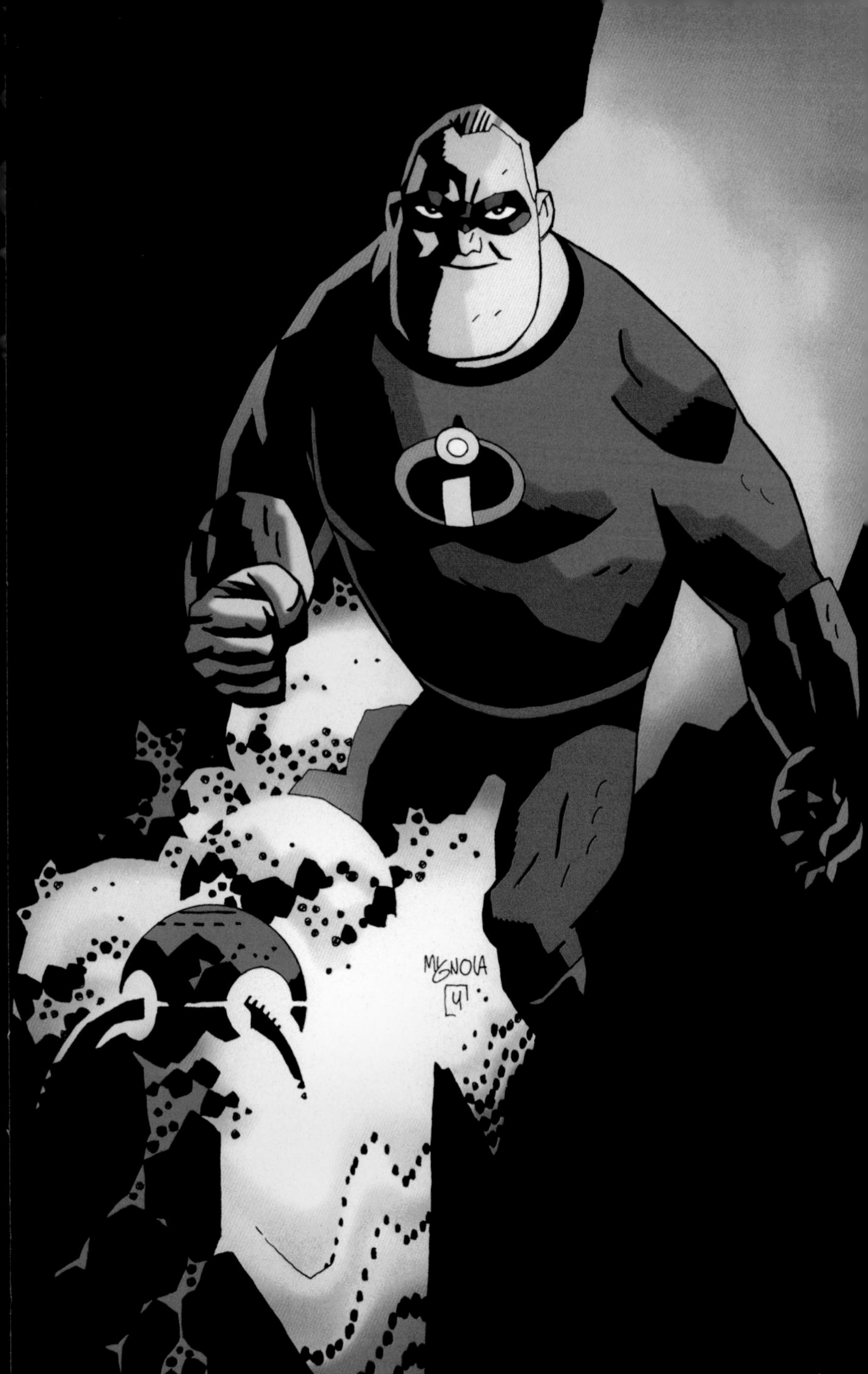
MIGNOLA

COVERS 1A-1D: MICHAEL AVON OEMING

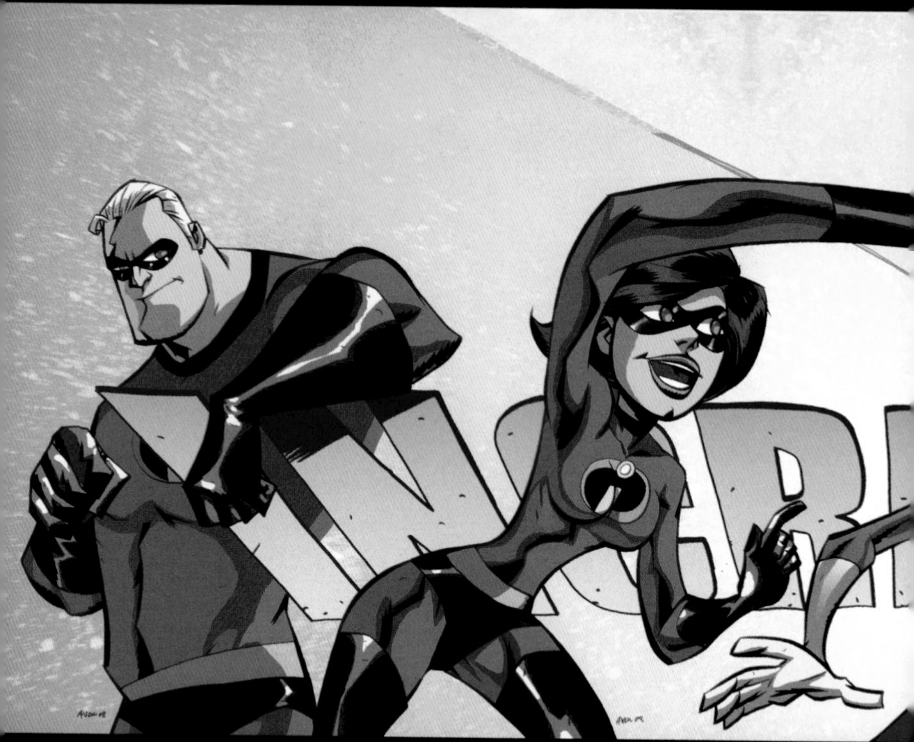

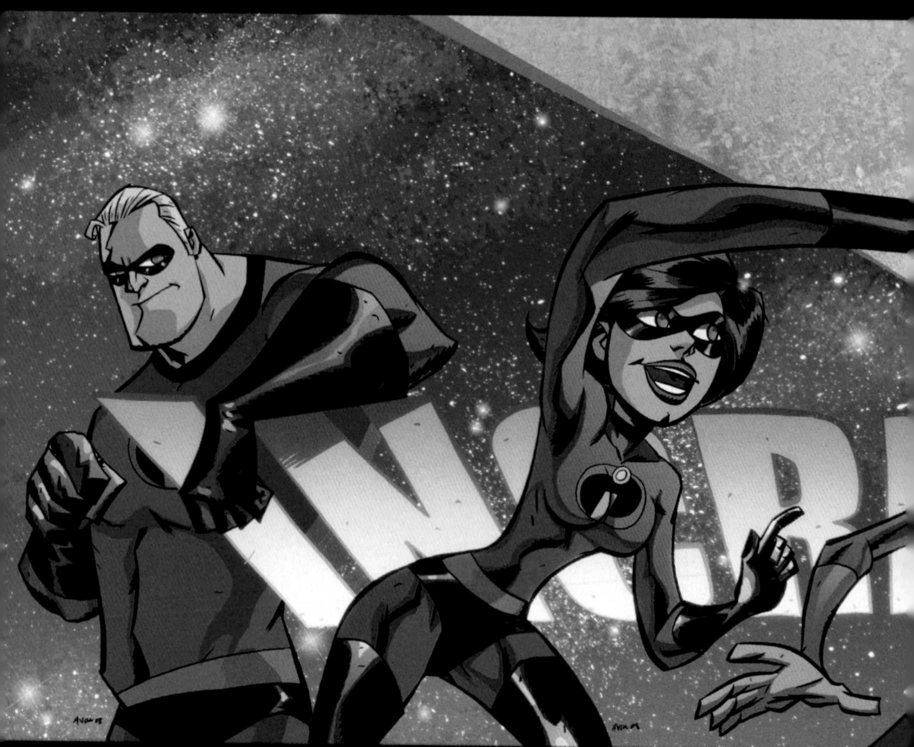

2ND PRINT 1A-1D: MICHAEL AVON OEMING

COLORS BY: NICK FILARDI

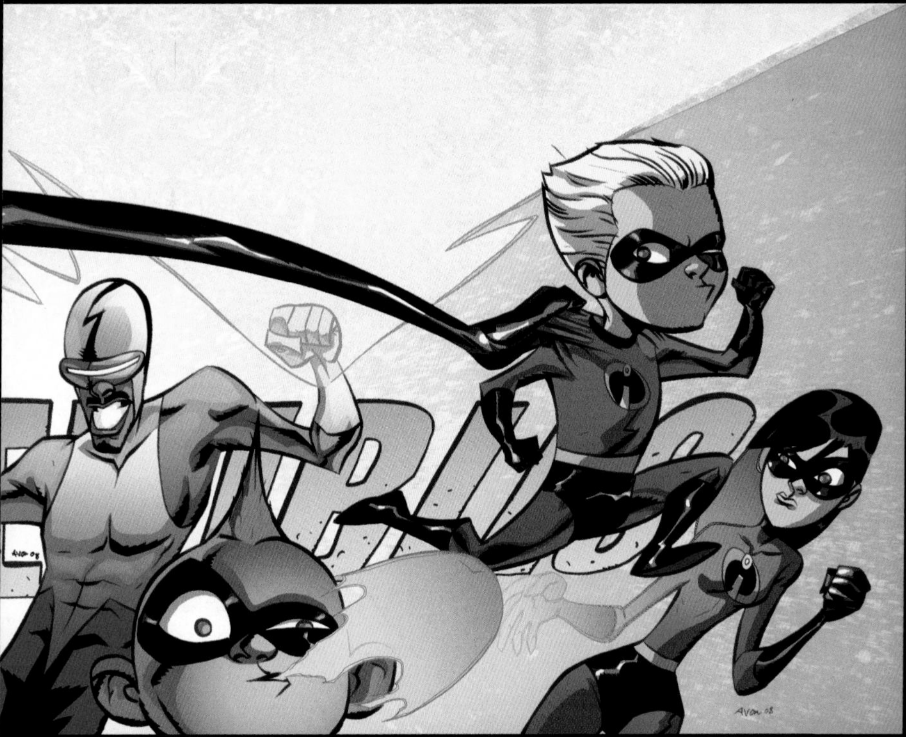

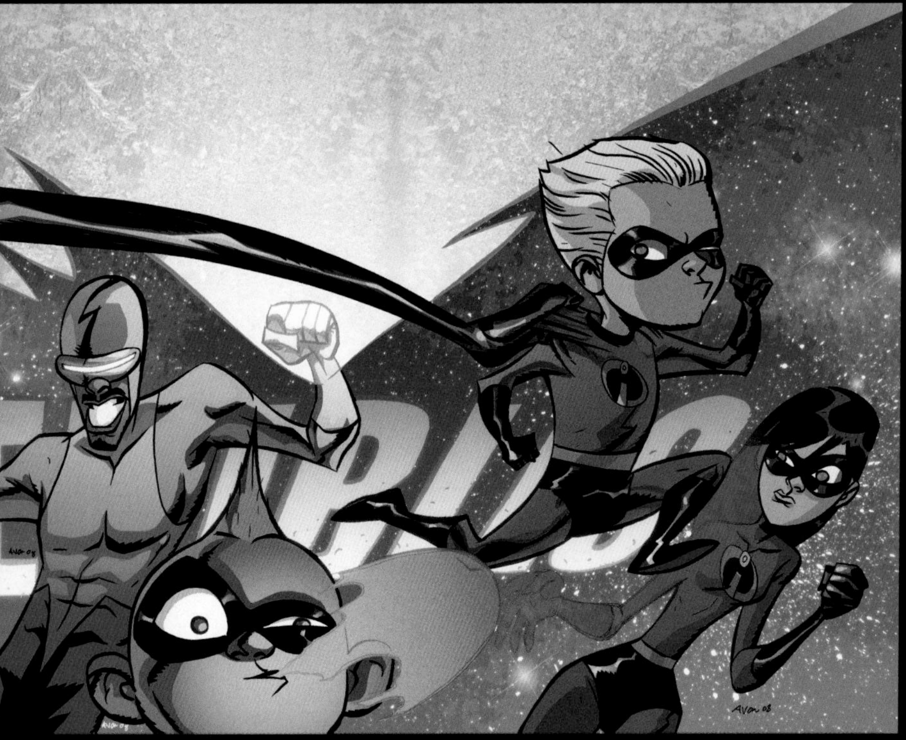

COLORS BY: NICK FILARDI

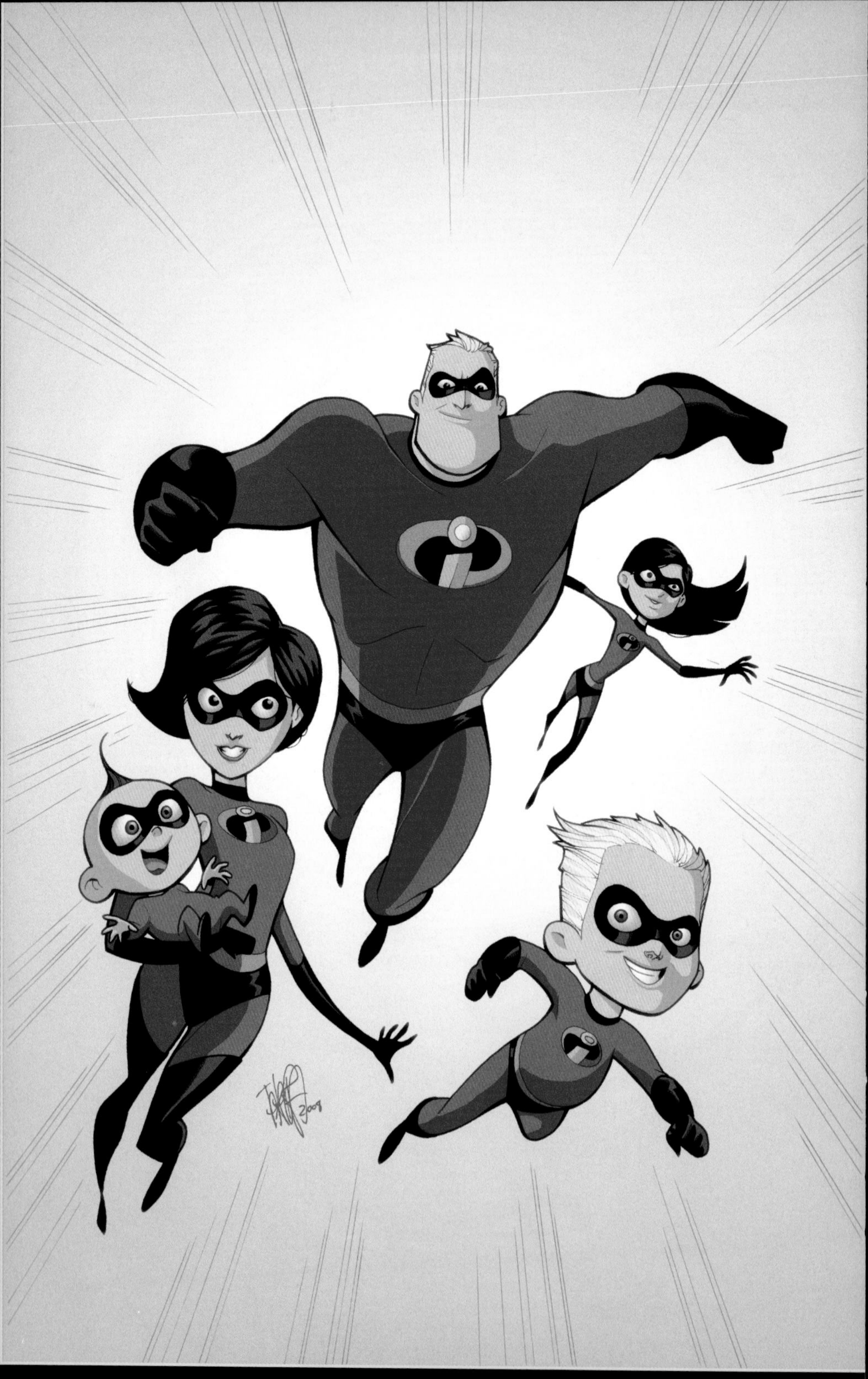

LONE STAR COMICS EXCLUSIVE: MARCIO TAKARA

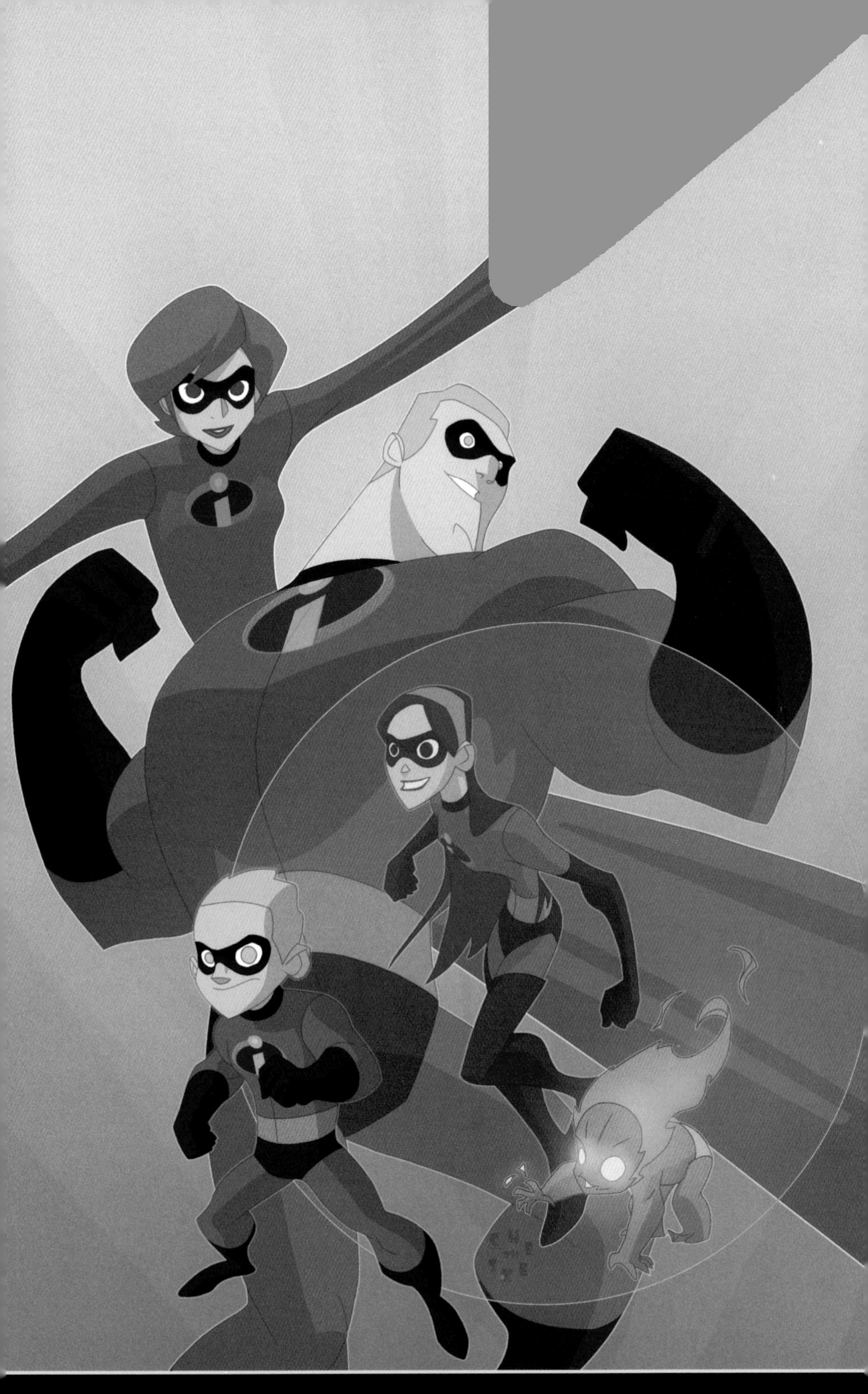

COVER 2A: SEAN “CHEEKS” GALLOWAY

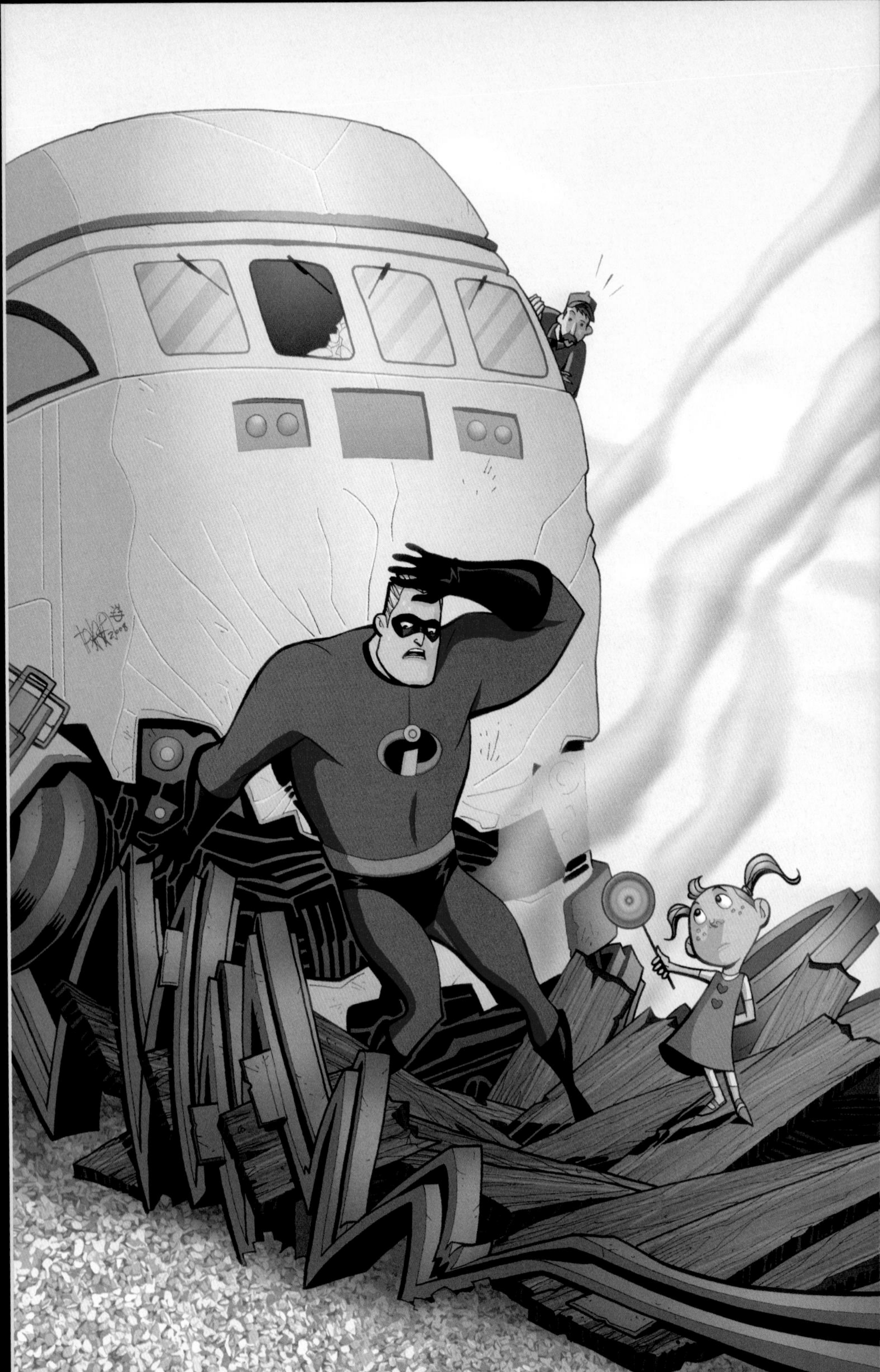

COVER 2B: MARCIO TAKARA

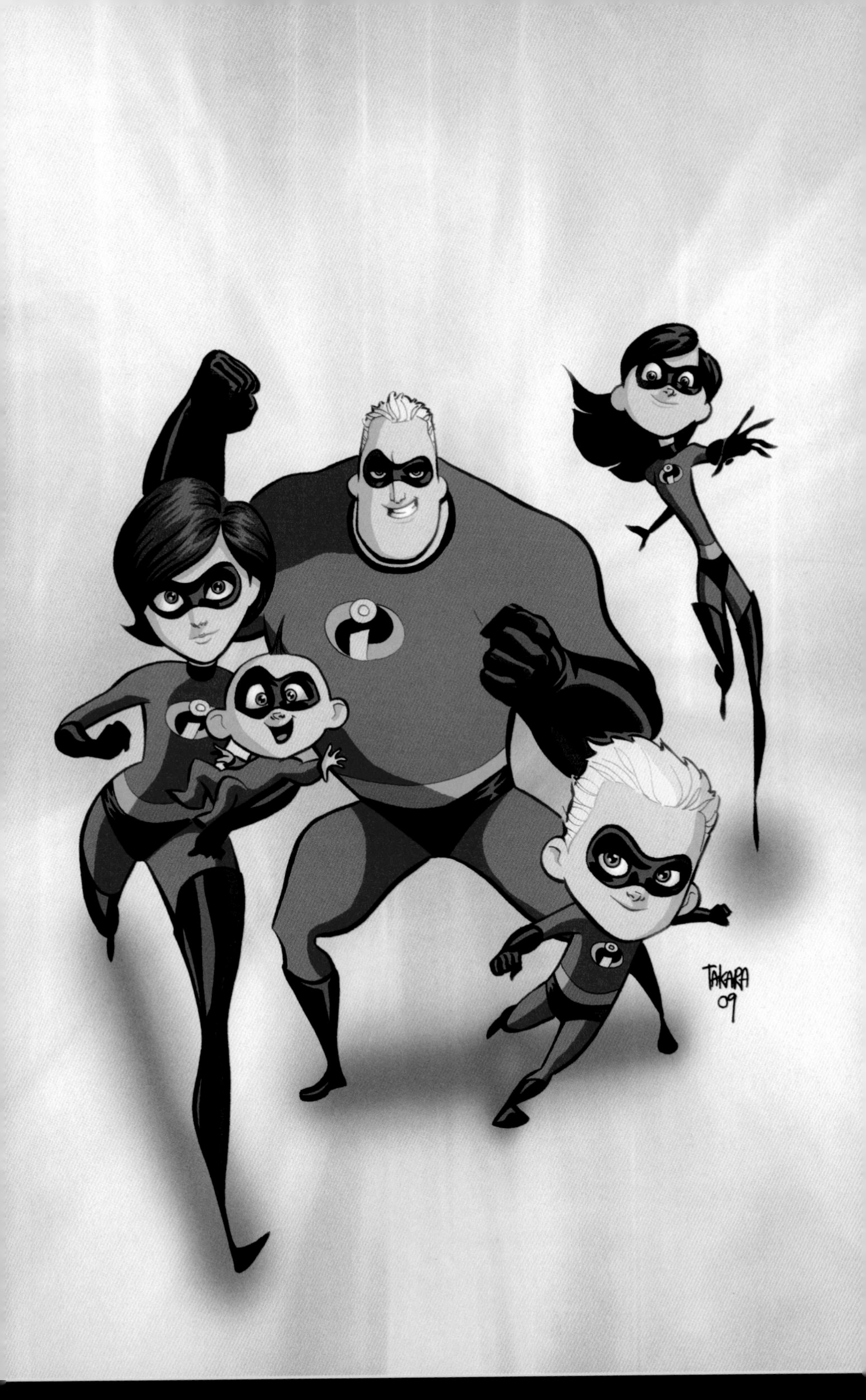
TAKARA
09

ONE STAR COMICS EXCLUSIVE: MARCIO TAKARA

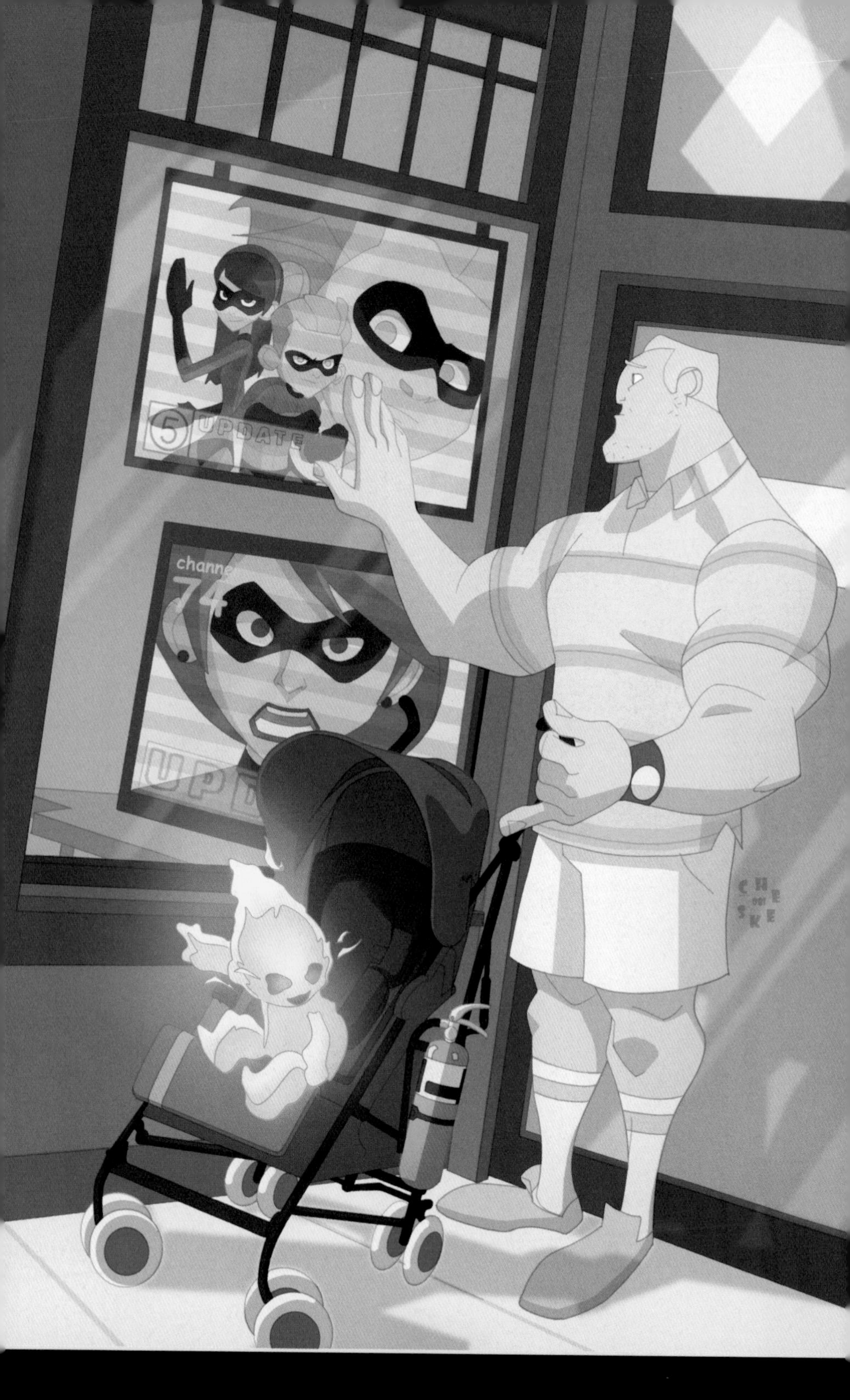
5
UPDATE
channel
74

COVER 3A: SEAN "CHEEKS" GALLOWAY

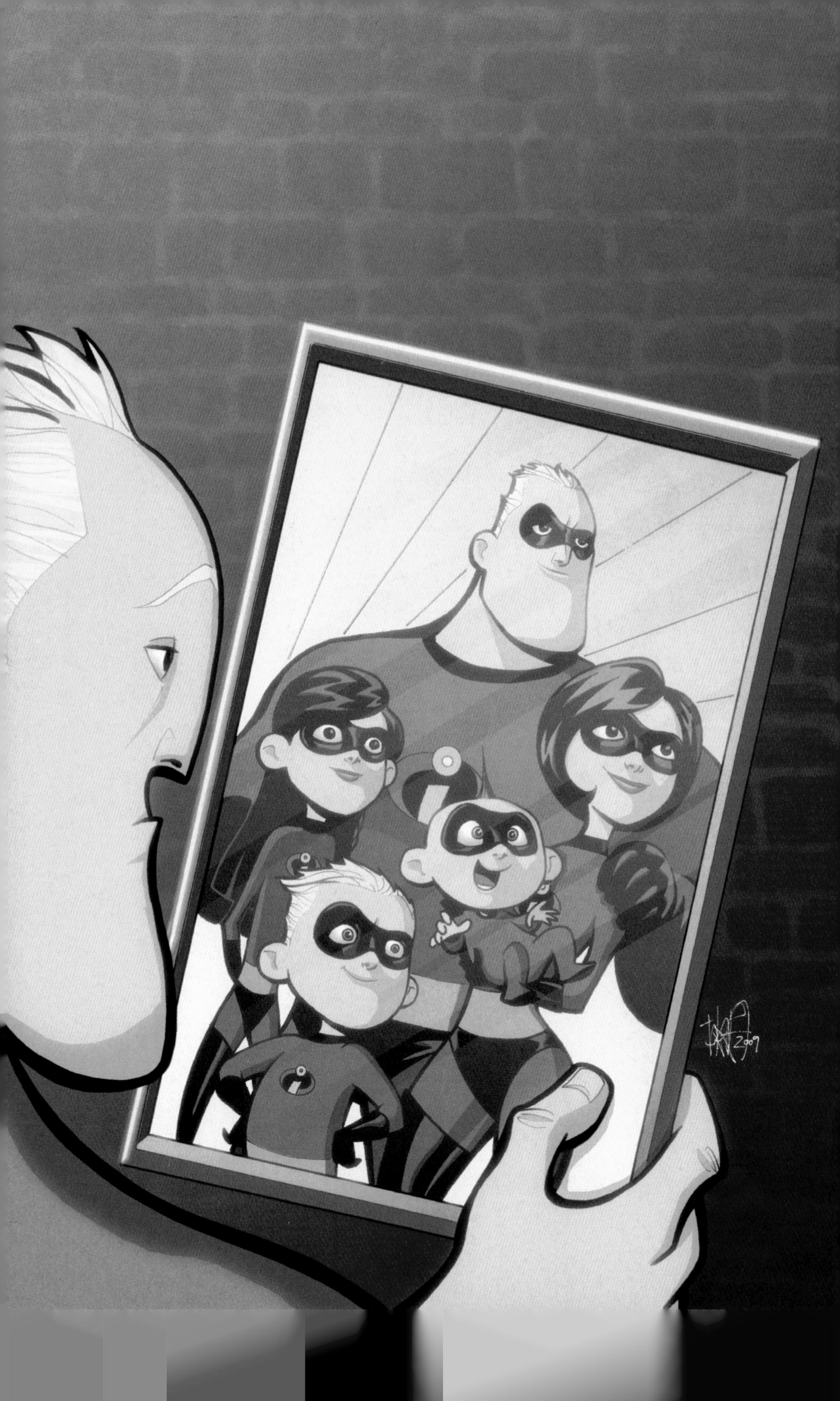

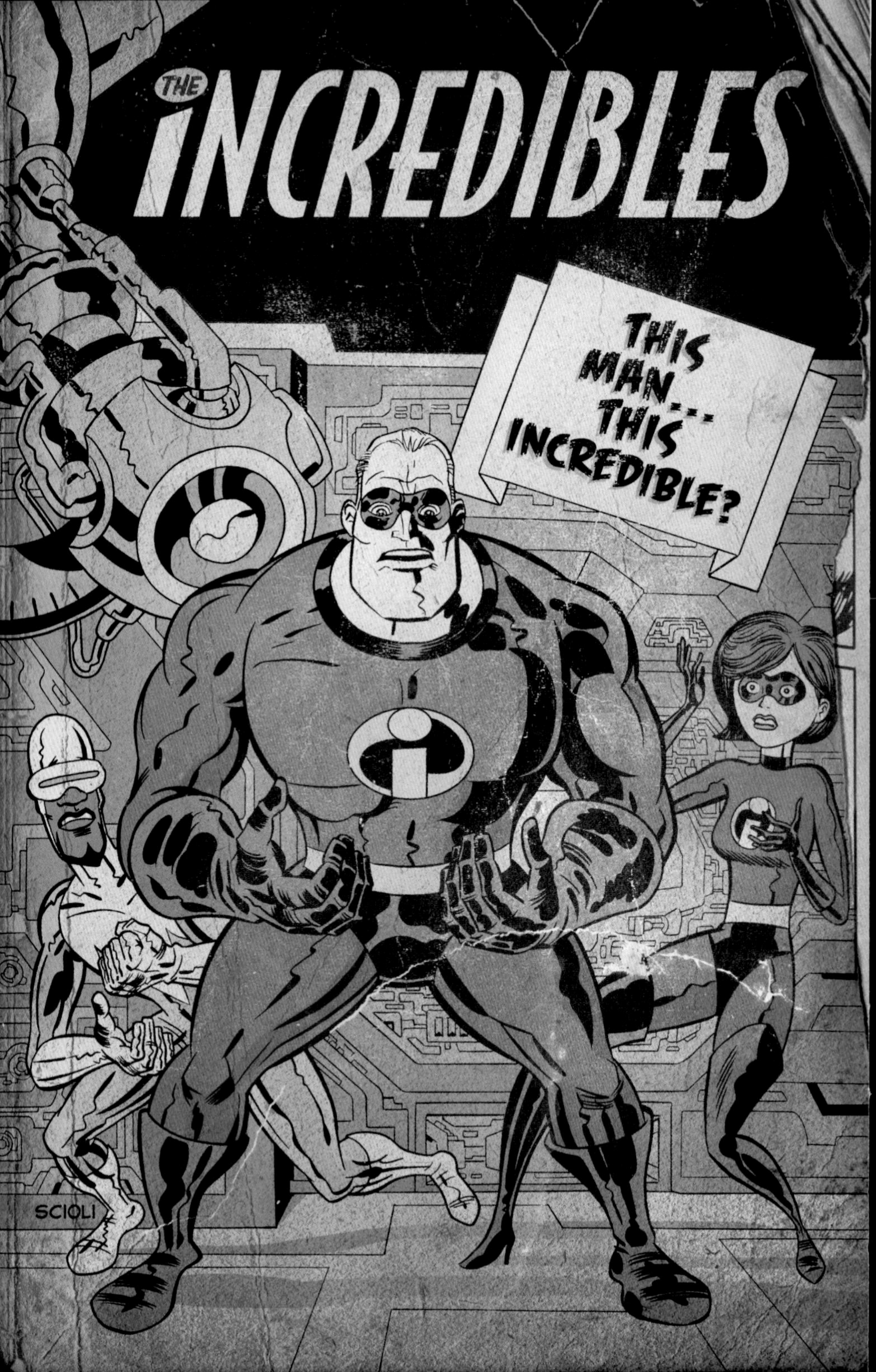
THE INCREDIBLES
THIS MAN... THIS INCREDIBLE?
SCIOLI

COVER 2C: TOM SCIOLI

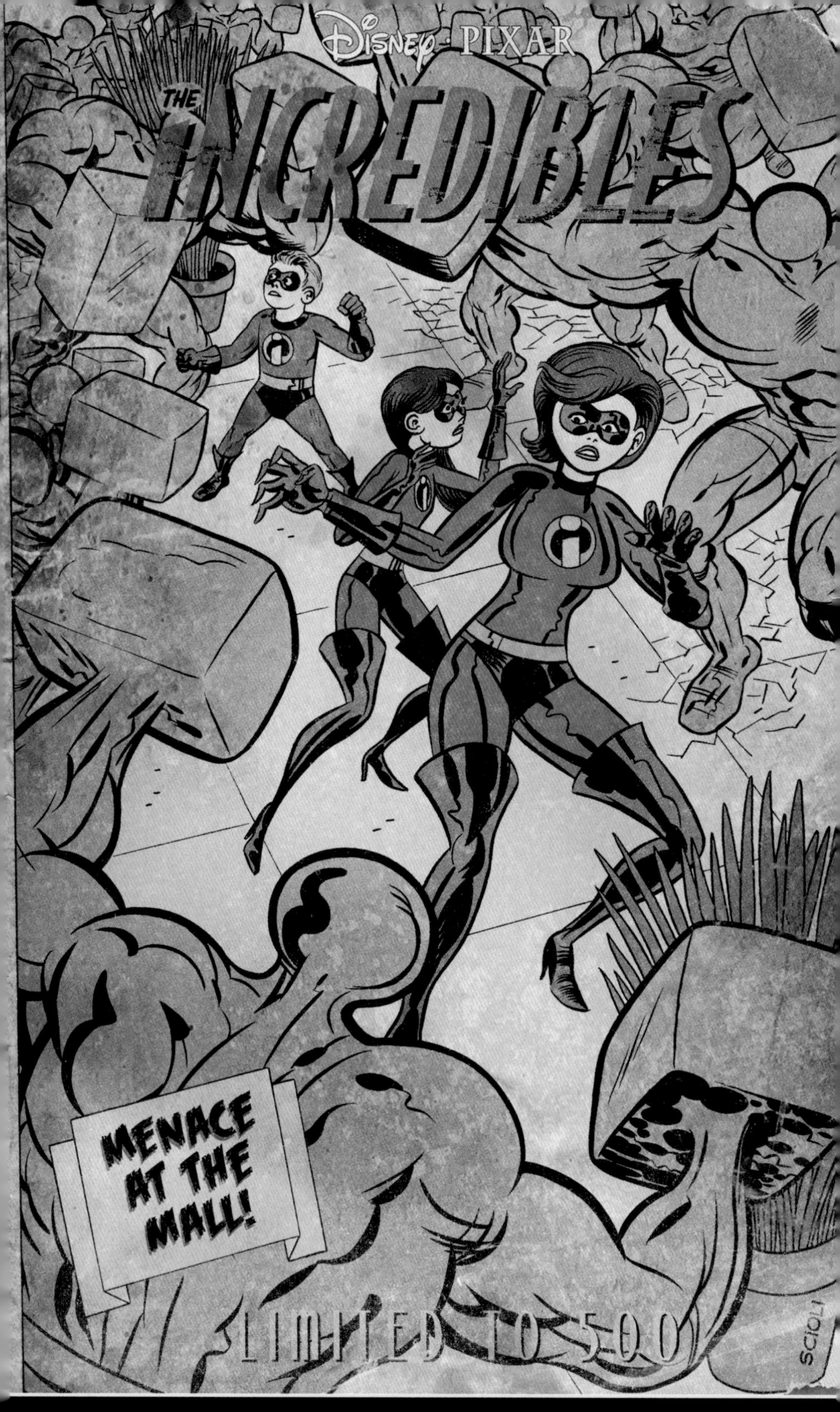

Disney · PIXAR
THE INCREDIBLES
MENACE AT THE MALL!
LIMITED TO 500
SCIOLI

ONE STAR COMICS EXCLUSIVE: TOM SCIOLI

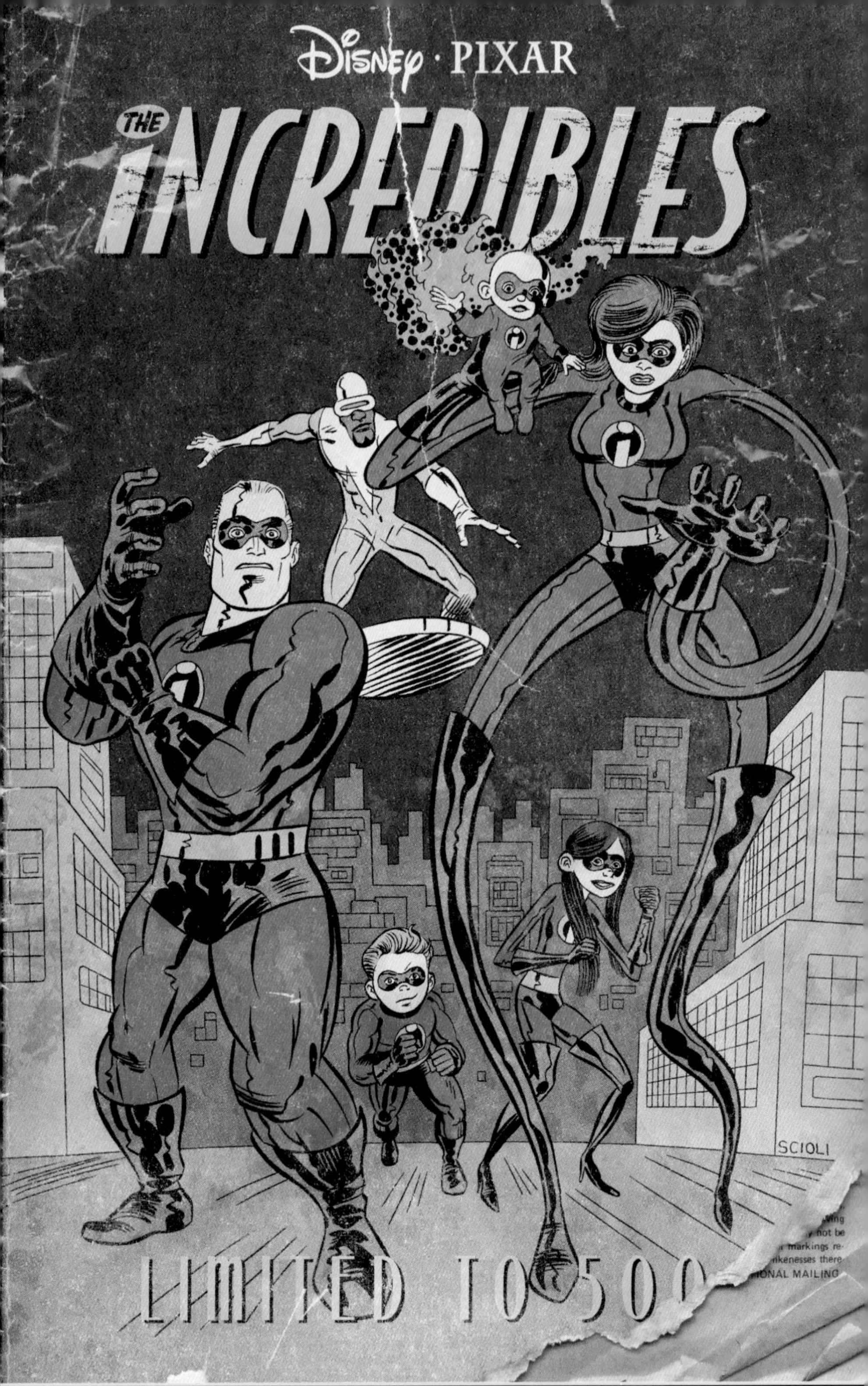
Disney · PIXAR
THE INCREDIBLES
SCIOLI
LIMITED TO 50

HEROES CON COMICS EXCLUSIVE: TOM SCIOLI

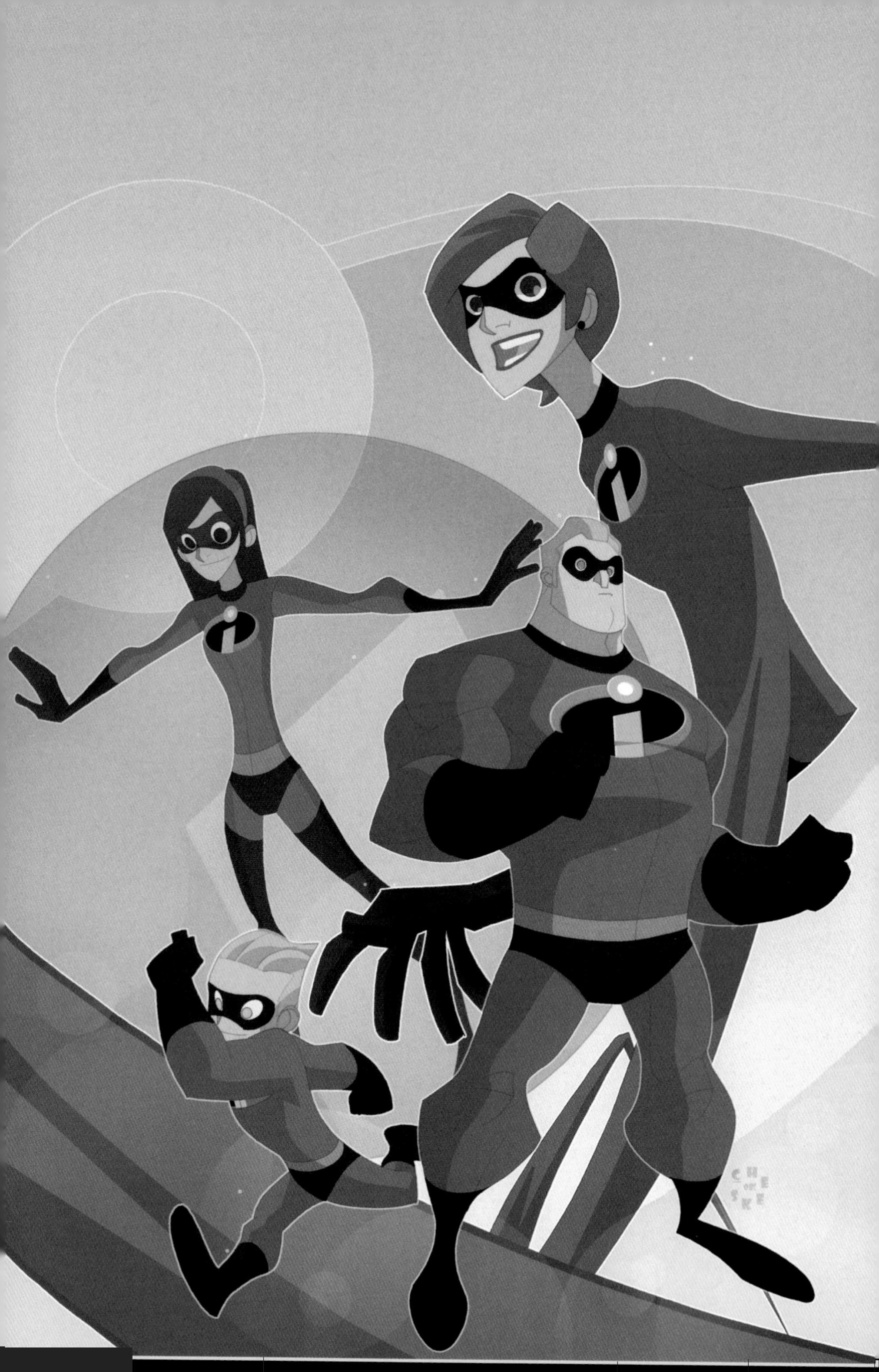

A: SEAN Y

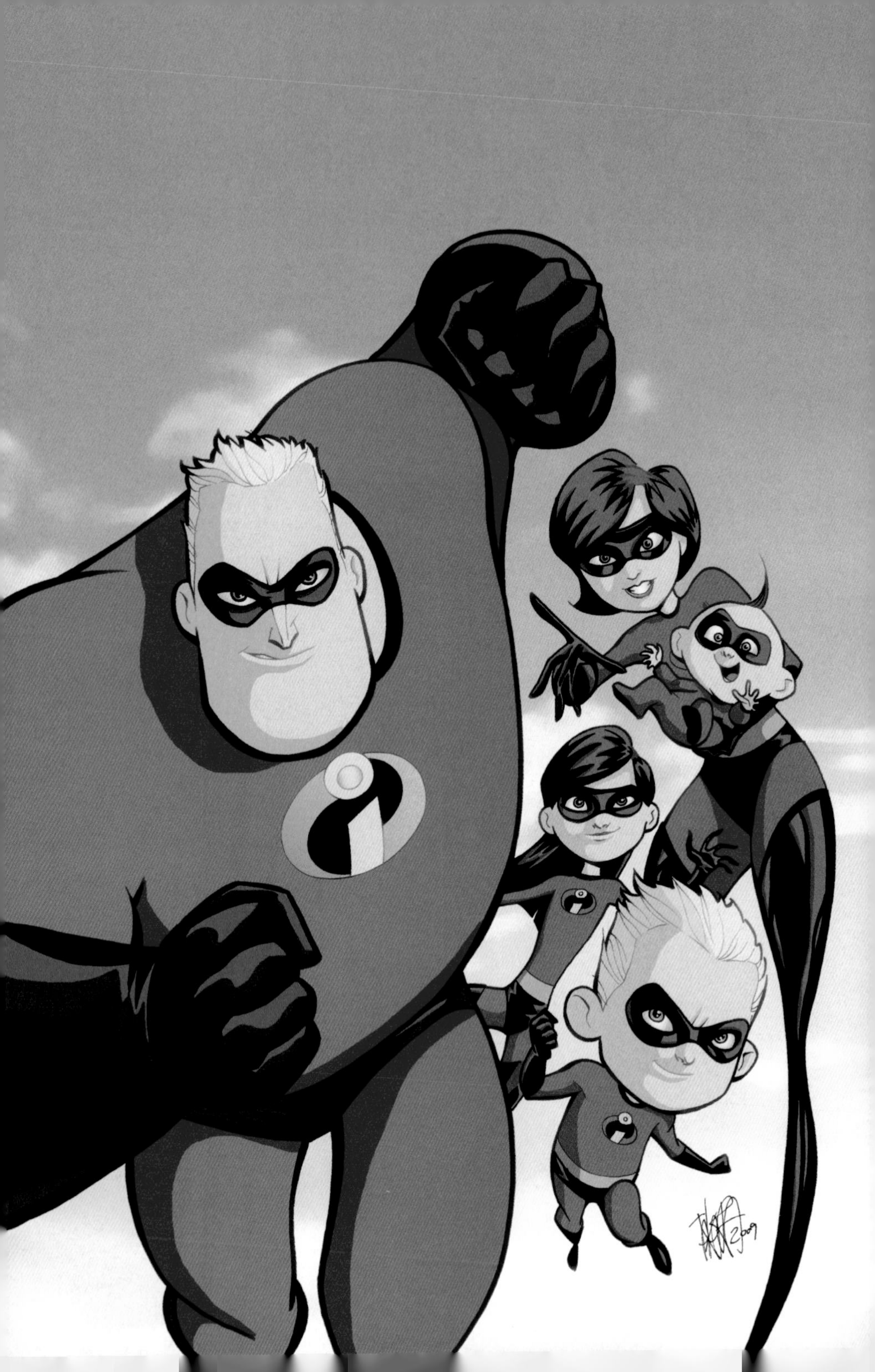

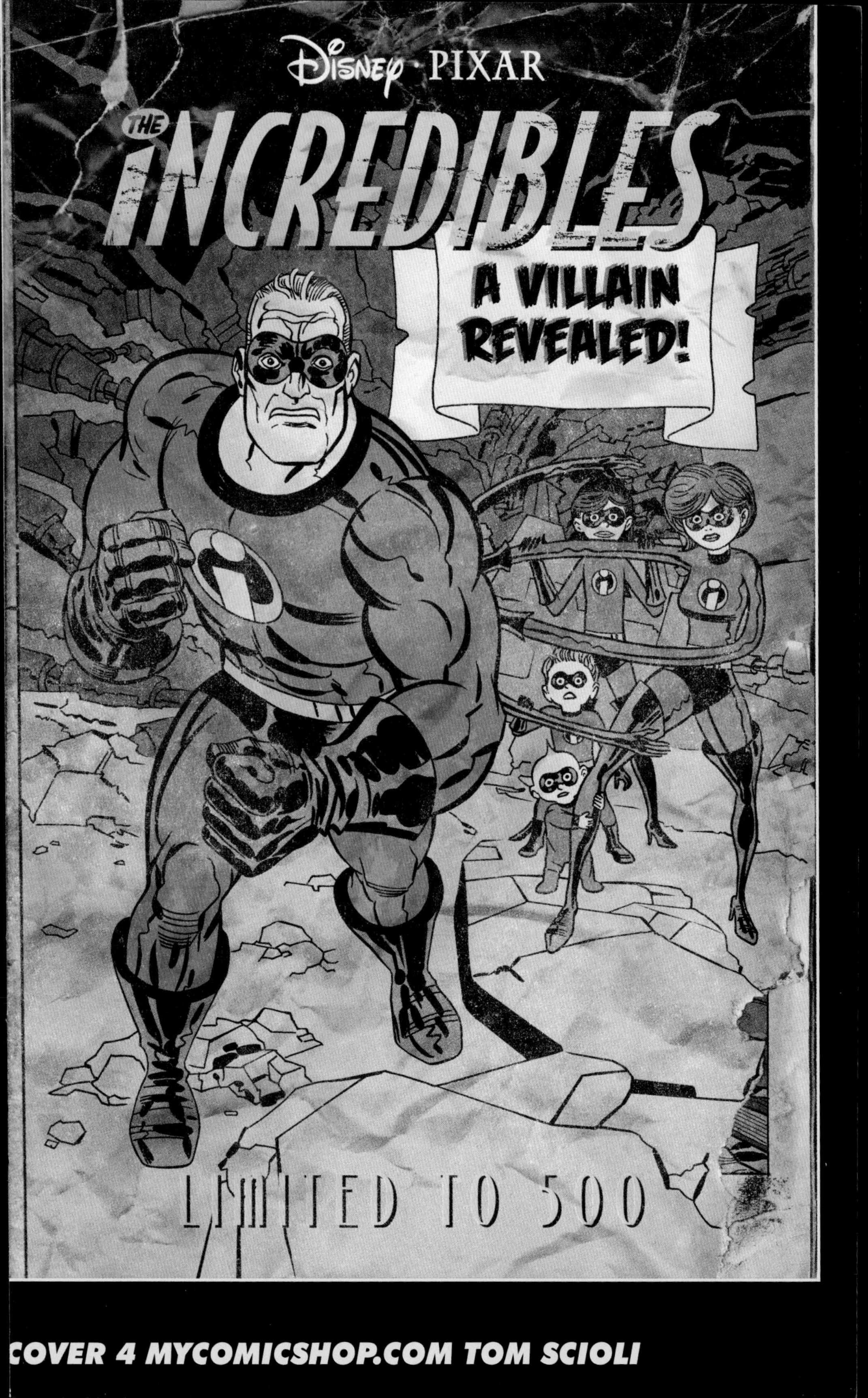
DISNEY · PIXAR
THE INCREDIBLES
A VILLAIN REVEALED!
LIMITED TO 500

COVER 4 MYCOMICSHOP.COM TOM SCIOLI

MARCIO TAKARA CHARACTER SKETCHES

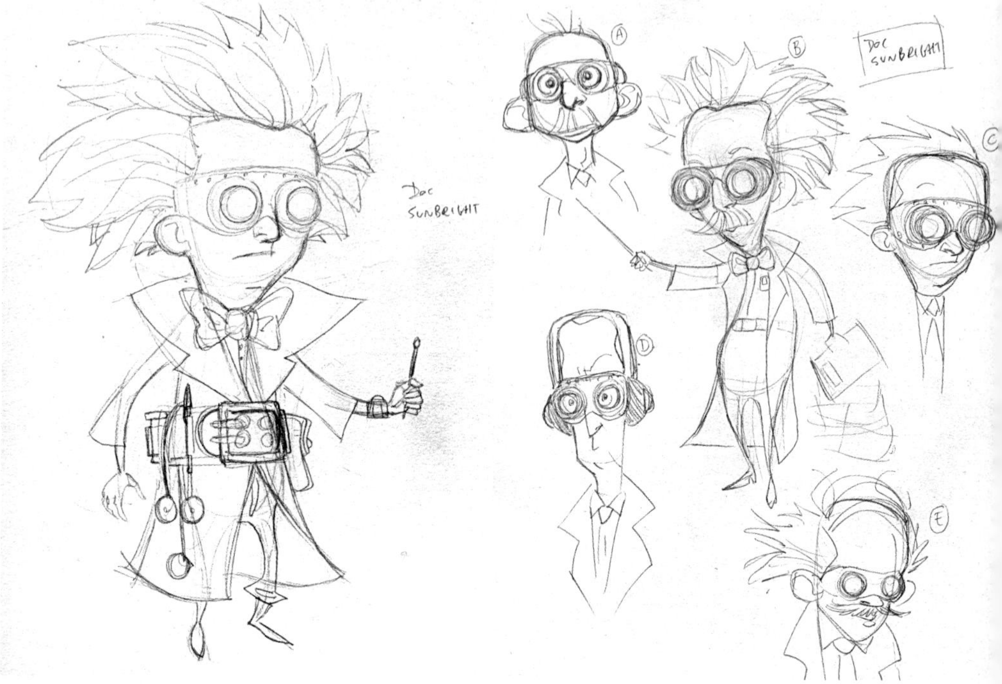
Doc SUNBRIGHT
A
B
DOC SUNBRIGHT
C
D
E

- Doc Sunbright

The idea was to make him look a little like Edna but I did the first version too much like her. So I tried some different versions before picking the final one.

- Nurse

I know it would be a brief appearance, but I really wish the fish head nurse would have been approved. Just one of Mark's crazy ideas.

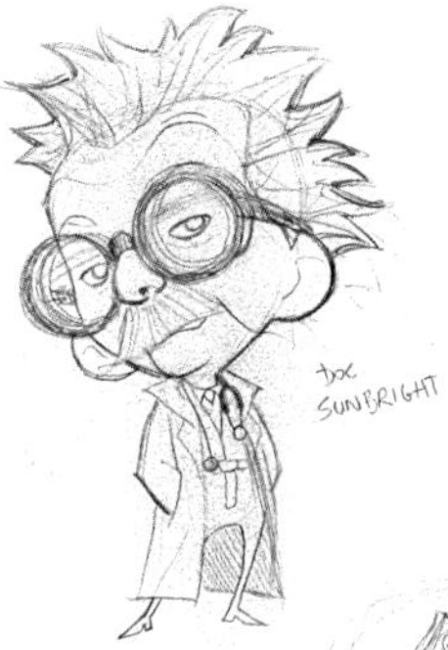
Doc SUNBRIGHT

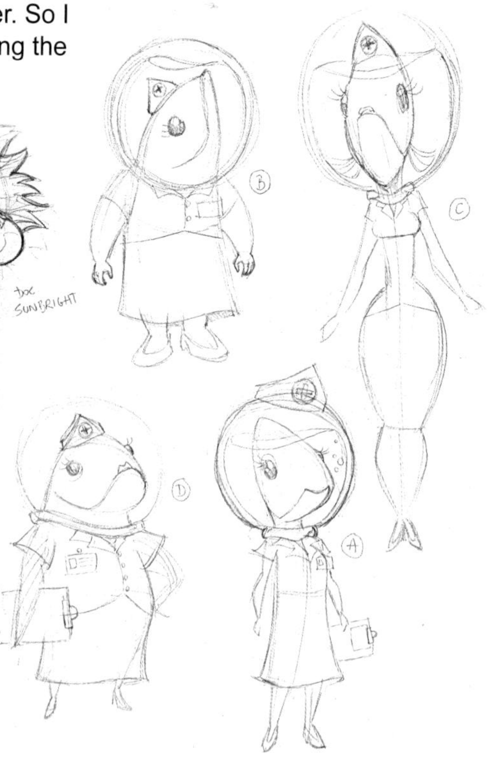
B
C
D
A

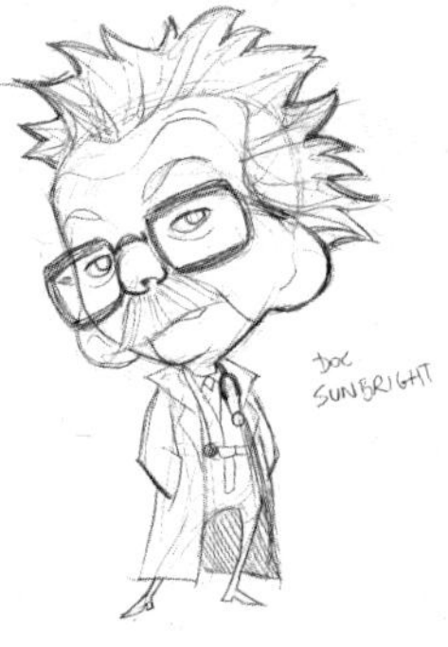
Doc SUNBRIGHT

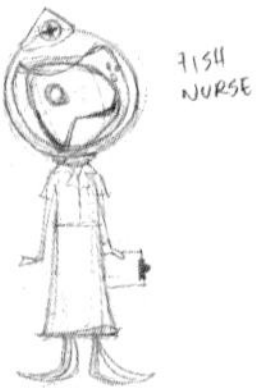
FISH NURSE

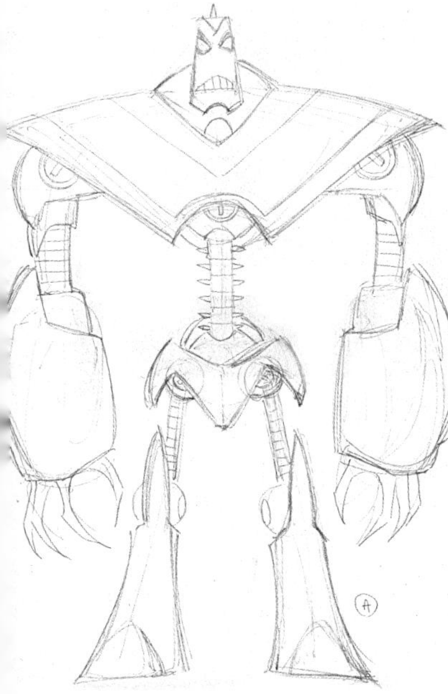
A

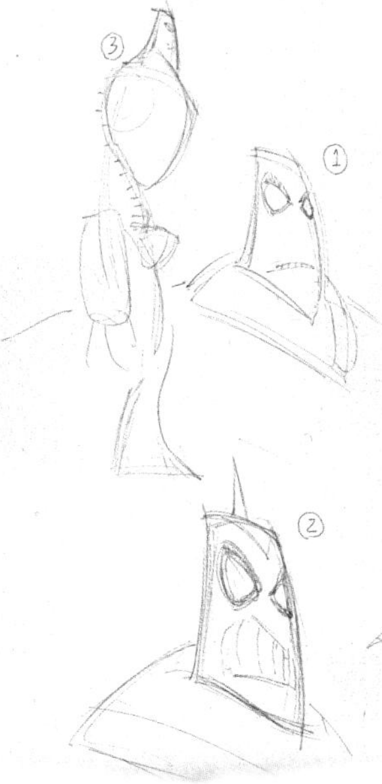
3
1
2

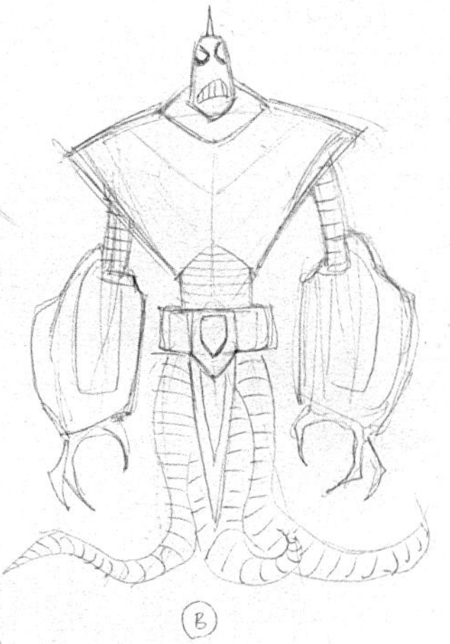
B

.C

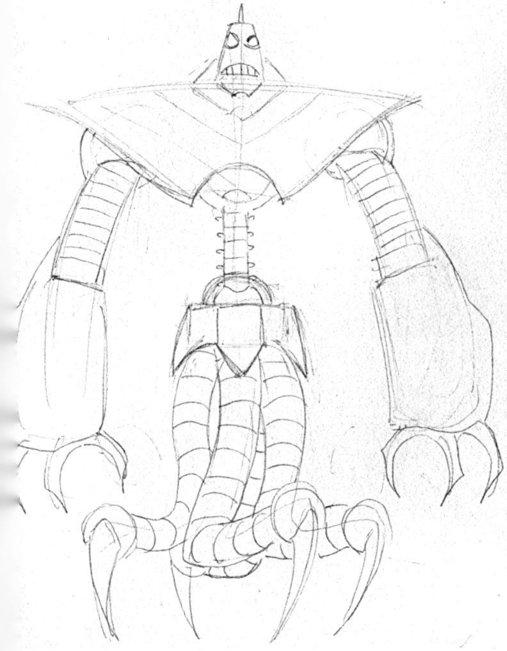

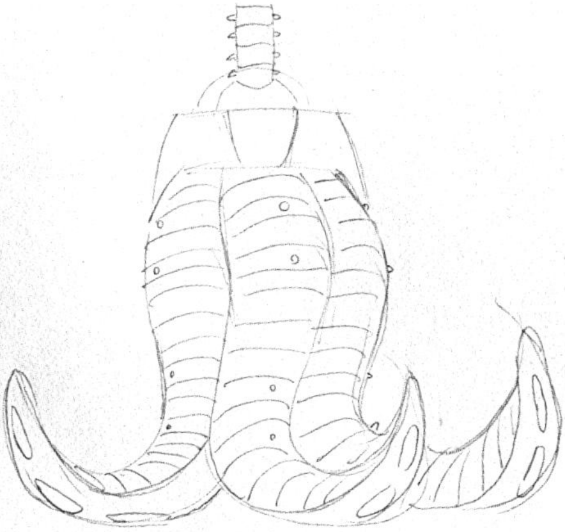

.D

- Futurion

For the main villain of the first issue I was asked to draw someone who'd look like a crazy tyrant from the future or something like that. My idea was to give him lots of sharp edges to make him aggressively looking. Contrasting with the roundness of the Incredibles world.

I think the tentacle legs would have look awesome! but still, I think he looks cool.

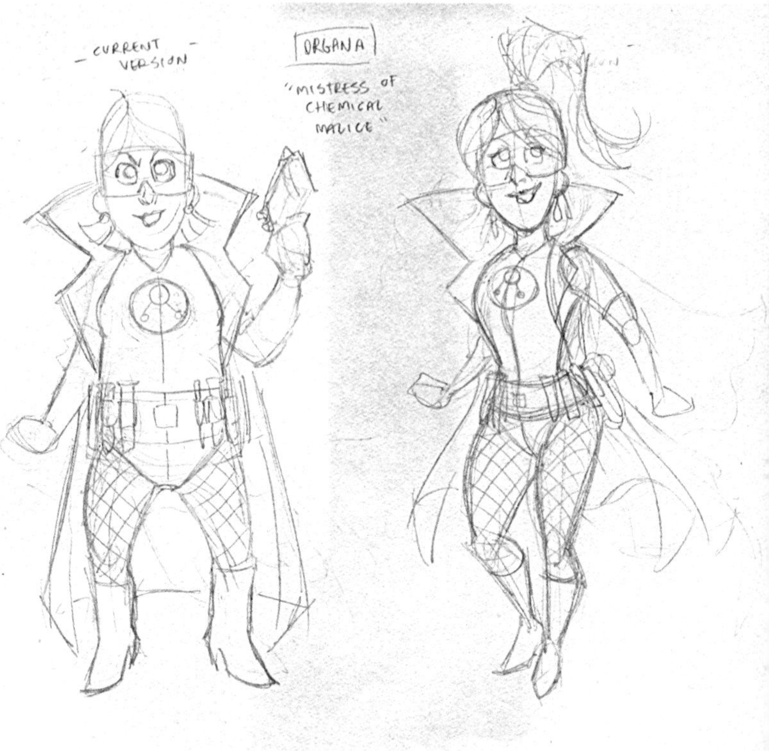
- CURRENT VERSION -
ORGANA
"MISTRESS OF CHEMICAL MALICE"

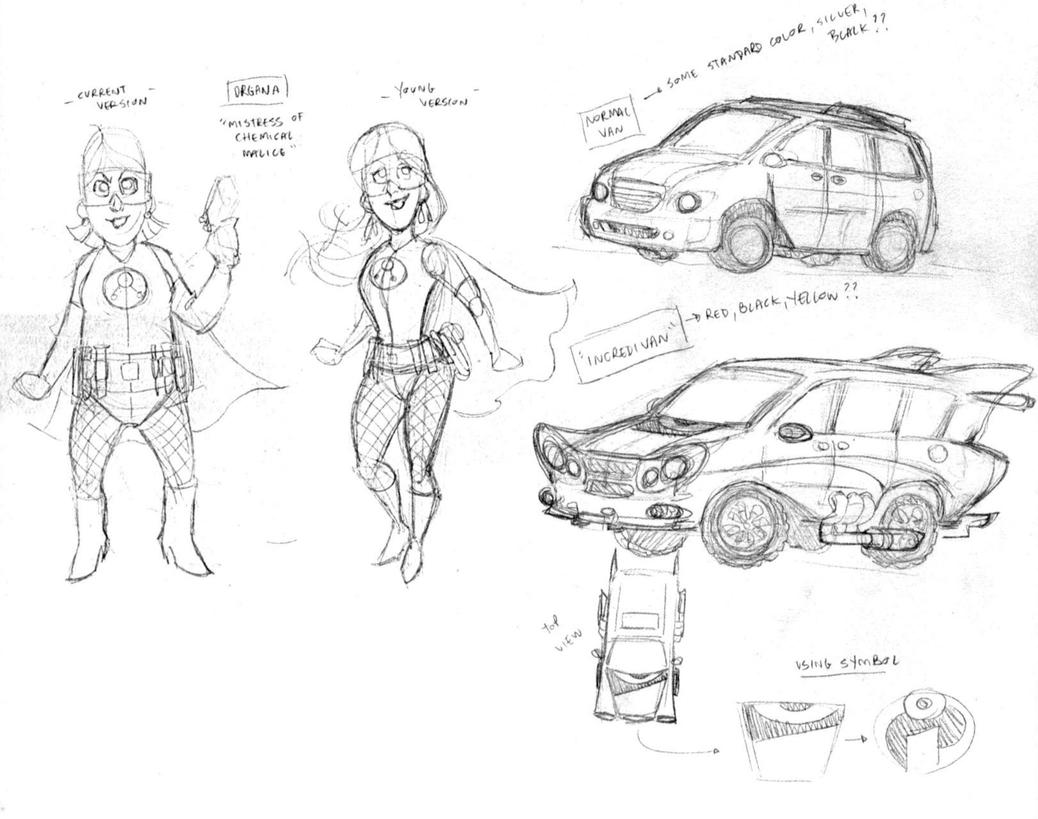
- CURRENT VERSION -
ORGANA
"MISTRESS OF CHEMICAL MALICE"
- YOUNG VERSION -
NORMAL VAN
SOME STANDARD COLOR, SILVER, BLACK??
"INCREDIVAN"
RED, BLACK, YELLOW??
TOP VIEW
USING SYMBOL

- Sketch pages

This is how they all start. I do something, I don't know 7"x5", just to show the editor my overall idea for the page... usually it's clear enough so that he can see if the storytelling is working...

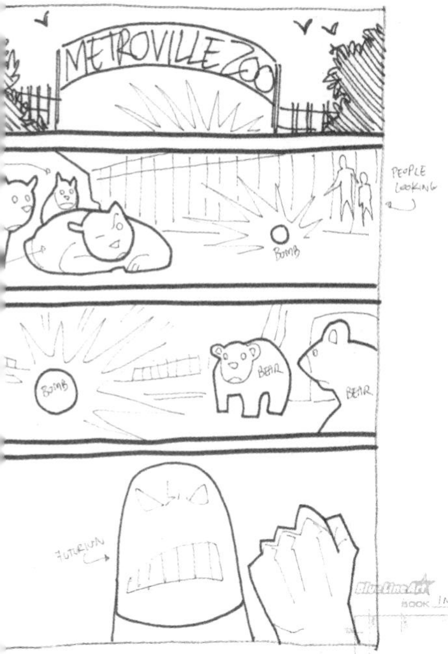

METROVILLE ZOO
PEOPLE LOOKING
BOMB
BOMB
BEAR
BEAR
FUTURIAN

Pencil pages

ly pencils are very loose.)ne of the reasons is ecause I'm inking myself ater, so there's no need to e too specific. What you ee here is good enough or me to ink right after it's pproved.

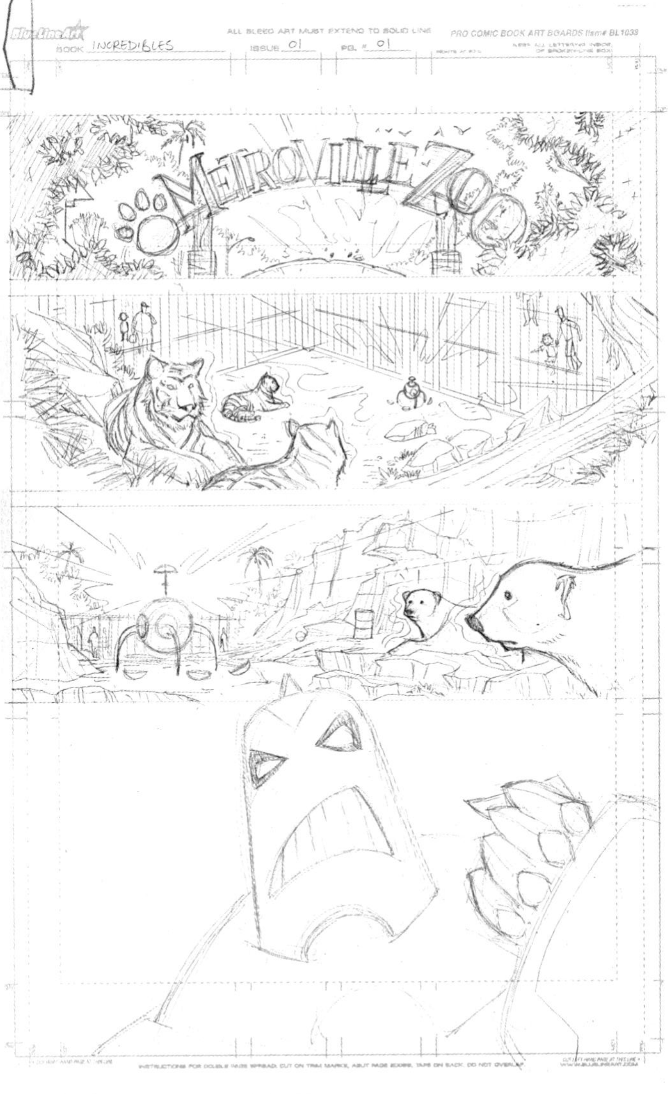

ALL BLEED ART MUST EXTEND TO SOLID LINE
PRO COMIC BOOK ART BOARDS Item# BL1033
BOOK INCREDIBLES
ISSUE 01
PG. # 01
METROVILLE ZOO

The pencil stage is the fastest one. I can do two or three pencil pages a day and sometimes even ink the three of them before going to bed. So yeah the inks, they take I'd say twice the time to finish.
All my pencils are done with a regular HB 0.5 mechanical pencil.

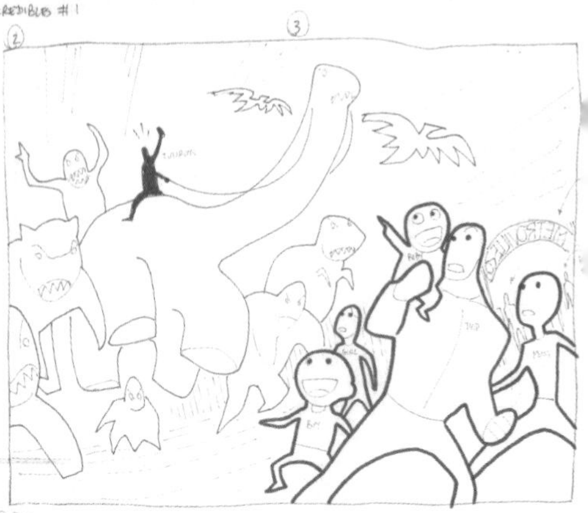
INCREDIBLES #1

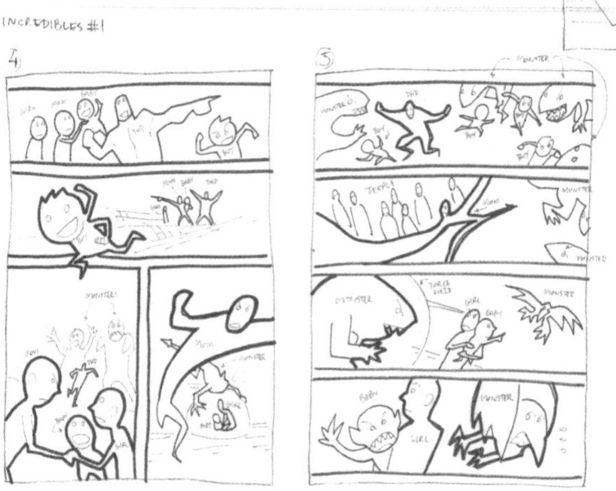
INCREDIBLES #1

- Inked pages

For the inks I'll use Micron pens from .005 to 1.0, Pentel brush pen and some cheap brushes to fill the black areas.

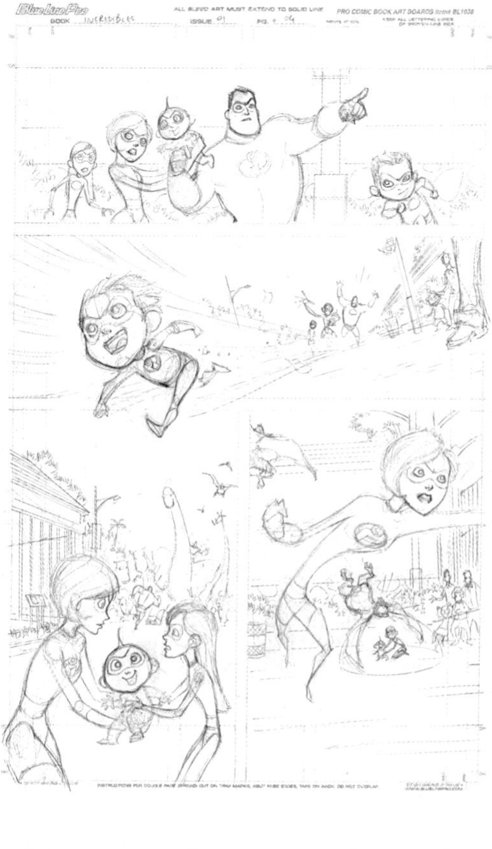

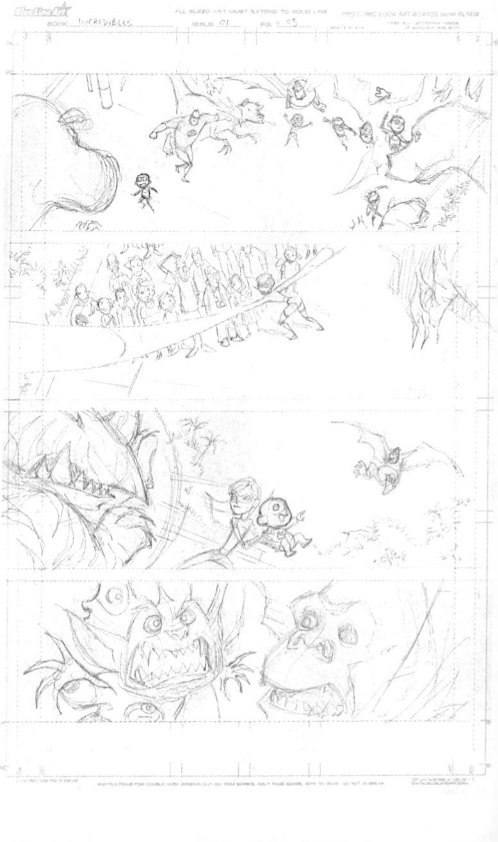

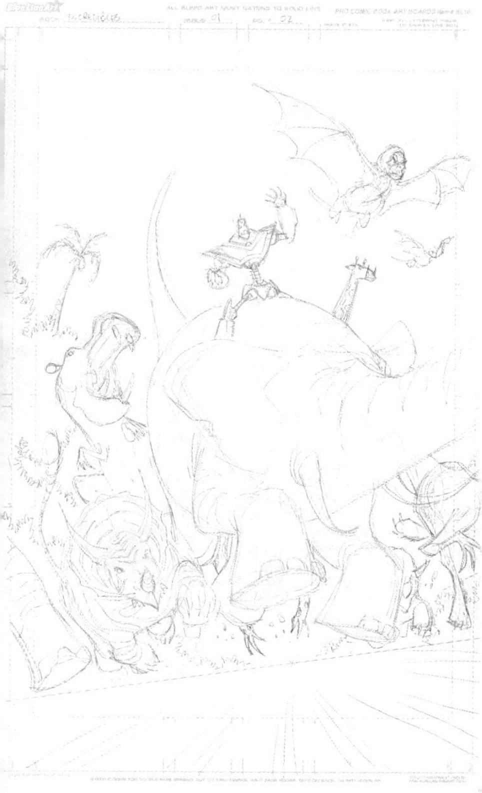
ALL BLEED ART MUST EXTEND TO SOLID LINE
PRO COMIC BOOK ART BOARDS

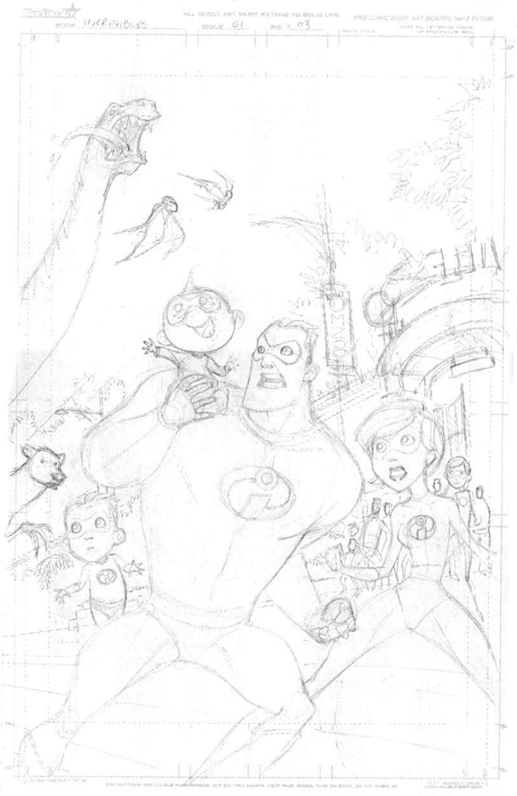
ALL BLEED ART MUST EXTEND TO SOLID LINE
BOOK INCREDIBLES
ISSUE 01
PG. # 03

INCREDIBLES #1

(6)

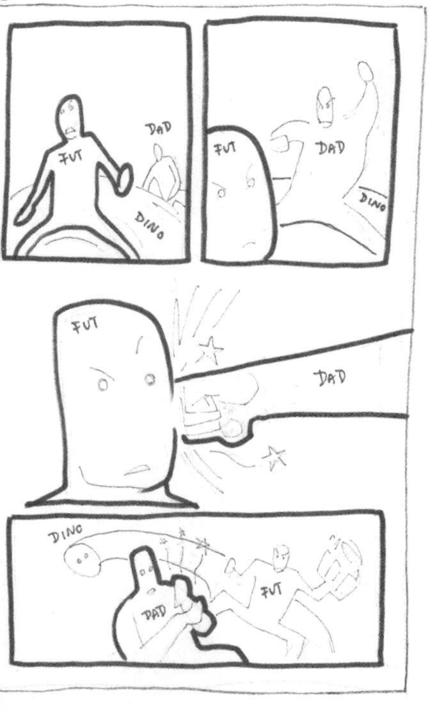
FUT
DAD
DINO
FUT
DAD
DINO
FUT
DAD
DINO
DAD
FUT

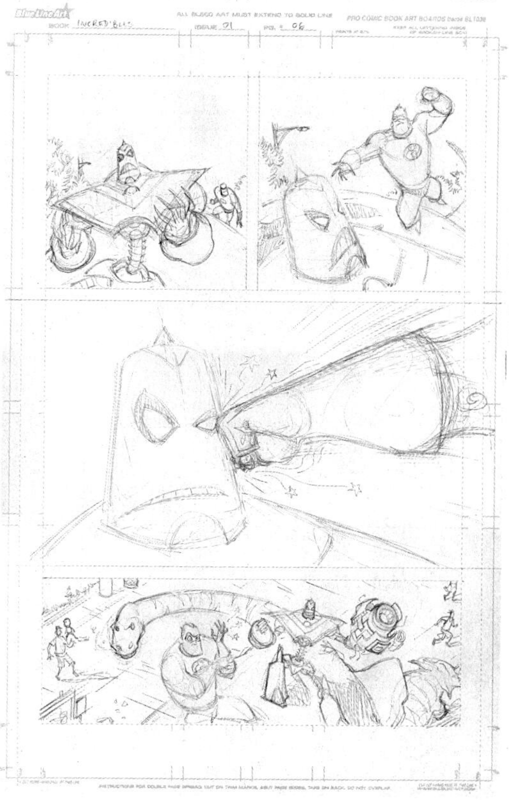
ALL BLEED ART MUST EXTEND TO SOLID LINE
PRO COMIC BOOK ART BOARDS
ISSUE 01
PG. # 06

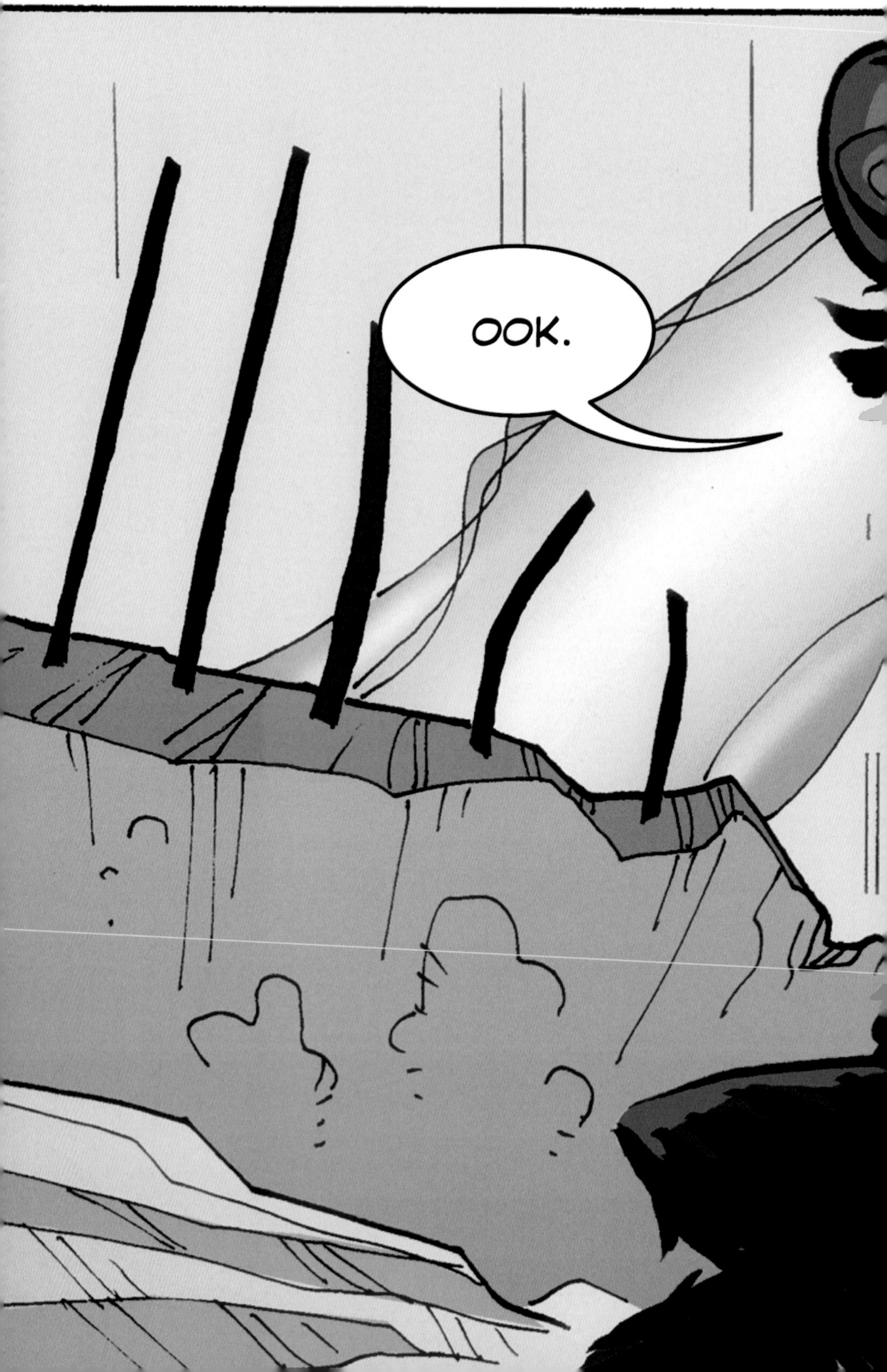
OOK.

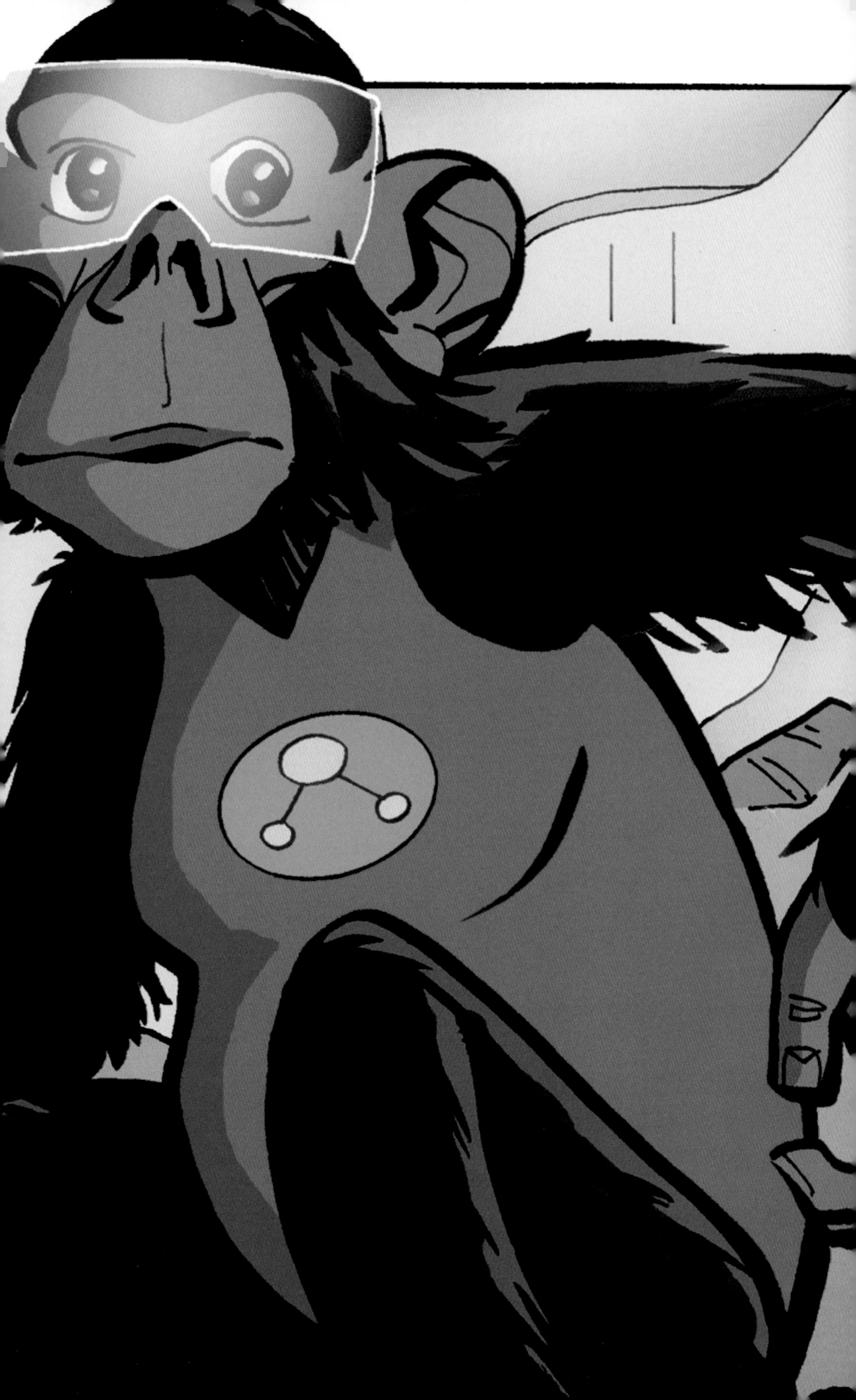

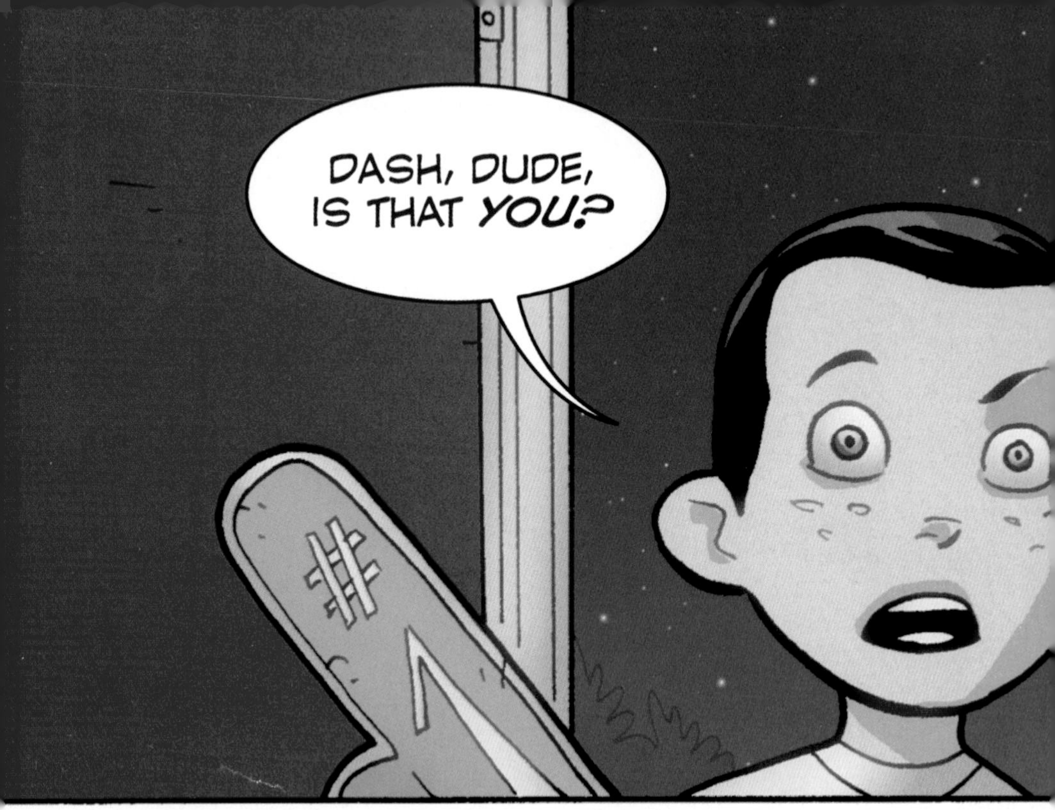
DASH, DUDE, IS THAT *YOU?*

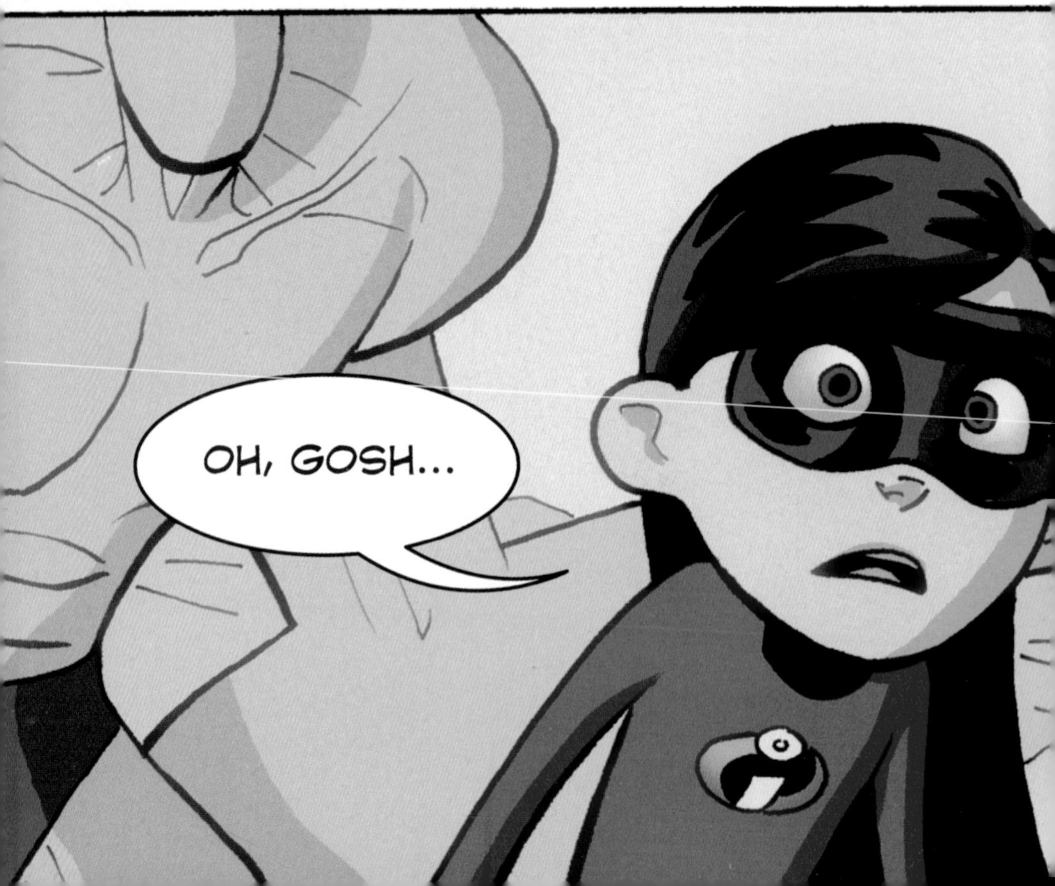
OH, GOSH...